MAN
of
ARMS

To my Mother

MAN
of
ARMS

The Life and Legend of
Sir Basil Zaharoff

ANTHONY ALLFREY

WEIDENFELD & NICOLSON
London

First published in Great Britain in 1989 by
George Weidenfeld & Nicolson Limited
91 Clapham High Street, London SW4 7 TA

British Library Cataloguing in Publication Data
Allfrey, Anthony
Man of arms.
1. Military equipment industries.
Zaharoff, Sir Basil, 1849–1936
I. Title
338.4'7623'0924

ISBN 0-297-79532-5

Printed and bound in Great Britain at
The Bath Press, Avon

Contents

Illustrations

AUSTRIA-
HUNGARY

Budapest

Kishinev

R. Dniester

R U

Odessa

Belgrade

RUMANIA

Bucharest

R. Danube

BLACK

BOSNIA

Sarajevo

SERBIA

MONTE-
NEGRO

Sofia

BULGARIA

Adrianople

Dede
Agach

Bosphorus

Constantinople

THRACE

Ankara

ALBANIA

MACEDONIA

Salonika

Gallipoli

Dardanelles

Eskishehr

Corfu

THESSALY

GREECE

Ionian Is.

TURKISH

Smyrna

Athens

Piraeus

Mughla

M E D I T E R R A N E A N   S E A

Nicosia

CYPRU

First World War 1914—18

Central Powers ☆
Allied Powers *

*Dates indicate when countries
entered the war*

GREAT
BRITAIN

GERMAN
EMPIRE

RUSSIA

FRANCE

AUSTRIA-HUNGARY

1916
RUMANIA

SPAIN

ITALY 1915

SERBIA

BULGARIA
1915

GREECE
1917

TURKISH
EMPIRE
1914

Alexandria

E G Y P T

R. Nile

S S I A

CASPIAN

C A U C A S U S

SEA

SEA

A R M E N I A

R. Tigris

Tehran

M P I R E

P E R S I A

Mosul

R. Euphrates

M E S O P O T A M I A

S Y R I A

Baghdad

Kut

Damascus

PALESTINE

Deraa

Basra

Jerusalem

Persian Gulf

aza

THE BALKAN STATES & THE OTTOMAN EMPIRE
National boundaries after the Balkan War 1912–13

0   100   200   300 miles

0   100   200   300   400   500 km

Acknowledgements

Pleasurable as it should be, it is nonetheless difficult to express proper appreciation with any degree of grace and sincerity in a bare catalogue of acknowledgements. I can only plead in extenuation of the laundry-list style that in many, if not most, cases I have personally rendered my thanks for exceptional kindnesses.

I owe a particular debt to Anne and Peter Thorold for their hospitality and forbearance over a long period, and to Anne for so tirelessly rooting on my behalf.

I am greatly indebted to Mr Hugh Scrope of Vickers Plc who, so providentially completing the tremendous labour of collating and indexing the company records when I first presented myself, has since patiently continued his assistance in his retirement. Mr William Scanlan Murphy has most generously contributed much information and an early photograph of Zaharoff which he acquired too late for inclusion in his biography of the Rev. George Garrett Pasha, *Father of the Submarine*.

I wish to record my gratitude to Lord Bonham-Carter for permission to quote from the Asquith Papers; to Mr A.J.P.Taylor (Beaverbrook Foundation) and Mr H.S.Cobb (House of Lords Record Office) from the Lloyd George Papers; to Mr Kenneth A.Lohf from the William Shaw Papers, Rare Book and Manuscript Library, Columbia University; and to the Keeper of the Archives, Oxford University. I also extend my thanks to the authors and publishers of the many works from which I have quoted, and the editors of those newspapers which have provided sources. I trust they will accept the fact of acknowledgement as sufficient evidence of my appreciation.

Every grubber in time past leans heavily on the generous support of librarians and archivists, curators and historians. I am accordingly grateful to Mr Giles Barber (Taylor Institution, Oxford University), Miss Elizabeth Bennett, (Churchill College, Cambridge), Mr D.M.Blake (India Office Library and Records), Mr K.V.Bligh (House of Lords Record Office), Mr Michael Brock (Nuffield College), Mr G.P.V.Collyer (Taylor Institution, Oxford University), Commander Richard Compton-Hall (HMS Dolphin, Gosport), Mr Oliver Everett (Royal Archives, Windsor Castle), Dr R.W.Ferrier (British Petroleum), Mr Henry Gillett and Mr John Hodgson (Bank of England), Mr J.P.Hudson (British Library), Ms Helen Langley (Bodleian Library, Oxford), Mr Ian Low (The Ashmolean, Oxford), Mrs P.J.McCrory (Rugby School), Ms Phyllida Melling (Guildhall Library) Ms Dorothy Norman (British Museum, Natural History), Mr A.E.B.Owen (Cambridge University Library), Mr H.Sykes (Bristol County Library), Ms Ruth Vyse (Bodleian Library, Oxford), Mr Adrian Whitworth (Imperial College of Science and Technology). I would also add my thanks to the staff of the British Library, Reading Room and Newspaper Library, the Public Record Office and the London Library, the expatriate's lifeline.

I am indebted to yet others, many of whom selflessly gave up time, all of whom took great trouble to satisfy what may often have seemed trivial points. I thank the Rev. W.M.Atkins (St George's, Hanover Square), the Hon. Richard Beaumont (James Purdey & Sons Ltd), Mr Michael Behrens (Ionian Securities Ltd), Mr Victor Blank (Charterhouse Japhet Plc), Mr Nicholas Bratza QC, Mr J. Coleman (Plenty Ltd), Mr A.H.Cundy (Henry Poole & Co.), Mr Hugh Curran (Laing & Cruickshank), Mrs S.Ferneyhough (West Midlands Police), Prince Yuri Galitzine, Earl Lloyd George of Dwyfor, Mr John Grigg, Ms Mary Hunt (British Embassy, Paris), the Rev. Martin Israel (Holy Trinity Church, Prince Consort Road), Mr Michael MacQuaker, Mr G.F.Miles (Barclays Bank Plc), Mr Iain Mitchell (Ellis Peirs & Young Jackson), Major General D.H.G. Rice (Central Chancery, Orders of Knighthood), Mrs James Sherwood (Orient Express), the Duke of Valderano, Ms Georgina Yates (Metropolitan Police) and Mr Morris West.   In France I owe many thanks to Mr Pierre Salinger and Mr W. Dowell (ABC News); also to Maître Jean Beauvillain, M Joseph Biaggi, M Jean Daubigny (Préfecture de Police, Paris), Général Delmas (Service Historique de l'Armée de Terre), Professeur Jean-Baptiste Duroselle (Institut de France), Mme Nadia Lacoste (Centre de Presse, Principauté de Monaco), M Laurent Morelle (Académie de Paris), Mme Patricia Oliver and M F.Rosset (Société des Bains de Mer, Monte Carlo), Mme Martine Savary (Editions Bernard Grasset), M Marcel Wormser (Musée Clemenceau) and the Secrétariat du Conseil Général, Banque de France.

Nearer home again, I am grateful to HE Rahmi Gumrukcuoglu, the Turkish Ambassador; also to Dr Victoria Solomonidis and Captain

G.Togas, HN, of the Greek Embassy, as well as to M Alexandre Sgourdeos.

Across the Atlantic I would like to thank Mrs Adele Bellinger (New York Public Library), Mr David J.Bishop (Department of the Navy), Mr Bernard R.Crystal (Columbia University Library), Mr Nicholas Field-Johnson (Merchant Bank of California), Ms Katherine Loughney (Library of Congress), Mr Vincent T.Malcolm Jr (Electric Boat Division, General Dynamics Corporation) and Ms Caroline Marks (Morgan Guaranty Trust Company).

I would like to add my final thanks to Mr Kenneth Rose, in whose company I profitably browsed; to Mr Anthony Blond for his initial encouragement; to Mrs Jacintha Alexander; to Mrs Venetia Pollock; to my agent, Mr Andrew Lownie, and of course to my publishers for their pre-natal ministrations.

Prologue

'Bloody Week'

BERLIN, 10–17 January 1919

Smudges of smoke hung in the sharp air over the Kaiser's palace, small-arms fire sounded sporadically around the city. Scattered groups of fugitives, some in workers' overalls, others in sailors' uniforms, dodged among the buildings in search of shelter, pursued by grim grey-green-clad units of regular troops and Freikorps volunteers. Otherwise the streets were deserted, the shop-fronts boarded up – not that there was much to loot that winter. Other groups, herded roughly by guards, stood about in sullen silence, avoiding the eyes of their comrades. This was civil war in which scant heed was paid to the nicer conventions of formal warfare. These people had been so close to success; now they plainly registered the despair of defeat soured by foreboding.

A little more than two months before, the Kaiser had been forced to abdicate and flee the fatherland. Almost by accident a republic had been proclaimed. But now revolution was dawning. Berlin was paralysed by a general strike. Just a short distance from the Reichstag, the revolutionaries of the Spartakusbund, led by the Marxist–socialists Rosa Luxemburg and Karl Liebknecht, had been preparing a Soviet republic from their entrenched refuge in the former imperial stables. In December the first Soviet Congress of Germany had met in the capital and put impossible demands to the temporary government, foremost among them the abolition of the regular army. Two days before Christmas, mutinous sailors constituting the People's Marine Division, now under the control of the Spartacists, occupied the Wilhelmstrasse, broke into the Chancellery and cut the telephone wires – but overlooked one direct line to army headquarters. An attempt to oust them by regular troops of the Potsdam garrison had been easily repulsed.

The insurgents remained in fateful ignorance of the pact made by the generals with the socialist leader, the saddler Friedrich Ebert, that the civil administration would put down anarchy (and Bolshevism) in return for the support – temporary, as it turned out – of the military. The army now accordingly called on the government to honour the agreement. The government, appalled in its turn by the prospect of outright revolution, obliged. Two days after Christmas, Ebert appointed Gustav Noske, a master butcher by trade, as Minister of National Defence. Early in January he struck. The Spartacists were crushed in a neat mucking-out operation.

The surviving ringleaders were apprehended. Rosa Luxemburg and Karl Liebknecht were escorted to the Eden Hotel to be interrogated by Captain Waldemar Pabst, the officer in charge of the sweep. They were next ordered to the Alt Moabit prison. They never reached their destination. On their way they were despatched in the Tiergarten.

The official explanation was that 'Karl Liebknecht was shot while trying to escape and Rosa Luxemburg was killed by an unknown person. . . .'

An enquiry was set up by the provisional government which led to a court-martial. A Lieutenant Wilhelm Canaris, later head of the Intelligence Bureau of the Wehrmacht High Command, took his seat among the judges. The four officers charged with the killing of Liebknecht were acquitted. The officer held responsible for the death of Rosa Luxemburg, a Lieutenant Vogel, was sentenced to a light prison term for 'disciplinary failure and abuse of power'. He escaped a few days after this sentence was pronounced.

But was their death the spontaneous happening it at first appeared?

At the time Canaris was widely suspected of having instigated the killings and he was later openly accused by *Die Freiheit*, with Pabst, of having contrived Vogel's flight. This allegation was taken up at the subsequent Reichstag commission of enquiry into the conduct of the war. Canaris replied flatly that this incident was outside its terms of reference. With that respect for authority that was ingrained into every good German, the matter was not pressed. An official communiqué from the Reichswehr Ministry, exonerating Canaris from any complicity in the affair, formally closed the case.

Another incident throws light on the matter.

A few weeks before the storming of the stables, a smartly dressed gentleman made the difficult journey to Berlin through a devastated Germany. He boasted the button of a Grand Officer of the Legion of Honour on his lapel and was approaching the age which many might have considered more suited to a rewarding retirement. He witnessed the very conditions he had foreseen, and so feared, on an earlier clandestine visit in the closing months of the war, a view which he had strongly impressed on the Allied leaders, precipitating the final autumn offensive. Once in the capital he called on a German naval officer, the same Canaris, whom he had already met in neutral Madrid in the winter of 1916–17. The two had much in common, not least a passion for intrigue and secrecy. The nature of their talk was not such that either party would necessarily have wished to keep a record, but, before leaving Berlin, the visitor addressed an aide-memoire to a colleague of Canaris' in the Abwehr, Otto Störmer:

The immediate problem is to counteract the Bolshevik propaganda which deliberately seeks to make mischief so that all forms of arms trade are controlled, or disbanded. Speak to Canaris about Liebknecht; the latter should be in no position to talk further by the end of the year.

The visitor's name was Basil Zaharoff.

'Never before or since in history', ran a later blurb, 'has a single man, who was neither monarch, politician nor general, achieved such a powerful and sinister influence over the nations of the world.' And yet, fifteen years after he had willed the disappearance of Liebknecht, the chairman of the US Senate committee investigating the private manufacture of arms, could ask: 'Who is Zaharoff?'

On his death the following year, in 1936, no one was left in any doubt. The passing of few men can ever have gone so unlamented in public print. The 'mystery man of Europe' was one of the milder epithets thrown his way. Front-page headlines proclaimed that 'Millions Died That He Might Live'. 'Death', ran another, 'has lost his last great recruiting agent'. 'The gravestones of a million men shall be his monument,' sang a lyrical American author, 'their dying groans his epitaph.' Biographers acknowledged him as the *High Priest of War* and the *Pedlar of Death*.

And yet the object of this impeachment was unknown outside a small circle until the latter years of his life. Even those propagandists for peace who, inspired by Liebknecht's earlier revelations of an international armaments 'ring', made it their business in the years preceding the Great War to expose the war 'trusts' and arms traders, remained ignorant of his existence.

His trade was arms, anything that fired faster, floated (or submerged) and, later, flew. For fifty full years he developed a colossal worldwide empire as principal overseas agent of Vickers Ltd (and its predecessors), nursing the original steel company into the greatest arms manufacturer of the age. He was power broker, banker, newspaper proprietor and oilman – with other less salubrious trades, so legend pretends, on the side. He pitted nation against nation, arming the competing combatants. A master of disinformation, he ruthlessly made use of the press to manipulate governors and governed. He dealt as a matter of course in bribery and blackmail. He had passed through the Old Bailey, married under an assumed name (and title) in London and committed bigamy in New York. Flamboyant and profligate, he offered thrones to his friends and Monte Carlo as a wedding present to the Duchess of Marchena, having waited patiently for forty years while her husband languished in lunacy, before marrying her in his seventy-fifth year. Above all, it was believed, he engineered, prolonged and finally put an end to the Great War, for which he was weighed down with riches and adorned with honours. Paradoxically for one described as the Allies' foremost munitions agent, he took a break from his career once the carnage commenced. Instead, he devoted himself to bullying the Greeks into renouncing their neutrality before embarking on a remarkable adventure to buy the Turks out of the war. In its aftermath he set Greek against Turk, resulting in the bloody humiliation of the Greeks and the downfall of Lloyd George. Rumour added its own gloss to this already unusual career, and if it exercised men's minds more than their tongues, it was a natural precaution: his agents were seen to be everywhere.

In short, he was the archetypal warmonger and capitalist profiteer of popular imagination. Shaw, it was supposed, used him as the model for the (not unsympathetic) armourer Andrew Undershaft in *Major Barbara*; H.G.Wells sarcastically excused his excesses: 'Indisputably this man has spent a large part of his life in the equipment and promotion of human slaughter ... but in no sense is it a personal condemnation. Millions of his contemporaries would have played the same game had they thought of it and known how.'

How did this legend arise? What was the reality? This is not such an easy question to answer. For one who attracted so much odium, his life is exceptionally sparsely documented; published references are meagre, much of the often quoted source material is of doubtful authenticity. In addition, he perversely destroyed his personal papers shortly before his death. Contemporary stabs at his biography resembled those efforts of ancient cartographers who, when faced with the unknown, excused the lacuna with the inscription 'Here be Monsters'. A later biographer pleaded that 'he remains an enigma that is hardly flesh and blood, a sketchy, shadowy figure which is a potpourri of fact and fiction'.

Zaharoff himself was not a little responsible for the mystification.

'I admire power that is secret', he professed, 'and doesn't advertise itself, for, above all things, I detest publicity.' This might justly be attributed to fear of revelation, yet a distinguished banker who knew him well attested to his possession 'of that kind of reserve which is the result of natural dignity'.

When notoriety overtook him suddenly and unexpectedly, he retaliated against the intrusion. As his reticence stoked speculation, he teasingly twitched aside a corner of the curtain to let in just sufficient light on his career to distract or deceive the inquisitive. He did not strive for consistency and as he never issued a disclaimer or correction, the legend branched and flourished like the green bay-tree amid the pacifist passions of the 1930s. Neither did he stoop to justification; he was not known ever to boast about his considerable benefactions or his real services to the Allies in the Great War.

It is not altogether unnatural that this should have been misunderstood. His conduct was deplored by many of those closest to him. The combative Georges Clemenceau complained about his friend's lack of response: 'He is himself a great deal responsible for all the malicious slanders that circulate. He should come out in the open, take action. Instead, what does he do? Refuses to lift a finger in his own defence.'

If fame came late, it stuck. It is now half a century since Basil Zaharoff, as he was known, was found dead in his bath in Monte Carlo at the age of eighty-seven. Over this time, his legend, which has passed into fiction, has become wilfully and sometimes inextricably interwoven with what little was known of his career, overshadowing the man. The essence is lurid enough for several villains to share and still leave something over for the life of an average Renaissance pope.

1

Origins and Youth

The first mystery to be tailored for the Zaharoff legend suitably surrounded his birth. Any records have long disappeared or, it is suggested, have been destroyed. Their absence was construed, without any allowance for the hazards of fire, earthquake, war and political disturbance, as one more of those occult, and to some sinister, coincidences which marked his career. Few reference books can even agree on his origins. (They may be forgiven; his own death certificate erred in regard to the day, year and place of his birth.)

In his middle age he procured a document, a mere confirmation of the fact of his birth in the absence of surviving witnesses. This established for the satisfaction of all but a handful of determined sceptics that the man to be known as Basil Zaharoff was born of Greek parents in a small town in Asia Minor in the middle of the last century.

Since before the days of Homer, colonies of Greeks had settled along the Asian shore of the Aegean and the Black Sea. The family Zachariadis had chosen Constantinople, the capital of the Ottomans since the fall of the Roman Empire in the east. In 1821 their less comfortably set-up fellows in Greece proper raised the flag of revolt, a fracas which dragged on for more than ten years, chiefly remarkable for a series of atrocities by each party. This commotion put all other Greeks under Turkish rule at risk and, hot on the heels of a wholesale massacre of Moslems by rebel Christians, the Turkish mob in the capital exacted prompt retribution.

The Zachariadises fled across the Black Sea to the free port of

Odessa, where they set up as tailors. They next turned up in Kishinev, then Romanian Bessarabia, before returning south to the small port of Ochakov, and finally back to Odessa itself where they prospered in a small way in the early 1840s.

The war for Greek independence won, the family, now with two sons in tow, recrossed the sea and cautiously settled in their former quarter in Constantinople. As an insurance, and sceptical of the first tentative constitutional reforms, they Russianized their name to Zacharoff in order to be able to invoke the protection of a great power. Nevertheless, impelled perhaps by unhappy memories of the mob, they moved on to Mughla in Anatolia, the centre of a modest trade in olive oil and tobacco inland from the Gulf of Kos.

The elder of the two sons had by this time married Helena, the daughter of one Antoniades. It was at Mughla that their first child was born on 6 October 1849. In accordance with custom he received his grandfather's name, Zacharias, and his father's, Basileios. When the infant Zacharias was some three years old, the family made another and final move back to the capital.

Zacharoff himself later scrambled this straightforward record. On the innocuous question of his origin, his putative ancestry would, on the strength of his own word, have made him into a unique cosmopolitan cocktail. 'My father was Russian,' he wrote to a young lady who had engaged his fancy in his old age, 'and my mother was Greek of the Byzantine family of des Brassinos.' Around the same time, in a posthumously published interview, he claimed in reply to a straight enquiry about his true nationality: 'I have almost forgotten. I was born in Anatolia. My father was of Polish origin. My mother was French with a Levantine strain.'

Legend fastened on to the Russian provenance. He was painted as a Jewish revolutionary from Odessa, otherwise a Jewish conscript in the imperial army – then a virtual life sentence – who was caught thieving and sent to Siberia, whence he escaped to Constantinople. Yet another version credits him with Lithuanian birth followed by service in the Russian army.

The toddler Zacharias Basileios Zacharoff was meanwhile on firmer ground in Constantinople. The capital was a great cosmopolitan port and trading centre, the gateway to southern Russia and the Balkans, and the seat of government of a sprawling, ramshackle, corrupt and repressive empire. Much of the commerce was in the hands of racial and religious minorities, the Turks content to staff the civil service and the armed forces. Usurious Armenian bankers had cornered credit; with the prosperous Greek merchants they were settled in the up-market suburb of Phanar, while more modest commercial and professional Greeks sheltered in the ancient quarter of Tatavla, present-day Kurtulus. It was here that the Zacharoffs set up house with the mother's prosperous brother in one of those finely wrought timber buildings which so often fed the flames that periodically swept the old city.

The mystery woven round Zacharoff's birth extended to his education. Once again he provided the raw material, this time for a ritual rags-to-riches romance. 'We were poor,' he recounted, 'and my father could only send me to an ordinary Greek school.' This is inexact. The family, although its fortunes may have fluctuated, was comfortably off and if the son of the house attended an 'ordinary' Greek school, he graduated to a grander establishment.

His obituarists in *The Times* and the *Daily Telegraph*, otherwise rarely unanimous, agreed that the family was educated and prosperous. Though far from amassing great wealth, they nevertheless shared in the profits generated by the Crimean War, which would account for their return to the capital from Anatolia. The father – small, dark and uncomely, as his son recalled – was an importer of attar of roses, a sought-after and costly essence (250 lb of petals from the most extensive rose gardens in the world in southern Bulgaria produced just one ounce of oil). When business took him abroad for prolonged periods, his family accompanied him; one of Zacharoff's sisters, according to family tradition, was born in England.

His mother, whom he took after, was by contrast tall and fair; a portrait painted some years later shows her as a model middle-class Victorian matron. She was also blind and made her son repeat to her his daily lessons, an exercise which sharpened his memory.

The Times obituarist was to state flatly that he was 'educated in London and Paris' – and that it was all that was publicly recorded of his early days. (Unfortunately, he omitted to indicate where it was recorded.) The rival obituarist in the *Daily Telegraph* hazarded that he was educated at Rugby, a canard that Zacharoff himself threw out in old age. (The school records refute this. It may be far-fetched to imagine that the Greek identified with the good Dr Arnold, who had the 'tact to make himself both loved and feared', a speciality of the adult Zacharoff.) In the same vein of minor conceit, he also told Sir Francis Bertie, British Ambassador in Paris during the First World War, that he had been 'at the University of Oxford'. He may well have got as far as the Mitre, but no further.

Legend insists that while Zacharoff was still in his youth, the family fell on hard times. If so, poverty would have been relative. Whatever the risks of the luxury commodity trade, the father practised also as a notary, a steady and gainful standby. And although there were now three daughters – Sevasty, Zoë and Charikleia – to feed, their education was not stinted in favour of their brother's, as would have been the case if funds were short. Despite this, the legend runs that a rich fellow countryman – a distant cousin, or even customer – from posh Phanar, one Iphestidi, now took up the boy and paid for his education at the English school. He would not have needed to do so. All foreign schools were run by various breeds of missionaries and, suffering some difficulty in filling them, waived the fees for those willing to brave their outlandish faiths.

A more reliable source, however – Zacharoff's own family – confirms that he did attend an English school, and the presumption points to one in England. He was clearly experienced in the essentials. Some years later, pointing out to a friend the expense of the Greek school in Cyprus – £100 a year – where he was then based, he was able to recommend 'plenty of English schools in & about London where the boy with clothing books & etc [sic] would cost' less than half that fee. His foreign name attracted the unwelcome attention of the other inmates and he was ragged, innocently enough,* as a fag whose duty it was to light the dormitory stove, a chore with which he was unfamiliar. He took two immediate measures to counter this mild roasting. He adopted his middle name of Basil and arranged for boxing lessons for himself. He was thereafter treated with corresponding consideration. He so relished his triumph that he recited it (in English) often enough for his grandchildren to remember it half a century after his death. (In fact, his memory may have played him false. Zacharie is more plausibly a schoolboy's rendering of his surname; he certainly clung formally to Zacharias as his Christian name for many more years.)

Education he did acquire, even if his finishing schools were the courts and capitals of Europe. Many years later, Prince Christopher of Greece wrote: 'it is difficult to believe this' – he imagined him to have started life as a pageboy in an Athens café – 'of one so deeply cultured in almost every subject, with such a wide knowledge not only of modern languages, but the classics'.

Legend contrarily credited him with being largely self-educated – in the streets, predictably barefoot. This process completed, he earned a subsequent living by scraping and scrounging in the same habitat. A French obituarist described this demurely: 'He first tried

* Zacharie, blow the fire, puff, puff, puff.
 First you blow it slowly
 Then you blow it fast.
 Zacharie, blow the fire, puff, puff, puff.

his hand at those thousand little roving trades with which all young Levantines are familiar.' Others identified these trades less prudishly as money-changer, brothel tout and tourist guide. If the young drago-man's margins were modest in the fiercely competitive climate, he would have reaped one bonus: the rudiments of those many tongues of which he was master from the earthy clients on shore leave from the ships of a dozen nations.

Another legendary trade he tried his hand at was fire-fighting – and, if rumour be true, fire-lighting. The local brigade, of which membership was much sought after by the adventurous young, was regarded as a lucrative source of salvage. Its excesses occasionally attracted the attentions of the police. A major fire in 1865 was followed by arrests and even executions. It was later claimed by his fellow dowsers that Zacharoff left hurriedly that year and did not deem it safe to return for four or five years.

However rude his apprenticeship, he was a survivor. He had, too, his share of good fortune. 'I have been lucky all my life,' he acknow-ledged with disarming frankness. 'If I hadn't been, I should have been murdered long ago, or else serving a life sentence in some prison.'

If a fraction of this lore were true, his family must have hoped that he would put his freelance initiatives behind him and adopt a more settled and respectable way of life. In his late teens, it is generally accepted, a maternal uncle, Sevastopoulos, offered him a job in his cloth business in the busy Galata district by the port. The merchant was delighted with his astute and aspiring relation and for two or three years everything went well. And then, suddenly and myster-iously, the young man vanished, and for several years all trace of his career vanished with him, conveniently creating one of those vacuums in his life which legend so avidly filled.

One tale had it that he had absconded with his uncle's cash, was caught and sent to prison from which he made his escape; it was even hinted that he had taken the life of a warder in this bid. The least sensational view was that he had committed some misdemeanour but had managed to flee abroad with the proceeds to embark on a new career under another name.

Less pressing motives may have prompted his departure. Multi-lingual, quick-witted, ambitious, he took off to dabble on his own account in commodities with parental blessing and a purse as a parting present.

'I began by using up my patrimony,' he recalled, 'and then came the struggle for life with all its risks and dangers.'

2

Nuptials and Newgate

Constantinople at this time hosted a multitude of commission houses operating on short credits regularly renewed in London. The funds thus available were mostly applied to commodity speculation. In his 'struggle for life', Zacharoff ensured that others shared the risks and dangers of this trade. He persuaded them to entrust him with commissions in England, Turkey's major trading partner, which he is known to have first visited in the year or two before 1870. These associations continued, peacefully if precariously, for several more years.

Along the way, the Greek, approaching his majority, had made the acquaintance of a young lady, Emily Ann Burrows, the daughter of a well-to-do Bristol builder. Zacharoff was a personable youth, above middle height, athletic and well set up, fair haired with a commanding nose and eyes of 'vivid cornflower blue that met yours with a candour so child-like that you wondered what was behind them'. He was, moreover, an accomplished charmer, his voice soft and caressing; he had fine hands, long and slender, firm and cool to the touch. To supplement this vision, he had adopted a style above his station. This promotion and his own presence made an impression. And, although living on borrowed time (and money), he gave the appearance of possessing the wherewithal to support a partner. The relationship ripened into a proposal of marriage.

According to the testimony of Emily Ann's niece, Mrs Henrietta Greenslade, made many years later (she was aged twelve at the time of the events she described), the couple were supposedly married first in Paris. They repeated the process from the bride's home at

4 Hill Street, Mayfair, at All Saints, Ennismore Gardens, Kensington, on 14 October 1872. This marriage, Mrs Greenslade recalled, was 'planned in a great rush. My aunt seemed agitated about something. She wanted to wait a little longer, but Basilius was pressing her to marry him.' This hesitation is strange if they had already gone through a civil ceremony, unless she had still not brought herself to share her good news with her parents. Indeed, but for the presence of these, John and Kate Burrows, as witnesses, it might well have seemed a hole-in-the-corner affair; All Saints was at the utmost limit of the sprawling parish of St Margaret, Westminster, in which the couple had residence, and an inconvenient distance, it might be thought, from Hill Street.

That there might have been some reason for this suspicion is evident from the marriage register. The name of the groom is given as Zacharias Basilius Gortzacoff, bachelor, rather quaintly described as 'General de Kieff', son of Basilius Gortzacoff, officer.

The Burrows family is likewise a surprise. John Burrows carried on his father's craft as carpenter and builder, working from, and living in, York Street, Bristol, a district of small tradesmen and artisans. Around 1870, if Mrs Greenslade's memory can be counted on, he set up his second daughter, Emily Ann, in the heart of fashionable Mayfair a few paces from Belgrave Square with Earl Cornwallis for her neighbour. It was a sudden and startling step up in the world. And if her parents neglected to make enquiries into Zacharoff's background, it must have been that they were overawed by his ostensible station.

Emily Ann was twenty-seven when she married, that is, four years senior to her groom, with one foot on the shelf. She appears in her only known photograph as a robust, self-possessed and determined woman with a quizzical air; she was certainly allowed an unusual degree of independence for the age.

A minor curiosity of this marriage is that it escaped attention, or at least mention, in Zacharoff's earliest biographies published in the last years of his life, as well as the newspapers which took such a close interest in his each movement and were not above airing implausible hearsay. And yet the record was available; journalists were familiar with the details but held their hand, incomprehensibly hoarding one of the few substantiated facts of his salad days.

Gortzacoff was also in the circumstances an uncharacteristically ill-considered choice of name for a serious imposture. Prince Michael Gortschakoff, as it was more usually spelt, famous for the stout defence of Sebastopol, had been dead ten years but his cousin, Prince Alexander, was still very much alive and active as one of the most

7

powerful ministers in Europe. His devious diplomatic manoeuvres were given wide and wary notice in the contemporary English newspapers.

There is reason to believe that, Emily Ann having secured her man, the Burrows were anxious for her to give up Hill Street and return to her roots in Bristol and that a quarrel developed on the groom's objecting to this unalluring prospect. In Hill Street they remained, the bogus boyar, Mrs Greenslade recalled, accompanying himself on the piano and entertaining his wife and her niece with talk of life on the steppes and the gay goings-on in the court at St Petersburg. This idyll lasted little more than a month. Then, scenting trouble, perhaps alerted by news from Constantinople, Zacharoff persuaded his wife that it was imperative they leave the country; he gave the impression that he was engaged on important diplomatic missions for the Russian government and had acquired enemies who, abetted by the police, were on his trail. Accompanied always by Henrietta Greenslade, they moved to Brussels where they were royally treated. The brave Belgians were very soon relieved of this charge.

On 20 November 1872, Sir Sydney Waterlow, Lord Mayor of London, signed a warrant in the Mansion House for the arrest of 'Zacharia Basilius Zackaroff, alias Prince Basilius Gortschakoff'. His cover had been blown.

When the Belgian police arrived, he tried bluff. Mrs Greenslade thought that he imagined he was safe in Belgium, having overlooked a recently completed extradition treaty with Britain. (His was, in fact, the first arrest under this treaty.) He was brought back to London to be charged. To his wife, dreaming of droshkys and borzois, samovars and sables, it must have come as an unwelcome surprise, but Basilius managed to convince her that it was all the result of a misunderstanding. Nonetheless, money would be required for the defence. Loyally, she obliged.

On 14 December, he appeared on remand before the Lord Mayor, charged with defrauding Manuel Hiphestidez, Greek merchant and judge, of merchandise – gum and gall-nuts – to the value of some £1,000 and of stealing securities worth between £6,000 and £7,000 – a very considerable fortune.

Much mystery has been made of this trial. Many vital papers are said to be missing for a variety of sinister reasons. In fact, each of his five appearances in court, although he was competing for space with the Tichbourne claimant and the arrest of Lord Alfred Douglas, was fully covered in *The Times* law reports, overlooked only by the mythmongers.

Fresh evidence on the family emerged. Zacharoff himself, the plaintiff's solicitor acknowledged, had the reputation of being very clever; already the master of seven or eight languages – he was then just twenty-three – he had worked as an interpreter in London for a few years. The father was a notary of great respectability; his own client acted as his exchange broker and accountant. This confirms a degree of affluence that Zacharoff later denied and that legend, not surprisingly, never conceded. There was a more startling revelation. A letter from Moscow, surmounted with a coronet, was produced in court. It was dated fourteen days before Zacharoff's marriage and bore the signature Gortschakoff. Hiphestidez testified that he recognized the handwriting as that of the defendant's father.

Unfortunately this does not seem to have aroused the curiosity of the court and it is now impossible to guess what reason or motive the family had to assume this name so overtly, and in Russia of all places. There were many stories of Zacharoff's Russian connection. The rest is conjecture.

The accused, it transpired, had been in Constantinople in June when he had offered to act for Hiphestidez, to whom he was well known, as agent for the sale of merchandise. He then approached Heinrich Bluhm of Faber & Co. and, representing himself as the owner, obtained advances amounting to £896 odd.

In September, the month before his wedding, the accused had returned to Constantinople, where Hiphestidez had requested an account of sales. Zacharoff, pleading that he was unwell and needed a rest, promised to do so in good time. He then vanished, taking with him a large sum of money and the securities from the plaintiff's safe, which the accused himself had purchased previously in London, retaining for his own use one of the two keys with which it was supplied.

The court was informed that the accused had next gone to Smyrna where he had tried to induce an English lady to join him with a view to marriage. She declined, but afterwards wed him in Paris, a ceremony which was subsequently solemnized in London. A 'remarkable notification' of it appeared in some English papers which fell into the hands of Hiphestidez. (*The Times* of 17 October 1872 briefly announced the marriage of 'Prince Zacharius Basilius Gortzcoff' [*sic*] on the 15th – one day out. None of the Bristol papers followed this up, although that city was given as the father-in-law's hometown.)

A detective officer gave evidence that he had traced the accused to Brussels where he was arrested at the Hôtel de France by the Belgian police. Faced with the charges, he had insisted that they were 'wrong from beginning to end' and that, though registered as Gortzacoff, it was a case of mistaken identity; his real name was Vassil. He had in his possession a case of jewellery, twenty-four Turkish bonds to the value of £1,680 and a revolver loaded, capped and cocked. The 'Princess' informed the police officer that it was fortunate he had brought sufficient assistance for otherwise he would have received the contents of one of the barrels, a casually cold-blooded assessment from a newly-wed. Returned to London a few days later, Zacharoff was charged with unlawfully pledging the merchandise with which he had been entrusted. He maintained his innocence.

On his fourth appearance, the defence asked the court to overlook the matter of the assumed name and the offence which had been committed in Turkey. On the remaining charge, the accused, who spoke very creditable English, pleaded that as Hiphestidez had not arranged for a commission – Hiphestidez had sworn in evidence that he had – he had simply drawn 12 per cent of the proceeds to defray the cost of the return journey to Constantinople and his expenses for two months' residence in London, and that this advance could not be said to be pledging goods.

The Lord Mayor disagreed. Zacharoff was committed to Newgate for trial at the Central Criminal Court.

At his first hearing at the Old Bailey before the Deputy Recorder, Sir Thomas Chambers, the accused withdrew his plea of Not Guilty. Something was afoot. At that Mr Straight, appearing for the prosecution, requested the judge to refrain from passing sentence until the next session because, in the interval, certain evidence would come to light that would allow a nominal sentence to be passed. The judge complied.

Zacharoff came up for judgement before the Queen's Bench early in February 1873. The prosecuting counsel, back-pedalling, declared that in consequence of the accused being a foreigner, the complainant (evidently considering himself a cut above fellow foreigners) was now graciously disposed to put the most favourable construction on his conduct. He suggested that the accused should be allowed to go free. Zacharoff's counsel did not dissent. The judge, taking note that he had made an offer of compensation, released him on his own recognizance of £100.

It is not, unfortunately, known what tipped the scales. Zacharoff had his own gloss to add. Many years afterwards, his first patron, Stephen Skouloudis, sometime Prime Minister of Greece, reconstituted from memory his friend's long account of this 'painful episode'.

It was somewhat more colourful in the telling than the general run of cases at the Central Criminal Court.

Zacharoff pretended that his 'uncle' had made him a partner by letter but had steadfastly refused to pay him anything on account for commission. The young partner, after waiting three years in vain for such recognition, paid himself off and, leaving an exact statement of account behind him, took himself out of range, as he expected, of his uncle's retribution. Unhappily, he lost the letter, important proof of his standing. Things looked very bad for him indeed, but he was saved by the severe English winter. Wrapping himself in a warm cloak for the short journey from his cell to the courtroom, he thrust his hands deep into the pockets. His fingers touched a paper, he gave a shout of joy.

The confrontation from the dock was dramatic. The uncle was about to testify when Zacharoff cried out: 'Mr Chairman, do not permit him to take the oath, for he will certainly commit perjury!' The uncle, thunderstruck, broke down and was obliged to acknowledge the authenticity of the letter. 'This', related Zacharoff, 'concluded the trial. The court ordered that I should be set free immediately.' Years later he was to sum up the case more succinctly: 'The head of the Stamboul firm was my maternal uncle. He owed me money and I took it. That was all.'

If plaintiff and accused were so closely related, it was never, surprisingly, revealed in court. Zacharoff always insisted on this point, perhaps to aggravate the impression of unjust persecution. Was Hiphestidez the same wealthy Iphistidi who was said to have sponsored his education? The record is silent.

A bizarre theory has been put forward to explain the discrepancies between the trial reports and Zacharoff's account. The Greek community's sense of solidarity was outraged that one of its kith and kin should be victimized by a fellow countryman before alien justice, and the uncle as a result had already had his shop windows smashed as a foretaste of its displeasure. If Zacharoff were found guilty, he would face a trade boycott. He therefore smuggled a predated letter to his nephew in prison which would get them both out of a spot while still ensuring that the debt was recognized.

This theory, far-fetched as it may seem, is, however, plausible. Zacharoff's behaviour, his sudden flight to Belgium and especially his artless bluster at his arrest, was not that of an innocent man. Then came prosecuting counsel's volte-face at the Old Bailey. Acting on instructions, he was playing for time. Hiphestidez, having returned to Constantinople, might have reached a settlement with his client,

11

Zacharoff's father. Counsel did not submit his new 'evidence' for the court's consideration; instead, he merely advocated Zacharoff's release, implying that as a foreigner he could not be expected to know any better. The Greeks, perhaps, acted out this little farce for the benefit of English justice to save the accused's skin and the plaintiff's remaining panes.

This is supposition. All that is clear is that Zacharoff made a promise of at least partial restitution, and there is little doubt, parental indulgence so recently overtaxed, of its probable source: Mrs Zacharoff, late Princess Gortzacoff, née Burrows. This, and her husband's legal expenses, according to Mrs Greenslade, swallowed up her aunt's money.

3

Island Interlude

His character discredited, his (and his 'uncle's') resources depleted, Zacharoff was forced to make a fresh start. He chose neutral ground where the ambience was nonetheless familiar. He settled with the compliant Emily Ann in Cyprus, which was to be his base for the next seven years.

An American author, Charles Merz, first signalled his arrival on the island in 1873 'using a British passport in the name of Z.Z. Williamson' where he was 'trying to sell military equipment' to General Wolseley; another source has it that he sank his wife's remaining funds into a small store and launched out as a salesman of 'superb specimens of sporting guns for the British Army officers in the island' to speed the extinction of the wretched moufflon, and 'then, through these contacts, he tried to sell modest items of military equipment at cut prices, apparently with little success, but at least gaining experience all the time'.

He would have gained little else.

This early introduction to firearms, conveniently foreshadowing his ultimate career, is too neatly contrived, for there is one snag. Cyprus was leased to Britain by Turkey, in the wake of the latter's defeat in the Russo-Turkish war, in exchange for British guarantees against Russian encroachment. Lieutenant-General Sir Garnet Wolseley was the first High Commissioner and as a former quartermaster-general would have proved a hard nut to crack for a débutant dealer in surplus stores, the more so as he was at this date subjugating the Ashantis in West Africa before a brief posting to Natal. Cyprus was not occupied until July 1878, and Wolseley left again the following year to overawe the Zulus.

There is, however, other more reliable evidence that Zacharoff was on the island, but before the cession to Britain. A later colleague, Sir George Owens-Thurston, who first met Zacharoff only many years after this period of his life, recollected that he went into property speculation.

An observer of the local scene, Sir Harry Luke, recalled that the suspicion of the British Consul, who had not been kept in the picture, was aroused by an unusual influx of visitors from the Turkish capital to Larnaca, avidly buying up all the real estate they could lay their hands on. Among the first of these dealers, acting perhaps on official leakage from the Sublime Porte, was a young Ottoman Greek then known as Zacharias Vasilios Zachariadis. Yet another Cyprus hand, Sir Ronald Storrs, described 'Mr Z.Williamson' as a local contractor whose fortune was founded on the erection of the High Commissioner's residence, a prefabricated wooden hutment destined for the officer commanding the garrison in Ceylon. That shrewd soldier procured a stone substitute for himself, and the freight, diverted to Cyprus, was carried up to Nicosia from the beach by camel.

As in the case of the Gortzacoff* impersonation, Zacharoff clung fondly to his own initials, the foundation for the 'ZedZed' by which he was later known in the boardroom of his employers at Vickers for half a century. The Williamson he adopted from a member of a family with old Anglo-Levantine associations. The daughter of John W.Williamson wrote many years after that 'my family was not in any way connected with Zaharoff. My father was in Cyprus at the time of the occupation, and possibly before that, and was there when Zaharoff came to the island, calling himself Z.Z.Williamson. I do not know why he chose that name . . . Anyway, my father was not at all pleased about it.' The wrath was retrospective; her father had less reason to be displeased than Zacharoff. The pair went into partnership. At first things went well. 'Little Williamson', Zacharoff considered, 'deserved great credit for the way he worked in the matter' of a commodity deal which turned sour; two months later, he thought him 'a stupid and ignorant idiot'. Zacharoff formally cast him off together with another unappreciated partner and had 'Johnny up before the High Court for wicked and malicious slander' for spreading the tale that Zacharoff's business had failed and that he had fled the island; although Williamson recognized his error and besought

---

* By a double irony, among the 2,000 White Russian refugees from the Black Sea escorted to Cyprus by the Royal Navy in 1920 was another HSH Prince Gortzacoff.

forgiveness, Zacharoff demanded 'an humble apology' in court. (It may be that he was not so grievously wronged as he made out; 'the law', he remarked, 'is very clear about slander, & provides up to two years hard labour for those, who actually tell the truth against another man.') Thereafter, Zacharoff continued for a time to trade (and travel) under the name Z. Z. Williamson.

Nothing more is known about his early years on the island except that it was here that he made the acquaintance of a seasoned English merchant, William Shaw, who was indirectly to provide Zacharoff with his main chance, although it was not immediately recognized. The two combined their talents in an informal relationship of rare affection, frankness and trust.

It was through this contact that Zacharoff met his principal benefactor, a family friend of Shaw, Stephen Skouloudis, a rich and already influential figure in Athens. This improbable pair had a common background, Constantinople, where Skouloudis, Zacharoff's senior by a bare dozen years, was born. A founder of the Bank of Constantinople, he had sold out a few years before and was at that time a respected commentator on the newspaper *Ora*, and within five years was to enter the Greek parliament and pursue a distinguished public career.

These first years, until he had established roots in Cyprus, were undoubtedly lean and uncertain for the young Greek. Skouloudis admitted that he was leading a hand-to-mouth existence and that his new friends often had to help him over the next day. Zacharoff was in no position yet to return other than trifling services, he had no prospects; there was little to recommend him save his charm, presence and quick wits. There is nothing certainly to indicate a marriage of minds between the scamp and his patron. Far from it. Skouloudis was pontifical and priggish. (A wartime British minister at Athens, Sir Francis Elliot, found his character so exasperating that he was seized 'with an almost irresistible longing to take hold of his long beard and tweak it as hard as he could'.)

Rumour, meanwhile, was busy and soon reached the ear of the older Greek. Zacharoff, his character once more at risk, put on a bold front and threw himself on Skouloudis' charity and credulity. 'You, my dear Monsieur Skouloudis,' he exclaimed in anguished accents, 'have also given credence to these infamous suspicions which pursue me everywhere. Good. Listen to the truth. I'll give you a good account, for you have given me so many proofs of your kindness. Listen to me and judge for yourself.'

Early biographers have evoked a most touching scene. The older man sternly surveying the accused, Zacharoff pulling press cuttings out of his pocket, 'objectively, soberly, almost drily, like a police report' recounting his experiences in Constantinople and London. Skouloudis listened, examined the evidence and was finally convinced. His protégé had been traduced; he deserved support. Zacharoff, with tears of gratitude, embraced his protector.

Half a century on, Skouloudis, full of years and honours – a former Prime Minister of Greece – himself described this encounter:

He was young, enterprising and intelligent, but opinion about him was divided. ... Some treated him with the mistrust with which the most disreputable individuals are regarded, while others thought him the victim of malicious misunderstanding. Basil Zaharoff had just come from trial in London, where he had emerged as the moral victor from a scandal disseminated by ill-informed or evil-minded persons. I took the trouble at the time to investigate carefully the records and the reports of the trial in the English newspapers and to study all the details of the affair which led his calumniators to spread scandalous stories. ...

Since then our personal relations have developed most cordially, and I must confess that I have read with increasing astonishment the untruths, inaccuracies and malicious reports which have been published in the newspapers about the origins, the past, the achievements, and the character of Basil Zaharoff, by whose friendship I am honoured.

Even if the rumours had been wildly exaggerated, this is still a somewhat generous interpretation.

While Zacharoff was successfully salvaging his reputation, war clouds were blowing up. Russia had long claimed a right to interfere in the affairs of the Ottoman Empire on behalf of the Sultan's Christian subjects. Her object was nothing less than Constantinople itself with the promise of warm-water access to the sea through the Straits. In the name of pan-Slavism she exploited nationalist rivalries in the Balkans to open up the way for her. An eruption of Serbs in 1875, speedily crushed by the Turks equipped with Krupp's latest artillery, led to direct Russian intervention and war with Turkey two years later.

This engagement produced feverish excitement in Greece, but the government was determined to remain aloof in view of the country's military unpreparedness. However, the fall of the Turkish fortress of Plevna after a heroic four-month siege brought about a change of regime. The Greeks now prepared to turn on the battered Turks in the expectation of pickings. But with the tsarist forces in sight of the gates of Constantinople, Britain, with a hawkish Queen Victoria breathing fire, declared that she could not remain neutral and as an as an earnest of her intentions sent the fleet through the Dardanelles. She also more discreetly put a damper on the war mood in Athens. The end of the hostilities left Greece in the air but, hopeful of at least pushing her claims to a favourable adjustment of frontiers at the peace table, she continued to marshal her forces. Thoroughly rattled, the great powers settled down in Berlin to make a first shot at the arbitrary Balkanization of that troublesome quarter and at the same time deprive Russia of the fruits of her victory.

One effect of the war had been to demonstrate the superior fire-power of modern weaponry, which was apparent for the first time on such a scale – at least in the European theatre; the lessons of the American Civil War were largely ignored by the Continental armies. The Turks had made devastating use of 1866-model Winchester repeating rifles and, for longer range, the American Peabody-Martini. The Balkans became overnight a happy and rewarding hunting ground for arms dealers. The timing could not have been more providential.

By happy chance, Skouloudis counted among his friends a Swedish sea-captain who acted as agent in Athens for a small enterprise founded by a fellow Swede, an inventor–engineer, Thorsten Vilhelm Nordenfelt. Its trade: the manufacture and marketing of arms. The captain was about to be rewarded with promotion elsewhere – an ill wind, as it turned out – and he therefore consulted the worldly-wise Greek on the subject of his replacement.

Skouloudis did know the very man. He recommended the resourceful Zacharoff – with one reservation. He touched on the rumours surrounding his candidate and suggested that the Swede should make his own researches. 'If they turn out favourable, do not hesitate to appoint Zacharoff. The man will be useful to you.' Zacharoff was spared any awkwardness. The departing sea-captain did not leave himself time to make even the most perfunctory enquiries; it has been suggested that, for lack of other references, Zacharoff let it drop that he had connections with British Intelligence. The very next day he was offered the job of agent for the Balkans at the handsome salary of £5 a week. The date was 14 October 1877. (Typically, Zacharoff later contested this. He claimed to have joined the company on 13 October 1878.)

Skouloudis recounted that Zacharoff came round three days later to express his thanks, threw himself on his knees and, bursting into tears, covered Skouloudis' hands with kisses. This scene must have been played in Cyprus. Zacharoff had been in Greece only once before August 1880 and he was then, by his own admission, in hiding.

17

While the Congress of Berlin – where Benjamin Disraeli squared up to the authentic Prince Gortschakoff – was carving up the Balkans, Greece continued to rearm. Almost as an afterthought, the powers decreed that Turkey redraw her frontiers with Greece – a net Greek gain of over a quarter of a million in humankind – but the continuing tension over demarcation led to recurrent bouts of armament and mobilization. At the time of the Congress, the Greek army was a ragtag of 20,000 semi-combatants, the majority without uniforms, almost all without maintenance; the state supplied only rifles and cartridges. Within three years its strength had been quintupled on paper, with an appropriation of sixteen million francs, or four-fifths of the budget. An order worth two million francs for the most modern artillery was placed with Krupp, for which the war had provided such a good advertisement, including eighty-four of the latest cast-iron cannon, of which most serving artillerymen sternly disapproved (bronze had been good enough at Austerlitz). At the same time, a strong home government under Skouloudis' patron, Charilaos Tricoupis, who was to remain in power, with short breaks, for the next dozen years, instigated economic reform which inspired confidence abroad. When a fresh conflict with Turkey threatened in 1885, a loan of one hundred million gold francs was raised for the army and navy. (The crisis was short-lived. The powers invited Greece to disarm and, to prevent any possible misunderstanding, blockaded the Piraeus.)

Contrary to legend, however, Zacharoff had not spotted these opportunities. For the next three or four years he devoted himself exclusively to his own affairs in Cyprus. He exerted himself just once, supplying a shipload of rifles to a 'very grateful' Greek government in 1881. They were not, though, Nordenfelt's wares.

From 1879 sudden rare light is shed on Zacharoff's character and career in a long, intimate and minutely detailed series of letters, hidden from view for over a hundred years, from 'Z.Z.', then aged thirty, to William Shaw, rising fifty. Gaining confidence and sometimes commissions, he had spread his wings beyond the island, leaving Shaw to look after their joint ventures and separate stores – Zacharoff in Limassol, Shaw in Larnaca – in his absence, while the latter's nephew acted for them as agent in Liverpool. July of that year found Zacharoff once again in Constantinople visiting his dying mother (his father had died the previous year). He was relieved, but not surprised, that his experience at the Old Bailey was a thing of the past: 'My affair (the old job) was quite forgotten as it would be in such an immoral den, others who had done worse & still continue ditto are well received in what they choose to call society ... Constantinople', he preached,

18

'was no good at all, people are starving, thieving, borrowing, cheating, I was quite disgusted.' He was, however, alive to opportunities in such an environment: these he diagnosed as 'money lending (usury)' or a shipping agency, which he interpreted as 'robbing Captains & owners'.

In August he was in London 'playing hide & seek' with his wife. 'I have seen her twice but she has not seen me & I take good care to keep out of her way.' (Emily Ann's health had broken down, according to her niece, Henrietta Greenslade, and the couple separated, Emily Ann returning to London. There is reason to believe that her husband had bought a property on the island in her name. The hapless woman was no doubt in search of the deeds and, by now, financial support.) A surprise awaited him at his lodgings at 92 Piccadilly. He found 'another person had registered themselves there as zig-zag' – a practical joker? – 'so I want you to alter your code to Zealous.' He was still preoccupied with his wife. Although he was alarmed that 'a private enquiry chap'* had 'got wind of my domestic troubles', he was 'persuaded that if I work my cards well she will lose all scent of me & think I am still at Constantinople where she dare not show her nose as she is mortally afraid of my people'. (His attachment to the name Williamson was as much an evasive measure to cover his tracks.)

He had developed into a versatile and alert trader, turning his hand to grasp any chance of a profit or commission. He dealt in commodities: exporting carobs – 'I humbugged the London lot nicely' – and importing barley from Beirut, which was 'badly managed . . . the thing is to get out of it without loss, if not to lose as little as possible, & if not to lose no more. This is the whole affair, we must not expect everything to turn out profitable.' He was not always so philosophical regarding the errors and omissions of his fellow middlemen; still less so with those against whom he had a real or imagined grievance: 'by God I shall make it hot for him', he bristled about an uncooperative manager of the Ottoman Bank. 'I have the bugger but he does not know it.'

During his ever shorter stays on the island – 'Would you believe it ... I have somehow taken to the place' – he managed his store with his Greek partner, George Rossides, scrupulously mindful of any bargain: 'vegetables ought to be most profitable. . . . Jams & cigars required at once . . . condensed Milk *cheap*. . . . Where are the sardines

---

* A curious advertisement addressed 'Strictly confidential: Z.Z. You can consult Mr Ward daily at his Private Enquiry office ... on Divorce, Loss or robbery' appeared on two successive days on the front page of the London *Evening Standard*.

you promised to send? We have not a single box here.' Judging the price of butter too high, he urged caution: 'quality must be superior & it will injure us, as if they get good stuff, they will always expect it & then we shall be working for the "Roi de Prusse" or may be even lose money.'

To supplement these modest margins, he diversified into catering, winning a lucrative contract to supply the canteen for successive British regiments on garrison duty, as well as that for the transport of troops. (He hoped to recover the customs duty on orders for the army, 'a good job, as it increases the profits materially'.) On the side he picked up agencies for earthenware and 'Scotch flannels, clothes & linen'; he made a try for the local agency for a Liverpool marine insurance company; he 'secretly' bought the waterfront Club in Limassol. All this was successful enough to encourage him, despite Shaw's pessimism, to open another small store in Nicosia, 'something like our Limassol place with not too many goods'. He found he was even sufficiently prosperous to practise a mild measure of philanthropy: the Greek school 'are making a God of me' – he had given them £5.

He pursued a parallel career as building contractor, though with some hesitation: 'it will be extending our operations, when it is our wish to confine them to a small focus'. Although he secured a contract for the Limassol water works worth in excess of £3,000, cash flow was as usual the main difficulty. One bank reneged on its promised advance on the security of the contract for the purchase of pipes; when Zacharoff in London had finally sorted out that in an exchange of telegrams with Shaw in their ad hoc and haphazardly concocted code which he had trouble interpreting, he could not find a ship to carry the pipes from England. Succeeding at last in this, he saved £75 on the freight but, obliged to pay £60 to a second bank for insurance, wondered 'if the damned ship will go down, what a lark if she should'. Next he was fortunate to fall in with the area manager of the Eastern Telegraph Company, Gibbs, who was to prove a loyal friend. Zacharoff called on the company's head office in London where they 'treated me wonderfully well, they think very highly of me & have covered me with invitations'. He was confident of the contract for 'laying down telegraph poles' in Greece and, when next in Constantinople, determined to 'feel my way about purchasing the Turkish line'.

He courted at the same time the Colonial Church Society on hearing the news that it intended spending £5,000 in the island on construction: 'a very good thing,' he judged, '... & I mean to have £2,000 out of it, if its only to show', he added to refute any slur of materialism, 'that I take an interest in religious matters, & you know I do.' He acquired, and paid for, land for the Society before leaving for London in December 1879, but his journey and the terrible weather took their toll: '... I cannot utter a word, my throat is quite closed up, awful pains in the chest, all my bones ache, & a strong attack of Cyprus ague, a thing I have never suffered from in Cyprus . . . I never was stout but I am now a perfect skeleton. [I] have lost courage which for me is a dreadful & unusual thing.' He found the missionaries 'very nice people & call every day & sit by my bed & keep me company'. The Society's secretary, indeed, invited the invalid to pass Christmas with them, but he 'excused myself as he has a church & I am not well read in finding the places in the prayer book etc. However I go to church now & in a week I shall be ready for him, I have another invitation which I will accept ... these chaps live like fighting cocks.' Such devotion evidently impressed his hosts for he was provided with the Society's power of attorney, entrusted with paying the Armenian 'parson' his £75 quarterly stipend and with the building of the 'church without tender & charge what it costs + 10% for my trouble you understand . . . if the Armenian trys to play with ZZ I will pay his passage & send him home, my powers are full and', he repeated to a sceptical Shaw, 'I am religious, & you know it.'

William Shaw, the owner of a small coaster, fostered his interest in another element in which Zacharoff would soon make himself at home. The *Pera*, Zacharoff thought, was 'too big for a little boat & too small for a big boat' but 'regular service and judicious manage-ment may in a short time turn out profitable ... the great thing in a boat,' he confidently lectured the shipowner, 'is regularity'. He also put himself out to find cargoes for overseas owners to induce them to call at the island, Shaw and Zacharoff taking 5 per cent on all forward cargo. When Shaw wished to expand, Zacharoff asked, 'but why buy a boat? I think I can get 2 boats ... sent out to us to work on commission & I believe that is better than risking your own capital.' Zacharoff's contribution was to suggest flat-bottomed steamers 'that will run up to the pier & discharge without lighters'. Shaw had his eye on the island's sole tugboat but his partner poured cold water on the idea: 'we w'ont [a persistent idiosyncratic construction] get a soul here to part with it, you know that as well as I do, if not better'. In Alexandria he spotted another monopoly, and a chance: 'there is only one ship chandler here, Ross & they are having it all their own way, I must work into their affections.'

All this might argue that he enjoyed some degree of affluence. He certainly did not deny himself comforts. Payment was always the problem. Some of his creditors were as much as eleven months in arrears; his expenses for foreign travel were high and the eventual returns uncertain, while at home he kept a groom to tend his five horses, as well as a faithful factotum. His three unmarried sisters were also a drain; they visited him at his expense and when he recovered £75 from the 'Religious Society' he proposed to send part of it to them as they were 'in want of funds'. He was unfortunate, too, with his other trading associates. He once feared that, with £500 unaccounted for, they had squandered the capital in his absence, leaving him only enough to meet his liabilities. Anticipating a reward of five years' hard labour for the miscreants, he was somewhat mollified to find that his capital was intact but that 'the profits are all buggered up'. He retrieved his deed of partnership from the aberrant bookkeeper '& he can go to h.ll [*sic*]. He recovered quickly. He received bills for £1,100 from Shaw which he endorsed and sent to a London bank for investment in 3 per cent government funds '& I'll see everyone damned first before I'll touch them'. With the payments for carobs, water works and troop transport, he paid off the local bank, leaving George Rossides 'to sack all the other buggers' and within a month had '£600 or £800 to my credit, this is better than I expected'. But just two months later in January 1880 he was 'boxed & fixed' in London. Shaw evidently lectured him on his extravagance. 'I am much obliged for your kind hint as to economy,' Zacharoff replied with dignity. 'I have put down every penny I have spent, been *most* economical.' 'Do for goodness sake', he pleaded later, 'send me the £100 I asked for & by telegraph otherwise I shall have to starve here I suppose. If you have to sell the damned place let me have it, I have not spent one penny on myself ... & it is damned hard to think that when they send up for my board & lodging I should have to pawn my watch.' Yet when he heard that Shaw had offered to go to Constantinople to raise £1,000, he would not hear of it: 'I have said repeatedly that I w'ont have anything of the sort, it is very kind of you, but we must do without it.'

Despite being short on substance, some of the leading Greek merchants and financiers in London 'wanted to pump me for their own benefit' on the prospects for a Bank of Cyprus. Zacharoff, unusually diffident, 'kept quiet & ... went up in esteem of Greek clique'. He was asked to dine that same night. 'It is curious that I know all these men & not one recognised me' (he was still passing himself off as Z.Z.Williamson). His advice evidently favoured an agricultural bank and he secured for himself a 'certain position & privileges', not least

1,000 fully paid-up shares, to which his hosts, after hard bargaining, assented. Six months later, the scheme was still hanging fire.

He had, indeed, a still more grandiose idea up his own sleeve. It was clear and audacious, and he went straight to the top to sell it. Cyprus had been assigned to England in return for the payment of all excess of revenue over expenses on the island, in the region of £100,000 a year barring natural disasters. If, however, Russia were to restore her conquests in Armenia to Turkey, England would evacuate Cyprus. This was a faint prospect, but the contingency discouraged British capital investment. Zacharoff's 'grand idea' was that the British government should offer the Turks a lump sum as compensation to amend the treaty in such a way as to render the occupation irrevocable, and the total annual revenue would instead be channelled into public works through a well-known and respected local contractor. For a small storekeeper who would shortly have need of recourse to a pawnbroker, this was a brazen ambition.

On the day of his arrival in London in December 1879, Zacharoff secured an introduction to Nathaniel Rothschild through a friend and Piccadilly neighbour, Frederick Gray. 'Rothschild received me very well, said my plan was an excellent one, but he was very sorry he could not mix in it, as the negotiations for the purchase of Cyprus ... were carried on through them ... that though this stopped them from lending their name to the plan, it would not stop them taking an interest in it through 3rd parties.' Rothschild sent Zacharoff to Julius Beer, the proprietor of the *Observer*, to whom he had already been introduced. The scheme hinged on whether the revenue of Cyprus had in any way been pledged to the foreign bondholders of the Turkish debt before the occupation, and whether the British government – a breathtaking presumption – would pay the rental into the Bank of England 'to the credit of *my* company'. This second question, even Zacharoff acknowledged, would require 'tact & influence'. Baring, Rothschild's principal rival, promised Zacharoff to sound out the Foreign Secretary, Lord Salisbury. Beer – 'the cleverest man I have met ... [he] has taken a great fancy to me' – undertook 'to bring out the bank for me' whether the master-plan succeeded or not.

Early in the New Year, Beer and Zacharoff were themselves received by Salisbury, but the original plan had 'taken quite another form, leaving less profit but making the affair more practical, I am at any rate leaving something for these big chaps'. Zacharoff understood that Parliament would be asked to vote half a million pounds for improvement in Cyprus which 'will receive great opposition, but it will be carried'; private finance was to be allowed to acquire the island's freehold. The government would 'lend their assistance as it suits them ... but it will be optional for them to buy us out at a profit'. Zacharoff was instructed to make an offer to the Porte, all his expenses being paid by the 'promoters of the Grand Idea which has taken a very favourable turn'. He was equipped with introductions 'to the best people & Pashas, Bankers etc'. If all went well, he was to return to London without delay; if the Porte did not 'come to terms, I will return straight to Cyprus & give up all idea of becoming wealthy in a day & stick to my business & I w'ont leave Cyprus again for a trifle, I can assure you. England w'ont see me for a few years.' He had not, however, parted completely from reality in pursuit of his chimera: 'You cannot imagine, how hard I have worked lately at the grand idea & how bothered I have been about not finding a ship for the water pipes.'

There was, however, an unsuspected fly in the ointment. 'The Liberals', Zacharoff wrote confidently at the end of January 1880, 'have no chance of getting in ... they have no leader & they say so. I would rather they did come in, I believe they would do more for Cyprus than the present party & have good reasons for saying so.' (He had already, in his thorough fashion, furnished himself with 'a capital source ... from which I get all foreign office news'.) Travelling by way of Paris and Marseilles, he had arrived in Smyrna by 12 February. For five weeks there is no sign of him. The first bad news he must have had was that of the death of his patron Beer on 29 February, aged just forty-four; this blow was followed a week later by the intelligence that Disraeli, similarly misjudging the direction of the wind, had called a snap election. His confidence sapped, Zacharoff did not await the results. He moved instead to Alexandria where, deferring his dream, he at once attended to his more immediate prospects. Staying with his friend Gibbs of Eastern Telegraph, he learned that the company's Cyprus manager had informed Zacharoff's host of all the rumours concerning him on the island. Fortunately this gratuitous gossip had the contrary effect on Gibbs who gave 'his *word of honour* that I shall build the house at Larnaca & Limassol'. Zacharoff decided to open an office in Alexandria '& soon too as the ETC have 800 miles of new lines to lay down & Gibbs has promised me the job. ... he does not care a damn what they say about me, he knows me & would rather trust me with the affairs of the C^{oy} than any living man. ... there is £2,000 to be made out of the ETC buildings.'

Zacharoff was back in Cyprus before the English election results were known. William Shaw set off for Alexandria to weigh his

24

partner's opinion of the place. 'God bless you old chap,' Zacharoff wired him, 'and a pleasant passage to you.' Shaw was not optimistic about their opportunities, but thought something might be done 'with a good deal of pushing & cheek & I flatter myself', Zacharoff considered, 'that I have a little of the former & heaps of the latter'.

It was only in the first week of April that Zacharoff had news of the decisive Liberal victory. He was 'quite astonished at the result but nobody was more astonished than the Liberals themselves. ... The poor Cypriotes [were] shaking in the shoes, for fear Gladstone should give up the island. ... Even at Headquarters this idea prevails. ... I do not believe in anything of the sort.' He was right, but he was shortly to be too disheartened by other setbacks to profit.

Shaw was away for most of seven weeks. Zacharoff missed him: 'the d––––d place looks so funny without you, Larnaca & our store miss you, I have got so accustomed to you old fellow that I'll shut up shop till you come back.' Gibbs, however, was as good as his word. Zacharoff got the contract for the new company house, taking 10 per cent on the value of the building, and, to keep his hand in, the would-be empire-builder set about painting the company's poles and bought the old Telegraph house for £50 where he 'made a lovely garden'. He warmly welcomed his partner's return: 'My dear old Shaw ... it will do my heart good to see you ... Go straight to the new house, take any room you like, all are at your disposal, & when you have had some grub & plenty to drink read the remainder of this letter.' This happy picture was soon shattered.

Another of his commodity deals was turning out more troublesome than usual. He fled to Beirut, intending to stay away 'till the matter has been squared with Burnett for £100 if he will accept ... If he once gets me into court, then Cyprus will be too hot for me.' He was still able to put aside his cares for other pleasures: 'I get on very well with the ladies, one is a perfect charmer, Venus herself & divorced from her husband, happy woman.' Finding that his hotel would not charge him for a servant, he urged Shaw to send over Abdul Kerim *without fail* as I feel lost without that young bugger'. He was, however, upset at hearing that Shaw was considering quitting Cyprus himself ('I shall be awfully cut up') and he returned three weeks later to face the music. Burnett having refused his proffered *douceur*, the case against Zacharoff had come up and he was enraged to hear that that same evening his persecutors had blackguarded him in his own Club, thinking he would not return. Recovering his spirits, he took out a 'criminal summons' against a couple of the sinners. Burnett's claim was not admitted by the court, but there were other pressing financial problems. He set about liquidating his affairs; the Limassol business went for over £900 and 'young Lansdowne' made him an offer of £521 for the Club. Thus armed, he 'passed my bankruptcy & returned ... with my discharge in my pocket'. But in a rare fit of pessimism he had already decided to abandon Cyprus himself. He was uncertain where next to flee: he contemplated Alexandria, Smyrna, Constantinople and Athens, 'but I begin to give up the idea. It is useless staying in any place where although you may do your best some chap turns up who knows your antecedents ... putting it about that you were this & that & more than the truth. My present idea is to have finished everything here, get all the cash in & then stay in the Levant for a couple of months & think seriously.' He even began to consider Russia, America or Australia. Shaw had already moved to Athens. Zacharoff left the island himself for the last time in September 1880.

All this prodigious activity was packed into little more than a year. It is no wonder that he was so inattentive to the affairs of his patient Swedish employer, or even had no leisure to indulge his priapic pleasures: 'I suppose that old dog of a Maltese has been getting into or onto the Widow, I wish I had the time to do the same ... [she] has the qualities that are necessary for scientific poking.'

There is a touching simplicity and warmth about his affection for the older Shaw. He was as spontaneously responsive to kindnesses as he was liable to occasional impulsive outbursts. Following some minor annoyance with Customs, he boasted that 'I'll lick those fellows before I leave, I'll give the b——————s such a hiding ½ an hour before I embark ... that they will remember Z.Z.' The officials were in little danger; his threats were nothing more than native braggadocio. He admitted, indeed, in a footnote that he was in an 'awful temper & I really do not know why'. He could, on the other hand, coolly deflate pretension. He faced a 'little breezy Scotchman' on Shaw's behalf 'who appears very fond of fighting'. He 'made a demonstrational speech lasting ¾ hr [and] when I finished I asked him if he had omitted to add anything to his very elaborate discourse – old boy turned downright nasty but shut up.'

He was a considerate and generous employer once his trust and affection were engaged. His assessments were indulgent, pithy and droll: Maltass 'would not suit you or me', he advised his partner, 'he is honest & straight but by the Lord Harry he left his brains in Smyrna or is keeping them in reserve'. Shaw differed, Zacharoff did not demur. He could also be unpredictably compassionate. Shaw complained to Zacharoff that an employee, Paul Samuel, had been 'suffering from drunkenness' in his absence. Zacharoff, who had 'very great confidence in him & would have trusted him with all I have', now decided 'he must go'. He was instead given another chance, but as he continued to give trouble, Zacharoff advised Shaw to dismiss him if he did not do 'entirely & exactly' what he was told. Samuel sulkily informed Zacharoff that he would not remain if he went away again, so his employer again decided to give him notice '& he can go as far as Smyrna with me, *since he is so fond of me*'. On the eve of his next departure for London, Zacharoff finally made the break, gently chiding Samuel for insubordination to the incompatible Shaw and advising him to look out for another situation. 'I regret being obliged to take this step & remain, Dear Paolo, very truly yours. ...' Zacharoff excused his action to Shaw: 'it is no use putting it off any more. I am not married to him, nor yet bound in any way.' Yet, before the month's notice had expired, Zacharoff, hearing from Paolo that he had no money, instructed Shaw to give him £5 or £10, and long after Zacharoff had left the island for good the two continued to correspond. He could be as sensitive as he was considerate of others' feelings: 'dear little George Rossides,' he wrote to Shaw about his associate, 'complained that I did not put enough confidence in him – on the contrary I love the boy dearly & I have more confidence in him than I have in myself, tell him I am hurt by his letter.'

Much of the malicious rumour that dogged him was undoubtedly due to envy. He enjoyed a perfectly amicable relationship with Wolseley's successor as High Commissioner, the Gunner, General Biddulph. His troubles arose with the rival English traders and agents on the island. The boom that came in the wake of the occupation was already subsiding. Their merchandise was often unsuited to the needs of the poor and thrifty Cypriots who, not speaking their tongue, were, as Sir Samuel Baker remarked, wary of them, while the Greek shopkeepers were content with smaller profits and less elaborate establishments. This would be enough to account for the resentment and spite, for his moral principles were not such that would have been wholly foreign to many other budding entrepreneurs of whatever nationality: 'I d'ont object to *doing* people, but I certainly object to being caught at it & in this case' – a trivial and apparently inadvertent overcharge for customs clearance – 'we have been already caught.' And yet twenty years later he was moved to protest when informed that a Greek naval officer would expect a commission on an order for warships; he was 'very shocked that any Greek should take a commission under the circumstances which simply means robbing his country & consequently serving it badly'.

He offered an illuminating glimpse into his selective sense of honour and impish humour at this time in a letter to Shaw from London in January 1880:

Do you remember my telling you of 2 disagreeable affairs I had in London a long time ago, & which I have [been] paying off since I have been in Cyprus. Well I sent for these people a few days ago, trying to compromise the matter. I squared the £3,000 man by paying him £150 cash down & have got a receipt in full, he asked me for I d'ont know what, but I was prepared for him, I was laying in bed & I know I looked like death. I had arranged also for a friend of mine to call while he was here, this chap pretended to be my doctor, & told my creditor in confidence that he had serious doubts about my recovery. I had planned all this, the 'Dr' prescribed & went away, & no sooner was he gone than the creditor jumped at my offer of £150 cash for fear I should die & he should get nothing.

The other man to whom I owed £400 (a dirty piece of business) had received since I have been in Cyprus £75 & I have given him £25 since, he has been very good to me in olden times & I will pay him in full by degrees & he says he will wait & never ask till I send him what I can afford [Zacharoff had just £34 left in the bank]. I am glad of these two jobs being settled as they were on my mind, a proof that I still have an ounce or so of conscience left.

The £3,000 man thinking that I would not live to accept his invitation foolishly asked me to stay with him for a week's shooting in the Country, & he will be damned wild tomorrow as I am writing him tonight accepting his invitation.

The disabused dupe was obliged to put up with his guest, along with his manservant, 'the black boy', for three days. Zacharoff 'quite enjoyed it. I think I managed that job capitally.'

After leaving Cyprus, Zacharoff spent the next nine months drifting around the eastern Mediterranean: Beirut, Athens, Alexandria, Constantinople. His expectations were raised when he heard on the Ionian island of Zante that a tramway was to be built: 'a sure fortune is to be made,' he confided to Shaw. Although in April 1881 he furnished the Greek government with a shipment of rifles, just two weeks later he was asking Shaw for repayment of a loan, and to lend him in addition £150 for six months. In June he plumped for a change of air in Paris; but tongues were still wagging and his health was now playing him up. 'The moment I leave a place things are said about me that if true ought to have sent me to the gallows long ago. ... [it is] impossible my dear Shaw for me to start fighting everybody, or stop peoples mouths – let it die out.' He was doing little to refurbish his reputation.

Mrs Jeherine [?] whom I was fool enough to poke a few times immediately after my arrival at the hotel, had her knife in me & Mrs MacCraith for my giving her up with the latter. ... You appear to be under the impression that Mrs MacCraith was divorced & I might marry her. You are wrong, I would not do so if she had millions – I poked her because it was my caprice. I poke her still & when I want a change I shall give her up. I am under no obligations to her or her family, as she costs me what an average whore would do & I pay her in one way or another & I have no doubt that if another man chose to court her & pay for it he could have her if he paid more than me, [and] she would turn me up.

The doctors soon put an end to this dalliance. Anaemia was diagnosed. He was advised to be 'very careful for a year. I am to avoid the least excitement ... to take gentle exercise & avoid all stairs & if I want to kill myself I am to have a woman, this last is strictly enforced, I am to give up women altogether, & in fact to avoid them so as not to get excited.' He also had to forego smoking, cold baths, spirits, coffee and tea; this bleak regimen was relieved only by an immoderate intake of cocoa. 'This is a blooming sort of a life, is it not?' he lamented to Shaw. 'I really don't think I shall have the patience to continue it, I might as well go into a monastery.' His enforced abstinence was short-lived (he later recommended Shaw to 'have Tassilaki [?] cut, for if he resembles ... Shaw or Z.Z. his tool will be his ruin'): after three weeks, he complained that 'damn it, it is an awfully insipid & monstrous life for a chap that has knocked about a bit. . . . I am afraid I shall have to go back to women & c & c [sic].'

He was again short of money, and was not finding the Parisian summer to his taste: 'the streets have not been watered for 10 days & the place stinks like fury'. He pricked up his ears on learning that Lesseps was to cut a canal through the Isthmus of Corinth, although Skouloudis, then also in Paris, warned him it would 'end in smoke'. He also tipped off Shaw that the French Rothschilds were 'going in for the Greek railway (this up to now is private & not even [Skouloudis] suspects it)'; Zacharoff made the acquaintance of the surveyor, Comte de Rohan, 'a Capital fellow ... we are now very friendly & I see him almost every day'. Apart from such flashes of sunshine, he was dithering about his future and at a loose end. 'I have nearly decided what to do . . . it is useless throwing away time & money in idleness.' Then, towards the end of July 1881, he wrote exultantly to Shaw: 'Fortune at last appears to be smiling on me again.' He was off to the Panama Canal (on which work had begun five months earlier) 'at my own expense' as agent for the Compagnie Générale de Ciments de Grenoble. He was to receive commission (12½ centimes) on each bag of cement, with a guarantee of 13,000 francs (over £500) each year for seven years and was at liberty to represent other French companies. Money was as usual the problem; he needed at least £600 for his passage and expenses. He raised only £125 from Skouloudis on his own draft on Shaw, Skouloudis – 'more than kind' – charging bare bank-rate for discounting the bill. With this, the prodigal 'went & ordered a few summer things for a hot climate'. He was once again on top of the world, 'all of a flutter & awfully excited. I don't remember being like this before & if I write much nonsense you must excuse me old boy. ... I feel', he added as a postscript, 'I shall get an attack of nerves ... & will go at once for a long drive.'

While this euphoria lasted, the Paris agent of the Eastern Telegraph Company received a cable: 'Search for Z. Z. Williamson late of Cyprus and Athens and wire when found.' He was wanted in Alexandria. Zacharoff, chary of trading a concrete proposal against an uncertain prospect, requested precise details.

By 24 July his contract was drawn up, but not signed. He never reached Central America. There is no word from him for three weeks and no subsequent hint of what had gone wrong. With hindsight he was fortunate; the malarial swamps were even less wholesome than the neglected Paris streets and his reputation was spared further stain by association at whatever remove with the greatest financial scandal of the Third Republic. Stoical as ever in adversity, he shrugged off his disappointment and made for Alexandria to sort out the affairs of the New Telephone Company: 'dear old Gibbs told Pender [the chairman] I was the best man they could get'. Fresh turmoil faced him. He found 'the thing has gone to pot, the staff sharing plunder'. Once his power of attorney arrived, he was determined to dismiss the manager and all the staff. His confidence had for once deserted him: '[I] cannot see things as clearly as I used to do & the slightest thing makes me lose courage – I suppose it is the 12 months lazy life I have lately had.' He faced up to the 'scoundrels', however, discharging twelve of his employees. Next day the remaining staff struck. After he discovered that they should have given three months' notice, they 'all cooled off in prison'. On their release, the recalcitrant 'rascals' cut down twenty-three wires while their employer was 'out in the sun all day to find out the fault'. Then the subscribers revolted, obliging him to give in to their demands for rebates. This activity acted as a tonic: 'I am always well when I have plenty of work & excitement. I suppose the reaction will come in as usual when all is right.' He travelled to London to explain the problems to the company, returning through Constantinople, Athens and Bucharest. He had not been back long before he was again betrayed by rumour and reputation. His friend Gibbs received a cipher telegram from Pender, chairman of the Eastern Telegraph Company: 'Have nothing to do with Z.Z. Williamson. You must not admit him on the Company's premises.' As Pender was also chairman of the New Telephone Company, Zacharoff expected 'to be discharged on Thursday's mail'. Even before this latest blow fell, he was suffering from his accustomed need: 'Want to get a little money together – if sisters ask say I'm in India.' Resignedly he packed his bags and continued his trek in an attempt to efface his past.

Pausing at Constantinople to take leave of his sisters, who provided him whenever he was low in mind or health with 'a little comfort & family happiness', he gave the next sign of life across the Atlantic almost three years later. Sloughing off his recent past, he had reverted to Z.Zacharoff. 'A fellow like you', he wrote to Shaw from New York at the end of December 1884,

laborious & economical need never want, yet Greece is too small a place for me, far too small. This is the place for me. Money is made not with work but with intelligence. I have done wonders here & am already being called the 'Little Railroad King'. The Yankees claim to be the smartest fellows in the world, they must be indulged in their fancy, but 'entre nous' they see little further than their noses. There is nothing on earth which could induce me to leave this country for good. I go to Europe now & then, & have been to Nicaragua repeatedly, but God bless the United States & Canada.

He had invested his savings from track-laying in Texas real estate, acquiring an interest in a large cattle ranch, and oil. His shares in an oil syndicate in Philadelphia, for which he had paid $4,000 the year before, 'went to hell', he afterwards admitted, '& I could not get $500 for my interest'. (Three years later he informed Shaw that he was 'on the point of making a little pot of money'. The Standard Oil Company was negotiating to buy him out and with 'no less than 3 fellows telegraphing me daily for my shares ... in competition have reached $20,500. ... Bakallum how much I will get.') Meanwhile, Lord Aylesford, representing an English group, had made him an offer for the ranch. Zacharoff's operations were seldom straightforward. The ranch owners, Zacharoff and his associates, would not get the title deeds until 1888 so he was 'endeavouring to get the government to join me in the sale – that will take me to Washington to do a little wire-pulling'. The outcome is not known; Lord Aylesford died at Big Springs ranch – possibly Zacharoff's property – two weeks later.

This transaction delayed his anticipated return to Athens, where the yeast of scandal was still active.

There had already been rumours in his last years in Cyprus that he was wanted by British law. These had been so persistent that Zacharoff had taken the precaution in Paris of asking an English judge of his acquaintance to 'find out quietly from Scotland Yard if there was any truth in the warrant affair' before chancing his nose in London. It transpired that Witt & Company had indeed applied for one back in 1874 and, although there was insufficient evidence to grant it, he was 'put down as a suspected person'. Zacharoff had later settled with Witt – the £3,000 or £400 London creditor – who had, however, omitted to withdraw the 'sworn information' until prompted by Zacharoff in 1881. Zacharoff's enemies in Cyprus, learning of this outstanding charge, had 'worried [Witt] out of his life' to proceed with the prosecution. A similar rumour that the law was after him surfaced in Athens in the late autumn of 1884. 'Who the devil said that a Scotland Yard man came to Greece after me?' Zacharoff asked Shaw. 'What the hell did he want? I fear no man living or dead. ... I say Shaw,' he continued in high humour, 'fancy my picking pockets when there are thousands of safes full of money waiting to be picked. What makes you believe that they murdered that poor fellow in prison?'

Unfortunately, Shaw's letters to Zacharoff have not survived and even Zacharoff found parts of this lurid account difficult to follow. But for once legend momentarily converges on real life. A sensational escape bid had been reported in the Athens press. The attempt was foiled, the runaway shot dead. The name of the deceased was given as Zacharias Basilius Zacharoff. The begetter of this fiction was Stefanos Xenos, a former financial operator in London turned author and journalist. The news must have surprised rather than alarmed Zacharoff's sisters, who believed their brother to be in America, but nevertheless they prevailed on Skouloudis to have the body exhumed and examined by Zacharoff's dentist.

I fail to understand how those damned fools arrived at the conclusion that that poor chap they murdered was me, & especially how they identified my effects. Will you oblige me by seeing Xenos at once & asking him to contradict in the most emphatic manner all that he thought fit to say about me. He was a friend of my late father & owes it to his memory & to my sisters, who are wickedly burdened down with the calumny. You know that I am not a man to be trifled with. By God I will have no nonsense. I shall be in Athens in a very short time & if I do not hear before then that Mr Xenos has in a gentlemanly & becoming manner contradicted all those vile slanders, I swear to do that to him which will prevent him from ever hurting another man, woman or child. A man of Mr Xenos brain & fertile intelligence cannot fail to understand that his reports are galling to me & to mine & he is sensible enough to see that I am justified in asking him to atone in part, or rather, to redress the wrong done me. Hand this letter to Mr Xenos, let him read it & if he is the man I take him to be he will act uprightly & justly – Demand it, do not beseech or press him. If he does properly well & good, if not may the devil help him for God cannot. I have nothing to lose in taking vengeance & if I had I would not care one damn. Let him be wise while he has time, on his own head be the consequences if not. . . .

Mr Skouloudis & Dr Agaley acted in a way I would expect of nobody, not even my best friend. To dig up the grave of a man buried 2 months, descend into it & pull the teeth of a decomposing corpse is a noble action & should I live to be 100 years old I can never forget their kindness, the outcome of which was to save my sisters the pang if not the sting of this uncalled for scandal.

The sequel is not recorded, although legend obliged with a comic confrontation between a triumphant Zacharoff and a cowering Xenos, who was let off with a stern caution and a public retraction rather than the threatened drubbing. More curious still was the alleged motive for the false claim – that Zacharoff had planted it himself on Xenos as he was still undecided which identity to preserve, William-son or Zacharoff, the resurrection of one requiring the interment of the other. It is no more evident why he should have been concerned for his nominal identity when he had made a new career in the New World. At all events, his mere reappearance in Athens, where his true identity was well known, would have given the lie to his reported death.

Early in 1885, Zacharoff returned to New York. There the late rancher and railroad king straightaway embarked on an untypically incautious adventure which nonetheless escaped the eye of the legend. At the end of August the *New York Herald* announced the marriage of Zacharias Zacharoff to Jeannie Frances Billings at the Madison Hotel one week before on 21 August. He had not given his hand lightly; Miss Billings, of 'excellent family and position', was further blessed with a fortune. The union, unhappily, was destined to be as brief and eventful as his legal London marriage thirteen years before.

The announcement of the happy event came to the attention of a Philadelphian businessman, formerly a resident of Bristol. He was reminded of a certain 'Prince Zacharias Basilius Zacharoff Gortschakoff' whom he had known well in that city and who had married the daughter of a local tradesman before falling foul of the law. He communicated his misgivings to the Billings family, who called on Mr Zacharoff – or Count Zacharoff as he was now sometimes known – for an explanation. The groom, indignant, protested his innocence with his usual vehemence. The performance was not convincing enough to still all doubt; family and friends of the young lady insisted on an investigation. Zacharoff went so far as to agree to live apart from his wife until he could clear his name.

The busybody from Bristol next interested a Mr Jenks of the law firm Crow & Jenks of Broadway, persuading him to pursue the enquiry in Bristol itself. The pair set sail for Liverpool on the *Servia* on 5 September. The victim of these malicious charges also took legal advice, evidently without letting his counsel completely into his confidence. He was urged to follow his detractors to Bristol with his wife, there to confront and confound them. This advice, with some modification, was deemed sound. Zacharoff, on the day his accusers sailed for Liverpool, took ship with his wife on the *Leerdam* for Rotterdam. Jenks was alerted by cablegram to this flight on arrival in England, but he had some time in hand before the *Leerdam* was due in Holland. He made the best of this, collecting first the evidence that the 'Prince' and the 'Count' were one and indivisible and next the former Mrs Zacharoff in London. On 10 September the two Americans, Emily Ann and her brother accompanied by a detective officer crossed to Rotterdam.

As Zacharoff's ship had still not docked, his adversaries enlisted the support of the American Consul. He agreed to deliver an invitation to Zacharoff on his arrival to meet him in his office; it was thought he would have no hesitation in complying as he would be likely to be well aware that no extradition treaty existed between Holland and the United States. The ruse succeeded. Shortly after his landing on Saturday, 18 September, Zacharoff – or Schwar as he now styled himself – presented himself at the Consulate. The other party burst into the room. In spite of such heavy odds, Zacharoff gamely tried to outface the opposition but was obliged to concede defeat. He left the Consulate hurriedly; he was no doubt concerned in part that, having entered Holland under an assumed name, he risked being shown across the border into a country where he would not enjoy immunity; his faith in Belgium as a refuge had already once been sadly misplaced.

The American faction, including the young lady whose fortune, possibly as much as $200,000, was at least intact, returned to Liverpool in time to catch the *Gallia* for New York on 20 September.

This gripping adventure made the front page of the *New York Times* on the day before the *Gallia* was due to dock. Although delayed for twenty-four hours by storms, the story was not followed up by the *Times* or any other New York paper. The attention of the reporters was taken up by the actress Mary Anderson returning on the same ship from a successful English tour. It was this débâcle that prompted Zacharias Zacharoff to convert himself into Basil Zaharoff in the hope of avoiding further unwelcome attention.

A clue to this curious episode is contained in Zaharoff's correspondence with Shaw. In 1884, Zaharoff wrote: 'You say the British Consul [in Athens] told you that female fiend who was the curse of my existence is dead. The Lord be praised or the Devil, it is immaterial.' He urged Shaw not to lose one moment in gathering all the particulars so that he could get positive proof from England. It is reasonable to suppose that this referred to Emily Ann Burrows. It is an explanation, no excuse; at the least he was guilty of gross carelessness and irresponsibility. Within three months of his brisk parting from Miss Billings, he had given his heart elsewhere: to a high-born lady wed to a grandee of Spain, in what was to be, after these two false starts, the one great and lasting passion of his life.

There is one conspicuous lacuna in his spicily varied career from his enlistment by the arms manufacturer, Thorsten Nordenfelt, in 1877 until the autumn of 1885: a singular absence of activity on his titular employer's behalf. It is plausible to presume that he had long ago forfeited his £5 weekly wage. Now, however, the inventive Swede reactivated his sleeping salesman. In September 1885, following the confrontation in the Consulate in Rotterdam, a chastened Basil Zaharoff made for Swedish waters where Nordenfelt's first submarine was about to be put through its paces. With his rich experience in so many fields and foreign lands, Zaharoff was an instant success underwater.

4

Submergence

We now arrive at what may be described as the backbone of the legend – the notorious *système Zaharoff*. Philip Noel-Baker, the former socialist politician and academic, castigated this as 'one of the most plainly anti-social, not to say detestable, but also one of the most effective methods of soliciting for armament orders ... playing one country off against another'. In the case of Zaharoff, the carrot was the submarine.

Many years later, Zaharoff recounted his part in opening up this market. 'I sold a submarine to the Greeks. And then', he added with a conventional chuckle, 'I went to the Turks and sold them a couple.' Russia presented the next obvious target. From a less reliable source we learn that Zaharoff, with bland impudence, expounded the situation as he saw it to the Navy Minister in St Petersburg: 'My firm is the agent of no one power. The Turks have bought two submarines from my firm. In the event of war the Turkish Navy can, thanks to these submarines, menace your ships in the Black Sea and strike where you least expect them. What the Turks possess you, too, can have, in greater numbers, if you wish. I propose that while two submarines are sufficient for the local needs of a small power like Turkey, four should be necessary for your own security as a great power.'

Legend relates that Russia fell for this logic. This would have made a total of seven submarines, a phenomenal tally for a first sale of an untried weapon.

It has been seriously suggested that Zaharoff's interest in these machines dated back to his youth by the Bosphorus, where he had been much taken by the ingenuity of petty thieves in escaping justice by swimming underwater with home-made snorkels. 'If only', he is said to have concluded, 'someone could develop a small craft capable of navigating below the surface, a navy could launch a surprise attack and achieve victory before the enemy knew what had hit them.'

This genial idea was not, of course, original, as Zaharoff himself was aware. His friend Lampsas, who rose from porter to proprietor of the Hotel Grande Bretagne in Athens, was so impressed with his knowledge of the subject that he wrote down verbatim the conversations he overheard. Zaharoff, so it appears, had commissioned a model submarine with which he entertained businessmen by performing with it on some pond, and on more than one occasion in the bath of the hotel. 'Everyone at first was merely amused and sceptical, but at least he made people think. . . .' Lampsas even remembered that, when one of the Vickers steel family came to Athens, there was an argument about submarines. (There is every reason to suppose that Zaharoff had met Colonel Tom Vickers, chairman of the company which bore his name since 1873, on the terrace of his Athens hotel in the mid-1870s. Vickers, noticing 'a very young man fidgeting around and looking rather upset', addressed him: "Young man, you are looking rather cross. Come and have a drink with me!"') Vickers, Lampsas recorded, argued that the submarine was the ridiculous invention of two mad Frenchmen.

'On the contrary,' replied Zaharoff, 'it is an invention of your own country, Britain. As long ago as 1596 John Napier,* a Scotsman, published a treatise on "devices of sailing under water". What is more, in James II's† time an attempt was made to row a boat under water, and in 1774 a submarine boat was built at Plymouth.'

The American Robert Fulton fathered a rather more effective contrivance with which he tried to engage General Bonaparte's interest. His *chariot d'eau*, the *Nautilus*, could remain under water propelled by a hand-operated propellor for three hours, and was armed with a torpedo to be embedded in the enemy's hull. The trials were successful; he had less success with the naval establishment. When he sought permission to sink two British frigates blockading Brest, he was ordered by the naval officer commanding, a republican of surprising

---

* Mathematician fondly remembered by schoolchildren as the inventor of logarithms.

† It was James I who was said to have taken a trip on the Thames in an enclosed wooden-framed vessel covered with greased leather. Designed by a Dutch doctor, Cornelius van Drebel, in 1620, it was successfully manoeuvred up to 15 feet beneath the surface. It is not recorded whether the monarch submerged.

sensibility, to do nothing of the sort: 'This fashion of making war ... carries with it such reproach that those who undertake the enterprise and fail in it would be hanged.'

However, Fulton had as little impact on the Admiralty, although the objection was not on humanitarian grounds. Lord St Vincent loftily considered that Pitt was 'the greatest fool that ever existed to encourage a mode of warfare which those who commanded the seas did not want, and which, if successful, would deprive them of it'.

The first successful sinking by a submarine was in 1864 when the Confederate *Hunley* accounted for the Federal corvette *Housatonic* blockading Charleston, by using a torpedo suspended from her bow as she rammed the Yankee boat, a hazardous operation. Both ships, indeed, sank.

The lack of a suitable means of propulsion continued to limit progress. It was another twenty years before any sensible advance was made. Then, two men of very different backgrounds, George William Garrett, a Manchester clergyman, and John Philip Holland, a diminutive Fenian who had emigrated to Boston, experimented with steam, using coal-fired boilers with retractable smoke-stacks.

Garrett's first prototype, *Resurgam* ('I shall rise again'), sank in 1880 on its way to be shown off to Nordenfelt. In the following year the Swede took out a patent for 'Submarine or Subaqueous Boats or Vessels' in collaboration with Garrett. Their original innovation was the idea of arming their submarines with torpedoes intended to be fired as distinct from being fixed to the hull of the prospective victim like a limpet mine. (This had been made feasible by the invention of gyro stabilizers for self-propelled torpedoes by a Lancashire man, Robert Whitehead, with whose company Zaharoff was to be closely involved.) A major flaw in the Nordenfelt design was its reliance for final control in a submerged state on a horizontal screw like a roof-fan, unlike the Holland models which incorporated rudders; the least malfunction caused the boat to bob to the surface, a not inconsiderable embarrassment.

Nordenfelt and Garrett – as his father's curate, he was spared more onerous church duties – laid down their first boat near Stockholm in 1882. Sixty-four feet in length, weighing 60 tons, it took a crew of three and was armed with one torpedo and a 1-inch Nordenfelt gun. Although it was launched next summer, it was not considered fit (or safe) for demonstration until September 1885 when the over-optimistic Swede showed it off to a distinguished naval gathering of the greater and lesser powers, in the presence of his friend the

Prince of Wales, off Landskrona. Its performance did not match its promise. Owing as much to basic design flaws as to the understandable prudence of Garrett and his fellow crewmen, it covered a mere 300 yards, perilously submerged, at a crawl.

The submarine had to contend against two prejudices, one practical, the other snobbish. The Big Ship – the Dreadnought had not yet been conceived – was a status symbol, for those who could afford one. The new-fangled weapon, if it was indeed as effective as its makers believed, could only prove a threat to these costly creations. It was, in addition, uncomfortably cramped, quite apart from the danger of carbon monoxide – and it had 'no deck to strut on'. There remained, however, lesser powers who were forced to cut their navies according to their cloth. Enter Zaharoff.

It is related that he persuaded Nordenfelt to let the initial sale go through cheaply in order to create a market; other sales would follow naturally, when the price could be increased. For his first victim he picked on his native country, which was once more making warlike noises in the direction of Turkey. To the Greek Minister of Marine he emphasized his patriotism as well as the prestige such an acquisition would carry with neighbours – and all on special terms. He clinched the sale with a demonstration of his model in the bathroom at the Grande Bretagne, despite the less than enthusiastic report of the government's own observer at the Landskrona trials. The boat was cut into sections and shipped to the Piraeus, arriving two weeks before a Royal Naval blockade was imposed to dissuade the Greeks from any rash action. The Greek navy had paid £9,000 for its pride; it is not obvious it got a bargain. On the naval experts expressing their grave doubts, she was never commissioned and was surreptitiously retired until broken up in 1901.

The Greeks had, notwithstanding, achieved some strategic value from their purchase and, through orchestrated and exaggerated claims for the new weapon, the Turks were made uncomfortably aware of the threat confronting them. Zaharoff proceeded to work on these fears. He persuaded Hassan Pasha, the Minister of Marine, to order two boats, in every way superior (on paper), with double the armament and a crew of five. The first of these was already nearing completion at the Naval Construction & Armaments Company at Barrow; the second was, at the Turks' insistence, confided to a Chertsey yard. The contract was drawn up by Zaharoff in January 1886, to specifications which were unrealistic, indeed unrealizable. On the understanding that delivery would be within two and a half months, the Turks were prepared to pay £11,000 for each boat. They were shipped, many months late, for reassembly under the occasional direction of Garrett in Constantinople. This was not so straightforward as the customer had expected; parts were missing, drawings were often sketchy in the extreme, Garrett, reassuringly evasive, was seldom at hand when most needed and Zaharoff, responsible for the workmen's wages, remained as elusive as ever. Complaining with justifiable bitterness, the Turks did their best to cope on their own. Although the Barrow-built boat was launched in April 1886, the official trials of both submarines did not take place until January 1888. They failed their main test; it was evident they could not dive. Apart from the danger to the crews, which had not escaped the notice of the Turkish commission, it flatly reported that 'they have no naval use'. They were still, however, commissioned – as the *Abdul Hamid* and the *Abdul Medjid* – and were promptly drawn up on shore for safety and left to rust. But, for the same reasons that motivated the Greeks, the Sublime Porte could not afford to acknowledge the boats' shortcomings, and so bluffed the European press with a positively radiant report on their performance. Garrett was himself even commissioned as a commander in the Imperial Ottoman Navy.

Nordenfelt, meanwhile, had already embarked on a more ambitious 'submarine torpedo warship' at Barrow – up to 230 tons – with confidence undiminished. It was, in the event, misplaced. As partial compensation for the Turks' natural disappointment, he offered them the option on his new creation, christened *Nordenfelt* and launched in March 1887. They declined it, although they had it in mind to insist on it as a replacement for their duds. Zaharoff again rode to the rescue. Combining a visit to St Petersburg in May as agent for the Austrian Mannlicher rifle, he there put his proposition to the Navy Minister, who expressed an interest, subsequently confirmed by the Russian Naval Attaché in London. With at least hope buoyant, the SSS (Submarine Steamship) *Nordenfelt*, with Zaharoff in her wake, took up station for the Golden Jubilee Review at Spithead in July. Steaming sedately past the ironclads, she caught the fancy of the Tsar. Not to be rushed into a bargain, a year passed before the boat was inspected by a Russian naval delegation, always a tricky exercise in deception. In an effort to bounce the reflective Russians into a decision, Nordenfelt announced that they had decided to buy her. This elicited a public denial in *The Times* and a forthright condemnation of the boat as 'entirely unsuitable for naval and fighting purposes'. Zaharoff was once more called on 'to work the oracle'. The best he could manage was to induce them to accept her on approval. The *Nordenfelt* accordingly set off with Garrett, his young son and a drunken crew in October

1888, en route for Kronstadt. She got as far as the Borkum Flats off Jutland before she ran aground. Although not badly damaged, the insurance company was persuaded to settle with the Barrow builders, of which Nordenfelt had been a director since the beginning of the year.

Nordenfelt's attention was, perhaps fortunately, distracted from further experiments in this uncertain medium by other more pressing problems. The submarine had always been a sideline. His own principal operation was now threatened, his independence sapped by his helpful Greek agent.

J.P.Holland of New Jersey launched his first underwater boat, just 14 feet in length, in 1875. His work had been financed by Irish patriotic societies in America with the idea that the infernal machines should be carried across the Atlantic in a mother ship and let loose among British warships at the other end. (A later model, the *Fenian Ram*, was stolen by Fenian dissidents; the possibility that Zaharoff was behind this coup has never been explored.) In 1889 he developed the *Plunger* and the *Holland*, precursors of all subsequent submarine design.

At about the same time, an entrepreneur, Isaac Rice, who had cornered the storage battery business in the United States, came on the scene and took the plunge. He formed the Electric Boat Company,* acquiring Holland's patents. Owing to his persuasive powers, and political pressures, the American navy bought the Holland submarine in April 1900. (It was considerably smaller than the Nordenfelt – 63 feet in length – and was driven by gasoline-powered engines on the surface, by electricity when submerged.)

Later the same year, the American company, under the auspices of the first Lord Rothschild, signed a licensing agreement with Vickers – which by then had absorbed Zaharoff and his employers – for twenty-five years, covering the whole of Europe as well as Britain. As there were no further orders forthcoming at the American end – the Navy Department feared that if the claim of the submarine was pushed, Congress might clip the cost off the battleship budget – Vickers supported Electric Boat by buying a considerable minority holding, and by 1903 held, with Isaac Rice, an absolute majority.

Not that the naval establishment on the other side of the Atlantic regarded the machines with complete favour: 'a low-class of weapon, underhand, unfair and un-English' was one not untypical verdict.

* Today part of General Dynamics Corporation, one of the largest US defence contractors.

41

(Admiral 'Jackie' Fisher's vehement advocacy was the exception.) But they had two distinct material advantages for the builders. They could be run up quickly; later, Vickers was able to deliver to the Admiralty six boats within eight months of any large order being placed. And in addition, as Albert Vickers was soon to confide to Zaharoff, 'these boats . . . afford a very wide margin of profit'.

Through this connection the American company would acquire Zaharoff as a business asset, and a very cosy arrangement on commission was reached which would last until the day of his death. Isaac Rice wrote to Vickers that he would defer to Zaharoff's opinion in the matter of sales policy and would be 'guided absolutely by this advice'. The submarine had by then come of age.

5

Arms and the Men

The first industrial revolution had not fathered any innovation in weaponry; the guns and ships that served in the Crimea would have been familiar to the veterans of Trafalgar and Waterloo. But the half century that followed witnessed the most lethal revolution in warfare, reinforced by such innocuous expedients as the steam engine and electric telegraph, between the invention of gunpowder and the atom bomb; muzzle-loading smooth-bore cannon throwing solid round shot were succeeded by rifled breech-loading guns* using shells with smokeless powder; at sea the wooden-wall broadside navy gave way to ships encased in massive armour – 'Floating Gun Carriages' as their builders boasted; on land, fire-power was multiplied by automatic weapons, which had had to wait for the metal cartridge. By the end, the services had taken to the air.

Two early birds in this field were an American, Richard Jordan Gatling, and a Swede, Thorsten Vilhelm Nordenfelt, whose inventions were soon to be overtaken by another American, Hiram Maxim.

Gatling, born in 1818, first turned his hand to agricultural machinery in his native North Carolina. With the outbreak of the Civil War he conceived the notion of a rapid-fire gun and within a year had perfected a weapon consisting of a bundle of from five to ten barrels which fired in turn when revolved. Hand-cranked, with a rate of fire

---

* The father of modern artillery was William Armstrong, a Newcastle solicitor. He produced his first gun in 1855 whose trials established its accuracy as sixty times greater than the old pieces. The Commander-in-Chief, the Duke of Cambridge, enthused that the new marvel 'could do everything but speak'.

43

of 350 shots a minute, it was fed by gravity from a hopper. By the time the Federal government endorsed its use, the war was over. In 1870 W.G.Armstrong & Company, of Elswick, now with Alfried Krupp the world's leading heavy armament manufacturer, became the sole British licensee for the Gatling.

Thorsten Nordenfelt, twenty-five years the American's junior, left Sweden for England at the age of twenty. The first patent for the gun which bore his name was issued ten years later. The weapon was a battery gun of ten barrels in a parallel frame resembling a horizontal row of organ pipes. It was compact and mobile, but still needed a crew of four men to handle it. Later, Nordenfelt took out a succession of patents for two-, five- and seven-barrel guns up to $1\frac{1}{2}$ inches in calibre, as well as for a 6-pounder. These early models were manufactured in Sweden.

In the year after Zaharoff had been nominally recruited by Nordenfelt in 1877, official trials of all rival 'quick-fire' guns were held at Shoeburyness. These favoured neither the Gatling nor the Nordenfelt, but the Gardner, made by Pratt Whitney of Hartford, Connecticut. Functioning on similar principles to the Nordenfelt, it was recommended by the War Office on the grounds of its greater mechanical simplicity, despite a particular proneness to jam when worked precipitately. This choice was a serious disappointment to Nordenfelt, not least because the prestige of official endorsement would have provided a fillip for foreign orders. For all that, the Nordenfelt was still popular in colonial wars, and other armies were flirting with it. Some idea of the pattern of this trade emerges from a later record of sales for the period April 1885 to July 1888, for most of which time Zaharoff was busying himself in the market. The War Office was still the largest customer over this three-year term: 100 guns with spares, mostly for India; the Crown Agents bought the odd one for the Gold Coast and Nigeria; there were orders from Victoria and New South Wales in Australia. Russia and Japan acquired the occasional gun for trial, followed by a modest quantity of assorted weapons; Italy took fifty guns, for delivery in parts; lesser clients included Uruguay, Spain, Portugal, Brazil and Romania; armament was provided for revenue cutters for the Chinese Customs.

The potential was considered sufficiently promising, in conjunction with Nordenfelt's preoccupation with his submarines, to naturalize the operation. In March 1886, the Nordenfelt Guns & Ammunition Company was registered in the United Kingdom at 53 Parliament Street, Westminster, with a nominal capital of £300,000, of which £150,000 was taken up. A gunnery expert and recently retired First

Sea Lord, Admiral Sir Astley Cooper Key, was put up as chairman; Nordenfelt, who brought his patents to the company, retained a majority block of shares. The new company so prospered that a dividend of 27½ per cent was declared for the first year, and in August the following year Nordenfelt acquired a ten-acre site at Erith within convenient range of the Woolwich Arsenal for his British plant. Zaharoff, too, had moved to London by this time and thrown himself with zest into his new trade as if to make up for lost time and opportunities.

Undoubtedly a major motive for this switch of domicile was the unwelcome appearance of competition. Until the mid-1880s, there was little to choose in performance between rival semi-automatic quick-firing weapons. That was to change abruptly. A cloud showed up over the Atlantic horizon that was not to challenge but totally eclipse all existent models. At the same time as Zaharoff was undergoing the severe trials brought about by anaemia in the French capital, an unquiet American – a 'brash Yankee' from his own description – made his first European trip as the chief engineer of the US Electric Lighting Company to the Paris Electrical Exposition of 1881. An eccentric, caustic,* boisterous and irreverent personality, Hiram Maxim was also to help found the fortunes of Zaharoff.

The Maxim family, Huguenots driven out of France by the revocation of the Edict of Nantes, had settled first in Canterbury before emigrating to Plymouth, Massachusetts, where, Hiram later wrote, 'they could worship God according to the dictates of their conscience and prevent others from doing the same'.

Leading a rough, self-reliant life, the young Maxim became a master of many trades. An oddity in a pioneering community, he grew up a non-smoker and non-drinker; he even disapproved of coffee. He found compensation as an inveterate card-player, picturesque liar and agnostic. Above all, being blessed with a strong physique, he enjoyed brawling. Apprenticed to a coach-builder, he made astronomical instruments in his spare time and supported himself as a part-time barman and bouncer.

But he was more than this: in his own words, 'a chronic inventor'. Cutting his teeth on an ingenious mouse-trap, he beat Edison to the patent office and, if we can believe him, installed the first electric lights in New York City. Already in Paris he had made the first drawings of an automatic gun, and, moving across the Channel to cast a critical eye on the state of the electrical industry in Britain, took

* Surprising the junior clerks at play while the telephone was ringing, he exclaimed: 'Don't you answer it, my poor boy. I know you're tired, I'll answer it for you.'

45

first a room in Cannon Street before moving into his own premises at 57d Hatton Garden.

The weapon that resulted from this doodling was revolutionary: it was the first fully automatic gun, all the functions being performed by the recoil energy of the 'kick' in contrast to its hand-cranked predecessors. By this method he was able to raise its rate of fire to a phenomenal 600 shots a minute, delivering a more accurate and concentrated fire than fifty riflemen. It was also lighter, and required a smaller crew than the Nordenfelt. Maxim took out his first British patent on 26 June 1883, the weapon, if not to end all wars, at least to end them more quickly – or so it was hoped.

Maxim's friend, Randolph R. Symon, vice-president of the Mexican Central Railway, introduced him to Albert Vickers. The trio forthwith incorporated their company in November 1884 with a capital of £50,000 in £20 shares, buying Maxim's goodwill for £35,000. Among the shareholders were Nathaniel Rothschild and Ernest Cassel, two of the shrewdest operators of the day. The company bought works at Crayford for the wonder weapon.

Social success was almost as rapid as the gun's consumption. The Commander-in-Chief, the Duke of Cambridge, was one of Hiram Maxim's earliest visitors. He was followed by the Prince of Wales with Burke's Peerage in tow, among them the Dukes of Edinburgh, Sutherland and Devonshire. Lord Wolseley liked it, society was ravished; the fashionable thronged to take turns on the trigger, burning up 200,000 rounds, the equivalent of five and a half hours of continuous fire at a cost of £5 per minute for ammunition – a colossal promotional budget. There was one notable absentee from the scrum, Basil Zaharoff, who was engaged in Maxim's own country with his private affairs. He was not left in ignorance of the little marvel for long.

It might be thought that with patronage of this order, the product would take off, but British government orders for the gun were few in spite of improvements to its weight and performance; a 40 lb version was produced which shot 2,000 rounds in three minutes – a record which was to stand for upwards of thirty years.

There remained foreign sales. The Maxim team's first essay was in Switzerland where they won an order against the Gardner, which had already beaten the Nordenfelt and Gatling. Then, in 1886, came trials at La Spezia for the Italian navy. Maxim only heard about them once they were completed: Zaharoff, now in harness, had carried the day with the Nordenfelt. Undaunted, Maxim, accompanied by Albert Vickers, arrived toting his weapon. After the usual procedure, which included immersion in seawater for three days, it smartly out-performed the Nordenfelt. Maxim had returned to London in triumph, having left the gun in the charge of an old friend, Nicholas de Kabeth, the Russian Consul at Spezia, when he heard that Admiral the Duke of Genoa had requested a personal demonstration. Unable to return himself Maxim, forever apprehensive of idleness and insobriety, sent down a marksman and mechanic with strict instructions to Kabath to keep the men under his eye. However, the visiting team managed to escape his vigilance and became so royally drunk that they were unable to hit the target for the Duke next morning. Twenty-four hours under lock and key steadied them. The episode ended on a happy note with an order from the Italian government.

The results of this trial, despite the hiccups occasioned by intemperance, constituted a clear warning to Nordenfelt's new salesman. Zaharoff's product was manifestly outclassed. Official trials for the Austrian army were scheduled to open at the Steinfeld range outside Vienna. Zaharoff went gunning for his rival.

The occasion was a full-dress affair attended by the Emperor Franz Josef himself with his brother, Field Marshal the Archduke Wilhelm. The Maxim gun did not disappoint the spectators. To polite applause, Hiram personally cut the Emperor's initials 'FJ' into the target with short bursts. The Archduke pronounced himself more than satisfied: 'Only too fast and true. It is a marvellous gun, the finest piece of mechanism I have ever seen.' He then went on to relate an experience he had had the previous afternoon. The 'agent of the other gun' had called at his office to dissuade him from venturing out in such heat, especially as the 'Maxim gun never works, and you will be greatly disappointed . . . So you can see', the Archduke happily confided, 'how much we can believe what we hear.' A check for Zaharoff.

The Austrian military, however, required a weapon which would fire their own cartridges. Maxim therefore returned to London to run up another gun and, on his arrival back at Steinfeld, prepared to give a further demonstration of its virtuosity. After he had fired only a few hundred rounds, it began to show disquieting symptoms, and finally stopped. Maxim stripped it down and found 'much to my surprise and disgust' that the fault was due to an example of shoddy workmanship which had been blackened over to deceive him. Once again he had to take the gun back with him as luggage to London where he discovered that 'this vexatious trick was the fault of my English foreman', who had dropped off at his bench from drowsiness induced by the liberality of his Greek host at lunch. When he awoke the damage had been done by the machinist, himself generously

47

rewarded. 'In fact it was the greatest trouble I ever had, as it brought into my life an individual who caused me an immense amount of vexation and trouble, and the loss of thousands of pounds in money.'

Maxim's trials, and tribulations, were not yet over.

The gun restored to working order, the operation was resumed. This time there was a witness to the display. The agent of the other gun, Maxim recorded, 'was on hand like a sore finger, not on the grounds, but looking through the gate with a lot of newspaper reporters'.

As the roar of the firing died away, the agent outside the gates rhapsodized: 'A wonderful performance, gentlemen. Marvellous! Nobody can compete with this Nordenfelt gun.'

'Nordenfelt? Isn't the inventor's name Maxim?' enquired one of the more alert newspapermen.

'No,' replied the informative stranger. 'That is the Nordenfelt gun, the finest weapon in the world.' And for the benefit of any remaining doubters, he repeated in English and French: 'The Nordenfelt gun has beaten all the others.'

And so it was reported.

Having handled the press relations, Zaharoff next turned his attention to the consumers. One of these officers subsequently reported this conversation to Maxim:

Do you know who Maxim is? I will tell you. He is a Yankee and probably the cleverest mechanician on the earth today. By trade he is a philosophical instrument-maker. He is the only person in the world who can make one of these guns, and make it work. Everything has to be of the utmost accuracy – one hundredth part of a millimetre here or there and it will not work – all the springs have to be of an exact tension. Suppose now that you want a quantity of these guns, where are you going to get them, as there is only one man in the world who can make them? Maxim goes into the shop and actually makes these guns with his own hands, and of course supply is limited. Then again, even if you could get them, do you expect that you could get an army of Boston philosophical instrument-makers to work them?

This was excellent intelligence on the part of Zaharoff. Oliver P. Drake of Boston, a precision-instrument maker, was an early employer of Maxim.

It was a singularly effective argument to put to the military whose concern, after operational performance, was quantity and continuity of supply, simplicity and robustness in action. That this line certainly had an effect on his audience is evident from a confession that one of the senior artillery officers made to Maxim: 'A colleague of yours from London, who witnessed the whole thing, thinks that nothing can be done with your invention – that it is a device for trick shots, but not for ordinary soldiers.'

Zaharoff had surely poohpoohed the fancy shooting which might have delighted a few court toadies, but which to the less respectful professionals must have smacked of cheap showmanship rather in tone with 'Buffalo Bill' Cody's Wild West Show, which had just hit Europe.

Maxim himself, Zaharoff conceded, was 'furious, but he forgave me'. It is not so surprising. The American was one of that species which is righteously persuaded that the natives are forever intent on swindling him; the theme constantly recurs in his memoirs. (And, of course, he invariably triumphed over such dark forces.) This incident could only have given him the satisfaction of proof for his opinion. Annoyed, as he had every right to be, he must also grudgingly have admired Zaharoff's ingenuity and tenacity. It was much of a piece with his own aggressive nature, and his simple homespun philosophy soon overcame the animus. He was shortly referring to the agent of the rival firm as 'my friend Mr ZedZed'. He could anyway afford to be generous. In spite of the best efforts of the Nordenfelt representative, Maxim came away from Vienna with an order for 160 guns. He feigned disappointment, but this quantity was sufficient to equip the greater part of the Austro-Hungarian infantry at the accepted level of provision at the time and up to the First World War.

If Zaharoff was cast into a thoughtful mood by his rival's success, he was kept too active to brood excessively. By August 1886, his recent itinerary had taken him from London to Paris, Madrid, Lisbon, Brussels and The Hague (he makes no mention of Vienna); at the end of the year he was ordered off to Constantinople with breaks in Athens and Berlin. He had been 'engaged for S. America but they found out I could be more useful here & have twice annulled my passage, taken & paid for'. He confided to William Shaw in Athens that 'they all like me exceedingly & well they might for I have pulled off things that they never expected'. It is not at all clear from the order book what he did pull off: Spain, Portugal and Italy were the only markets he is known to have visited with discernible success. He had another justifiable grumble: 'Yet this does not pay me, as in each country I have mentioned they have their local agents who get all the commissions while I do the work. Thus our Madrid agent who has been there 3 years scratching his balls & never did a thing now goes & gets a commision of £3,050 on a contract that

I got.' It was 'natural I want to get to America where will I get all the commissions for my work'.

In spite of this injustice, he was happy to be properly appreciated. 'I'm getting on famously in fact, I am consulted in everything of importance & my opinion is generally acted upon. I am much liked by the Chief & all the others & if I continue to like the business as I now do, I can always remain at the top of the tree.' He continued to look to the sea for commission. This, as he pointed out to William Shaw, 'mounts up to thousands' on government orders. He offered Shaw the agency for the Fairfield shipyard – 'sooner or later the Greeks will be building ships' – whose 'proprietor ... Sir William Pearce a new Jubilee Baronet & worth several millions' was a good friend. 'Unfortunately I have rather encouraged [him] in the belief that the [Greek] government intend building 2 fast cruisers – please keep this up ... it suits my purpose as have other things on hand with him at moment.' He was also trying to procure agencies for his friend for different insurance companies, though pessimistic over the prospects: 'if you can persuade the Greeks to be provident in an accidental risk you will merit a monument'. Even so, if Shaw thought he could do anything, 'I want a share.'

His three sisters descended on him. Zoë returned to Constantinople after three months, Sevasty and Charikleia he installed in a house in Paris, 'a very nice one & beautifully furnished but it has made a big gap in my savings'. He was himself, now approaching forty, more provident; he was even considering buying 'an annuity in some good [company] & thus be prepared against a rainy day'.

The spring of 1888 was a watershed in his career. He had settled comfortably into his *métier* and was enjoying a measure of steady prosperity. 'I am still alive are you ditto?' he asked Shaw. He went on to list 'notable events' concerning himself:

1. I continue to make a little money.
2. I have 5 decorations (if I get a few more, can stick them on my backside)
3. I have a charming house in Paris 54 rue Bienfaisance.

Two months after Zaharoff had been touting for the Fairfield yard in Greece, it had been agreed that the Barrow Shipbuilding Company, which had launched two of Nordenfelt's submarines, could make use of their agents, and in 1888 Nordenfelt, with Lords Brassey (a recent Civil Lord and Secretary of the Admiralty and founder of the *Naval Annual*), Hartington (the Liberal statesman and friend of the Prince of Wales) and Zaharoff's old acquaintance Rothschild (created the first Jewish peer three years before), bought the Barrow yard. In June of the same year Zaharoff was buying the land for another shipbuilding yard at Bilbao in northern Spain, where he had already won contracts for four men-of-war.

In the same year, a merger, equally portentous for Zaharoff's fortunes, took place between the Nordenfelt and Maxim gun companies. Zaharoff is supposed to have acted as the marriage broker in order to bridle his rival and it is indeed most probable that he forced his employer's hand by a direct approach to Rothschild, who was persuaded of the good sense of harnessing the sometimes wayward gifts of the two inventors to a more practical commercial management. He was already on nodding terms with the Vickers brothers. At an extraordinary meeting on 12 July 1888, the Nordenfelt shareholders voted to wind up their company and merge with Maxim. Although the Maxim company's capital had been raised to £80,000, Nordenfelt was still the much larger and more prosperous enterprise. Yet Maxim, with his patents valued at around £1,000,000, was admitted to the ensuing partnership on equal terms. One week later, the Maxim–Nordenfelt Guns & Ammunition Company was floated for a solid £1,900,000 and was fully subscribed within two hours of opening the books. Rothschild and his fellow banker Ernest Cassel, who had joined him in the promotion, were rewarded with shares roughly equal in value to the combined Vickers family holding. Zaharoff, for his part, must have been rubbing his hands in anticipation of the assault on the worldwide markets on land and sea which now lay at his feet.

6

First Love

Zaharoff's interest in Spain, where he rapidly established a fiefdom, may have been awakened by his friend Skouloudis, Greek Minister in Madrid from 1883. The year before he had been setting up his shipbuilding operation near Bilbao, he had been prospecting the fortifications at Cadiz. And this was not, by his own account, his first visit to the peninsula. He had recently undergone a brief, romantic and, if he is to be believed, bloody encounter with the one woman to whom he remained constant until her death forty years on.

Whatever picture this woman, petite and vivacious, presented to the besotted eye, her name was a mouthful: Maria del Pilar Antonia Angela Patrocinio Fermina Simona de Muguiro y Beruete, daughter of the Count of Muguiro. She was married aged a bare seventeen on 7 January 1886 to Don Francisco Maria Isabel de Borbon y Borbon, Duke of Marchena, son of the Infante Sebastian – and sympathetically described by one biographer as a 'sickly, late-born scion of a worn-out stock'. The wedding would have taken place in the palace had the court not been in mourning for Alfonso XII.

There was little formality surrounding the sequel. Zaharoff himself recounted the story of their first encounter in two incomparable versions. Others have placed the scene on board the Orient Express, whose compartment No. 7 became Zaharoff's home from home on wheels over the years.

The adventure opened, he recalled in later life, on the stairs of the Escorial Palace outside Madrid. A girl with 'the loveliest and saddest face I'd ever seen' was accompanied by a man so ablaze with orders that people drew aside to let them pass. 'Suddenly the man took the girl's arm brutally and crushed it – she gave a little cry, and, before I knew what I was doing, I'd hit him across the face. ... Image the commotion! I'd struck a Prince of the Blood, cousin of the King of Spain, merely because he'd been rude to his wife.'

Honour was requited next day at dawn. Zaharoff, with the choice of weapons and wary of the effect of firearms, plumped for swords – and was promptly pinked by the sickly scion. He had plenty of time, he philosophized, to repent his folly in hospital. 'I'd been there a fortnight when they told me a lady wanted to see me. She wouldn't give her name and she was thickly veiled, but I'd have known her anywhere – it was the Princess. She told me that she and her husband were going away that night and that she had come to say goodbye – but we never said that word.'

Determined to complicate his life, he bribed his way out of hospital and on to her train. Rather imprudently for one already once wounded, he had her carriage filled with flowers and managed to speak to her while the Duke had his back turned. 'After that, wherever she went she found my flowers waiting for her.'

His second putative adventure is almost prosaic. Alerted by the thunder of hooves in Madrid's Prada, so he informed a young temptress in later life, he 'turned to see a carriage and pair with the coachman tugging at the reins. I was ... much younger then, and so I dashed into the road and managed to pull up the horses. The young lady riding in the carriage had been badly frightened . . . She was very beautiful and we fell in love.'

After this it is easier to sympathize with the confession of his more conservative friend and colleague, Sir George Owens-Thurston, that the hero really was an extraordinary man, but that it was difficult to believe him always.

Other favoured versions place the encounter on a train. The two editions of this rail romance open in a similar vein. A young girl, dishevelled and frightened – and in one case rather unfortunately attired in a (torn) mauve peignoir – fled into the corridor. On one train she shouted 'Socorro ... Dios ... Salve!' – she was lucky to have fallen on an accomplished linguist – while on the other she addressed the nearest source of succour more composedly: 'Monsieur, please help me. Hide me, I beg. My husband wishes to kill me.'

In the first instance, without waiting for an invitation, she pushed past Zaharoff into his compartment, while the husband erupted into the corridor with a jewel-encrusted dagger, his face mottled with fury, where he was overcome by the alert sleeping-car attendant and the bodyguard of his wife's saviour. On the other express, Zaharoff silently opened the door of his compartment and, bowing stiffly, said simply: 'Please come in.'

Remaining impassively – and properly – in the corridor, he was accosted by an irate husband. 'I am the Duke of Marchena. Have you seen my wife?'

'No, I am afraid I haven't, *monsieur le duc.*'

'She has not passed by here?'

'No.'

'I demand that you open the door of your compartment.'

'I regret that I must refuse to gratify your request.'

'If it were in Spain—'

'But we are not in Spain. We are in Switzerland and about to enter France.'

'Alors,' replied the Duke resignedly, if not at his most gallant, 'perhaps she has jumped off the train. So be it. I shall go back to sleep.'

Shortly after this, as Zaharoff recounted the sequel, 'my lovely lady's husband went mad. He was put in an asylum until he died ... She was a Catholic. I implored her to get a divorce, but she refused.'

After these harrowing incidents, the Duchess's immediate future is obscure. In one version her husband was consigned to an asylum near Granja staffed by nuns pledged to devoted nursing and complete secrecy, while the Duchess, held to blame for his unstable condition, was shunned by the Regent Maria Christina, widow of Alfonso XII, and forced into exile. Other sources accept that Zaharoff persuaded her to use her influence at court to press his own cause. As a result he brought Spain into his empire, which was to prove the most long-lasting and profitable source of commission.

However, following the Maxim–Nordenfelt merger, Zaharoff had little time for philandering. He crisscrossed Europe, often in company with Hiram Maxim, with his guns for baggage. In addition to his work for the new company, he also held an agency for the Austrian Mannlicher rifle as well as for the Barrow shipyards; and he had been recruited by Vickers some time before as agent for that company's new armour-plate for naval shipbuilding, a field in which the French were at that time the market leaders. It was on the seas rather than on the land that Zaharoff was to found the bulk of his fortune.

Zaharoff had already met Tom Vickers in Athens over ten years before, and his brother Albert, an entrepreneur of decision and daring, would have been known to him, at least by name, as chairman of the Maxim Gun Company. The story of his first meeting with Albert was recorded many years later by Albert's nephew, and was confirmed in its essentials by Sir George Owens-Thurston, naval designer for Vickers from 1905.

Zaharoff went to the Vickers offices at 28 Victoria Street, Broadway, just two doors down from Maxim–Nordenfelt, to beard Albert in order to try to obtain the agency for arms for Turkey or Russia. Albert replied that he would talk it over with his colleagues. He came back later to inform the suppliant that his request had been granted, whereupon Zaharoff went down on his knees: 'Mr Vickers, I am starving. This has saved my life.'

This episode is difficult to place. Albert Vickers, chairman of Maxim Guns since 1884, had acquired Zaharoff's services directly with the merger with Nordenfelt of 1888 – and he would not have swallowed his story of starvation. Vickers own ordnance department was only formed in that same year along with the development of the new all-steel armour in which there was stiff competition with Cammells, John Brown and other major steel companies. The scene therefore most plausibly relates to Zaharoff's winning the agency for armour plate at some date in the mid-1880s. Doubtless Vickers was amused by the Greek's histrionics. Subsequently a very intimate relationship grew up between 'Don Alberto' and ZedZed which was to last for upwards of thirty years.

7

Bagman

The Maxim gun and its variants quickly acquired an ascendancy, and then a near international monopoly, and held this position until the Great War. The principal problem, as with every fresh development which upset entrenched notions of tactical warfare, was to get any perception of its utility through to the military mind, still very much obsessed with the gospel of mass – preponderant, and ponderous, conscript armies.

Professional observers of contemporary battles in the Prussian victories over Austria and France, and later in the South African and Russo–Japanese wars, read these lessons correctly, but their views did not succeed in percolating through to the monastic seclusion of the war ministries. Even when the mandarins were faced in person with the effect of the machine-gun on the battlefield, their scepticism remained superbly impervious to experience. The future Field Marshal Haig, as an army commander in France, considered as late as the spring of 1915 that the machine-gun was a much overrated weapon (there were only three hundred in service in the British army in Flanders). It took a civilian, David Lloyd George, to break the mould. Informed by Eric Geddes, whom he had conscripted to the Ministry of Munitions, that Lord Kitchener's opinion was that four to a battalion might be useful, but more than that a luxury, he advised him: 'Take Kitchener's maximum; square it; multiply that result by two – and when you are in sight of that, double it again for luck'.

Following his success with the Italian and Austrian armies and navies, Hiram Maxim next set his sights on the German market. Although competitive trials had been held for automatic weapons, there had been no orders. It was the Prince of Wales, on his visit to Berlin in March 1887 to celebrate the ninetieth birthday of Wilhelm I, who dropped a word into his host's ear. Impressed with this endorsement, the old Emperor and the Crown Prince attended trials at Spandau. 'That is the gun,' exclaimed the Emperor, patting the barrel fondly. 'There is no other.' The German army was equipped and, in the year of the Maxim–Nordenfelt merger, Krupp acquired a licence to manufacture the Maxim.

When Friedrich Krupp, the son of the old man Alfried who had died in 1887, came over to England for a personal demonstration, he remarked admiringly to Maxim: 'I do not believe any of your associates appreciate the great value of that invention.' (He was wrong in at least one case.) In the following year the British army, too, cautiously adopted the weapon.

In 1888, Zaharoff and his new managing director, Maxim, their differences buried, and no doubt passing the time topping each other's stories, took off on their first joint sales mission to St Petersburg, accompanied by the Russian Consul, Kabath, presumably by this time also on commission. Maxim already had an agent, Hartmann, in Russia but had effected no sales although the Russians had dabbled with the Nordenfelt. They made a redoubtable team, the gunman and the bagman.

The latter much later outlined his own recipe for his sales technique: this was to make a beeline for the woman behind the throne. 'How did I do it? By flattering the wife or mistress of the Minister in power. ... I got introduced to her, sent her flowers or jewels, courted her and eventually sold whatever I wanted to her husband or lover!'

His target in St Petersburg is discreetly described as the Grand Duke S. (Serge Michaelovich, *Monsieur Tant Pis*, Russian artillery commander in the Great War). Having already ascertained that the Grand Duke was installed with a ballerina, Zaharoff secured an introduction to her and proceeded to pursue her. Overcome by such attention, the belle from the Bolshoi passed him on to the Grand Duke. A week later, the legend runs, the first Russian order for guns went to London. With mere ministers he could afford to shed such subtleties. One well-known example of his efforts to ingratiate himself with venal officialdom was to propose a bet he was certain to lose: he would lay a large sum on, say, a Tuesday that the next day would be a Sunday. (Any honest functionary he dealt with must have suffered doubts about his sanity.) Another endearing trick was to offer his case containing the new-fangled product of Turkey to his particular pigeon; each would be wrapped in a high-denomination banknote – the first king-size cigarettes.

He might have amused himself in this way, and certainly wasted a lot of money, but the orders, unfortunately, did not come so effortlessly.

Affairs in fact moved slowly for the home team. Two weeks passed without any manifest sign of interest. Maxim was then called up before the police. Their suspicions were aroused by his Christian name, Hiram, and reinforced by that of his father, Isaac, and his grandfather Samuel. Local regulations, they pointed out, forbade any foreign Jew to live or work in Russia. He indignantly protested that he was an innocent agnostic. Worse still, he was told: no one without a religion was permitted to stay in Russia. He then cheerfully confessed to being a Protestant.

Having established this credential, Maxim and Zaharoff were presented to the Tsar for an audience of three-quarters of an hour and stayed on for a lunch of raw fish. (The ruler's frugality was deeply deplored by the court.)

The incongruous couple must have presented a curious spectacle at the stolid tsarist court: the American, a bit of a bruiser with a spade beard, ebullient and incurably loquacious in just the one language; the Greek, very much at home in faultless French and Russian (the last tsarist Foreign Minister, S.D.Sazonov, testified that he spoke 'with the purity and fluency of a native'), with a polished manner and sober dress in keeping with his new station in life. 'Quiet clothes', his friend T.P.O'Connor, the journalist and Irish Nationalist MP, wrote, 'immaculate boots, full-cut trousers, short dust-coat buttoned up and fitted with a broad collar almost à la Byron; there is nothing in this regular attire of his to attract the slightest attention. Only if you studied him carefully, would you give more than a passing thought to his hat, which is of the semi-clerical type, but with broader brim and higher crown.' Another friend considered his taste in hats and shoes – flat rubber-soled bootees – eccentric; he suspected that he had bought the whole stock at one sweep and was determined to wear them out.

For Zaharoff this pilgrimage marked the beginning of a long-lasting attachment to, and even affinity with, the country. Prince Christopher of Greece considered that he 'certainly had the mysticism, the superstition and the artistic strain one so often finds in Russians'.

Neighbourliness dictated their next move – an offer to arm the Turks against the Russian menace. As the train service to Constantinople had been interrupted by cholera, they embarked with their hardware at Marseilles in a very old and dilapidated steamer, sharing the accommodation with sheep, cattle, 'a real English Admiral of the Fleet, retired [Admiral Sir John Commerell, VC, GCB, chairman of Maxim–Nordenfelt], Monsieur ZedZed, a clever and entertaining Russian gentleman [Count Nicholas de Kabath] and an expert French mechanician who never got drunk.' They packed with them Maxim's latest creation, the 37 mm weapon which was to win renown as the 'pom-pom' on the South African veldt. Maxim, expecting to be cheated, was much struck with the honesty of the Turkish soldiers in refusing tips for helping him to set up the gun for the trials. Impressed with his prowess, the Sultan 'Abdul the Damned' rewarded Maxim with a decoration and Zaharoff, mindful of essentials, with a more tangible order.

After Turkey the team, trailing their pom-pom, proceeded to Paris and on to Spain, from Spain back to Spandau, returning to Cadiz in time for naval trials. Barely drawing breath, but still finding time to perfect a smokeless powder, they took their weapon to Portugal, where the King was allowed to try his own finger on the trigger; this indulgence resulted in the bestowal of another decoration. Happy, footloose days.

Towards the end of September 1888 Zaharoff figured for the first time in the company's minute book, one of the few records to survive from that pioneering epoch. After his previous cancellations, it was finally proposed to send him to Chile and Peru 'with one or two guns after he has called at Rio and Buenos Aires'. These places were to become over the years a most lucrative market, and one as volatile as the Balkans. The political situation in Chile in particular provides a vivid vignette of the arms game in action.

The incumbent President, a reformer with autocratic methods, was engaged in re-equipping the army and navy and at the same time quarrelling with both Houses of Congress in the run-up to the presidential election of 1891 in which he wished, in time-honoured fashion, to impose his own candidate. The opposition, led by the Vice-President of the Senate and the President of the Chamber of Deputies, supported by most of the navy, countered by recruiting an army among the labourers in the nitrate fields whose revenues also conveniently contributed to finance the force. They first sought to obtain arms in the United States, but the vessel bringing them in was unable to land them. They finally succeeded in obtaining arms from Europe, with which they overwhelmed the presidential faction. The loser abdicated on the eve of his defeat and took refuge in the Argentine Legation, where he ended his life and administration with his own hand on the same day as his term expired. The brief but bitter contest had cost 10,000 lives.

The outgoing President had been within a hair's breadth of regaining supremacy of the sea, which he had lost with the defection of his fleet. He was awaiting the imminent delivery of the most powerful ship in the Chilean navy, the somewhat curiously named *Arturo Prat*, and two fast cruisers. These were lying incomplete in European dockyards and did not make the civil war. But as the ousted President's successor was the promptly promoted admiral commanding the victorious naval forces he was not ungrateful for stylish new additions to his command. The new government therefore magnanimously honoured all debts from both sides, and the payment of full commissions.

Zaharoff was also preparing the ground for the future by setting up a local organization of agents. In Santiago he recruited no less a star than the brother of the later Cardinal Merry del Val. These were to serve him well when the great naval shipbuilding boom almost swamped the region. Whether it was due to his success in South America or some other field, in December 1889 the company made him a present of £500 'in recognition of my carrying out satisfactorily a certain transaction. It is not the money I value,' he told Shaw, 'but the compliment.'

In the New Year he found that the two inventors had fallen out in London through incompatibility of temperament. Zaharoff, as he later described it, chose the stronger man and stuck by Maxim. In fact there was a more practical reason behind the split. Nordenfelt, it seems, had managed, doubtless at a price, to retain some degree of independence and with it control of his original works at Carlsvik. He continued there as a sub-contractor to Maxim-Nordenfelt, but lean times in the arms business, which nearly brought down the main company, forced him into liquidation, a state of affairs which he blamed, probably unfairly, on his erstwhile agent. Zaharoff is supposed to have snapped up his disposable assets. The Swede took himself off to Paris with his nephew and turned his hand to farm implements and, lastly, an unsuccessful motor car, retiring to his homeland in 1903. Whatever Nordenfelt's feelings, Zaharoff nevertheless contributed a not ungenerous payment of £100 a year to his first employer, in the nature of an ex gratia pension, until his death thirty years later. A difference of opinion at once arose over the ownership of patents, the British company taking an action in the French courts against Nordenfelt, which dragged on. As compensation for the time Zaharoff was obliged to devote to this, his guarantee of commission was increased by £50 a month for the suit's duration.

In the same year, he was reporting on prospects from Spain and Romania while his promotion was being considered behind his back in London. In October 1890, he accepted an engagement for two years as foreign adviser, and in the following May his fee, always excluding commission, was settled at 'not less than £1,000 per annum with full powers to act for the company'. In September 1892, his contract was renewed indefinitely, but was made subject first to three and next to six months' notice and an assured minimum commission of £1,000 per annum.

In December he returned to familiar haunts in Athens and Constantinople, a different figure in his Sunday best made by Henry Poole of Savile Row from the recent fugitive from scandal. He lunched with the royal family at Tatoi, the county palace outside Athens, 'a handsome man, looking younger than his forty-odd years'. He appointed his old friend, William Shaw, as the company's representative; the terms were not over-generous – just 2½ per cent commission and £25 a year to cover all expenses, whereas the agent he chose at the same time in Constantinople drew 5 per cent commission with a guaranteed minimum of £300. But then, although Skouloudis was now Minister of Marine, Zaharoff had no serious expectations of the Greek market bearing any fruit so long as the country enjoyed only fitful bouts of political and financial stability.

Spain was a different matter. Business was blossoming. The government, harassed by Cuban rebels, solicited arms. For five years, so it is said – a useful period of grace for the Cubans – Zaharoff and Krupp's star salesman, Friedrich von Bülow, fought ferociously for orders until almost every Spanish officer above the rank of major had become the minion of one or the other. This, as might have been foreseen, led to stalemate with each warily circling the other watching for a break. Zaharoff provoked it. Purchasing some Krupp arms for his own account, he arranged for them to be distributed to the Cuban insurgents, and then betrayed them to the Spanish officers on his payroll. This expedient elicited an order from the government. Zaharoff's real edge more probably lay in the fact that he could undercut the Germans by supplying arms from the company's native plant – Placencia de las Armas – in the Basque country. (The ill-used Bülow suffered further misfortune. Finding himself in London in 1914 as agent for Krupp, he was charged with spying and put away for four years.)

Zaharoff carried the fight to the camp of his principal rivals, not only Krupp in Germany but the French Schneider of Le Creusot. The German navy adopted the Maxim and the French the 37 mm

Maxim as well as the 6-pounder Nordenfelt. From April 1893 he was assured of 1 per cent commission on all contracts with the French government.

By the summer of 1893 he was back in the South American ring. He suffered his first contretemps in that market due to a rare omission on his part. He was accused of bribery and arrested. He had been denounced by another British arms agent acting for the rival Armstrong, who had preceded Zaharoff to Chile and Argentine, Robert Lawrie Thompson. Thompson, who doubled as a special correspondent of *The Times*, had already had cause to be jealous of the Maxim agent whose path he had crossed in Spain. Now, piqued at the newcomer's renewed success in winning orders in spite of charging higher prices, he was determined to trip him up. However, after suitable arrangements had been made, Zaharoff was released. Disgusted, the Armstrong agent took himself off to follow the Chino–Japanese war. (He was fortunate enough to arrive at a peak period so that within a month of the outbreak of hostilities he could afford to relinquish his post with *The Times*, although ten years later he had to recover his commissions in the Chancery Division.)

The Zaharoff legend fattened on his supposed South American career. He was credited with an original technique – fighting by rounds. Whenever he came on a war, it is supposed, he would arrange a restorative truce in which the principal performers would re-equip themselves before resuming hostilities. One practical difficulty he must, of course, have faced was to complete and deliver the resulting orders from half-way across the world in good time; there must have been nail-biting suspense in the savanna. The beneficiaries of this consideration, extending fancifully over a period of some thirty-five years, were supposed to have included Paraguay and Bolivia, Argentine and Chile, Panama and Columbia. There is no supporting evidence for this.

In spite of all this bustle and Zaharoff's best efforts, all was not well with the Maxim–Nordenfelt company. Orders were sporadic; at the machine-gun factory at Crayford there were constant slack periods, and even temporary closures. A more important contributory factor was poor financial control and loose management. Maxim was not an administrator; his inventor's itch so interfered with production that he was eventually banned from the Erith works and allocated a shop at Crayford. He was unreasonably optimistic. He dubbed his more realistic joint managing director, Captain F.E.Acland, 'Captain Calamity'. Even his own inventions were not always entirely practical; one for extending the life of his guns was not universally popular with the marketing department. Although Albert Vickers sat on the board, with the Hon. Algernon Mills, a partner of the bankers Glyn Mills, there was no day-to-day oversight of the company's operations. As a result the company posted losses of £21,000 in 1894 and £13,000 the following year. Accounts, and presumably commission, were not paid promptly, and one annual general meeting at the Cannon Street Hotel was prolonged for two and a half hours by dissatisfied share-holders. It was Lord Rothschild who provided a solution in the form of a young protégé, Sigmund Loewe, younger brother of Ludwig Loewe, founder of the celebrated German arms firm Deutsche Waffen. He was appointed general manager and, in October 1895, full-time managing director. Within just one year he had turned the company round to show a profit of £138,000.

In order to achieve this happy end, various economies had to be made, and the axe fell impartially on Zaharoff. In January 1894 the board proposed to withdraw his guarantee of commission; Loewe, the executioner, was left to deliver the notice 'as soon as ... special reasons ... have ceased to exist'. He owed this postponement to the continuing lawsuit with Nordenfelt in Paris. (In July 1895 Zaharoff informed the company that judgement had gone against them, but that an appeal had been lodged. He was rewarded with a cheque for £250 for his services, with the promise of a further £250 on the final settlement of the case.)

Three months later there were five dismissals among the London staff and agents, and Zaharoff, along with two surviving colonels, was shifted on to fixed payment. As if this were not already a bitter enough pill, in June the secretary was instructed to inform him that the board had reluctantly come to the conclusion that the present condition of the company did not permit them to continue his agree-ment. He was given six months' notice. This was doubtless a ploy to facilitate Loewe's surgical pruning of dead wood and paring of extravagance. However, in October he was reprieved and it was resolved to continue his employment in the company in Continental Europe – no mention of South America or other overseas markets – on terms which Loewe formalized within a week: Zaharoff was to receive commission of 1 per cent on all orders from Europe, pay-ment to be made each month only as cash was received, and terminable at three months' notice. There is no mention of any fee, although it would reasonably have been restored to its original level of £1,000 per annum. (This was still generous. A head of department earned not more than £400, which would buy a three-bedroomed house with a large garden.)

He would not, however, have been destitute if he had not been spared. In 1891 he had founded the Express Bank and bureau de change in the Place de l'Opéra; he was agent also for the American Bank Note Company: he supplied specimen notes at the request of the National Bank of Greece, but failed to win the contract: 'the Greeks want cheap work & don't mind how bad it is – no honest man', he lamented to Shaw, 'ever made a penny out of Greece.' But he was prepared to put up half a million francs with four associates to acquire the emery monopoly from the Greek government. Shaw was to act as the syndicate's agent on a fixed salary – 'what frankly do you think you should have' – and a share of profits. He expected to be cheated by the government unloading their stocks during the negotiations, depressing the price and spoiling his market. On the death of his chief French partner, which put him to much inconvenience, he suspended the affair. He also considered trading in tin, berating the Greek government for their failure to control production and thereby being forced to sell at a loss. They were 'too idiotic to see this ... [it would] take 2 or 3 years to sell what is now in Europe. ... one day they will see which side their bread is buttered & then we may be able to deal with them'. Although he might have despaired of his fellow countrymen, he nonetheless offered to contribute 25,000 francs towards the Greek pavilion at the Paris Exhibition, if he were appointed 'Royal Commissioner', so that 'she can show that notwithstanding her troubles she still occupies an honourable position among civilised countries'. Despite his promise to 'do everything in a proper & grand style & bring credit to the nation', his largesse was spurned.

Having repaired his fences with Maxim–Nordenfelt, at the end of 1895 Zaharoff received another jolt. This time it was Vickers' turn to experience a hardening of the market. The company was dismissing its agents for ordnance and armour plate, preferring to make special arrangements as business arose. It was only in the next year that the situation improved marginally for him. In July he was confirmed as director of the Spanish Placencia company. And in March 1897 his efforts were materially recognized: he was voted in testimony of the board's appreciation of his services, in Russia and Spain especially, a gratuity of £1,000. His cup by now over-flowing, he was offered a new agreement: his sphere was extended to the whole of the company's business on a commission of half of 1 per cent. He drew breath and replied: 'The above conditions are perfectly satisfactory to me, and I hereby beg to accept them.'

If Maxim was at all put out by this tightening of the belt, and relative relegation, he soon threw it off. He was probably even relieved to have the routine cares of the business taken off his shoulders. It gave him more time at the drawing board.

The range of his inventive genius was remarkable. Apart from the many innovations he introduced into the military hardware department, he took out over a hundred patents on both sides of the Atlantic for such diverse products as hair-curling irons and a vacuum-cleaning device, pneumatic tyres and a forerunner of ships' stabilizers, coffee substitutes and 'Maxim's Pipe of Peace' – an inhaler for bronchial disorders. And he had another surprise up his sleeve: a heavier-than-air machine. This essay into a new element caught the imagination of Zaharoff, already soured by Nordenfelt's abandonment of his underwater warship; he claimed with near-truth to have been 'the first man to rise from the earth with Sir Hiram Maxim' (he was knighted in 1900). As with everything touching on the ingenious but ingenuous Maxim, there was a comic element about these experiments.

He had embarked on them at his 40-acre estate at Baldwyn's Park, near Bexley, as early as 1893. He first evolved a steam-engine plant which developed more power for its weight than anything before, although the sheer volume of water it was necessary to carry would have ruled out flights of any length. (And anyway, typically impulsive, he 'had made no proper provision for, nor study of, stability and control in the air'.) There was another restraining factor. The landlords insisted on being paid £200 compensation for each tree he felled in order to provide the margin of clearance for the uncertainties of free flight. He decided instead to provide a runway on rails as an economy.

At some cost to his backers – £20,000 was put up by his fellow directors and friends, including 'Mr ZedZed', who later not untypically boasted to a colleague that his outlay had been as much as £200,000 – he produced a giant craft which 'partook of the nature of a biplane'. It was an impressive sight. The boiler platform was suspended from a large central plane, with two adjoining curved planes on each side in addition to fore and aft elevating planes. In spite of its weight – three and a half tons, including water – the lifting effect of more than 475 square metres of plane surface was unexpectedly efficacious. The propellers were built to a similar scale; over 17 feet in diameter and 5 feet wide. With this contraption Maxim fondly expected to reach a speed of 40 m.p.h.

He entertained visitors, among them the sporting Prince of Wales, to trial runs down the track. (His own chairman, Admiral Commerell, was excessively alarmed at the speed he reached.) A large crowd gathered to witness his first controlled solo spin. With a good head of steam, Maxim recorded, 'on liberating the machine it bounded forward with great velocity' so that he found himself airborne, the one effect that had not been anticipated. A plank from the track then sprang up and smashed the screw, and the craft was wrecked. This, the pilot firmly concluded, was the 'end of my flying experiments'. This was eight years before the Wright brothers successfully took off.

Maxim's angels may very well have been reluctant after this mishap to dig deeper into their pockets, but he had also reckoned without the landlords. Foiled of compensation for the trees they must have hoped to see cut, they had sold the estate over his head to the London County Council, who required the land for a lunatic asylum. He turned his hand instead to captive 'Flying Machines' for fairgrounds until these too were declared unsafe by the Council's inspectors.

Zaharoff was impressed, but with reservations, by his colleague's wayward and egocentric enthusiasm. The possibilities of the new medium matured in his mind until ten years later he initiated with more method the earliest academic research into flight.

In the meantime he was more concerned with hard selling than sailing through the air to satisfy a wild dream, a priority no doubt shared by the London office. Maxim's heavier weaponry, ranging up to 14-pounders, was too cumbersome to take around the world as personal luggage, so visiting royals and notables had to be enticed down to the gun ranges at Erith and Shoeburyness on the company's steam-launch *Vectis*; otherwise special trains were chartered for outings to the ranges at Swanley and Eynsford outside London.

The most venerable of these was the pig-tailed Chinese statesman, Li Hung-chang, the founder of the Chinese navy and long-standing client of Krupp. His first auspicious words on stepping ashore were, 'I should like to see Hiram Maxim.' His wish satisfied, he presented him with the decoration of the Double Dragon. To Zaharoff's disappointment at least, it turned out that this honour was due to his admiration not for the artillery but for Maxim's vigorous views on missionaries: the Chinese should, he thought, be allowed 'to enjoy their own religion, in their own country, in their own way'.

After the demonstration, Li Hung-chang asked to see the explosive shells for the pom-pom. Handling a sample reverently, he enquired its price: 6s 6d. Although it was less demanding in ammunition than its smaller brother – about 300 rounds per minute – he countered: 'That gun fires too fast for China.' The King of Denmark had similar reservations: 'That sort of gun would bankrupt my little kingdom in two hours.' Another less honoured guest was the Shah of Persia,

Nasr-ed-Din, whose unorthodox habits – he blew his nose on the Duke of Montrose's muslin curtains – were disconcerting. After being lavishly entertained by the Rothschilds, a demonstration was even arranged for him in the grounds of Buckingham Palace. The Prince of Wales had warned Maxim that the acquisitive potentate would expect a gun as a gift, but a broad hint to this effect by the Shah was pointedly ignored.

A succession of minor and major wars which erupted sporadically throughout the world at this period also 'helped to reduce our obsolete or obsolescent stock of guns'. Maxim–Nordenfelt had no publicity or promotional department; even then it was felt that 'if we had advertised we would have been stigmatised at fomenters of wars'. Successful sales in an intensely competitive market depended entirely on reputation and demonstration as well as on more aggressive techniques of the agents under the overall direction of Zaharoff. But although a naval officer remarked that the Matabele had confessed that they could not face up to the 'choc-a-choc-a-choc' of the Maxim, orders for colonial wars were insignificant, and expenditure on ammunition was costed to the nearest penny by a scrupulous home government. A major campaign such as that which culminated at Omdurman was exceptional; here an unusually generous provision of forty-four Maxims enabled the 25,000 strong Anglo-Egyptian force to account for 9,700 Sudanese at a cost of 20 British officers and 462 other ranks. Civilians were often more enthusiastic – or bloodthirsty – than the military. Cecil Rhodes, describing how in the Matabele campaign each receding wave of Lobengula's warriors 'left a thick deposit of corpses on the ground', commented approvingly, 'There is no waste with the Maxims,' and H.M. Stanley considered them 'invaluable for subduing the heathen'.

8

Arms Amalgamated

Other, greater and older companies were also not immune to such pressures as sporadic recession, sometimes frank depression, and always severe competition. These conditions led to a rash of amalgamations and diversification among the big steel companies.

Vickers, based on Sheffield, made a first fortune exporting steel bars to the States during the rail boom of the 1850s. The decision to enter the field of armaments was taken as a rescue operation to escape the falling-off of this traffic which followed bank failures and the erection of tariff barriers. The entry was effected by two routes, armour plate and guns.

All-steel armour plate was a lucrative but intensely competitive business, in which all nonetheless happily joined. This rivalry virtually ended with the introduction of the new Krupp hardening process in 1896 under which Vickers and other British companies took licences, until Vickers produced its own light-weight nickel chromium plate, although under the terms of a pooling agreement the company was obliged to exchange information with Krupp on such improvements.

The entry into ordnance was by a bumpier road, the companies involved maintaining that they had been induced by the British government to invest heavily in the expectation of orders that were forthcoming neither in sufficient quantity nor in sufficient constancy to justify the capacity of the new plant. It was this conjuncture that forced the companies to look elsewhere – abroad – for alternative markets, a shift, indeed, actively encouraged by the government.

Vickers did, however, plunge in 1888, investing around one million pounds in the process and receiving in return modest orders from the government for guns. In spite of this, armaments remained but a small part of their total business. It was Albert Vickers, 'optimistic, daring and speculative', who determined to go the whole hog, and the recently revived debate on sea-power, backed by political and public sentiment, pointed the way.

As a first step forward Vickers acquired in 1897 the recently enlarged and re-equipped Naval Construction & Armaments Company Limited at Barrow, one of the most well-ordered shipyards in the country, for the bargain price of £425,000; and, as a natural complement to this, rounded off the process in the same year with the purchase of the Maxim–Nordenfelt company, of which Albert Vickers was already a director, and which was in turn linked with the Barrow yard, for £1,353,000, acquiring the works for guns and ammunition at home and abroad, the ranges, and one other shareholder (since 1894) – salesman-in-chief Basil Zaharoff. This deal, as the earlier Maxim–Nordenfelt merger, was masterminded by the team of Cassel and Rothschild through an issue of debentures and an increase in Vickers' issued capital to £2,500,000. The new company took the name Vickers, Sons & Maxim Limited. Maxim joined the board – an honourable burial, according to one writer – until, with his final retirement, the company restricted its name to Vickers Limited in 1911.

With this sudden aggressive sweep, Vickers was quite deliberately setting itself up to challenge the heavy-gun and big shipbuilding combine of Armstrong and Whitworth – wedded in the same year – and even, in good time, Krupp's itself. (In 1896 Krupp had acquired the Germania dockyard in Kiel and embarked in earnest on marine armaments.) Albert Vickers had thus achieved his ambition 'to supply ships with their engines complete and equipped with guns and armour plate, entirely manufactured by the Company in its own works'.

Vickers continued on this path of integration by picking up, in 1902, a half share in the naval shipyard of William Beardmore of Glasgow. The previous year the Wolseley motorcar company had been set up with more than half an eye on its military possibilities. Later still, when Barrow was deeply committed to a submarine-building programme, Vickers completed its design with the purchase in company with Armstrongs, and at the Admiralty's express request, of a controlling share in the Whitehead Torpedo Company, first of Fiume and then of Weymouth. This whole programme spawned a series of issues which, between 1899 and 1902, doubled the company's capital to over £5,000,000.

The manufacture of arms was not a passport to an easy fortune. The massive yet often minutely intricate and accurate engineering skills, the exacting standards, demanded a much higher level of capital investment, as well as research and development, than was normal in British industry. While orders from the home government were unpredictable and irregular, the companies were still expected to maintain additional capacity in reserve, which the Royal Ordnance factories and dockyards, kept at a steady level of employment, did not possess. The companies were therefore obliged to seek alternative markets overseas.

Until the early 1870s the British had enjoyed a virtual monopoly of the world trade in arms. But as this market expanded with the mounting nationalism of lesser powers, they met stiff competition from first the Germans and later the French. (The Americans made little mark until well into the new century.) But by the turn of the century the armourers, in stark contrast to their civilian counterparts, had recovered their market supremacy against even such entrenched interests, strongly backed by their governments, as the Germans in Turkey and the French in Russia.

And it was a substantial cake to share. Exports in just seven major markets in the period 1900–14 reached a little less than £60 million in warships and naval ordnance. Of this Vickers and Armstrong, separately or in association, took over 63 per cent, Vickers achieving something better than a half share. The French, Germans, Italians and Americans divided the remainder, not one achieving 10 per cent of the market share.

The rapid expansion of Vickers added significantly to Zaharoff's opportunities. He could now offer such a range of armaments that no other single company in the world could match, from the rifle-calibre Maxim – later developed into the company's own Vickers machine-gun of the First World War – up to the latest and largest battleship, home-made from masthead to keel, from jack-staff to poop. For it was exactly on his foreign sales that the positive results of the company often depended; like any tide, that of prosperity receded as often as it advanced, but less predictably. With the rising threats to Britain's naval supremacy, the year of the merger witnessed such a prodigious leap in the Naval Estimates – a direct response to Admiral Tirpitz's shipbuilding programme – as to envisage the laying down of a whole fleet of five battleships, thirteen cruisers and twenty-eight destroyers; and the following year a further four battleships and etceteras were contemplated. Most of this immense effort, in a fairly constant ratio of about two to one, fell on the private firms.

However, following the Boer War, there was a period of general stagnation in the general trade of the country. Then a slow improvement took place which lasted until 1905 when the dividend came out at a total of 15 per cent, these welcome results being 'largely due to the increase of business done with foreign countries'. In 1908 there was a downturn once again, a depression of world trade which lasted until 1911 when the improved results for Vickers were once more owed to the flourishing foreign business of the company.

In return, Zaharoff was well rewarded. Early in 1898 he was offered, and accepted, a small percentage of the profits of the company – nine-tenths of 1 per cent – in full payment of all current commissions, plus an allowance of £1,000 per annum for local expenses in Paris which included his new home at 41 avenue Hoche, between the Arc de Triomphe and the Parc de Monceau. In the previous year he had also acquired a *pied-à-terre* in the fashionable heart of London, installing himself in gentleman's chambers at 22 Ryder Street, now the site of the *Economist* building.

He was able to indulge in other foibles. In keeping with his new estate, he adopted the appurtenances of high life, with them a pair of Purdeys. An unaccustomed weapon, he briskly fired off 500 rounds, but 'bumped his cheek so badly' that, disillusioned and pained, he gave the offending guns to the Vickers family. In Paris he was often to be seen driving in the Bois de Boulogne on the box of a high buggy drawn by three horses after the fashion of a Russian troika; according to his friend Lady Napier, he had even brought a string of horses from Russia to complement the image, but the wretches had all inconsiderately died of consumption.

He was by now comfortably off. As a result of his arrangement, Vickers, Sons & Maxim paid him £34,000 in 1902, £35,000 in 1903, £40,000 in 1904 and a staggering sum of £86,000 the following year. (By 1902 his personal savings were already so considerable that he was able to purchase outright a block of shares worth £25,000 offered to him by the banker Saemy Japhet.)

Today it requires a most difficult projection of the imagination to gain any true picture of just what these sums represented at the time; no facile conversion – multiplication by, say, a conservative factor of thirty – can give more than an approximation, and a very rough one at that. The bar was the most richly rewarding profession. Asquith, practising at this same epoch with all the prestige of a former Home Secretary, was earning a figure which fluctuated between £5,000 and £10,000 a year, high without being sensational; income

71

tax was a mere 1s in the pound, soon to be reduced by Asquith himself to a more reasonable 9d.

And what, also, do these great sums represent? Like much else it is a matter for speculation. Taking the year 1905 as a base reference, his share of the company's profits from the previous year would have barely exceeded £6,500. He would have also collected a fee of a few thousands, and expenses – by no means slight. But that still leaves an unexplained payment in excess of £75,000. If, in addition, to his share in the company's profits, he was also collecting commission of 1 per cent on his personal sales, then he was generating overseas business to the tune of around £7,500,000 – or the equivalent of three battleships a year, a couple of cruisers and a handful of submarines. This is simply not a reasonable supposition. In 1904 the Maxim division had actually registered a loss (although this was retrieved in the next year) and the profits at Barrow, where over three-quarters of the work in hand was anyway for the account of the home government, had barely exceeded £400,000 for a turnover of just over £1,500,000; and the only foreign subsidiary in existence at that time, the Placencia small-arms works, more often showed a loss than a profit.

Could part of this payment then be explained away as his share of the dividends on his own holding in the company? That is another grey area. A quarter of a century later he was painted as 'le principal actionnaire' of Vickers, but it is less easily proved and still less probable. The only holding in his own name, and in an exceptional year, was some 69,000 ordinary shares in the annual returns for 1908, well under 2 per cent. After that he seemingly reduced even this to a nominal 2,000-plus, with minor variations in mere hundreds, so that at the outbreak of war he owned only 2,913 – in his own name – as opposed to the 550,000 odd ordinary shares held by the family and directors. (Zaharoff was never a director of the Vickers parent; he would have had to forego his commissions.)

In 1920, sensitive to criticism that effective control of the arms firms was exercised by the hidden hand of a small elite of scheming profiteers, the board carried out an analysis of the share register: this revealed a spread of 47,000 shareholdings with an average 265 shares each. Zaharoff's nominees might, of course, have multiplied with the ease of the nimble amoeba – he also bought small holdings in his sisters' names – but if he did indeed acquire a larger holding than the books reveal, it would have taken him quite a number of years of heavy investment to build up any significant holding to match the family's. Zaharoff evidently was, however, a substantial shareholder in Deutsche Waffen; Saemy Japhet described his purchase of a line in these shares, which he acquired from 'our Paris friend', as an 'important deal'.

If he was ever a sinister and occult influence in any company, he managed to fox the responsible officers who already had an eye on him. At the senatorial enquiry into the munitions industry in 1934, the chairman, the dyed-in-the-wool isolationist Senator Nye, closely questioned Henry Carse, president of the Electric Boat Company, on Zaharoff's role:

'How much stock do you suppose he had?' asked Nye.

'I have not the faintest idea,' replied Carse. 'I was not able to trace it. He told me he was interested in the stock and I went over the stock list to see whether I could analyse the names to find out whose might be his. I thought I was a little conversant with that business ... but I could never check out anything that gave me an idea of how much belonged to him.'

Would some part of these payments have represented bribes or other more subtle subsidies? It would have been very surprising if they had not. There has been as much woolly thinking on this subject as on every facet of the ethics of arms. One sweeping accusation, put out in the name of the League of Nations, was that 'armaments firms attempted to bribe government officials, both at home and abroad'. No supporting evidence was ever put forward for this at home, and a subsequent Royal Commission gave it short shrift. Quite apart from other considerations, the scrupulous system of estimates and tenders very largely precluded any opportunity for corruption. Abroad, however, less precise procedures allied to alien mores did little to discourage the practice. The Vickers' historian, J.D. Scott, wrote: 'It would be naive to imagine that the standards of business ethics in the Balkans and South America in the seventies and eighties were the standards of Whitehall or the Bank of England. Bribery was not accidental or occasional but essential and systematic in every field of commerce.' This is uncommonly tactful. Things have scarcely changed in one hundred years, except that the field has broadened. Gifts and favours were a convention of the market place. The habit indeed was so universal and comprehensive that it might have been thought to provide an inherent immunity against undeserved advantage, some crude system of safety in numbers. The aim was not so much to gain such advantage as to avoid disadvantage. Indeed, the system prejudiced the more innovative companies whose tenders and costly designs were seldom treated with strict confidentiality. (Vickers were invited to participate in the Greek naval competition of

1911–12, Zaharoff being received by King George along with the naval architect Owens-Thurston. Their plans were circulated to the opposition, the order went to Germany.) And, a fact often wilfully overlooked, graft was not the monopoly of the arms trade. It sullied all sectors of commerce from the sale of steam engines to sewing machines.

China and Japan were the leaders in this sordid trade, but there is no indication that Zaharoff was himself ever personally involved in any transaction of any nature in these countries, or even that he ever set foot in them. In his known preserves, however, he was 'greasing the wheels' in Russia in 1900, 'doing the needful' in Portugal in 1906 and in Spain as late as 1925, and 'administering doses of Vickers to Spanish friends'. Scott states that in addition he paid baksheesh in Serbia in 1898, and probably in Turkey, in sums running from £100 to possibly several thousand pounds, but 'it would be equally naive', he cautioned, 'to imagine that when Zaharoff paid bribes, the money paid appeared under a ledger entry of "Bribes" in the books in London . . .'. Naive indeed.

Zaharoff was also, of course, in overall charge of all the company's overseas agents, all of whom worked on commission which they split when it became desirable or necessary. In a lax if not unashamedly acquisitive climate, a very fine borderline exists between corruption, the offer of money as an inducement to a government's agents to favour a product, and commission, the subsequent consideration for such preference.

However exceptionable, the practice – commission or corruption – existed, and no amount of pious hand-wringing and preaching would make it go away. It was, as Clive Trebilcock has written in a close study of the problem, 'customary and conventional . . . a formal preliminary to business, not a determinant of business. . . . The process was rather that governments decided to buy arms, and officials then expected the usual tokens of good will; the firms could not create the demand simply by offering the tokens.'

While they may reluctantly have accepted the prevalence of the custom, the British arms companies more practically considered it an unnecessary and irrelevant overhead. They had no need to fear foreign competition, they would have preferred to fight it out on the relative all-round excellence of their products. Their problem was that they could not afford to disregard the practice. The situation was further weighted – Zaharoff complained to Albert Vickers of 'terrible odds' – when their French and German rivals were acting at the same time as the expression of their governments' political ambition; this pressure was especially acute in Russia and Turkey, both important targets of rival diplomatic offensives by Paris and Berlin. Krupp, indeed, regarded all German diplomats abroad as his salesmen; a military mission to Turkey in the 1880s under General von der Goltz had precise instructions to 'get the Turk to buy their guns from the firm of Krupp'. The British companies, even when presenting a united front against foreign opposition, enjoyed no such solid support; their ambassador in St Petersburg could only send up a gentlemanly wail that the behaviour of Krupp and the French Schneider was 'too disgusting for words'.

It may have been no more than a coincidence that the happiest and most fruitful period of Vickers' collaboration with the Turkish government came only after the Young Turks' revolt in 1908 had attempted to restrain the incidence of ingrained corruption in the old Ottoman Empire.

Apart from commissions, 'by far the commonest and by far the most dangerous form of bribery', in the view of Philip Noel-Baker, 'is that of money gifts disguised by the name of "loans"'. The evidence available, he continued in his indictment of the *Private Manufacture of Armaments*, 'leaves no doubt that such direct money gifts have in the past been accepted by all grades of persons concerned with armament purchase, from Ministers of State ... to humble Government Inspectors who have to pass the goods when they are made'.

The evidence does support the view that loans were offered and accepted – or requested and granted. But there was one significant difference. In the only two surviving records of any similar transactions it is quite clear that such loans as were made were expected to be repaid, and in one case at least they attracted interest in the interim. 'You must not forget', Zaharoff wrote rather anxiously to Trevor Dawson, former naval gunnery specialist and a director of Vickers from 1897, in an undated note, 'that I agreed to lend B——*£160,000 and that you are to give me this money.' Sinister, at least superficially – except that Zaharoff's concern was more mundane. He had seemingly issued a cheque in six figures without provision: 'B' had promised Glyn Mills the cash before the end of the month, but in case of delay in the mail – Zaharoff was about to leave Paris for the country – he wanted 'Don Alberto' Vickers to pay in funds to cover Zaharoff's cheque.

In March 1907 Zaharoff was writing to Philip Thaine, Vickers'

---

* The name is difficult to decipher in Zaharoff's hand. The debtor could be Budeassa, Vickers' Bucharest agent, although Vickers had no significant business with Romania until the 1920s.

company secretary inherited from Maxim–Nordenfelt, who had sent him an extract of the accounts for Russia, on the matter of another outstanding loan. 'The £8,370. 18s. 8d. balance of a special "B" account, although appearing in your books against me, is, as you know, lent to a high personage, whom I cannot dun, but as he has paid off I part, feel certain he will pay the rest.' He was evidently a naturally slow payer. Two years later Zaharoff wrote again to Thaine. 'The high personage in Russia who owes us a certain amount of money has just paid into my credit at St. Petersburg the interest of same for one year, amounting to Rbls. 4,500 [around £500], and enclosed I send you cheque for equal amount.'

If the high personage in Russia had hoped to be rewarded with a 'disguised loan' in return for some past or future service, he must have been cruelly deceived.

Zaharoff, in spite of the riches that flowed his way, often found it difficult to make ends meet. In 1908, he addressed a homely, even poignant, appeal to Dawson:

I have had to pay for the Gold Cup for the *Rurik** and largish sums on account of the Electric Boat Co., etc., etc., and as I have been very much fleeced of ready cash, I would like ... if possible ... a cheque for £4,000 on account of expenses for the six months ending the 30th June next.

I would not bother you in this matter if it were not that my friends have drained me almost dry.

Please consider this as between you and myself, and believe me, my dear Dawson,

    Truly Yours,
      ZedZed

It is most probable that the large sums paid to Zaharoff were not all necessarily destined, or at least designed, for his personal pocket, but were expenses to cover the whole of the foreign sales organization. In May 1901, Douglas Vickers wrote to Zaharoff that in order 'to provide liberally during good times for the extension of the business, we will put at your disposal quarterly a sum equal to one per cent of the gross selling value of the company's output in war material from their works in England and at Placencia'. This was to be effective for five years so that he might make 'stable arrangements'; thereafter it was subject to two years' notice.

If this interpretation is correct, then his net personal earnings in

---

* Barrow-built armoured cruiser, 15,200 tons, completed for the Russian government in January 1906, delivered, owing to teething problems, in November. In return for the gold cup, Zaharoff received from Fabergé an engraving of the ship on a silver plaque.

this period have been grossly exaggerated. Before this time limit was up, in July 1905 the board again reviewed Zaharoff's remuneration as foreign adviser, which was fixed at an amount equal to the sum payable to a junior managing director.

It is a Sisyphean task to disentangle his finances. The boundaries are blurred. It would be comforting to believe that he had little idea himself of where he stood at any moment. He never seems to have been much of a money manager; his friend Owens-Thurston estimated that he was 'no financial genius', but then he was not the best qualified judge; he uttered this judgement on the steps of the London Bankruptcy Court. Neither did he ever collect money for mere pleasure; he genuinely revelled in the good things that it could provide as well as the power and prestige it attracted. There is no doubt that he was free and open-handed, and while he often practised a certain flamboyance, his generosity was usually more discreet.

Just two years before he was complaining to Trevor Dawson that his friends had drained him almost dry, he had helped Vickers over a presumed spot of trouble with their cash flow with a loan of £100,000 at 4 per cent. Even by his own standards this must rank as an extraordinary gesture, and extraordinary also that it should ever have been needed. There was Vickers, his employer, one of the most successful and dynamic British companies capitalized at over £5,000,000, having declared a profit after tax of £787,776 for 1905 – increased to £879,905 the following year – on which an ordinary dividend of 15 per cent was paid, yet grateful to accept a loan of such magnitude from its own foreign adviser to tide it over a temporary difficulty. He might well have crowed over this small service, particularly as bank-rate had moved up to 7 per cent in the autumn of 1907. He never did.

He repeated this amazing offer in 1913 for the same amount on the same terms. On this occasion his offer was turned down: the company was expecting considerable sums from the Admiralty as well as the first money from a new share issue. 'In fact,' confided Sir Vincent Caillard, the financial controller who had inherited Loewe's mantle, 'we ought to be very well off in cash henceforward for at least two years and I believe I shall have to sit heavily on some coat-tails in order to prevent a certain rushing at expenditure in sight of so much gold.'

The sorry, if provisional, state of Zaharoff's pocket in 1908 was owing to his self-indulgence and generosity. He had become a man of multiple property. In 1898 he had set himself up in comfort and style in the avenue Hoche (now renumbered 53). Four years earlier, emulating the *haut monde*, he had acquired a sumptuous summer seat, the Château de l'Échelle, on the Arne some three miles from Roye in that flat and featureless landscape, before it was seeded with war cemeteries, between St Quentin and Amiens. He still had charge of all three sisters, who had moved from the rue Treilhard to Chalgrain, where they occupied themselves – as a penance, legend might say – with good works. And to complete the happy family circle, the lively, dark-eyed beauty he had met so dramatically, the Duchess of Marchena and the incapacitated Duke, who was said to be 'very platonic', had taken up residence at 11 rue Dumont d'Urville off the États-Unis with their two surviving daughters, Christina, who married into the Walford shipping family in 1911, and Angèle, born in 1895.

Zaharoff's relationship with his Duchess naturally gave rise much later to gossip. At the time it seems to have been generally accepted – it was, after all, the tail-end of the *belle époque* – by his friends and, more significantly, their wives. She is said to have accompanied him on his travels, occupying suites on different floors in their hotels and an adjacent compartment, No. 8, on the Orient Express.

And inevitably there was speculation surrounding the identity of the true begetter of her daughters. In the 1930s, the Paris correspondent of the *Evening Standard* wrote a private note to his paper to the effect that Zaharoff was generally supposed to be the father of her children. Their parentage is not pertinent. Zaharoff treated them as his own family, and later adopted them.

By 1911 at least the ladies were very much at home and often on hand *en famille*. In the new year, Albert Vickers, off to Algiers 'to get away from this terrible winter', sent his 'kindest regards to Madame and the young ladies'. He must have broken his journey at Marseilles because two months later he wrote to thank his friend, 'also the Duchess, Carricula [Charikleia] and Angelina', for having him to stay at the Hôtel Metropole at Monte Carlo where Zaharoff had taken to wintering since at least 1895.

Zaharoff's secretary, Archie de Bear, has left an intimate pen picture of life at the château where the family spent three summer months each year until the war intervened. It was here that de Bear first met the Duchess, to whom his employer 'gave his heart and many years of patient devotion'. The Duke, under constant medical supervision, was rumoured to have occupied a distant wing, but de Bear was never able to confirm this story.

There were never large house parties, three or four guests at the most at any time; and there was usually a motive – business. Zaharoff never left the precincts of the château except for his daily croquet.

There was no one to touch him at this on his own ground and he took the sport with the utmost seriousness: 'even if war had been declared, he would have received the news unmoved'.

Every year one of the Vickers directors came with his family for two to three weeks. On one occasion, de Bear recalled, the child of one of Zaharoff's guests had become dangerously ill on returning to England. Zaharoff, showing great anxiety for news, ordered his secretary to stand by at the nearest post office in Roye. After several hours of suspense, a telegram arrived announcing the death of the child. De Bear bicycled back the three miles through a blinding rainstorm and handed over the missive to Zaharoff who, after dismissing him with a gesture, sat just staring at it. Later, handing de Bear a cheque for £25, Zaharoff said: 'That's for what you did today.'

On the same day one year later, Zaharoff sent for his secretary. Silently he handed him a cheque. It was for £25. De Bear attributed this to his 'extraordinary sense of fairness and the consequent desire to avoid the possibility of causing disappointment after creating a precedent'. A strange insight into the 'merchant of death'.

9

Eastern Empires

While Zaharoff was perfecting his cannons on the croquet field, the Balkans were bubbling over once more. The most contentious problem was the hopelessly mixed population of Macedonia, which fed violent irredentist sentiments in Serbia, Bulgaria and Greece. While Greece's designs on the disputed territory were ripening, she attempted a diversion against the Turks in Crete. She was forced to abandon this at the insistence of the great powers, coupled with the positive attitude of an international naval squadron in the proximity, but the popular discontent this aroused led to outright war with Turkey. This promptly degenerated into a débâcle, the Turkish troops giving proof of the benefit of their German tuition. A peace treaty was arranged by the European powers, from which Turkey won an indemnity of £4,000,000. Zaharoff's sympathies were engaged: 'It is peculiar,' he wrote, 'but in my case, my patriotism has arrived at a very high pitch, & I have done much for the good cause & intend to do more.' But when the practical William Shaw suggested that the Turks might be persuaded to devote this windfall to restore their losses in arms, he was scornful: 'I do not think the game is worth the candle ... so many thieves will be after the small sum available ... [that it is] hardly worth while to fight for the pittance.'

Neighbouring states were infected by Greek ambitions. Serbia, her claims secretly endorsed by Austria-Hungary, increased her army by one-third; Bulgaria, hovering on the brink of war with Turkey herself in 1903 over Macedonia, was obliged to keep up an army which served only as a drain on her economy.

Legend pretends that 'it was in the most eloquent language of all the Balkans – the language of bribery – that [Zaharoff] proved himself most skilled' and that as a result he came to arm the full complement of combatants in their intermittent wars. In reality, Krupp the Cannon King had the lion's share. Ten years before the death of the founder's son, Alfried, in 1887 the company had produced over 25,000 guns of which over half had been sold in eager markets the world over. In Turkey, Krupp enjoyed a monopoly and also had a tight hold on the Greek and Bulgarian markets. In Serbia, the fast-expanding Austrian company, Skoda, managed to secure a preponderant share. Until Vickers' marriage with Maxim in 1897, Zaharoff could not offer medium or heavy ordnance, but he had a world-beater in the Maxim. Krupp already held a licence for their manufacture; and in 1901 Deutsche Waffen, related to Vickers through the Loewe family, was granted the exclusive rights, subject to agreement with Krupp, to manufacture the Maxim and the licence to sell it anywhere outside the British Empire, France and the United States. Therefore, in the Balkans, with the Germans already strongly entrenched, Zaharoff was competing against himself: in 1899, a time of feverish rearmament in the region, royalties from Deutsche Waffen and Krupp paid to Vickers totalled £45,596, and Zaharoff was, of course, sharing in the profits of Vickers.

A major coup that was indirectly attributed to Zaharoff at this time, but at some distance, was the destruction of the cruiser USS *Maine* in Havana in February 1898, which cost America the loss of two officers and 258 crewmen, and Spain the loss of Cuba. The American court of enquiry found that the ship was destroyed by a submarine mine, although it was 'unable to obtain evidence fixing the responsibility ... upon any person or persons'. The Spanish enquiry, boycotted by the Americans, found that the explosion had an internal origin. Spain, certainly, had no hand in it. The Cuban insurgents had the motive, but themselves believed that an American *agent provocateur* had been responsible. There were many in the States who sought war. The gentle Senator Thurston foresaw that it 'would increase the business and earnings of every American factory', while Pulitzer's *New York World* competed for circulation with Hearst's *New York Journal* in urging revenge. In view of Spain's contrition, some such outrage was essential to persuade President McKinley, whom Theodore Roosevelt accused of having 'No more backbone than a chocolate éclair', to go to war.

The unfortunate result for Spain was the loss of her entire Pacific fleet in Manila Bay, shortly followed by the Atlantic fleet – four old cruisers, the best of which lacked her main battery – at Santiago de Cuba.

The natural sequel to the loss of Spain's colonies and her navy was that one-fifth of her annual budget was forthwith devoted to rearmament. The major British shipbuilders were the beneficiaries. Vickers, with Armstrong and John Brown, formed in 1908 the Sociedad Español de Construcción Naval to refurbish the dockyards at Ferrol and Cartagena for the construction of a new Spanish navy, and the national arsenal at La Carraca. The British provided one-quarter of the capital, skilled management and labour. SECN became the country's largest shipbuilding and engineering undertaking, for which the Placencia arms plant, of which Zaharoff was a director, became a major subcontractor. The new company also embarked on a programme to build Holland-type submarines under licence from the American Electric Boat Company, for which Zaharoff was to draw commissions and cross-commissions until the end of his life.

In 1902 Zaharoff was reported back in South America up to his old tricks arranging temporary truces in hostilities between Argentine and Chile. If he was in Chile, then he was frying bigger fish. In February, the Chilean government put its signature to a contract for two battleships, one the *Libertad* for Barrow, the other for Armstrong's Elswick yard. Their design – displacing 11,800 tons, they foreshadowed the all-big-gun Dreadnought – compared favourably with the current class of ship in the Royal Navy and, able to throw more tons of metal around per minute, were two knots faster than the best of their foreign counterparts. The Admiralty was not best pleased at the prospect of their passing into other hands, but the British government resisted a call in the House of Commons for their purchase. In the end they had a change of heart and beat the price down from £2,200,000 to £1,875,000 per ship, which the First Lord thought a 'good bargain for the country'. (The saving indeed represented the cost of ten of the new Holland-type submarines which Vickers had now begun to deliver to the Royal Navy.)

Whether Zaharoff too had had to cut commissions and other traditional expenses, he was unable to persuade the Chileans to replace their losses. His team, however, compensated themselves five years later in Brazil with an order for the 19,200 ton post-Dreadnought *São Paulo*. In the South American market, Vickers and Armstrong joined forces to face the growing American competition. The contract for the *São Paulo*'s sister ship, the *Minas Gerais*, was formally awarded to Armstrong's Elswick yard, while Vickers supplied the turbines, roughly equivalent to a third of the total cost; they did the same later for the monster 27,500 ton *Rio de Janeiro*, which was sold to Turkey and so brusquely requisitioned as HMS *Agincourt* in 1914.

Three years before their entry into the Spanish market, Vickers had struck up a partnership with two Italian companies to form the Vickers–Terni Società Italiana d'Artiglieria ed Armamente. The English company took a 28 per cent holding and pledged its designs and patents for which it was granted 10 per cent of the net annual profits, although such a position was barely reached before the outbreak of war. Zaharoff, with Albert Vickers, was nominated to the board. Between 1906 and 1910 Vickers–Terni erected a complete arsenal at La Spezia when work started on the first government order for the complete armament for two warships (the armament accounted in round figures for one-third of the cost of a ship). The cause of this exertion was that the Italians had announced early in the century their plans to spend over £50,000,000 over the following ten years to refashion their navy.

In Japan Vickers, with Armstrong and local finance, founded a large ordnance factory at the request of the government. Here Zaharoff held himself aloof. He would have had to make his choice; if any suspicion of his providing comfort and aid to the enemy, especially after Russia's naval disaster at Tsushima in 1905, had reached the ears of the court on one of his visits, his career might have come to a frosty end in Siberia.

He was well dug in at St Petersburg, casting his spell, 'working the oracle' and 'greasing the wheels' while leaving the nuts and bolts of the arrangements to his team of agents: the 'Nobleman, Engineer, Secretary of State' General Balinsky, Baron de Nordwell, possibly still the peripatetic Kabath and, on a lower level, Maxim's old agent, Hartmann. Zaharoff himself stuck close to the court. He cultivated two Grand Dukes, Michael Nicolayevich, president of the Imperial Council and Inspector-General of Artillery, and his successor in the latter post, Serge Michaelovich; also General Nicholai Kuropatkin who, as Minister of Defence in 1904, vainly attempted to restrain the Tsar from taking on Japan.

One of Kuropatkin's successors, General Vladimir Soukhomlinov, a member of the Rasputin set, was a less attractive proposition. Judged intelligent by Maurice Paléologue, political director at the Quai d'Orsay, but 'lazy, hypocritical, sly, venal', he was surrounded by speculators and adventurers with whom he spent weeks at Monte Carlo gambling away his gains. Despising this weakness for the tables, Zaharoff would have cynically exploited the streak. The Greek's circle was completed by Arthur Raffalovich, Financial Attaché at the Russian

Embassy in Paris and, a most enviable position, agent for the Russian loans. Paléologue, from the moral fastness of the Quai d'Orsay, castigated this respected economist and corresponding member of the Institut de France, as the great corrupter of French journalism and politics. The victims showed no inclination to resist their seduction.

After the gradual estrangement between Germany and Russia which followed Bismarck's overthrow, the French, delighted at the chance to implant themselves on their foe's furthest flank, gladly took up the running and the French banks, with their bias for foreign investment, responded to the challenge. Few conditions were imposed for the loans: strict political allegiance – that is, loyal opposition to Germany – with a corresponding obligation to 'Buy French'. In the course of the delicate negotiations for the 'loan which saved Russia', huge sums were lavished on promotion with French editors to gull the small investor with the tacit approval of the government, which had after all connived at the same device for the Panama Canal loan. As a result, as much as a quarter of the total of French savings were diverted to Russia, never to be recovered.

It is ironic in view of the oft-repeated charge that 'the arms firms manipulated or controlled the press' that the Paris press played a prime part in the propagation of the Zaharoff legend. The newspapers were not just susceptible to corruption, they courted it; one editor of *Le Figaro* was only satisfied if every item in the paper was paid for. And there was a lot of money to be made. For their foreign news, all newspapers relied on one source, Agence Havas, which provided a free service in exchange for the right to insert other material of a paying nature without charge. When the revolution of 1905 in the wake of the disasters of the Japanese war made it harder for Russia to raise her loan on the French market, she was forced to increase her usual sweetener to the fourth estate by twenty times. The Germans, indeed, continued their not disinterested subsidy of the French newspapers well into the war; *Le Journal*, with one of the largest sales in Paris, and the left-wing pacifist *Le Bonnet Rouge* lost their over-confident, careless proprietors to the firing squad.

Zaharoff is supposed to have a played a sinister role in this sordid scene. As much of this as is visible is innocuous enough. In a sober biography of Clemenceau it is stated that 'through the purchase of a harmless non-political paper, *Quotidiens Illustrés*, [Zaharoff] secured secret control of a second journal, *Excelsior*, which served as a lever for moving public opinion when it was necessary to employ the technique of "incitement"'. The truth is more prosaic. Zaharoff did invest 250,000 francs to acquire a minority interest in the company *Quoti-*

diens Illustrés, which he used quite openly to found in 1910 an entirely non-political paper (which may well have been one of the reasons for its lack of success) to satisfy a presumed desire for illustrations; the editor favoured photographs while the public's taste, as it transpired, leaned towards strip cartoons. Zaharoff himself, in face of the most vituperative and sententious press in the world, claimed simply that he had created it 'in order that his daughter might have a morning newspaper fit for a *jeune fille* to read'. He might also have hoped to make some money out of it.

In 1920 he unloaded *Excelsior*, on which he complained he had lost £300,000, on to *Le Petit Parisien*, one of the very few mass-circulation papers to eschew subsidy and to succeed in offending only a few people. 'Look here,' he told its proprietor Senator Dupuy, to whose son he was godfather, 'I have lost a good deal on the *Excelsior*, because I do not know how to manage a newspaper. You take it, make it pay and give me what I have sunk out of the profits. If there are no profits, then, of course, you need not pay.' Dupuy apparently made no more of a success out of it; *Excelsior* sank just eighteen months later.

Zaharoff was also accused of holding a share in *L'Echo de Paris* and *Le Temps*, for which Clemenceau wrote and on which his protégé, André Tardieu, served as foreign news editor and leader writer from his desk at the Quai d'Orsay. This is not improbable. What is not clear is what it proves. If he had wanted to place pieces of 'incitement', he could more simply have paid over the counter through one of the ubiquitous agents of Agence Havas.

But before he became a proprietor of the fourth estate, he was quite in his element, lording it at the court of the Tsar. Zaharoff's own secretary recorded that the Grand Duke Serge travelled to Paris expressly to see him, staying at the Hôtel Continentale in the rue de Rivoli, and that his employer always travelled alone on his trips to Russia, surrounded by absolute secrecy, as the personal guest of the Tsar. He was, needless to say, accompanied with 'gifts of great price': jewels from the rue de la Paix, and the rare and costly toys which were so popular at the court. (He seems to have taken a simple pleasure in showering his friends with his favours; Albert Vickers wrote to tell him how 'perfectly delighted Izme [his Bostonian wife] was this morning to receive your magnificent present. She is simply dee-lighted.')

All this was before the Japanese war unleashed the armaments boom. It is perfectly feasible that the court and administration, labouring under the chafing diplomatic restraints of the Quai d'Orsay and the commercial pressure of the French banks and industrial groups, happily leaned on Zaharoff as a counter-balance; he had no political axe to grind and was fully conversant with the quicksands of French politics, while his links were with London, with which the Tsar was seeking a better understanding. After the Russian defeat, he was well placed when the time came to re-equip the shattered imperial forces. Armed with power of attorney from Vickers in October 1906 – the contract for the *Rurik* had been signed in January – he had already suggested to the Russians during the war that his company should put in hand the immediate construction of destroyers for delivery in parts by rail to Port Arthur. There was no time for such stratagems. Before this the Russians had taken delivery of Holland's submarine *Fulton* which had arrived in Vladivostock overland six weeks before, but too late to take part in Tsushima; by 1908 they had six of the latest American-made Holland submarines at Kronstadt (on which Zaharoff earned his commission), as well as a mixed underwater fleet in the Black Sea.

It was in the year of the great naval disaster – the same year in which Vickers was completing two battleships, the *Katori* and the *Kongo*, for the victorious Japanese navy – that Sir George Owens-Thurston, its chief naval designer, accompanied Zaharoff to Russia, the first of many such visits which witnessed an increasing participation by the British in a hitherto French *chasse gardé*. Zaharoff liked to boast to the Vickers chiefs in London that, entering Russia, his pockets and suitcases were stuffed with banknotes for bribes. Thurston was evidently sceptical. 'Not many men', he remarked, 'could prevaricate in quite such a convincing manner and with such an honest expression.' And the *Rurik* contract was put through without a rouble being paid under the counter. Owens-Thurston was present when the Tsar invested a nervous Zaharoff with the Order of St Anne.

Zaharoff had one success to his own gun. He negotiated an agreement with the Department General of Artillery, no doubt with the approval of the Grand Duke Michael and the disreputable war minister, Soukhomlinoff, for the manufacture of Maxims at the Tula arsenal, for which the English company was paid a royalty of £80 a piece. It is known that in 1913 the arsenal produced 800 guns for which Zaharoff collected a commission of as much as £9,300, close to 15 per cent on the royalties. This was no doubt intended to cover sub-commissions to the venal Minister and others in his entourage – only to pass the wrong way over the green baize at Monte Carlo. However, lest he should have been thought greedy, he devoted the equivalent of two years' full commission to the creation of a chair of aviation at the university of St Petersburg.

Thereafter the Greek maestro appears to have withdrawn again from the front of the scene and remained shrouded in the wings with his eye open. He passed the reins to a Vickers director, Francis Barker, who was to become another close friend, Zaharoff standing in as godfather to his son Vere. (He was not generous in this role, considering his handshake in itself sufficient to confer 'luck and money'.)

The Tsar had led Russia to the brink of self-destruction. After the abortive revolution of 1905, the Little Father had conceded a representative assembly, the Duma, which loyally responded by nodding through snowballing budgets for rearmament until by 1913 the defence programme was consuming 35 per cent of the national income. However, the new wave of nationalism insisted in the same breath that such orders should be undertaken in Russia by Russian industries. For this they were dependent on outside capital and technology. The French were already installed in place; Schneider, along with Krupp and Skoda, had a share in the Putiloff ordnance works, the largest private enterprise but also a centre of subversive activity and too close to the capital for the comfort of the court. The British companies – John Brown and Armstrong, Vickers and Beardmore – swarmed in to fill the gaps. Vickers had one Greek ace up its sleeve and it was Vickers on its own which pulled out the plums by offering a sophisticated package around a superior product. It won in turn the rights for the financing and construction of complete dockyards to increase the Black Sea fleet (depleted when its pride, and flagship, the *Potemkin*, was scuttled by mutineers) by three battleships and lesser vessels of Vickers' design; and an arsenal which was promised as 'the most modern and most effective ... a private factory such as no other country possesses excepting England'. It was no idle boast.

Vincent Caillard, tying up the financial strings in London, showed himself to be perfectly aware of the diplomatic reverberations. In March 1911 he was conferring with Zaharoff about the formation of a French limited company for 'acquiring, installing, administering and exploiting' the naval shipyards. The resulting Société des Ateliers et Chantiers de Nicolaieff attracted not only the major participation of one of the most important French *banques d'affaires*, the Société Générale, but the Banque de l'Union Parisienne, which was intimately associated with Schneider and of which Zaharoff was a shareholder. This French interest was also represented on the board of the new company: Eugène Schneider was appointed a director along with Paul Doumer, a former Minister of Finance and President of the Chamber of Deputies. Schneider's partner Putiloff also joined them.

Vickers themselves took a 10 per cent shareholding in return for guaranteed profits, along with design fees, while carefully absolving themselves from any responsibility 'owing to Russian methods, management and labour'.

There was, of course, a shrewder reason for this French presence other than a good-natured desire to assuage Gallic pride. Russia's savage repression of the 1905 uprising had made her very unpopular in England and an embarrassment to the British government in the course of negotiating the Anglo-Russian convention. Rothschild, to whom Vickers might otherwise have turned, had refused Russia a loan on account of her persecution of her Jews; Cassel was the only Jewish financier to break ranks with an offering of £7,500,000 to the Tsar in 1909. It was correspondingly easier to harness the support of French bankers, particularly with a prod from the Quai d'Orsay for any reluctant starters; even the French Rothschilds had been whipped into line. Indeed it must have been the later realization of their losses which was to aggravate the French sense of grievance.

The Tsaritsyn* complex, the Russian Artillery Works Company, which was to stretch for two miles along the banks of the Volga, envisaged an investment of £2,500,000. Vickers was to take a 20 per cent holding and contribute its patents, innovations and expertise in return for a hefty design fee and 10 per cent of a decade's worth of guaranteed profits. This only got off the ground in the autumn of 1913.

Zaharoff, in spite of his grand connections, his 'greasing the wheels', his energy and enthusiasm, still faced frustrating obstructions. Raffalovich wrote to Minister Davidoff:

I have met Mr Zaharoff. He complains of the difficulties he is having to encounter in getting the bill of 1,500,000 roubles put through the Admiralty....

Zaharoff thinks that it will take three to four years to build armoured cruisers on the Black Sea in sufficient strength to overawe Turkey. That so far nothing has been pushed on. That Russian factories and banks concern themselves more with the Bourse than with anything else. Zaharoff must have been a little disillusioned here.

This sudden rude Anglo-Saxon eruption on to the steppes, regarded as inexcusable poaching in a French preserve, gave rise to howls of outrage in Paris. All the earlier accounts of this period, drawing for inspiration on French sources and pacifist propaganda, are correspondingly partisan. One especially tortuous interpretation would have

* Later Stalingrad, later still Volgograd

it that Zaharoff, squeezed out of the Russian shipyards by a resolute French defence, avenged himself with the monopoly of the rival Turkish fleet, thereby so terrifying the Russians that they sought to placate him with the monopoly for the imperial artillery. If there is any interrelation it is that the successful conclusion to the planned Russian naval programme acted as a spur to Turkish determination to counter it.

Essentially, the triumph of Vickers was seen as a check to Schneider Le Creusot in particular, and an affront to national pride in general, though this largely ignored the fact that French aspirations, sound or not, had been served and secured by the presence of the French banks. Furthermore, Beardmore of Glasgow, in which Vickers had a half interest, had joined with Schneider for a shipyard and arsenal at Reval.

The socialist Deputy, Albert Thomas, provided an insight into the depth of the chauvinism over the competition between Vickers and 'our Creusot', which he deplored as evidence of 'little respect for French interests by our allies'. He was more specific still: 'the Russian papers have described, as the most active agent, the most enterprising broker of the house of Vickers, the most redoubtable rival of Le Creusot, M. Zaharoff'. In an unusual overt intervention by Zaharoff in the pages of *Excelsior*, the paper published a detailed *démenti* that French interests had in any way been neglected by Vickers.

Zaharoff was also blamed, by remote association, for what became a *cause célèbre*, the so-called Putiloff affair, a crudely transparent but apparently effective ruse to throw a scare into French political and public opinion in order to loosen the purse-strings. The first card was played by *L'Echo de Paris* which published a telegram in January 1914 reporting 'a rumour that the Putiloff factories at St Petersburg will be bought by Krupp. If this information is well founded, it will cause great concern in France.'

The reaction of Schneider was curiously cautious. The company announced that it had no information but admitted that the news, if confirmed, would be very serious in view of the fact that the Putiloff works possessed the secret of French arms manufacture – just the kind of clarification calculated to raise goose-pimples on the French flesh. (In fact, there was little if any secret. French factories had for a long time been delivering 75 mm guns – the first field-pieces to absorb their own shock, thus eliminating the need to re-aim between shots – to Italy, a member of the Triple Alliance, and Bulgaria.)

The issue of *The Times* which described the 'no small excitement caused in Paris today' also carried reports from its correspondents in Berlin and St Petersburg categorically denying the rumour. In face of this, Schneider was forced to admit that negotiations were taking place, not for the purchase of the works by Krupp, but for an increase in its capital with the participation of the German company and the Deutsche Bank. Obviously, the French insisted, gamely sticking to their guns, any such transaction would inevitably bring the Putiloff enterprise under the control of German interests.

The same Deputy Thomas later declared that the principals in the affair had confessed to him after the war that the rumour had been confected late one night at the *Echo de Paris* as Schneider were threatened by another French group. This group could only have been the Société des Ateliers et Chantiers de Nicolaieff, in which Schneider and his bank were already involved. Despite *The Times'* revelation that the plot had no substance, Vickers again felt obliged to issue a statement in Frank Barker's name absolving the company from conspiring against legitimate French interests: 'I say most emphatically that the Vickers company has nothing at all to do with the Putiloff business. In Russia it has no relations with the Krupp firm and has never had any intention of combining its interests with that firm.'

A suitable role for Zaharoff in this imbroglio was only attributed to him nearly twenty years after the event by the Union of Democratic Control, a pacifist pressure-group in London which sustained its spirits by sincere but emotive moralizing. The false report, it claimed, was provoked by Raffalovich in collusion with Soukhomlinoff 'after an understanding had been arrived at with Zaharoff. The news was sent through from St. Petersburg that the Putiloff works required another £2,000,000 and would be pleased if they could obtain it from Schneider–Creusot. Schneider–Creusot accordingly put the required capital at the disposal of Putiloff and at the same time a new Russian loan of £25,000,000 was raised in France....' It is note-worthy that, years later, Zaharoff, in a critique of the Union's report, *The Secret International*, to a director of Vickers, wrote: '[I] agree with you that 25 per cent of the facts and 75 per cent of the conclusions are incorrect, yet many of its allusions are correct.'

It may well have been that the French company was hoping to increase its own holding in Russia and needed to soften up the market in order to be able to raise the stake. It could certainly not have found this sum – many times Vickers' financial commitment in the shipyards and arsenal – from its own resources. But why Zaharoff should have helped Schneider to achieve this, or why Schneider should even have needed his help, is less clear. The evidence of his engagement is slim; it hangs by the thread of hearsay from a flagrantly partisan source. If he was privy to the plot, the most reasonable explanation

90

is that Schneider was acting throughout with the knowledge and approval of the French government, and the latter turned to Zaharoff who, having no obvious direct stake in the issue, would have been seen to be playing the part of Caesar's wife. It might or might not be relevant that on 31 July 1914, Zaharoff achieved his third promotion in the Legion of Honour under the auspices of the Ministry of Foreign Affairs for 'services exceptionnels'. There are no other discernible meritorious services that he rendered to that ministry during that period.

Another and better documented press scare in which Zaharoff would certainly have had a motive was revealed in the Reichstag by the independent socialist deputy, Karl Liebknecht. He had intercepted a letter written as long ago as 1907 from Paul von Gontard of Deutsche Waffen, licensees of the Maxim. The writer wished to arrange for the insertion in 'one of the most read French papers, if possible in the *Figaro*', of an item that the 'French Army Command has resolved to speed up considerably the equipment of the army with machine-guns and to provide double the number originally contemplated'. This was considered too crude even by the standards of the French press and it was not accepted in this form.

There was indeed throughout these pre-war years constant clamour in the more jingoistic newspaper columns which fattened a host of false alarms about the rival qualities and quantities of arms and armaments as between the French and German armies, while Britain enjoyed its share of naval shipbuilding scares. This stirred an easily inflammable public opinion and led inevitably to clamour on all sides for increased expenditure on similar weaponry. It also led later to questions about the control of the press by the arms firms. In the case of the British press, no such charge was ever made, but Zaharoff himself was described after the war by French press sources as 'the proprietor of several great French newspapers'. No instance was cited, no evidence offered, apart from the *Excelsior* of which incidentally he had already divested himself at the time this claim was made, and which he stands accused of using 'to great effect in the famous Putiloff scare'. (It would have taken a sharp-eyed reader to have spotted it.) By contrast, Krupp did control two German newspapers and one Belgian, and was in a position at least to influence the emanations of the Wolff News Bureau. Schneider seems only to have acquired newspapers, and then mainly in Belgium, after the war. But then, in the context of the peculiar practices indulged in by the Paris press, ownership was not a requisite for commanding editorial policy.

Meanwhile, back in the Balkans, where Zaharoff was impatient to 'overawe Turkey', a multiple arms race was engaged. Krupp and Skoda, Schneider and Vickers all had a hand in equipping the competing states. In Greece French military and British naval missions were remodelling the Hellenic forces; another British naval mission was in place in the rival Turkish camp, while the Ottoman army was still under German tutelage. Schneider, in what he described as his 'stroke of luck', was arming Bulgaria. This achievement nicely illustrates what may be described as one of the vicissitudes of this capricious trade. 'Foxy' Ferdinand, the Tsar of the Bulgars, paid a state visit to Germany in 1909 with a shopping list for Krupp in his pocket. At a banquet at Potsdam in his honour, the Tsar, incautiously leaning down the better to admire the view from the windows, received a smart buffet on the royal rump from a playful Kaiser. Foxy, his honour stung, walked off in a huff, taking the contract with him to the French.

The British companies were playing their part. Vickers, with Armstrong, was closely engaged in the 1910 shipbuilding competition in Turkey, while Owens-Thurston was ensconced in Athens overseeing the inevitable sequel, the Greek competition of 1912. The Turkish deal resulted in the order for the *Reshadieh*, displacing 23,000 tons, wrested from under the nose of Krupp at the last minute. The British terms were the decisive factor, Vickers in effect financing the construction for the Turks. ('If Zed wants to do any of this money,' Albert Vickers wrote to Trevor Dawson, 'he is very welcome.')

Zaharoff joined his friend in the Greek capital. They were received by King George, but the order went to Germany, the armament being contracted to the American Bethlehem Steel Company at 'an impossible price' in order to secure a footing in the Greek market. (Justice was done: war broke out before this order could be completed and the 14-inch guns were seized by the Royal Navy on their passage to Germany.)

All this activity and resulting tension contributed to a rough-house, another Balkan embroilment, in which the suppliers could sit back and clinically observe the performance of their wares in the hands of their client states. Bulgaria, Serbia, Greece and Montenegro joined in a transient union against Turkey; after the latter's defeat, the former allies turned on each other and were joined by Romania and Turkey.

When war broke out in 1912, all Macedonia, Albania and Epirus were still Ottoman, and the Turks, unable to introduce reinforcements except by sea, were thus obliged to fight three separate campaigns. To protect their southern front, and their shipping, they offered Crete to Greece to persuade her to remain neutral, but Venizelos, Prime Minister for the past two years, was shrewd enough to weigh the disadvantage of such inaction – the loss of a seat, and a voice, at the peace table. The Greek and the Bulgarian forces acquitted themselves with credit, the former, under Crown Prince Constantine, clearing Thessaly up to Macedonia and narrowly beating the Bulgarians into Salonika. Within five months Turkey was beaten on all fronts and signed away most of her territory in Europe, the lion's share going to Bulgaria. The latter, with the bit between her teeth and her eye on Salonika, turned against Serbia and Greece, but Romania, worried by Bulgaria's pretensions, entered the ring, while the Turks took advantage of the scrimmage to reoccupy Adrianople. All this second phase* lasted barely five weeks. Greece as a result emerged with large territorial acquisitions and a corresponding increase in population approaching two million.

The French, crowing, took this as worthy proof of the superiority of the Schneider product over Krupp's. The Turks for their part sombrely considered their military and diplomatic relations with the central powers.

During this conflict Zaharoff was said to have borne the cost of the Greek army out of his own pocket; another source more precisely claimed that he contributed $2,500,000 a year for the war (Greece's active participation in the first round barely exceeded five months, in the second as many weeks.) It would have been an inexplicably quixotic gesture: he had never held any high hopes of Greece as a market, although he was said to have nursed ambitions to see her emerge as a power in the region. And yet Prince Christopher, whose father King George, a man of moderation, had been assassinated at Salonika between the two Balkan wars, declared that 'he never posed as a patriot or claimed to have any special affection for Greece, or for any other country for that matter.... a freelance ... with an extraordinary instinct for backing the winning side'. Zaharoff's secretary, on the other hand, described his 'immense patriotic devotion to Greece'. By his own account his patriotism could be fired, especially at times of national humiliation, while paradoxically he held unflattering views about those 'Greeks inhabiting the Fatherland' in comparison with the 'foreign Greek', and with one exception had scant respect for their politicians.

There remains nonetheless the plausible hypothesis that his

---

* This scrap saw a notable 'first' in aerial warfare: bombing – by grenade, for which watermelons were later substituted with great psychological effect.

emotions had been enlisted by Venizelos. The Cretan politician not only a bore a marked physical resemblance to Zaharoff, but shared many of the same characteristics: a 'restless and subversive spirit; adventurous, often inconsistent, ardent and passionate with ambition and caprice unrestrained'. Added to this somewhat wayward streak, the Greek politician was also 'persuasive and plausible', and capable of exercising an almost mesmeric charm over his victims. The two had first met a year or so before the recent war; their relationship has been described as 'a curious partnership, each wary of the other, perpetually on guard, yet outwardly presenting a united front'. There is no suggestion in this of any personal attachment but rather an awareness that one might be useful to the other. Their association was to last for ten years, and to culminate in disaster.

Turkey, meanwhile, undergoing a moral renaissance under the Young Turks, would not accept the ruling of the London peace conference. She turned to Britain and France to redress her wrongs. This abrupt change of course towards a greater degree of independence if not an alignment, with the Entente powers, was fatally ignored by the politicians in Paris, obsessed with the Tsar, and by a disdainful London. The arms firms have often been charged with stoking and provoking belligerency, and it is true that their interlocking financial alliances did not necessarily correspond with the prevailing system of political alliances. In the instance of Turkey in the two years leading up to the European Armageddon, it is more painfully evident that considerations of self-interest dictated a switch in Turkish policy towards greater dependence for armament and administrative assistance on the French and British, an initiative from which the statesmen failed to draw any diplomatic advantage.

It is an additional irony that, immediately following the Balkan wars, Turkey had first applied to Berlin for a loan and had been recommended to refer herself to the Paris Bourse. As the way to the French pocket ran through the Quai d'Orsay, tough conditions were imposed: the purchase of French arms along with supervision of the Turkish gendarmerie and treasury and concessions for public works. These were swallowed in part. But in naval hardware Turkey sought complete independence.

Again Vickers joined forces with Armstrong to combat the formidable Krupp with Bethlehem Steel in tow. The British combination, battling those 'terrible odds', nevertheless carried this off. The indefatigable Frank Barker, born in Constantinople of a leading family of bankers, once more played the major role, although Zaharoff was credited by the opposition with this *Meisterstreich*. Barker earned a pat on the back from the master; he 'has certainly managed that business remarkably well', Zaharoff wrote to Albert Vickers, '... kindly congratulate him from me'.

The winning consortium undertook to renovate the arsenal at the Golden Horn and to construct a shipyard and floating docks with a monopoly of orders from the Turkish navy for thirty years, along with a promise of £10,000,000 worth of armament orders. The British companies each took a 20 per cent shareholding. There was a prudent long-stop: any deficits of revenue to cover the payment of interest and the amortization of the capital were to be covered by the revenues from taxation of the province of Sivas. The administration of the Ottoman Debt, over which Vincent Caillard had presided before his departure to Vickers, was entrusted with the collection of these taxes. A local lawyer, Count Léon Ostrorog, a polymath of Polish origin, was appointed legal adviser to the companies; his son was to become a member of Zaharoff's other family through his marriage with the Duchess of Marchena's second daughter Angèle. Ostrorog *père* went on to become Vickers' legal adviser for European affairs.

Contracts for the construction of one Dreadnought, two light cruisers, six destroyers and two submarines had already been signed and distributed before the world war broke out. (This, of course, triggered an alarmed reaction from the Greeks, who forthwith commissioned a battleship from France and torpedo boats from French and German yards.)

An interesting comparison lies between this straightforward commercial arrangement and the French system by which the government sought to obtain trading and political advantage in exchange for consent to touch the French peasant for his savings. In addition to the share capital put up by the British partners, provision was also made for the issue of just over £1,000,000 worth of bonds, of which half were already subscribed by the British public in July 1914. When the Turkish government confiscated the British holdings at the outset of war, the British companies, mindful that their good name was at stake, recognized their moral responsibility by making an offer to all subscribers to repurchase their rights to the bonds plus accrued interest. Small French investors had no such redress against their government; they simply lost their *chemises*.

This deal caused consternation in Berlin. The government-inspired *Kölnische Zeitung* warned:

This English concession is far more significant than the engaging of a German military mission. Not only do the English have de facto control of the Turkish fleet; they have now in their hands the entire output of Turkey's yards and arsenals. Thus they are in complete control of the Turkish navy. What in comparison with that is the fact that a German general is in command of a Turkish army corps?

Schneider picked up a not inconsiderable consolation prize: three-quarters of Turkish army contracts in the face of Krupp's 'embassy' and the German military mission. The burden of this programme would be met by yet another bond issue of 500,000,000 francs floated in Paris, with the usual consideration for the press. (Two-thirds of a 3,000,000 franc slush fund was distributed to French newspapers through Léon Rénier, a director of Havas, who retained 500,000 francs as commission; he was later rewarded with the Grand Cross of the Legion of Honour for his services to the Republic.)

The sequel was less friendly. A Turkish mission visited Schneider at Le Creusot and gave in its orders, but before they could be completed war intervened. The purchases were diverted to Krupp and Skoda – and paid for in francs.

10

Friendly Relations

Shortly after Zaharoff had established himself in Paris, he took the first serious step to provide himself with a background and to draw a line under his past. He acquired a birth certificate. This stated:

The undersigned, members of the old established community of Mouchliou [Mugla], bear witness on their oath as Christians that Zacharie Vasiliou Zaharoff, or Zaharoff Basile, was born in this town on 6 October 1849, the legitimate son of Vasiliou and Helene Zaharoff, and was on the 8th of that month baptized according to the rites of the Greek Orthodox Church by the priest Daniel, the pastor of the community, and at the ceremony his paternal grandmother was godmother. Mouchliou, 21 December 1892.

An Archimandrite Makharios bore witness only that the signatures to this document were genuine, and his Holiness the Oecumenical Patriarch Monsignor Neophytos bore witness to the genuineness of the signature of the Archimandrite. The identity of the 'under-signed' is not known, nor even whether they were witness to Zaharoff's baptism over forty years before. The church register itself is said to have been destroyed by fire some years before he obtained this certificate, a convenient coincidence for those who relish mystery. Zaharoff only produced this document for ratification before a French court in July 1908.

This move to secure a measure of respectability, or at least normality in law, is said to have excited the curiosity of Scotland Yard and the French Sûreté, possibly alerted by his enemies; if it could be proved he had falsified a document in support of his application for naturalization, he would have earned a stiff term of penal servitude. The British bulldogs – though why the case should have concerned them is not clear – were the first to turn up a trump. Their quest ended in Odessa; the archives of the Yard, it was claimed, held a photostat – a very early one – of a birth certificate for Zaharoff, in Yiddish and verified by the officiating rabbi, then aged ninety-one. Simultaneously the Secret Service, with small regard for expense, established that Zaharoff had been born in Constantinople of a Russian father and a Greek mother. The French, in an independent spirit, set their own hounds on the trail. This ended in Mughla. But nothing was as straightforward as it seemed. The French agent, one Nadel, who had regressed from pimp to police spy with a sinister appearance to suit – 'pock-marked and ugly' – only filed his own findings with his superiors after he had first cleared them with Zaharoff. This friendly gesture was occasioned by the fact that each shared a guilty secret. Nadel was an Odessa-born Jew who, eluding military service, had emigrated to France. He had also for some time past been on Zaharoff's payroll.

A variety of sources have credited Zaharoff with a Russian origin or parentage. He himself raised this spectre and his secretary, Archie de Bear, was 'sure' his father was Russian. Legend persists in this. One version painted him as an ardent revolutionary and deserter from the Tsar's forces. In 1924 the Soviet authorities in Odessa, unusually obliging, allegedly furnished the Turks with a dossier claiming he was the son of a Jew named Sahar from Odessa. Another tale, reputedly confirmed by a confidential bulletin of the Okhrana, the Tsar's secret police, identified Zaharoff as 'Basilius Zacharias, formerly of Odessa, Russian subject, born in Constantinople, wanted for desertion, theft and revolutionary activities'. (The police had long memories: Zaharoff was in his sixties at the time the Okhrana was formed to combat the terrorism unleashed by the Social Revolutionaries.)

He was fortunate that none of these rumours, later editions to the legend, were current in Russia before the Great War.

Then, just as this might be dismissed as a conspiracy to defame, a strange figure materialized from Lithuania by way of Leicester, demanding recognition.

The name of this intruder was Haim Manelovich Sahar, born on 15 April 1868 in Vilkomir, then a part of Russia, later to become, briefly, Lithuania before reverting. The family had emigrated from Kishinev in Bessarabia, not far from Odessa. Haim's father, Manel Sahar, had married Haia Elka Karolinski, a young Jewess of Odessa. Shortly before the birth of their only child, Manel was drafted into the army. The son saw little of his father, who finally abandoned his family when Haim was about six or seven, that is, in 1873–4. Another variant has it that Manel Sahar was sentenced to Siberia for theft in the army around 1872–3. Mother and son subsequently moved to London, where she remarried a Jewish cobbler. Haim himself took up the same trade and, marrying in Leicester in 1898, was blessed with five sons and four daughters.

Then suddenly, on 11 April 1911, Haim picked up the *Birmingham Daily Mail* and read about Basil Zaharoff. It occurred to him at once that he had found his errant father. So strong was his conviction that he changed his name to Hyam Barnett Zaharoff. Unfortunately, by this time his mother, Manel's old wife, had already died, so she was unable to be of much help with identification. However it was natural that he should have wished to contact his parent. He did not have a great deal of success. His card was returned. He took on lawyers, their letters went unanswered. Undismayed, he followed his 'father' to Paris, hanging around his house in the avenue Hoche until finally, bribing one of the servants for the telephone number in the family tradition, he managed to get through to his insensible parent in the presence of his lawyer. Zaharoff made an appointment in a neighbouring café; he did not keep it.

After the war Hyam took his troubles to Scotland Yard. Here he was informed that the British government and the police would back his claim, but not as long as Zaharoff was still alive. 'He is too important to be attacked now.' The reason adduced for this benevolent interest was that under French law 65 per cent of his French estate would descend to the deceased's blood relatives – and the British government was interested in collecting the death duties. Later, when Hyam moved to London, presumably to be within touching distance of his putative father, the two daughters of the Duchess of Marchena visited his shoe shop. Hyam's eldest daughter, Yvonne, and the elder Marchena girl were, so it was said, as like as two peas.

There are two curious coincidental features about these stories. There is firstly the constant recurrence of Odessa. It happened that the port was swarming with Lithuanians, driven south by famine and repression; and the physical characteristics of the race match Zaharoff's exactly. He did not pass on any of these to his 'son'. Anyway, in 1872 and 1873 Zaharoff was known to have been in London, occupying himself with his wife and his defence at the Old Bailey. Although there are unaccountable gaps in his life, he would have had to cover great distances at great speed in order to lead such a full double life. It happens also that there is no mention of Zaharoff in the *Birmingham Daily Mail* of 11 April 1911; more important, the earliest-known press photograph appeared in print only ten years later. If Hyam had indeed connected Zaharoff with his father Sahar through some casual newspaper reference, it would have been by name only, the similarity of which was slim enough ground on which to build a serious paternity case.

In the absence of any further evidence, it is simply not plausible.

It is a difficult task to uncover many of Zaharoff's ploys and plots in this pre-war period in any detail. There is little of any importance in the company minute books between October 1906 and March 1911. Later in life he claimed 'sincerely' that he had not tried to add to his possessions since 1900, the year of his own half-century. He did not have to try too hard; he was coasting on commission.

His secretary is again a fount of information for these years, much of which admirably fits the legend. But there was no rancour in these revelations. Archie de Bear found him 'a personality forbidding but lovable; approachable yet inaccessible'.

Nothing surprised de Bear more in his time than 'the fact that certain seemingly influential Englishmen journeyed to Paris with the object of soliciting Zaharoff's interest on their behalf – in England'. This is indeed surprising. The only obvious influence he exercised was within the boardroom of Vickers, a not inconsiderable source, but hardly unique or in any way special. True, he could hob with such nobs as the Rothschilds and Cassels, but so could many others nearer home. He had only a very small circle of friends, almost exclusively drawn from his business contacts, and no political influence at all. He was not yet even widely talked about. It is difficult not to believe that this power of the mythical *éminence grise* was largely presumed by his petitioners, their hopes built on the sands of the stories of his fabled wealth, greatly exaggerated by his eccentric ways and flamboyant style.

Even within Vickers his intervention was circumspect and oblique. A certain James Dunn, deadwood on the board, had resigned from the parent company in 1909 but had remained on the advisory board of the Spanish SECN – or, as it was known, La Naval. This was very much Zaharoff's sphere and the two men must have had a difference of opinion. In January 1911 Albert Vickers wrote to Zaharoff that 'your private letter to the directors ... is duly received, and I have at once written to Dunn to ask him, nicely, to resign ... and I have put your letter in the fire.' It may be noted that Zaharoff preferred to address himself to the directors collectively rather than to conspire privily with just those one or two with whom he was on the closest personal terms.

De Bear added that, to oblige his friends, Zaharoff acted as their broker in procuring honours, although he never benefited personally by one penny. This was hugely helpful of him, but unnecessary. True, the most notorious Patronage Secretary, the Master of Elibank – otherwise 'Oilybank' – was a friend, but the way to the Chief Whip's office was well enough known not to need pointing out.

The attentive secretary was also witness to 'huge sums' that were paid for 'immature' plans for shipbuilding and arms production and asserted that army and navy estimates, made available by highly placed officers of state disguised by code names, were known before they were even presented to their parliaments. In certain markets, particularly where the pay of civil servants and the armed forces was grossly inadequate to support a becoming station in life, such action was undoubtedly widespread. From a practical point of view it cannot have given the competing arms companies much of an edge; they all had access to the same information through similar channels; only failure to avail themselves of such opportunities would have been a positive disadvantage. Anyone with such scruples would have been politely invited to enrol in a missionary society and cede his place to another.

In France and Germany the system was more subtle. It was very much a family affair. The Wilhelmstrasse was stuffed with relatives of Baron Stumm, the principal shareholder of the Dillengen Hüttenwerke, an important producer of guns and ammunition, and owner also of the chauvinistic *Berliner Post*; Krupp, according to the peevish testimony of his rival Thyssen, had 'two brothers in the Ministry of War and the brother of the head of the German Naval Department'. In spite of this cosy arrangement, Krupp came a cropper and in 1913 was brought to trial for bribery of the civilian head of the War Ministry and other minor officers; the former got six months, the lesser fry getting away with a maximum of four months. In France, Schneider, whose function was, after all, the national defence, regarded the appointment of a member of the Chamber of Deputies' army commission as its perquisite.

These allegations of de Bear's aroused not a little interest in the House of Commons when they were published after the Great War (their author had by then taken to the music-hall boards). The Prime Minister was asked whether he would give time for the consideration of a motion for the appointment of a tribunal to enquire into the allegations that Basil Zaharoff had made corrupt payments to servants of the Crown. 'No, sir,' replied Stanley Baldwin. 'I have no intention whatever of taking any action on vague and irresponsible statements of the kind referred to in my hon. friend's motion.' This firmness was rewarded with a loyal 'hear, hear'. 'If, however, he is in a position to furnish me, on his own responsibility, with any information showing a prima facie case for enquiry, I shall, of course, be ready to consider it.' There was no such information forthcoming, there was no enquiry.

What about these sinister-sounding code names? Here history has been kinder. The text of just one telegram from Albert Vickers to Zaharoff, dated 28 November 1910, has survived:

JELLYFISH HAS YPOSKEPSE DIA AUTIN TIN EBDOMATHA 14 HILIADES
TONOUS THERAKOTA PIATA MISO DIA GLASGOW

This must satisfy any lover of mystery. A private cipher? A commercial code? Plain Greek. Even so the message is enigmatic: 'fourteen thousand tons of clay dishes, half for Glasgow'. Missiles for a Celtic–Rangers encounter? More likely a reference to plate of the armoured kind. The Krupp patent had run out that year and Vickers' own armour was adopted as standard by the Admiralty, as a result of which large orders came its way. The first such was placed in early November and half of it, 7,000 tons exactly, was destined for Beardmore of Glasgow. And 'Jellyfish'? Would it be too fanciful to put forward the name of 'Jackie' Fisher, the First Sea Lord? Albert Vickers had already discussed with Zaharoff the possibility of such an order in plain language. Why the Greek? Simple playfulness? Perhaps it was this cryptic communication which played on Archie de Bear's imagination.

About that same time, de Bear gave up his employment and joined Sir Wilfrid Laurier, the first French Canadian premier. He accompanied him to London for the first Imperial Conference of 1911. His former employer immediately materialized at the same hotel, the old Cecil, and suggested to his ex-secretary that 'if, without betraying in any way the obligations imposed upon me, I would keep him advised discreetly on the intentions of the Canadian government with regard to armament construction, it would be worth my while'. He reassured de Bear that he 'had no cause to doubt the normality of the procedure, or to regard it as a breach of confidence'. De Bear, less sure about this, turned the offer down. He noticed no perceptible change in Zaharoff's customary friendly attitude as a result.

It is a matter for regret that Zaharoff was not more pressing. If on the contrary he had been able to persuade the Canadian government

(and electorate) to pursue their shipbuilding programme more resolutely, he would have rendered the Allies a considerable service.

He had every reason to be anxious. In 1910 the Royal Canadian
Navy had been formally founded and two old cruisers, one Barrow-
built, procured as training ships. Vickers, at the request of the federal
government, engaged in the building of a drydock at Barrow and
yards in Montreal for a planned naval programme of cruisers and
destroyers. This led to a furore in fiercely isolationist Quebec which
contributed to Laurier's defeat in the election of 1911. His conservative successor visited Britain in 1912, where he was persuaded that,
in view of Germany's preparations, there was an emergency in naval
affairs. At the end of the year the new Prime Minister accordingly
submitted a proposal to build three warships at a cost not exceeding
£7,000,000; these were to be placed at the disposal of the empire;
thus the plan for a separate Canadian navy was shelved. This was
supported by the Commons but failed to pass the Liberal Senate,
so that when war broke out the only ship under construction was
an ice-breaker. Vickers' effort, however, was rewarded in the war
years in which the yards produced twenty-four submarines in record
time in collaboration with Zaharoff's friend, and former rival, Charles
Schwab of Bethlehem Steel.

A few years before this Zaharoff had even duped Vickers. The company had commissioned from Barrow as a speculation two special
cargo steamers but by the time they were launched there was little
demand for new bottoms. A picturesque old French sea captain, reek-
ing of garlic and with an extinct Gauloise stuck artistically to his
lip, appeared and agreed to recommend his company to acquire the
pair of them if they were first completely fitted out. He haggled in
the time-honoured manner, beating down the price until they were
sold at not much more than cost. Months later, Zaharoff's old friend,
Sir George Owens-Thurston, discovered that Zaharoff was the 'company', and had passed on the ships to the Grand Duke Michael as
Russian naval transports at twice the price he had paid for them.
It is not at all improbable that the wily Greek, enormously tickled
at the success of his ruse, actually confessed to this himself. Two
years later he retrieved his honour by helping Vickers with the
£100,000 loan at just 4 per cent.

His contribution to the company was not always so lighthearted.
He had his eye on the sky. He was about to assist another take-off
but before he launched himself, mindful no doubt of Hiram Maxim's
offhand attitude to control and stability in flight, he set about founding
his own chair of aviation. He chose his newly adopted country (his

French naturalization had come through in 1908). In March 1909 he confided his intentions to the Vice-Rector of the University of Paris through a third party and prayed to be received the same day. His wish was accorded.

'You know, Monsieur, what brings me here.'

'Yes, Monsieur.'

'How much would it cost a year, this creation?'

'21,000 francs all included . . .'

'21,000 francs. At 3 per cent that makes, in capital, 700,000 francs. I give them to you.'

As he left 'in the most courteous fashion', Zaharoff added: 'Neither you nor I have any time to lose.' The Vice-Rector later admitted that this expeditious way of doing business appealed to him. The chair was set up in November with effect from 1 January 1910. It is probable that Zaharoff's concern was prompted by his friend Louis Barthou, who as Minister of Public Works had set up a committee at the end of January 1909 to encourage research into aviation with a modest government vote of 100,000 francs; his brother Léon, another friend, was also a member of this committee.

Unfortunately the post-war paper franc, further depreciated by devaluations, devastated this donation; today the annual revenue of the Zaharoff foundation is just 211 new francs.

The same year provided a further example of Zaharoff's refreshingly incisive and confident approach to money matters. In June Saemy Japhet visited him in Paris to persuade him to help him over a hurdle. Counting on his past association with Zaharoff, the banker felt he could risk the question and launched himself into the deep end without preamble.

'I want you to grant us a loan for six, or better, twelve months. We have bought the holding of the Darmstädter Bank in our concern for the sum of £130,000, but cannot withdraw that amount of money from the business. I must be backed for that sum until I find new capital *en commandite*.'*

'Where will you find it?'

'At Sir Ernest Cassel's.'

'Have you any reason to believe he will give it?'

'I am relying on my efficiency to state the merits of my case.'

'Let me see: you want to repay a bank, which for ten years has made continuous and considerable profits out of your firm, but *I* am to refund their claim and take the risk? How much do you want?'

* Capital invested by a sleeping partner.

'£100,000.'

'On what security?'

'On none whatsoever.'

'Japhet my friend, can I do that?'

'Yes, quite safely.'

'Well,' replied Zaharoff after a moment's reflection, 'it's done.'

This exchange lasted no more than three minutes and by four o'clock the funds were placed at the disposal of Japhet. His confidence was justified: Cassel agreed to come in.

Vickers at this time was experimenting in a new, delicate and initially disastrous element under an Admiralty commission: airship design and construction. The No. 1 Rigid Naval Airship, ill-advisedly christened after that ephemeral insect, the *Mayfly*, broke her back in a crosswind before leaving her mooring mast. Zaharoff had a better idea. This, with Vickers in agreement, was to acquire an existing pattern of plane for manufacture under licence on the lines of the company's successful venture with submarines. France at that time was the leading pioneer in aviation design and the two most promising prototypes, or *oiseaux artificiels* as they were still called, were the Sommer biplane and a monoplane – a 'very elegant little aircraft' – designed by the celebrated pilot Robert Esnault-Pelterie, with whom Zaharoff, with that prescience that served him so well, seems already to have been on friendly terms. In November 1910 he reported to Barker that Esnault-Pelterie was 'very desirous of arranging for his English business with us', whereas 'Mr Sommer seems to make light of the very important position of the Vickers firm'. That, clearly, damned him.

Zaharoff's delicacy of feeling was at once exposed. 'I am always a fool,' he wrote disarmingly to Frank Barker, 'especially in this instance, as I have agreed to his suggestion that I should indicate the terms, and I regret it, because it is a question between my own firm, and my friend.' Pointing out the certain expense and doubtful result of undertaking their own experiments, he suggested that 'as he asks for cash down, it would not be excessive if we gave him £2,500 on signing the contract' with royalties to be paid once Vickers had successfully produced the first machine. In view of Zaharoff's conflict of interest, Esnault-Pelterie took up the running himself in London.

Vickers did not allow its enthusiasm for powered flight to run away with it. Barker informed Zaharoff that it might consider buying one monoplane outright for 29,000 francs, with probably another £1,000 for the rights of the plane and engine but, although 'I want to treat [him] well because I think he is a very able man, and can be useful ... to pay him £2,000 in cash, and to buy a monoplane, would be too much'. In December, Barker was able to tell Zaharoff that an arrangement had been concluded: 'we avoided handling him in too niggardly a fashion'.

As with other innovations, the main difficulty was selling a novelty to the services. Early in the new year, the machine walked away with all the records. The two-seater prototype, with 68 horses behind it, clipped a full fifteen minutes off the 80 kilometre record, covering the distance in just ninety seconds over the hour; it also flew, Zaharoff reported with wonder, 535 kilometres without a stop, 'which makes his machines absolutely the first in the market'. Vickers proudly re-offered its product, steel-framed and even capable of 'ascending from any of HM ships'. The Admiralty loftily replied that 'it was not proposed to acquire any Aeroplanes for the Naval Service at present'.

In spite of this official rebuff, Vickers persevered. Its first plane based on the R.E.P. design was produced at the old Erith works in the summer of 1911. It was purchased for Sir Douglas Mawson's Antarctic Expedition, but lost its wings during a demonstration in Adelaide due to gross pilot error and ended its days ignominiously as a tractor for the expedition's dog-sledges, 'appreciated mainly by the huskies'.

Vickers progressively refined its design until within two years it had produced the first model of the FB – Fighting Biplane – with a nose-mounted Maxim, which was the forerunner of the Royal Flying Corps' 'Gun-bus' of the war years, although by August 1914 it held orders for just half a dozen aircraft. In 1915 it was able to return the compliment to France by assigning to the Darracq company the rights to manufacture Vickers planes.

It has been said that there are two ineluctable fates – death and the Legion of Honour. In 1908, the ink barely dry on his naturalization papers, Zaharoff was initiated into the order as Chevalier under the aegis of the Ministry of Marine, rising to Officer in 1913 at the instigation of the Ministry of Public Instruction, and Commander in 1914 for services to the Ministry of Foreign Affairs. He had two further promotions to look forward to.

A less edifying role has often been ascribed to him, and not one that would on its own earn automatic public recognition: that of French brothel-keeper. His raison d'être in this field was not profit but pillow-talk to fuel his intelligence service. The motive is not probable. It would have been a messy hit-or-miss affair on the principle of the scatter-gun; it would have been far more effective to have cultivated selectively, as the Germans did during the war, the company

106

of those complaisant ladies close to men in a position of power. This was Zaharoff's own avowed recipe.

Zaharoff was also related to other Vickers' enterprises which figured in the balance sheet as 'Interests in Subsidiary and Connected Companies', worth over £4,000,000 by 1913. Colonel Tom Vickers, not a conspicuously communicative chairman in his day, used to brush aside shareholders in search of information with a brusquely dismissive, 'I do not think it is worth while giving a list.' But then he took annual general meetings at a gallop with one eye on his watch; his personal best was twelve minutes.

One of the major acquisitions was the Whitehead Torpedo Company. Robert Whitehead, an emigrant engineer whose name had become eponymous with his self-propelled weapon, had first opened a works at Fiume in Austria, but the Admiralty had insisted in 1891 that he must build a source of supply at home if he wanted further official orders; this he established at Weymouth. Then in 1906 Trevor Dawson was called to the Admiralty and informed that the business was for sale – in a run of bad luck many of the members of the family and senior management had died off in quick succession – and their Lordships were not desirous that it should fall into foreign hands. As a result of this appeal Vickers joined with Armstrong to purchase the controlling interest for £400,000, the minority holding remaining in the hands of the family. Zaharoff set up a French associate company at St Tropez in 1913 to handle the important orders from the French government.

A later rival to the Whitehead weapon was the German Schwartzkopf torpedo which had been prescribed for the Spanish navy. Zaharoff set out to break its hold. This, he foresaw, would 'need much diplomatic handling' – and supplementary commissions. In 1909, he wrote that 'we all know how difficult it is to persuade a government to change its armament, and ... although the prospects are not bad, the question is a very difficult one because all the officers, non-commissioned officers and sailors are accustomed to the [German] equipment, and are already in arms against another one being introduced'. Nevertheless, he seems to have succeeded in the face of this professional resistance; friends of La Naval who lent their support to the conversion split a finely tuned commission of $6\frac{1}{8}$ per cent.

There was one vital raw material offering toughness and corrosion-resistance for armour plate and guns in which France, until overtaken by Canada, held a virtual monopoly: nickel from New Caledonia. Rothschild had first set out to control this supply and in 1901 formed a syndicate with the French producer Le Nickel through which all the European arms companies would draw their material. Loewe joined the board and on his death was replaced by Albert Vickers. In April 1913, Zaharoff took Vickers' place as his 'great experience' would prove 'a most valuable acquisition'.

Within two months of the outbreak of war, a mysterious incident arose which gave rise to accusations of trading with the enemy. There is certainly a *prima facie* case for this charge. The matter was first raised in the French Senate in January 1917 by Senator Gaudin de Villaine, who alleged that on 1 October 1914, a:

Norse three-master loaded 2,500 tons of nickel in ... New Caledonia, consigned to Hamburg and intended for the Krupp works. Krupps had paid half the money in advance. The ship was stopped by the *Dupetit-Thouars* and taken to Brest, where it was declared a prize by the courts. Then the order came from Paris to release the ship. The local authorities refused. On that there came from the Minister fresh instructions confirming the order. On 10 October the ship resumed its voyage.

The Senator further charged that in 1915 4,606,834 kilos of raw nickel ore had been despatched from Noumea 'without that most important condition being laid down, a condition made obligatory in Canada, that the nickel should be consigned only for the use of the Allies'; and that 2,599,427 kilos had gone to the United States which for years had not bought from New Caledonia.

This set tongues wagging, and brought a sharp reaction from the Hauts Forneaux de Noumea, the only producers completely independent of the international trust. The company wrote to *Liberté* to protest that 'we have the honour to state that not a single kilogram of nickel from our Caledonian field has gone to America except with the provision that it is destined for France or one of her allies. ... It was not our company which had an agreement with Krupp as a result of which even after the outbreak of war certain consignments were sent to Norway.'

What prompted the Minister to release the ship? It was Zaharoff, it was later reported, who had run down to Brest to inspect the cargo and then influenced the Minister to intervene. He had been since the previous year a director of Le Nickel, if not also his company's representative on the users' association which regulated supplies and prices. He might have let the seizure proceed, pleading *force majeure* for non-delivery, and reclaimed the nickel in the name of the French company. It is more likely that he took the long-term view of the inviolability of established commercial practices over temporary expediency. Vickers was itself nominally paying royalties to Krupp on each time and percussion fuse manufactured; Deutsche Waffen was doing the same on Maxims, for which settlement would be required when the shooting ended.

There is a more intriguing possibility. In order to demonstrate that this was not a one-way trade, Zaharoff is said to have 'mysteriously' produced a letter from Senator Possehl of the German steel makers of the same name in Lübeck. It was dated a few days before the outbreak of hostilities and addressed to their agents, Bosshardt Bros of St Petersburg. 'The question of deliveries of steel', the letter warned, 'has now become very dubious since war on the Continent may break out any day.' It promised that 'in any case our Swedish works will do their utmost to speed up delivery, which at the present time we think will be very convenient for Messrs....' The letter urged Bosshardt 'to speak on this very confidentially with Messrs ... and you can be assured that nothing will be revealed by us. On that point you need have no fears.' The letter ended with the advice that 'we shall have to raise the price of nickel [ingots] very considerably. But there is no one who can supply these more cheaply.'

If Zaharoff produced anything, he owed his information to the German courts. L. Possehl & Co. were prosecuted at Leipzig. It transpired during the trial that the name left blank in the letter was Putiloff, in which Krupp and Schneider were partners. It is not inconceivable that the nickel impounded in Brest was destined for Russia.

Herr Possehl spun an ingenious defence which convinced the court. He was, he pleaded, faced with the problem of keeping his factories in Russia turning over as well as could be done by holding them at a not unreasonable level of production to avoid probable confiscation, or closing them down with certain confiscation. In the former case, he realized that an amount of steel would inevitably find its way into providing munitions for Russia; still, this was preferable to outright closure which would allow Russia to take over the works and devote them entirely to her military needs. He was held not to have aided 'of his own will' a foreign power at war with Germany. The Kaiser congratulated him on his patriotism.

Vickers indeed had reason to believe that in some of the years before the war Krupp had been surreptitiously increasing its purchases of nickel by obtaining supplies from outside the syndicate. The conclusion was inescapable; arms and armaments accounted for over 70 per cent of the world consumption of nickel. The company very properly passed this suspicion on to the government, as Admiral Sir Reginald Bacon, Director of Naval Ordnance at the time, later testified before a Royal Commission.

War was now around the corner. Zaharoff, over-confident or care-less, remained in residence at the Château de l'Échelle through August 1914. As the German cavalry surged in through the front gates, the owner, as he liked to relate, scampered off through the back with a manservant clutching a few belongings. He did not, fortunately, have quite such a narrow escape from the Uhlans. Roye lay immedi-ately behind the vital point in the Somme valley where the Allied lines turned northwards into Belgium, and the château was therefore regarded by the opposing commanders as a very desirable residence. Foch first made his headquarters there, and was soon dispossessed by Kluck, the commander of the German First Army. The French, however, returned once more into the breach, whereupon the Germans spitefully retaliated by shelling the château and village into rubble.

11

Private Lives

When the fateful year of 1914 opened, Vickers was a veritable giant among the arms companies. In enterprise and innovation it had overtaken Armstrong Whitworth to become the largest armourer in the British Empire; capitalized at some £7,000,000 it surpassed Schneider Le Creusot in range and size, and equalled, where it did not excel, even Krupp.

Like the country, the company survived and prospered on overseas markets, but there was a serious imbalance nationally which in the short term was to lead to delays and shortages of war material. 'The outbreak of war', Lloyd George later wrote in his *War Memoirs* with the advantage of hindsight, 'found this country totally unprepared for land hostilities on a Continental scale.' The reason was rather that very few prophets foresaw that a long struggle would ensue, still fewer that it was even possible to sustain. The war, the French and German generals promised, had to be over by Christmas. Lloyd George himself thought it might drag on for as much as nine months; only Kitchener considered that it could last three years. Zaharoff concurred. He is alleged to have told the Russian Minister Sazonov that 'these fool politicians think that when war comes, it will be short and sharp. How wrong they are and how little they understand the situation. It will be a long and hard war and only because of this will the central powers be defeated. They cannot hope to last in a long war, so logic decrees that a long war it must be.'

The General Staff's planning for a Continental war had envisaged an expeditionary force of six (in the event reduced to four) divisions,

111

or some 150,000 men; within just two weeks, and before even the Marne, this was scrapped. Kitchener announced that the aim was to put thirty divisions in the field. 'Our chief problem', he recognized at the same time, 'is one of *matériel* rather than personnel.'

Where was all this armament to come from?

Three-quarters of the War Office's supplies came from the Royal Ordnance factories; in the last ten years before the war, Vickers had supplied only eleven machine-guns a year to the army. (Even Portugal had done better for herself; in 1905 she had placed a second order for 72 Maxims and 100,000 rifles even though the final instalment of over £100,000 had not been paid, which Zaharoff optimistically attributed to a change of minister.) The only machine-guns available in 1914 were the Vickers and the now obsolescent Maxim; the lighter Lewis gun had actually been rejected for army use in 1912. (One of the advantages of the Vickers was that every part was interchangeable, a condition imposed on Zaharoff by the Russians for a large order.) Within two months of the outbreak of war, 1,792 were ordered. The very rate indicates 'a wild uncertainty': on 11 August, 192 guns were ordered; on 10 September a further 100; less than three weeks later another 1,000, and just a week after that 500 were added. In October an order for the French for fifty guns a week was allowed on the understanding that this would not interfere with the production for the War Office. (By the end of the war the output of machine-guns, heavy and light, had risen to just under 250,000. The generals by then had come to accept them.)

The companies' difficulties were further compounded by problems outside their control. First there was the shortage of skilled labour, aggravated by the fact that 'a thousand young men threw up their work for the trenches' at the Vickers' Sheffield works alone. Sir Trevor Dawson made an effort to retrieve this, with no official recognition, let alone encouragement, by importing Belgian labour and training women for the work. This in turn upset the trade unions. And, just as seriously, the steep rise in purchasing power resulting from the heavy overtime led to what Lloyd George in 1915 mildly lamented as 'the lure of drink'.

Within a year these teething problems had been overcome. But it is ironic that this unpreparedness of the munitions makers was so fiercely criticized by the same people who were later to castigate them for war-mongering. At the time, the companies' contribution was recognized, not least by the foe. 'Machinery was winning against man,' wrote one of the latter. 'In the cold and pitiless battle of the industries of blood and steel, the German industry was being defeated.'

One less appreciative source was the man who had provided the means of execution, the first Minister of Munitions. 'It is a lamentable story of failure,' Lloyd George, embittered by fifteen years in the wilderness, told the Royal Commission into the private manufacture of arms.

There are grounds to believe that Basil Zaharoff had made contact with Lloyd George, then Chancellor of the Exchequer, in 1909. This was the time of the Mulliner 'incident'.

Between 1906 and 1908, at a time of actual reduction in naval expenditure in Britain, H.H.Mulliner, managing director of the Coventry Ordnance Works, had passed to the Admiralty information which indicated that Krupp was taking measures to accelerate its rate of production of large naval guns and gun mountings, the most precise, intricate and delicate feature of naval shipbuilding. (It took eighteen months to complete a set of turret mountings as against twelve for the shell of the warship.) This information was very largely confirmed by the British Naval Attaché in Berlin. The resulting pressure for rearmament aroused a fierce debate in Parliament and the press – 'We want eight and we won't wait' become the popular cry – which persuaded a reluctant government to lay down first four, and then a further four Dreadnoughts. Disagreement then arose between Mulliner and the Admiralty and, disgruntled that the additional orders he had hoped for had not come his way, he spilt the beans in *The Times* after he had been forced into retirement.

Zaharoff is supposed to have impressed on Lloyd George the need to:

convince McKenna [First Lord of the Admiralty, 1908–11] that he is not helping our cause by giving way to the pressure from the men of Coventry. When the facts are shown to be other than Mulliner has stated, no one is going to believe any experts any more and when we really need extra ships and guns there is going to be greater difficulty in persuading any government to supply the money. They won't forget Mulliner's blunders in a hurry. If war came now through a silly scare, nobody would be ready for it. ... If war is to come, Britain must have a long time in which to prepare for it and to win other allies. But there is every reason for believing that, given time, the massive armaments potential of the Entente will, if it does not deter Germany from adventures, ensure her ultimate defeat.

Unimpeachable sentiments, and sound common sense, except that Mulliner was more nearly correct in his assessment than Zaharoff: the margin of superiority considered necessary to maintain British naval supremacy at the outbreak of war was 'little, if at all, above' that traditionally accepted.

This conversation is said to have been reported by T.P.O'Connor, Irish Nationalist MP and indefatigable journalist, in an unpublished letter in November 1909. If so, the sense was conveyed to him by Lloyd George himself; O'Connor did not meet Zaharoff until 1913. Legend has presumed much about the relationship of Zaharoff with Lloyd George. The evidence is tenuous. There is no indication even – rather the reverse – that Zaharoff ever had direct access to him; he seems to have managed any personal contact he wished to arrange through Vincent Caillard of Vickers or Lord Murray of Elibank, the former Liberal Chief Whip; and even after the war an appeal to the Prime Minister straight from Zaharoff's heart 'to do something for the Greeks' was passed on in a letter from O'Connor. The only sources detailing personal confrontations between the two men are Zaharoff himself, in his rare expansive moments, and the dubious authority of (missing) French documents.

It has been seriously suggested that Zaharoff had a hold over Lloyd George in the shape of knowledge that he had previously, if only briefly, had an affair with Emily Ann Burrows, Zaharoff's former wife. Lloyd George had an unusually lax moral code – and was something of a humbug to boot. The thought that the man who could attempt to foist his mistress on to a retired station master in marriage for the sake of the appearance of respectability could have been in the least abashed by such a revelation is comic; neither could Zaharoff have given a very convincing picture of the wronged party when he had abandoned his wife twenty-five years before. If anything it is Zaharoff who would have been the more diffident of the two even to admit to a relationship which he never acknowledged.

This, with other information of a scandalous and compromising nature, is said to have come to Zaharoff from one of his tools, a colourful scoundrel know as Ignatius Timothy Trebitsch-Lincoln. Born a Hungarian Jew, he became in bewildering succession a Presbyterian missionary, an Anglican curate, social researcher for Seebohm Rowntree, Liberal MP, wildcat oil prospector, bankrupt and forger, a wildly unsuccessful self-proclaimed spy, an adviser to warring warlords in China and finally founder of a Buddhist sect, the League of Truth. If he had ever enjoyed any association, however dishonourable, with Zaharoff, this irrepressibly indiscreet egocentric adventurer would have hastened to boast of it in his two autobiographies, the last written when Zaharoff's notoriety was at its zenith, and in which he delighted in portraying himself in the least flattering light.

The one undisputed link between Zaharoff and the seats of power was provided by T.P.O'Connor. Widely respected by even his political opponents, he managed to remain on varying terms of intimacy with the Greek, his contemporary, and with Lloyd George and Clemenceau, who esteemed each other's abilities as much as they distrusted each other's ambitions.

'T.P.' considerately left a record of his encounter with Zaharoff. He had expected to see 'an old, stooped, shy man, bent with years and work, and with all the aloofness of the voluntary recluse. Instead there entered with brisk step a very tall thin man with the air of a great fencer, with a long thin face, a slight grey moustache, and eyes of blue grey, steely almost in their strength, their penetration, and their courage.' The Irishman noted that he was 'English in his taste and tendencies, with all an Englishman's directness, frankness, and good humour'.

Zaharoff's relations with Georges Clemenceau, but especially with his brother Paul, were undoubtedly closer than those with Lloyd George, but again there is no documentary evidence; both men perversely burned their private papers. Clemenceau, unusually for a politician of the Third Republic, had a clear and consistent principle which he pursued with single-minded determination, but in spite of his formidable reputation as a fighter he had a generous and attractive personality. He 'thought coldly and believed hotly'. Zaharoff respected the old warrior. The pair most probably first met around the time of Clemenceau's 1910 lecture tour of South America. Zaharoff employed his scapegrace son, Michel, who specialized in cultivating the company's South American contacts, in the post-war Vickers Paris office; a later associate of Zaharoff, Nicholas Piétri, a self-made entrepreneur from Corsica, was an intimate of Clemenceau during his wartime premiership.

It was customary to reproach Clemenceau for his acquaintance with the Greek. Their relations were 'the subject of considerable speculation'; it was seen as 'sometimes sinister that he should have been on good terms with a "merchant of death"'. Zaharoff was not above letting it be understood that these relations were rather more intimate, that the two would break a *baguette* while running the war in harness. Clemenceau's last *chef du cabinet*, Georges Wormser, however, denied that his chief ever lunched with Zaharoff during his term of office.

The two main planks of Clemenceau's credo, in office and out, were to strengthen the Anglo-French entente, not from any feelings of tenderness towards the country but because he believed that France could afford no other policy; and to persuade the British to build a large enough army to intervene on the Continent in the event of the catastrophe that he foresaw as inevitable. It is said that, wary of

Lloyd George, he requested Zaharoff to furnish him with a dossier on the Welshman. Zaharoff reported that he:

could be a most formidable enemy. As long as he is tied to the forces of the Liberal pacifists, so he will remain. But his real ambition – and this over-rides all else, his beliefs, his morals and his principles – is to become Prime Minister. He will turn his policies to fit him for such a course. He would even ally himself with the Conservatives if the Premiership lay through their help.

He revealed another side of Lloyd George to O'Connor. He was, he considered, 'a far greater asset than Kitchener', who was 'so rooted in prejudices and military mish-mash that he could lose the war between sunset and sunrise, whereas Lloyd George could win it merely by his facility for changing his mind or trying something new. One can sell new ideas to Lloyd George. He ought to be in charge of munitions production, for he has a business mind.'

Zaharoff may well have held such views but the sources are only attributed at second hand.

In the spring of 1913, Clemenceau, who had already had experience as press proprietor and indomitable purveyor of polemics, produced the first number of his new paper, *L'Homme Libre*, with vehement and sometimes vitriolic attacks on the government of the day. (When he fell foul of the censor in the early stages of the war, he changed the title to *L'Homme Enchaîné*.) It was never easy for a politician out of power to find the capital to finance such a venture. Reports in the Paris police files referred to the possibility of an English group backing him for the *L'Homme Libre*. There can have been few English groups ready to volunteer for such a philanthropic gesture and, continuing with surmise, it is possible that Zaharoff had at least been sounded out. His answer, as T.P.O'Connor discovered, would have been a polite but firm thumbs down.

Just three years after the war, Père-la-Victoire, as he had become, founded another paper, *L'Echo National*, for his faithful protégé (and later premier), André Tardieu. It was at once rumoured, and subsequently repeated, that Basil Zaharoff had supplied the finance in order to influence French policy in favour of his Middle East intrigues. His interest was, indeed, remarked by the Foreign Office. Georges Wormser, who was entrusted with the arrangements for the funding, categorically denied this; the founding fathers were determined that the paper should not be linked with big business.

O'Connor also went fund-raising for a war weekly, *T.P.'s Journal*, he had started in 1915, and which within a year had lost £7,500.

'My associates', O'Connor wrote to Basil Zaharoff, 'do not desire to go further. I have put my last shilling into it and I have to keep it going, if possible, until the end of the war.' He was hopefully seeking a further £5,000, but added with fatalistic honesty, 'I frankly confess that this is, on business lines, a proposition of a speculative character.' Zaharoff declined, as he also did with another appeal for Irish political funds the following year. O'Connor took this rebuff philosophically, even generously. 'It was not that he baulked at the money ... but it is apparently an inflexible principle of his not to touch anything of a political character. He begged me not to press him and I could not go any further.'

After the war Clemenceau inherited Zaharoff's former chauffeur, Albert, as his valet. He set this transition down to Albert's love of contrast: 'For years he valeted for the richest man in the world and now he valets me, the poorest,' he confided to Stephen Bonsal, President Wilson's interpreter at the Peace Conference, 'and yet he is always smiling.' When Albert brought Clemenceau his customary soup at midnight, the politician tried to worm out of him how Zaharoff had coined his millions, but he would only tell him how he spent them, and 'in the spending line', Clemenceau ruefully admitted, 'I am not in need of instruction.' Albert informed him that throughout the war, day and night, Zaharoff's agents were on guard at the Paris stations waiting for the leave trains with no more sinister purpose than to hand out forty francs to each of the soldiers on leave.

And why? asked Clemenceau. Because Zaharoff:

could not sleep at the thought that our *poilus* on short leave in Paris would have to go without their beloved *pinard*. What a strange animal he must have been. He could not sleep at the thought that some of our *braves enfants* went thirsty, and yet the thought that hundreds of thousands of men are blown to bits by the bombs he manufactures never worried him in the least! A strange animal, indeed one of the strangest that the war has brought out of their caves.

Later, however, having reproached Zaharoff for not countering the calumnies concerning him, he remarked to another witness: 'But what has he so terrible to defend, after all? ... I do not blame him. I understand. Besides he was of great service to the Allies.'

Resigned to the irremediable loss of the Château de l'Échelle, the Zaharoff entourage set about providing themselves with another secure summer retreat out of reach of marauding German cavalry.

They found it near Pontoise, the Château de Balincourt at Arronville, a short drive from the capital.

Family connections had probably pointed the way. The château belonged to the mistress and later morganatic wife of King Leopold of the Belgians. In 1911 the elder daughter of the Duchess of Marchena, Cristina, had married Leopold Walford of the shipping family, whose father, George Paget Walford, had been closely associated with King Leopold in his lucrative exploitation of the Congo, and after whom he had named his son.

As the war opened, Basil Zaharoff made one final act of supreme self-sacrifice. He sent off his gold dinner service, which Sir Robert Bruce Lockhart considered 'probably the finest in the world', to the Bank of France to be melted down as his contribution to the war effort; it was, he used to explain, everyone's duty to make sacrifices up to his limit. Still, it must have been a wrench – and a weight: the centrepiece, the feet encrusted with lapis lazuli, was said to be so heavy that it required four men to lift it. Zaharoff related himself how he had found one perfect plate in a Paris auction; the design – or arms? – had so enchanted him that he had bought it and had it copied as a complete service for thirty-six persons by the famous Paris goldsmiths Boucheron. Unkind and idle tongues suggested that he consigned the service to the Bank of France for safe keeping after the panic flight of the government to Bordeaux in the early weeks of the war; if this had been his motive, it would have been safer still with the Bank of England.

However, patriotism rather than pessimism was most likely to have had the upper hand. In an extraordinary display of confidence in the long term, just eight months after the opening of hostilities, Zaharoff was planning for the future in the post-war world. His idea was to 'put a strong spoke in the German wheel in Spain' by forming an organization to oppose the AEG–Siemens monopoly of hydro-electric plant in that country. He planned to go to Madrid in the spring of 1915 to prepare all the elements so that 'the moment peace is signed we can form the Spanish company and begin working'.

But this was all further in the future than perhaps even Basil Zaharoff yet realized.

12

War Service

The most prejudicial wartime intercession attributed to Zaharoff concerned the Briey iron ore basin in Lorraine, which was vital to the French war effort and yet, once lost to the Germans, was never regained and which was, moreover, mysteriously spared from damage. It was a matter, understandably, which later aroused much emotion, was the subject of persistent parliamentary enquiry, and was never satisfactorily resolved.

The ore in the Longwy–Briey region, bordering the German industrial centre of Thionville, was worked by the Comité des Forges, the most powerful syndicate in France. Pre-eminent among the iron-masters was one of those rare great French entrepreneurs, François de Wendel, whose firms produced as much as 10 per cent of the total iron and steel output of the Hexagon. This, together with the secrecy with which the Comité conducted its affairs, gave rise to suspicions that a deal had been agreed for its blast furnaces in the German-occupied territories to be spared a rival blasting.

The architect of this immunity was supposed to have been Basil Zaharoff, who proudly bore the honorary title *maître de forges*.

The Germans had long settled on the Briey basin as a primary war aim and in the opening stages of the fighting surprised and routed two French armies, which retreated westwards to dig in around Sedan and Verdun. Thereafter the basin remained in German hands for four years and served to forge munitions without which Germany could not have fought for six months. (She imported roughly half of her needs in iron ore whereas France exported one-third of her output.)

119

There remains the very pertinent question of exactly why the blast furnaces were never subjected to artillery or aerial bombardment. There is ample testimony that the will existed at the highest level, and the occasional freelance effort was even made by the odd errant pilot who earned a reprimand rather than a ribbon.

A general idea of the muddled and ineffective system of command was revealed to a post-war parliamentary commission of enquiry by the Socialist, Albert Thomas:

At the end of 1916 ... when General Lyautey was Minister of War, I repeatedly intervened [as Minister of Munitions] to demand the bombardment of Briey, and the Council of Ministers was angered by the inaction of the aircraft. The Minister of War repeatedly declared that he had given orders for the bombardment ... but that these orders had not in fact been carried out.

This must rank as one of the most extraordinary admissions from a minister in time of grave national emergency. And Thomas was the man whom Lloyd George would have had Painlevé appoint Minister of War in his short-lived Cabinet in 1917. It was this attitude of weary fatalism, verging on defeatism, that Clemenceau dispersed with his thundering 'Je fais la guerre.'

Then, it may well be asked, did Clemenceau, his own Minister of War, fare any better in imposing himself on the General Staff? When he came to office in November 1917, the situation had changed. Russia had dropped out of the war and by the treaty of Brest-Litovsk in March 1918 Germany acquired at a stroke the major part of Russia's iron and coal.

What was Zaharoff's role in frustrating the entire French War Cabinet?

He was, it was claimed, a close associate of Robert Pinot, secretary-general of the Comité des Forges, who had been 'extremely agitated' by conversations he had had with General Malleterre, who wanted to bomb Briey. At Pinot's request, Zaharoff took informal soundings from German industrialists in Thionville, while at the same time putting up an alternative blockade plan to French headquarters: this was that the installations at Briey should be left intact, but that attacks should be launched instead on the railways. General Malleterre 'immediately and violently contested' this option.

This preference may have reflected the special interests of the Comité. The ultimate decision, however, lay with the ministers individually and the Cabinet collectively after taking into consideration the advice of their military advisers and the service chiefs. They neither pressed it, nor resigned in disagreement.

The same French source put another gloss on this affair. Towards the end of 1916 Lloyd George sought Zaharoff's advice on the chance of securing a token withdrawal of troops on both sides of the front on New Year's Day, an appeal which Zaharoff, with his customary agility, distorted into a mutual agreement between the Allies and the Central Powers to respect each other's arms factories.

Lloyd George, according to this version, 'finally concurred with Zaharoff's viewpoint and agreed it would be senseless to destroy industrial plant and to end the war with derelict factories and mass unemployment. Lloyd George was in favour of anything that would slow down the tempo of war on the Western Front, and it was better to have the means of supplying arms to the theatre of war which really mattered to him – vital salients of the Moyen Orient.'

Thus, instead of a mutual truce, there came to be a tacit agreement for a 'no bombardment' policy in the Briey basin. This still does not explain the French inaction. If they had disagreed with this policy, they could have been expected to represent their dissent in a matter of supreme national interest in a forthright manner.

There is possibly another reason to explain this immunity. In 1914 the French government had delegated the Comité as its official agent for the purchase of iron and steel abroad. There existed in parallel a curious surreptitious trade in essential supplies. During the first eight months of 1916 alone, some 150,000 tons of iron and steel were exported from Germany through neutral countries. A token fine of five marks a ton was imposed at the frontier but the high prices the French and Italian manufacturers were prepared to pay took much of the pain out of this. Switzerland was the centre of this trade*; a flourishing chalet industry developed for the removal of the stamps of origin from the metal. It was claimed that in exchange for this leakage, the Germans received much needed nickel, copper and rubber. It might well have been considered the wiser course to connive at this black market than to destroy or damage its source.

Basil Zaharoff's influence, malign or even benign, during the

---

* The barbed wire protecting the approaches to Verdun had been provided by the Magdeburger Draht-und-Kabelwerke through Switzerland just two months before the great battle for the fortress.

war years has been much exaggerated, and he himself did little to reduce the impression. 'I had always known my value,' he boasted. 'Now I became of inestimable value in the Councils of the Allies. Arms, arms, and still more arms they demanded – and I could supply them.' Everyone did indeed need arms, and still more arms. Vickers, with all the other arsenals and armaments manufacturers of the Allies (and America) was doing its best to meet the demand. The problem was one of production capacity and priorities in which Zaharoff had no hand; it was the day of the engineer and the manager, the planning specialist and the committee man – an alien animal to the individualistic Greek. Of course, in Europe, where he was regarded as *le principal actionnaire* of Vickers, he would inevitably have been courted at this time of material shortage, although he was in no position to furnish all the armament through simple goodwill.

After the demands of the War Office and Admiralty had been met, Zaharoff would have been able to cut corners in providing for his other friends, France and Russia. This alone would have been sufficient reason for cultivating his company. It was perhaps Zaharoff who had arranged for the order for fifty Vickers machine-guns a week for the French as their Minister of Munitions clearly did not know an arm from his elbow.

He certainly had a hand in diverting a substantial flow of arms to Russia. In 1915 the British government had placed an order through Vickers for 6,000 machine-guns which were to be manufactured under licence by the Colt Patent Firearms Company. The next year this order was taken over by the Russian government for delivery in March 1917. Before this the Russians had placed a first order for 10,000 guns through the same channel. Together these were worth over $27,000,000 of which $7,000,000 was paid in cash in advance, but the American company was only ever able to deliver 3,000 guns. This resulted in a squabble over commission with the suppliers after the war, Vickers acting for Zaharoff in pressing his claim for payment of the agreed $2\frac{1}{2}$ per cent commission – over $650,000 – on the whole order. It was contended that Zaharoff had been able to keep the client happy until the Americans were able to establish the plant but that, owing to the growing delays in the States, they had been obliged through no fault of his to accept cancellation of the order and return $2,700,000 of the advance. It appears that Zaharoff finally accepted a mere $95,000 in settlement which Vickers sternly intimated to the Americans was a 'very satisfactory adjustment' from their point of view 'considering

122

Basil Zaharoff's high position and the exceptional services he had rendered'.

During the Great War, another well-meaning admirer recorded, Zaharoff was actually the Minister of munitions for the Allies; his power and his influence were so great that the Allied leaders were compelled to ask his opinion before any great attack was undertaken; his change of residence was kept secret and he went from port to port in a British torpedo boat which had been placed specially at his disposal.

This is the quintessence of the legend of the *éminence grise*. An interesting illustration of how a dog acquires a bad name is afforded in the diary of Sir George (later Lord) Riddell, a member of the Press Committee. In April 1916, Riddell lunched at Carlton Gardens with Arthur Balfour, First Lord of the Admiralty, fresh from a Cabinet meeting; they were joined by Lord Lansdowne, minister without portfolio in Asquith's Coalition Cabinet. 'The conversation turned on the armaments firms. I told Balfour and Lansdowne about Zaharoff, the wonderful man who controls Vickers. ... They had never heard of him, strange to say, and were very much surprised and interested. Balfour said it was one of the most remarkable stories he had ever heard – like a novel, but that to be complete, the story should have included a statement that Zaharoff had engineered the war.' Riddell did not vouchsafe what he had told Balfour to leave this impression, but Balfour's dictum that 'Zaharoff had engineered the war' has often been taken out of context and used against him in spite of the fact that he had never heard of him before the hors d'oeuvre. (The legend was not above lending himself a bad name when in one of his perverse moods. 'I made wars so that I could sell arms to both sides,' he is reported to have boasted.)

Devious ulterior motives, owing little to altruism, were freely imputed to Zaharoff to explain his opinions and conduct in the war years: there was his supposed concern to preserve the industrial infra-structure of Europe, his aversion to any measure which might serve to force a premature dénouement on the Western Front so that he could further his nefarious ends in the Balkans. Lloyd George was seen to be a willing accomplice as such a diversion would have allowed him to push forward his own projects for a campaign in the east. Zaharoff perhaps had a clearer and more realistic view than many of his subsequent critics. Sir Francis Bertie, British Ambassador in Paris for much of the war, reported that 'Zaharoff is for the prosecution of the war *jusqu'au bout*: a lame peace would cause squabbles between the Entente Cordiale.' Clemenceau was similarly adamant that there should not be 'a half-peace'. On the other hand Zaharoff took a more apocalyptic view in a letter he is supposed to have written to Venizelos in mid-war: 'Germany', he considered:

was far more vulnerable in 1914 than she or the West realized. I could have shown the Allies three points at which, had they struck, the enemy's potential could have been utterly destroyed. But that would have ruined the business built up over more than a century, and nothing would have been settled. The world would have been ripe for revolution. Our policy is to contain the central powers, then to achieve victory without permitting industrial chaos in Europe.

It is natural that the enemy should be supposed to have had their eye on such a redoubtable opponent. It seems that Zaharoff had fears for his personal safety, going so far as to shave off his goatee after his precipitate exit from the Château de l'Echelle one step ahead of the German cavalry. And if he had stuck to his mythical torpedo boat, he might have avoided, in spite of the bumpy ride, a sensationally close escape from the jaws of the sea-wolves.

The scene of this improbable encounter is usually set on board a neutral ship, one day out of port and bound for Greece. (Steamers between Italy and Greece were on occasion stopped by enemy submarines and in at least one case their haul included a British military attaché – and the diplomatic bag, which, insufficiently weighted, was fished out of the sea.)

An ill-disposed person, so the story runs, informed the Germans of Zaharoff's movements and from that day orders went out that the man from Vickers must be captured at all costs. (It might be thought easier to have simply shot or sunk him unless the cunning Hun was counting on injecting him with truth serum to discover the secrets of the Entente.) Their perseverance was rewarded. His ship was tracked down and boarded by a U-boat with a courteous request to hand over 'Herr Zaharoff from Cabin 24'.

With this unpleasantness behind them, the remaining company steamed on. And who did the astonished skipper see but Zaharoff calmly taking the air on the upper deck and smoking a cigar.

'I thought they got you,' he cried.

'Oh, no,' replied Zaharoff between puffs. 'I was in my locker when they entered my cabin. But I'm afraid I lost an invaluable and very efficient secretary.'

A further example of his resourcefulness as well as a practical contribution to the war effort was his advice to Lyautey, briefly Minister of War but whose mind was still on Morocco where he was shortly to return. He complained to Zaharoff that his *poilus* became so sick riding their camels that they were soon rendered unfit for active service.

'What would you do?' he asked.

'Let the navy ride the camels,' replied Zaharoff helpfully.

13

Aegean Stables

Byplay in the Balkans meanwhile was running true to form. The rival states weighed the chances and prepared to take sides, sometimes short of an actual state of war, with two considerations evenly balanced: what was in it for them and what their neighbours were up to. Although caution was the keynote, it was on the other hand seen to be important to make some show of support if a seat and a say at the peace conference table were to be secured. There was no clear and easy choice. It was for a start unthinkable that Greece and Turkey should range themselves on the same side; Russia and Turkey would have made unnatural bedfellows.

Greece remained the centrepiece of this embroilment for the best part of three years. King Constantine, realistically considering the state of the armed forces, was staunchly neutralist. He was backed in this opinion by the majority of his people. (The offer of Cyprus by Sir Edward Grey, the Foreign Secretary, as an inducement to enlist with the Allies was seen in Athens as an excessive provocation to Turkey.) He was opposed in and out of office by Venizelos, genuinely believing in a swift victory for the Entente. France, determined to ensure the occupation of the country, supported Venizelos; Great Britain, with no policy of her own, allowed herself to be swept along in the wake, feebly protesting at each successive outrage without, however, disavowing her ally.

Austria opened the ball within a month of the outbreak of general hostilities by advancing against the reprobate Serbians, to whom Greece was tied by treaty. Turkey's entry into the ring opened the way to Allied intervention. This strategy was favoured by the 'easterners' in the British Cabinet, the formidable trio of Lloyd-George, Kitchener and Churchill with the backing of Maurice Hankey, Secretary of the War Council. They were resolutely opposed by the 'westerners', the British and French generals commanding in France, who refused to release sufficient men for any effective effort in any other theatre of war.

The prospect of participation in an offensive against Turkey in the Dardanelles was too strong a temptation for the Greek Prime Minister, Venizelos, who offered his assistance without consulting his King or Cabinet. This thoroughly alarmed Russia, who absolutely declined to allow Greek troops to play any part in the business in case they beat the Cossacks into Constantinople. Venizelos had no choice but to resign.

And thus began an adventure in which Basil Zaharoff acted the role of paymaster to browbeat Greece into renouncing her neutrality.

The excuse for such high-handed action was the alleged pro-German proclivities of King Constantine. This bias, cultivated in England by the censor and eagerly seized on in republican France, was false. (The views of the two men in the best position to judge, the British Admiral heading the naval mission and the Military Attaché, were dismissed as prejudiced.) Indeed if he had any personal leaning, it was rather towards England; he was on more friendly terms with his cousins George V and the Tsar Nicholas than with his preposterously pretentious brother-in-law, Kaiser Wilhelm. He tried to make his attitude quite clear. 'I'm neither pro-German nor pro-Allied,' he protested, 'but pro-Greek.' This was not considered an adequate excuse.

His neutrality had already been challenged by the Kaiser who, disclosing his secret alliance with Bulgaria and Turkey, threatened to treat Greece as an enemy if she did not declare for the Central Powers. (This crass attempt to force Greece into the same camp as her two arch-enemies could only have confirmed the King's resolve to stay outside the conflict.) Constantine's subsequent warnings of Bulgaria's alignment were ignored in London and Paris; instead, the Allies tried to buy Bulgarian support with an offer of territories in Macedonia recently won by Greece. (She, by way of compensation, was promised a slice of the Ottoman Empire in Asia Minor, a classic example of swapping the skin of the bear which, although an endangered species, still had some mileage left in it.)

Faced with Bulgarian mobilization, Venizelos, once more returned to power by the electorate, proposed a massive Allied intervention at Salonika in order to enable Greece, her flank secured, to join forces with Serbia. The opposition of Allied headquarters in France scotched this plan. Then in September 1915, the Austro-Germans in concert with the Bulgarians struck at stubborn Serbia. While Sir Edward Grey blandly promised 'to give our friends in the Balkans all the support in our power ... without reserve and without qualification', he was reckoning without the generals. Eventually a futile compromise was effected and in October 150,000 Anglo-French troops, too few to reassure the Greeks, too late to save the Serbs, were landed at Salonika. The British government immediately regretted this impulsiveness, whereas Joffre as suddenly waxed enthusiastic, reinforcing the French contingent with a further two divisions. These promptly took to the field under General Sarrail, only to find that the Bulgarian offensive had separated them from the Serbians, who were retreating through Albania to refuge in Corfu. The French fell back on Salonika in confusion.

Through this Greece remained uneasily but obstinately neutral: the Germans were unhelpfully insisting that the Allied troops retreating into Greece be disarmed, while the British were urging evacuation on the French, who were determined to stay put.

The Salonika garrison, soon swollen to half a million men by the survivors of the Serbian armies, played no further serious offensive role until the autumn of 1918. The Germans were content to leave it in peace under the watchful eye of their Bulgarian ally; they gleefully described it as their 'largest internment camp'.

As a result of this débâcle, Venizelos was once more dismissed and, after fresh elections in December, Zaharoff's old friend Skoulou-dis formed a government which declared 'a very benevolent neutrality' towards the Entente. This did not save his country. The deposed Venizelos threw his energies into plotting with the Allies. His unamiable attitude towards his own government was summarized in a conversation with Asquith. Coercion, he urged, must be brought to bear on the King; if the Greek General Staff created a problem, he would 'undertake to cause an insurrection in Athens, and the King would be torn to pieces'; and he advised the Prime Minister to 'reduce our resources more and more, allowing wheat, coal and money to reach us only in the smallest quantities – only what is strictly necessary to keep the people from dying of hunger ...'. 'Thus', Asquith laconically noted, 'M. Venizelos.'

Venizelos was not content, however, to sit back and let others do the dirty work for him. He fostered his own plans for deposing his monarch which the partisan Greek Minister in Paris confided to the Prime Minister, Aristide Briand, in the hope of attracting financial support. Briand had scruples but nonetheless handed over 350,000 francs as a token of sympathy.

The French premier's parsimony might well have derived from a decision he had already taken to tap other pockets. He had in mind a Greek patriot and naturalized French citizen. He turned to Basil Zaharoff, whom he introduced to his friend Henri Turot, a former Deputy, established undercover in the French Legation in Athens. Once assured of Zaharoff's willing co-operation, Turot convinced him that 'the most potent means of helping our propaganda, or rather of calling it into existence, was to found a Mediterranean news agency . . . to supply a counterweight in Greece to the infamous and demoralizing propaganda of the Wolff agency' in which Krupp had a stake.

Zaharoff rose to the occasion with characteristic munificence. 'It is not my intention', the Maecenas grandly announced, 'to create a wretched local agency. I shall extend your conception and give you the means to found an agency that will be worldwide in its influence.' Thus Agence-Radio came into being.

Three days after Christmas 1915, Briand was able to inform his Minister in Athens of Zaharoff's offer – most reasonably 1,500,000 francs' worth. Two months later the new voice of the Allies set about its task with bullish enthusiasm. The agency, the Russian Minister, Prince Demidoff, reported to St Petersburg, was trying to influence opinion by means of 'wildly imaginative news'; even the Venizelist papers were soon up in arms to condemn its methods. This persuaded the resourceful owners that the news agency alone was not sufficient as a weapon; newspapers, the end-users, had to be secured. The sequel to this was richly comic. The largesse scattered around the editorial desks aroused the envy of those who were left out, those very organs whose declared sympathy for the Allies rendered subventions seemingly supererogatory. When news leaked out that *Embros* was about to be bought up, the owners of *Patris*, the official Venizelist paper, trooped round to the French Legation and threatened to switch their support unless a suitable portion of plums was dropped in their lap. The project was abandoned and Turot, sourly condemning the Venizelist press as 'enterprises of extortion', had to advise Paris that they would have to be pacified with two or three hundred thousand francs.

Much as the Germans must have enjoyed this spectacle, they were roused to respond. Their propaganda chief, Baron von Schenk, was seen by the opposition as 'devilishly cunning' while his own Legation discerned 'increasing symptoms of mental aberration'. He anyway countered within his means – the Allies were said to spend fifteen times as much as the Germans – by buying up all the theatres, music halls and cinemas. But most of his success he owed to the Allies' excesses. When he was finally forced out of Athens, he remarked to an American journalist: 'Thanks to the able assistance rendered to me by the Allies, results have far exceeded my expectations. I cheerfully leave my work in their hands.'

There is no record of whether Zaharoff was aware of this blundering; although banker to the enterprise, he seems to have required no accounting and to have exercised no control. His judgement, indeed, appears to have deserted him even earlier. Before Briand had engaged his interest, he had sold a hare-brained scheme to the British government to nobble the Greeks. In the middle of December, Asquith informed Maurice Hankey of 'a secret known only to McKenna [Chancellor of the Exchequer] and himself, viz, that they have sent off a trustworthy Greek, a very large shareholder in Vickers who lives in Paris, with £1,400,000 in his pocket to buy the whole Greek administration and Government. Apparently McKenna knew the man to be reliable and had insisted on the PM's acceptance. . . .'

It is impossible to imagine what he can have hoped to achieve. True, his first patron Skouloudis had just formed his government but, although well known for his sympathy towards Britain, his first loyalty was to the King; he was not only a wealthy man, but a politician of undoubted integrity. He was also smarting from an Allied rebuff; the Germans had placed a credit of £2,000,000 at Greece's disposal, while Briand, true to Venizelos' injunction, had refused a new French loan. If in these circumstances Zaharoff expected to be able to influence Skouloudis, it was a grave error of judgement.

Unfortunately there is no further reference to this initiative, or to the fate of the fund. It is not likely that this was used to subsidize the subversive operations of what came to be called Zaharoff's private army, which is said to have included in its ranks a pretty cross-section of Athenian society: eight suspected murderers, twenty-seven thieves, ten smugglers, twenty-one professional gamblers and twenty white-slavers. This motley gang, which was anyway always short of money, was directed by the intelligence service of the British Legation under the care of the young author Compton Mackenzie,* who led his men with the verve worthy of one of his later plots of japes in the Highlands. The Germans, through the necessity of economy rather than principle, never worked through 'bullies and bandits', but still

---

* The confusion over the command of this private army, mistakenly attributed to Zaharoff, may have arisen from the fact that Compton Mackenzie came to be known as 'Z' in the mysterious alphabet of the secret service.

employed a few on dud missions to occupy the attention of Compton Mackenzie's braves.

The excesses of this band were matched only by the antics of their French colleagues under the Naval Attaché, Captain de Roquefeuil. This character, enjoying more influence than was usual for his rank by his marriage to a Mumm, reported, or more often misreported, direct to his friend the Minister of Marine behind the back of his own superiors. From the day of his appointment, the French in Athens forced the pace with the joyful connivance of General Sarrail ('I took as my directives my frankly republican views') in Salonika. This genial pair considered the assassination of King Constantine, while the French Minister independently outlined a scheme to the Quai d'Orsay to have him abducted; in July 1916, the summer palace of Tatoi was destroyed by arson, claiming seventeen victims, although the King and his family escaped.

There were some, of course, in England who were not averse to a show of violence. General Henry Wilson wanted to 'take Tino by the throat'; others believed against all the evidence that the King was an autocrat defying the popular will,* and most were happily ignorant of the methods being employed in their name to coerce Greece. When it was too late, the philhellene Hankey, no friend to the royal family, censured the methods of the French intervention as 'unscrupulous and unjustified'.

The Russians were the sole members of the Alliance to emerge with any credit. 'France's action in Greece', Prince Demidoff deemed, 'is not in accord with my conception of political morality ... [the Allies] are flouting the ideal of liberty and of the free self-determination of small nations ...' – original sentiments from that quarter.

All of this unusual activity persuaded the King that benevolent neutrality might well prove more dangerous than a state of war, as long as Greece could avoid exposure to the risk of being overrun like Serbia. However, the time for parley was past; Sarrail had the bit between his teeth. In August 1916, supporters of Venizelos with French military aid took over control of Salonika and a few days later, much to the surprise of her allies, the French fleet appeared off the Piraeus, troops were landed to protect the Legation and the Greek navy was seized. In October Venizelos raised the flag of revolt in Crete and was installed by Sarrail as head of a provisional govern-

* Bertie, British Ambassador in Paris, was one exception. While still convinced that the King was pro-German, he conceded that he was 'worshipped by the Greeks who do not want to fight ...'. But he did not question that they should be dragooned into battle regardless of their wishes.

ment in Salonika. The country was on the brink of civil war. Into this turmoil the British Legation launched a soothing declaration that 'It is not the intention of the Allied Powers to constrain Greece to abandon her neutrality.' This could hardly have convinced even its author.

On 1 December some 3,000 troops, French in the main, marched on Athens to seize a store of arms. They were resisted by 'guns and riff-raff'. Then, without warning, the French fleet opened fire on the capital, narrowly missing the Russian Minister, who forcefully protested. At home, the violation of Greece's neutrality was viewed with equanimity by those who had professed outrage at Germany's invasion of Belgium.

Other means of persuasion were introduced to cow an increasingly surly population. The Allies imposed a blockade. This was more successful; for the next eight months Greece starved. In April 1917, Prince Demidoff telegraphed his government: 'The Greeks are ready for any capitulation, provided that the King is left untouched.' The French were not so accommodating. In June, a French Senator, Charles Jonnart, arrived off Athens in a French warship and proclaimed himself 'High Commissioner of the Protecting Powers of Greece'. (The Greeks must indeed have wondered just whom they were being protected from.) In fact it was bluff. Jonnart, taking his allies' name in vain, presented an ultimatum demanding the King's immediate abdication, and threatening to order a military occupation of Greece and a further whiff of shell if this demand were not met. 'I come from the French invaded territories,' he told the Prime Minister. 'I have seen Arras, where not one stone remains on another. If the King does not at once abdicate, we shall make of Athens another Arras.' In the face of this, the King submitted. 'If I am the stumbling block,' he told the Crown Council, 'I must remove myself.' On 29 June 1917, Greece declared war on Germany, Bulgaria and Turkey.

It was against this background that a Greek politician is reported to have remarked that 'Zaharoff could claim for himself the glory of having promoted to a very considerable extent the participation of Greece in the war.' Unfortunately, as his identity is not revealed, it is uncertain whether he was speaking in a spirit of irony or of partisan political fervour.

Jonnart himself suffered a posterior qualm. 'Had this been known in Britain,' he declared, 'the decision to dethrone the King would never have been taken', and he wrote to his own premier: 'This has been a far from glorious page in the history of France.'

It would be comforting to know where Basil Zaharoff stood in all this. It is hard to credit that he was so out of touch with Greek opinion that he fell for his own propagandist fantasies; at the least Skouloudis, known to deplore the tactics of Agence-Radio, might have been expected to convey to him his concern at the turn of events. Did Venizelos, spell-binding at his best, lie to him as he did to the French press about his attitude and intentions towards the King?

He could never have hoped on past form to recover any of his subsidies through commissions. It is most likely that his ambition for Greece had become a ruling passion which was not to be deflected by any lesser consideration; he recognized in Venizelos the sole instrument for converting this zeal into reality. Zaharoff by this same action was piling up a debt of which he was soon to seek a settlement.

14
Talking Turkey

Zaharoff's end was now secured in Greece. But long before that he had another and complementary trick up his sleeve: while introducing one combatant into his own camp, he would cut out another from the opposing corner. He decided to tackle Turkey, a tougher nut. The same methods of intimidation would not serve; the country was already engaged. There was, however, that expensive alternative he had once before sold to the British Prime Minister. He would buy them out.

The idea for his 'Ottoplan' was probably born as early as 1916, but there is no record of how, when and where he made his first contact with his prey. There were disgruntled Turks aplenty floating around abroad, whose services were open to offer but who represented only minority factions within the ruling Committee of Union and Progress. But Zaharoff had had his own agents in Turkey for upwards of twenty years and he could have tapped the recent experience of the Vickers' directors, Frank Barker and Vincent Caillard, as well as that of Count Léon Ostrorog, the company's legal adviser, who would all have been familiar with the foibles and frailties of the top Turks; there was, too, Sir Ernest Cassel, who had furnished a first small loan to the Young Turks to engage their favour. Zaharoff put his plan to the British government in the summer one year before Greece entered the war. He was given a free rein.

The advantage to either party of Greece's shotgun marriage to the Allied cause was questionable; the accession of Turkey to the side of the Central Powers was calamitous. The supposition and its consequences seem never once to have crossed the mind of any political leaders at home until it was too late, an omission born of aversion, at best disdain; Liberal opinion was still coloured by Gladstone's ringing diatribes against 'the one great anti-human specimen of humanity'. And yet, for the past hundred years, Great Britain had, for sound reasons of self-interest, acted as the traditional friend, and often protector, of the decrepit Ottoman edifice. More recently, her influence had been dissipated, her place taken by a brash newcomer, Germany, pursuing a determinedly expansionist policy eastwards.

Then came the Young Turks. Their aim was the invigoration of a less dependent, nationalist Turkey, a process which disturbed her neighbours. They granted concessions to European companies, which brought in valuable foreign capital, much of it English; Vickers was entrusted with the reconstruction of the fleet, arsenals and shipyards; a British admiral was in charge of the instruction of the navy, a German general of the army.

The Turkish strong man was Enver Pasha, one of the founding officers of the Young Turk movement who in 1914 became Minister of War after a spell as military attaché in Berlin. Marriage to a daughter of the Sultan enabled him to live in palatial style. He was to become one of the triumvirate, along with Talaat Bey and Jemal Pasha, the Navy Minister, who ruled Turkey throughout the world war. Enver and Zaharoff were to play out an extraordinary final act together in neutral Switzerland.

Within the councils of the Committee, Enver, then in his early thirties, was the most resolute champion of an alliance with Germany. He was opposed by an anti-war party which would have preferred an alliance with the Entente – if it would buy off their acquisitive Russian neighbour. Talaat, Interior Minister and political 'boss', preferred the fence, seeing disadvantage on each hand and advantage on neither.

Turkey had proposed an alliance with Britain as far back as 1911. Winston Churchill, who had just taken over at the Admiralty, could see no need for this, and instead lectured the Turks on the value of British friendship. When in July 1914 the Turks, responding to earlier overtures, proposed a secret alliance against Russia to the Germans, the Kaiser instructed his Ambassador that 'under no circumstances at all can we afford to turn them away'.

While the Turk was havering, nervous at the last minute to put pen to the German treaty, the British obligingly gave him a push into the outstretched arms of the Emperor. Churchill summarily 'requisitioned' two first-class battleships laid down for Turkey in England: the *Sultan Osman*, already completed at Armstrong, and the *Reshadieh*, just preparing for her trials at Vickers' Barrow yards. Each had cost over £2,000,000 and had been paid for out of public subscription by the patriotic peasants of Anatolia in the aftermath of the defeats of the Balkan War.

On 2 August, the alliance with Germany, known only to Enver and Talaat, was signed. On 10 August, the German battle cruiser *Göben* and the light cruiser *Breslau*, having given the British Mediterranean fleet the slip, entered the Dardanelles. They were allowed to pass on the personal authority of Enver; entry was barred to the British. This did at last cause mild concern, but after all, they comforted themselves in London, Turkey having declared her neutrality, it would be enough simply to insist that this be strictly observed. This was not quite how the German Admiral, Souchon, saw it. Throughout, he retained a clear and definite view of the desirable objective: 'to force the Turks, even against their will, to spread the war to the Black Sea against their ancient enemy, Russia'.

Meanwhile, the peace faction in the Committee of Union and Progress, headed by the Finance Minister, Javid Bey, suggested to the Allies – a state of war had existed since 4 August – that they might make some gesture to strengthen their hand through modifications to the 'capitulations' (the foreign debt secured by revenues of the state) with the offer of a loan. The Allies parried this with a demand for the dismissal of the German military mission and the expulsion of the crews of the two German ships.

The Turks had no means to enforce this against the Germans, intransigent and unassailable. A genial compromise was then agreed – that Turkey should buy the two German cruisers. This was popularly acclaimed as just retribution for Britain's seizure of the Turkish ships. They were rechristened the *Jawus* and *Midilli*, the crescent flag was raised and their smirking Teuton crews were invested with fezzes. (And technically they thus passed under the flag of the Commander-in-Chief of the Turkish navy, the British Admiral, Limpus.)

Still the Turks were in no hurry to declare war on Russia as they were now bound by treaty to do. All the ministers other than Enver wished to avoid any overt act. Germany must suddenly have seemed a distant prospect, whereas the British and Russians were uncomfortably close at hand. The Russian and French governments themselves at last woke up to the crisis; they were prepared for the first time to join in a guarantee of Turkish territorial integrity, sweetened by 'great financial advantages at the expense of Germany'. So great was this belated Russian concern that she was actually willing not only to renounce her claim to Constantinople, but most handsomely to abide by it 'even if we are victorious'. England alone remained unmindful of the menace.

The Germans looked on with mounting apprehension, aware that the slippery Turk might yet elude them. They decided to force the issue. On 28 October the German Admiral, with Enver's connivance, led his fleet under false colours into the Black Sea, shelled Odessa and Sebastopol and sank a Russian gunboat. Appalled, the Grand Vizier, supported by a majority of ministers, tried to wriggle out of all responsibility, but the Germans, with the capital under the *Göben*'s guns and documents compromising the Committee in the Embassy safe, were not about to let them off the hook. The Russians formally countered by declaring war on Turkey on 4 November, followed by Britain and France the next day.

The opening operations of the war did not augur well for the reluctant belligerent. Prompted by her new ally and by Enver's megalomania, Turkey launched a mid-winter stroke in Armenia against the Russians. Over 80 per cent of Enver's command, mainly Anatolians, the finest fighting material of the country, were killed, wounded or frozen to death. However, the Russians had been sufficiently alarmed to appeal for an urgent diversion against the Turks by their western allies. This led indirectly to the Gallipoli adventure and provoked the partition (on paper) of Ottoman lands.

The attempt to force the Dardanelles also provided the first instance of an unusual, if not original, method of warfare which was to continue sporadically up to the eve of the Turkish final surrender three and a half years later, and in which Basil Zaharoff was to play a leading role. The warriors at Westminster and Whitehall had not learned to take the unspeakable Turk too seriously. Counting on the time-honoured cupidity and corruption of the eastern empire, it was thought that an appeal to their pockets would be fitting and effective.

The first revelation of this ploy surfaced briefly almost a quarter of a century later. Sir Basil Thomson, at the time head of the Special Branch, casually recounted that Captain Reginald 'Blinker' Hall, RN, Director of Naval Intelligence, had 'felt pretty sure' that he had 'bought' the Dardanelles forts in February 1915 through an Indian Moslem. Confirmation came only very much later with the publication of the diaries of Colonel Sir Maurice (later Lord) Hankey, Secretary of the Committee of Imperial Defence through the war. Early in March 1915, he had been told by Hall – 'a brilliant if none too scrupulous' man – that negotiations had been opened to bribe the Turks to evict the Germans. Two British agents – the different accounts do not agree on their names – had been authorized to commit the

British government to pay up to £4,000,000 to this end. (There is a certain endearing naivety – or shrewd calculation – about this sum; it represented rather less than the government could be said to owe the Turks for the two impounded battleships, by then flying the white ensign.) Although the bombardment of the Dardanelles forts had already commenced on 19 February the British agents sat down with the Turkish representatives in the middle of March at Dede Aghach in Thrace. This was elaborated into a more tortuous version by Hall's biographer. The agents, Griffin Eady, an executive of the contractors Sir John Jackson Limited, and Gerald Fitzmaurice, former dragoman at the British Embassy in Constantinople (already declared *persona non grata* by the Young Turks), made contact with a friendly minister through the son of the Grand Rabbi in the Turkish capital. They carried a letter from Hall, issued entirely on his own authority, pledging the sum of £3,000,000, with power to increase this to £4,000,000. Hall then suffered an onset of cold feet; he progressively lowered his reward by cable to his emissaries. His first offer on 5 March was £500,000 for the surrender of the Dardanelles and clearance of mines, and the same sum for the *Göben* (undamaged). Three days later he reduced his price for the *Göben* to £100,000, less than 5 per cent of its market value. It was only at this stage that his chief, the First Sea Lord, Admiral 'Jackie' Fisher, learned of this auction, and ordered Hall to offer £200,000 for the *Göben* and £100,000 for the *Breslau*. These were the final terms set before the Turks on 15 March.

The negotiations foundered for other reasons than their unattractive terms. The Turks simply requested that the British government guarantee that Constantinople would remain in Turkish hands at the conclusion of hostilities. This the British government was unable to do. Her Russian ally was already pressing for a similar deal. The secret treaty allocating Constantinople to the Tsar was signed a few weeks later. Thus it came about that Russia, in fulfilment of Catherine the Great's ambition, found herself dependent for all her supplies and munitions from her allies through Archangel, accessible only a few months of the year, and Vladivostock, some 5,000 miles from the front.

The second example of this odd propensity for paying out followed in what transpired to be a false start to the Mesopotamian campaign. A small Anglo-Indian force, having secured Basra, was tempted to push on to Baghdad. Checked, it withdrew to Kut where it was pursued and besieged by the Turks. After costly and abortive attempts at rescue, it was forced finally to surrender in April 1916, but not before the British government had made 'a vain and ill-judged effort' to bribe the Turks to let the troops go free. (The British brokers, led blindfold through the lines, were a Captain Aubrey Herbert and a young archaeologist, T.E.Lawrence.) The offer price on this occasion was £1,000,000 – for the wasting remains of one division – but this was doubled when the Turks met the proposal with an aloof silence. Although the news of this trafficking was kept out of the English papers, the Turks happily put the news about abroad. This would have reached Zaharoff's ears and served as an actuarial base to calculate the price of his own premium for peace.

When the forces besieged at Kut were halfway through their ordeal, Basil Zaharoff took what at first sight was a drastic and unexpected step. He prepared to sever the umbilical cord with his adopted family. His principal role was that of overseas agent-in-chief for Vickers, and this function, hitherto of such vital interest to the company in peacetime when orders from the home government alone were insufficient to support the capacity necessary to provide a reserve for national emergency, had ceased to exist on the declaration of war. Thereafter the problem of the armaments firms was instead that of actually achieving the unforeseen level of production that the allied governments so urgently and suddenly required. There was simply no longer spare capacity for third parties.

Pre-war sales of military equipment were infinitesimal; the average proportion of machine-guns in the major European armies in 1914 was two to a thousand men. The Maxim division of Vickers, even with worldwide sales and with the all-round superiority of the weapon, was often at a standstill; in only four of the years from 1900 to 1914 did profits reach six figures and in at least five of them there were losses.

Zaharoff in these years was therefore largely confined to negotiating orders for naval construction and equipment. As a result of these activities at the outbreak of war the Barrow yard was engaged on one battleship for Turkey – the unhappy case of the *Reshadieh*, subsequently commissioned as HMS *Erin* – three smaller vessels for Brazil and the main propelling machinery for a Brazilian battleship being built by Armstrong. The yard had other minor orders in hand for China, Italy and Argentina in 1914, and for Spain and Russia the following year, but by 1916 there was no work being undertaken for any foreign governments except for the completion of the Brazilian contracts. True, Zaharoff was still a substantial shareholder in Vickers Limited and would therefore expect to share in their distributed profits, but there was no longer a field or future for him in foreign sales.

There is no reference of any importance to Zaharoff in the company minutes throughout the war. As Vickers' evidence for the Royal Commission on the Private Manufacture of the Trading in Arms (1935–6) simply and plainly stated, 'Basil Zaharoff's services were at the disposal of the British government and were freely utilized.'

On 23 January 1916, with a heavy heart, Zaharoff wrote to Sir Vincent Caillard, through the forbidding-sounding company secretary, John Coffin, offering his resignation from the company with which he had been associated for so many years. Caillard must have communicated this extraordinary news to his fellow directors, but they seem to have taken no action; no doubt they regarded it as a temporary aberration on the part of the eccentric ZedZed – and put it away in a drawer till the war should end.

And other work was afoot.

Undeterred by the failure of his earlier efforts to suborn the Greek government, he determined on a similar coup across the Straits. At the same time he must have concluded that his terms might not have been generous enough, or that his new victims were worth more, for he doubled the stakes. We owe this information to Maurice Hankey, 'man of secrets', who noted in his diary for 2 June 1916 that the Prime Minister, Asquith, had told him, in the presence of Reginald McKenna, then Chancellor of the Exchequer, that 'the old Greek had now a more ambitious scheme to buy up for £4 million the whole of the Young Turk Party, who would hand over Constantinople and the Dardanelles to the Allies and bolt to America. It seemed far-fetched,' he noted mildly, 'and unlikely to come off, but as there was to be no pay until the goods were delivered there seemed no objection to letting him try.'

The scheme might well have appeared far-fetched even to such an original and thoughtful public servant; it is difficult not to imagine that Asquith might have privately agreed with him. On the other hand the political establishment was suffering from a malaise. They felt helpless in the face of events; they believed something different should be tried to break the deadlock; they had no clear idea what. They were in a mood to clutch at even a far-fetched straw.

The timing, however, would not seem to have been propitious. There could be little reason for thinking that the Turkish leadership just then might have been despondent over the course of the war. The Dardanelles adventure was in the past and not likely to be repeated; the Mesopotamian front was quiet; a small force under Colonel von Kress had made a boldly successful raid right up to the Suez Canal where the British were on the defensive. Only in the Caucasus were things not going too well, but, after the loss of

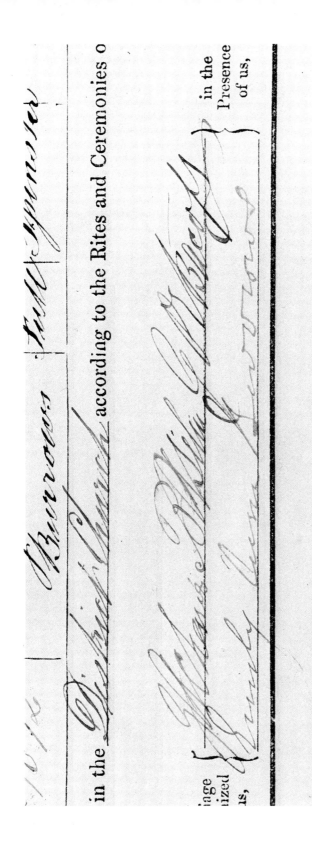

in the _District Church_ according to the Rites and Ceremonies o

in the Presence of us,

Marriage signatures of Emily Ann Burrows, a Bristol builder's daughter and 'Zacharias Basilius Gortzacoff, General of Kieff', alias Basil Zaharoff, in London, 14 October, 1872.

The *Abdul Hamid*, built at Barrow in 1886 for the Ottoman Navy. The first submarine to incorporate a torpedo, housed in the bulbous projection at the bow, it was also armed with two one-inch Nordenfelt guns (with no foothold for the gunner). Steam-powered with a retractable smokestack, it submerged by means of a primitive system of ballast tanks and vertical screws, visible on the deck. It was subject to 'some eccentric and dangerous effects'. It was no sooner commissioned than beached and abandoned to rust.

The Nordenfelt Submarine Boat sales and engineering team, Constantinople 1888. Seated, left to right: the Reverend George Garrett Pasha, Captain P. W. D'Alton and standing, left to right: Fond Eckerman, engineer Lawrie and Basil Zaharoff.

(*Above left*) The *Maxim*, patented 1883, the first truly automatic gun, with a rate of fire of 600 shots a minute. H. M. Stanley thought it 'invaluable for subduing the heathen' but the military establishment was not converted to the machine-gun's worth until well into the World War.
(*Above right*) The strong right arm of Hiram Maxim, boxer, brawler, bouncer and 'chronic inventor', with his revolutionary gun.

A demonstration of tree felling for the Chinese minister, Li Hung-Chang, with Hiram Maxim (right) and Sigmund Loewe (behind) at the latter's country house. When informed of the cost of the ammunition, the minister retorted, 'That gun fires too fast for China.'

Hiram Maxim's steam-powered 'flight' on rails at his country house near Bexley. The contraption, which 'partook of the nature of a biplane', unexpectedly lifted off from the track in spite of the weight of its boilers and was smashed.

Battlecruiser *Rurik*, 15,200 tons, was built by Vickers for Russia in 1906, but commissioned only in 1909 owing to problems with the gun mountings.

Sir Vincent Caillard (1856–1930), soldier, diplomat, banker, Near Eastern expert and protégé of Ernest Cassel. Financial director of Vickers from 1906–1927.

Albert Vickers (1838–1919), 'Don Alfredo', chairman of Vickers from 1909–1919.

(*Above left*) Enver Pasha (1881–1922), a leader of the Young Turks in 1908 and pro-German minister of war in the Turkish triumvirate.

(*Above*) Eleutherios Venizelos (1864–1936), a Cretan of mixed Turkish, Jewish and Armenian descent, four times prime minister of Greece, he successfully agitated to induce Greece to abandon her neutrality and join the Allies in the Great War. His ambitions for Greece coincided with Basil Zaharoff's until they diverged in 1923 over the Greek royal family.

Georges Clemenceau (1841–1929), an implacable opponent of German militarism and French defeatism, was appointed premier in the dark days of November, 1917. He lost office in 1920.

(*Above*) Sir Basil Zaharoff takes a brisk
constitutional in Monte Carlo.

(*Above right*) Basil Zaharoff, Honorary Knight
Grand Cross of the Order of the Bath.

Sir Basil and Lady Zaharoff, the former Duchess
of Marchena, caught unawares on the day after
their marriage; 23 September 1924.

ONE OF THE "MAXIMS" OF CIVILISATION!

OLD AND NEW.

"THINK of the glorious Mottoes," said a Major of the old school. "'*Nil Desperandum*,' 'Death or Victory,' 'England Expects,' and so forth!" Replied his friend, the modern Captain, "Bother your Mottoes! Give us the 'Maxims'!"

Cartoon from *The Modern Traveller*, H. Belloc and B. T. Blackwood (1898) The illustrator, Lord Basil Blackwood, shared Basil Zaharoff's chambers in Ryder Street, St James's.

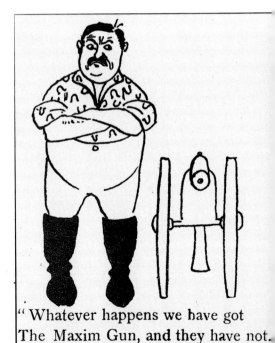

"Whatever happens we have got The Maxim Gun, and they have not."

Punch cartoon, 2 December 1893.

Trebizond and Erzerum, a new Turkish army was being formed to counter Russian encroachment. A major difficulty, even for the glib Greek, would have been to persuade Russia to surrender her claim to Constantinople. But the idea did not die.

In the course of 1917 a whole further series of peace negotiations with Turkey were put in hand which were to continue for almost eighteen months up to the eve of the armistice, and which were crowned by direct talks between Basil Zaharoff and Enver Pasha. These comprise a hitherto untapped dossier of history, high drama and humour.

Turkey was no longer such an essential physical and material prop to the Central Powers. Although the success of the German offensive against Russia earlier in the war had depended on keeping the Dardanelles firmly closed, this no longer held after the assassination of Rasputin had released that popular ferment which triggered the abdication of the Tsar and the revolution. As Turkey's value declined, so did German aid, soon replaced by financial subsidy and promises as Germany herself began to experience shortages.

An overwhelming force of a quarter of a million men entered Baghdad in March, providing a timely, if temporary, moral stimulant for the Allies at the peak of the submarine campaign which the German military confidently expected, and the Admiralty feared, would be decisive. (It was; it provoked a reluctant President Wilson.)

Then, encouraged by the revolt of the Sherif of Mecca, a similar-sized British force in Egypt began its stumbling advance to Gaza. On this front the British enjoyed an even greater superiority, sometimes as much as nine to one in men; there were indeed more Turks guarding the long line of the Hejaz railway from the attentions of roving bands of Arab irregulars led by a young English officer, T.E.Lawrence, than there were facing the mass of the British army. This force, much strengthened in men and command under General Allenby, entered Jerusalem in the last month of the year, again providing a welcome moral tonic after the futile losses at Passchendaele, the Italian rout at Caporetto and Russia's breakaway.

An early initiative by the British government to open peace talks, or at least to take the temperature of the water, got under way in the late spring of 1917, and immediately ran into difficulties. The English emissary was to be Captain Aubrey Herbert, the Unionist Member of Parliament who ten years before had served in the Embassy at Constantinople and enjoyed the friendship of many leading Turks. But before he could take a step forward, he was rumbled.

A representative of the Armenian Committee and Dr Chaim

Weizmann, the Zionist leader, descended on the Foreign Office and gave a convincing performance of being 'very much excited and very angry' while promising to do all they could to oppose Herbert and his designs and to make as much trouble as possible.

The Allies had already made it that much more difficult to detach the Turk from the German's side. Desperate for some sop to satisfy the suspected idealism of the American public – unnecessarily as it turned out; the loss of American ships was a more effective spur – the Allies had earlier in the year, and rather late in the day, spelt out their war aims, and these included the 'liberation of the peoples who now lie beneath the murderous tyranny of the Turks'.

Whether the Armenian–Zionist threat turned many Foreign Office bowels to water, Captain Herbert at least was not deterred. Hot from his seat in the Irish Office, he arrived in Berne in July and conducted a series of talks in a rather self-consciously cloak-and-dagger style with various Turks over the next week.

The Turkish spokesman, purporting to be acting for the gormandiz-ing Talaat Bey,* represented an influential anti-Enver group which, although interested in forming an alternative government, was not inclined to do so merely for the sake of the Allies, who might then proceed to parcel out Turkey. They desired guarantees.

Herbert presented the Turkish peace proposals to Foreign Secretary Arthur Balfour – 'interested and excited' – and Lloyd George who 'took it all in well enough'. Maurice Hankey was also present; he seems only to have warned his chief that the initiative, which evidently came from the Turks, might be a 'dodge to separate the allies'. (Lloyd George had already informed the French and Italian governments of this initiative and had secured their assent.)

But Lloyd George was also clearly keeping his own counsel. If he took it all in, neither was he giving anything away. Basil Zaharoff had been in touch with other Turkish leaders for some time. The Prime Minister had in his possession when he saw Herbert a memoran-dum outlining the results of Zaharoff's most recent meeting in Geneva with Enver's envoy, Abdul Kerim, a Pasha of the old school, which had taken place just one month before Herbert's Swiss rendezvous. Even the ubiquitous Hankey was kept in the dark.

The first of these records dates from June 1917. The Turks were awaiting Zaharoff's arrival in Switzerland, but he was delayed or un-aware of their interest. Enver had not lingered in Geneva, but had left

---

* He was reputed to sink a half kilo of caviar at a sitting, washed down by an ad hoc cocktail of two glasses of brandy and two bottles of champagne.

Abdul Kerim behind to hold the fort. Kerim, too, tired, and wired to Enver that he would wait no longer, upon which Enver, taking the waters in Herculesbad in Romania, instructed him to stay on and make fresh contact with Zaharoff. The two finally came together towards the third week of May.

Zaharoff opened the ball by asking Kerim, to his apparent annoyance, for his credentials. It would be sufficient, Zaharoff smoothly suggested, if he would show him Enver's telegram. This Kerim produced and allowed him to copy.

On Kerim returning the compliment, Zaharoff replied that he represented the 'Money-Bags' of the Allies. This, with Zaharoff's own reputation, satisfied him, although he enquired if America, which had entered the war the month before, was included. 'Peut-être,' replied Zaharoff cagily.

That this was not the couple's first encounter is evident from the fact that Kerim lamented their last failure. Things had changed since, he explained. Turkey was ruined and lost, and Enver and his faction were willing to throw in the sponge on 'reasonable conditions' and get out with their lives. The conditions were not unreasonable: a 'retaining fee' of $2,000,000 – they were now into dollar diplomacy – to be put down immediately, payable at Morgan's in New York.* Of this Kerim would personally appropriate one-quarter and, after putting Zaharoff in communication with Enver and Javid, the Minister of Finance, who were also acting for others,† he would 'curse the Turks and Turkey' and go to America, there to await the others. The remaining $1,500,000 would go to these others who 'absolutely needed every piastre of it to buy certain people who are indispensable'.

This second reference to America as a bolt-hole raises the interesting supposition that Zaharoff had already been in touch with the Turks even before he had proposed the idea to Asquith in the summer of 1916.

It is not clear at this stage whether Enver was to be included in this share-out; even without him the average is only a rough $250,000 per head – something of a bagatelle – out of which some 'indispensable' other people had to be squared. However, this was only a sweetener; in addition a further and final sum of $10,000,000 would 'pay for

---

* John Pierpont Morgan Junior's banking house acted as agent in the United States for the British government during the war.

† Among others Kalil, the victor of Kut; the Sheikh-ul-Islam, the Ottoman religious leader; Jemal Pasha, the Sheikh's son-in-law, third member of the triumvirate and then commander on the Palestine front; and, curiously, the Emir Husain, Sherif of Mecca and leader of the Arab Revolt. A notable omission was Talaat, second member of the triumvirate.

everything'. (In a tantalizing aside – no records exist of the earlier talks – Kerim declared that 'that which was possible last time was no longer so now, consequently the programme must be altered'. The assumption must be that the situation had become more difficult, or dangerous, to manage – and therefore more expensive.) Even so, in those happier days of the proud pound, Zaharoff was still well within his original margin of £4,000,000 sterling. It was good value. Although it is difficult to break down the costs of the war on the Middle East fronts, the subsidies to the Arabs and other incidental expenses of operations against the Ottoman Empire, the global cost of the war to the Allies was by then some £7,000,000 a day.

As soon as the retainer was paid over to Kerim, he and Zaharoff would meet with Enver or Javid. He gave 'simple indications' of the arrangements that might be made at this meeting, by which time Zaharoff would have been able to ascertain the views of 'Money-Bags' to allow them to settle the details. These arrangements were set out:

$XXX to be paid to their nominees when the Turkish troops have been with-drawn from the Mesopotamian front, to a line indicated by Zed.

$XXX to be paid to their nominee when the Turkish troops in Palestine have been withdrawn to a line fixed by Zed; this line not to be at a very great distance, so as not to excite suspicion in Constantinople.

$XXX to be similarly paid when the Turkish troops on both sides of the Dardanelles have allowed the Allies to land and have delivered the forts to them.

$XXX when our Fleet has passed through the Dardanelles and the Turks have asked for an armistice, which in Enver & Co's opinion will be certain to lead to a general armistice on account of the terrible state of Germany and Austria (not Hungary).

All as neat and tidy as a City takeover conducted under the nose of the major outside shareholder, with golden handshakes for the directors, executives and staff to be presented with a *fait accompli*. Object: asset-stripping. From this point in the exchange onwards the documentation is satisfactorily complete. It consists in the main of long memoranda from Basil Zaharoff in France to Sir Vincent Caillard in London, who in his turn dealt directly with the Prime Minister. Zaharoff's first memorandum was summarized and edited in London; thereafter, as the pace quickened, his reports were hand-written, often on the train bringing him back to France, and were typed in London for transmission to the 'chairman', Lloyd George. These reveal at last the authentic voice of the man of mystery.

Following his May visit to Switzerland, he was, on the evidence of a large cheque he drew on his personal account at the Bank of England, in London in June to receive instructions before he made a further trip to meet Abdul Kerim in the middle of July. The sticking point was the $2,000,000 'retainer' for the introduction alone, which would have been irrevocably lost had the resulting negotiations fallen through; and whatever discretionary powers Zaharoff held, he clearly shied at committing government money to such an uncertain end. 'If the money had been his,' Caillard informed Lloyd George in a covering letter of 1 August, 'he should have risked the two million dollars, as he thinks it would have been worthwhile.' Zaharoff's health, too, was giving him trouble; his latest journey had had 'a most unfortunate effect ... and he is obliged to go to bed for a fortnight.' (He was two years short of his seventieth birthday when he undertook these travels.) Caillard, looking forward to another meeting with Lloyd George, meanwhile enclosed Zaharoff's memorandum:

On meeting A[bdul] K[erim], Zed began proceedings by producing the Morgan telegrams etc. ... AK did not look at these, but said that once Z had the funds he was to deposit $500,000 to AK's credit at the *Crédit Suisse*, Zurich, and handed Z an envelope (in my possession. V.C.), addressed to the *Crédit Suisse*, Bureau Central, Zurich, adding that the $1,500,000 were to be deposited to Enver's credit at the *Banque Suisse et Française*. [AK] ... said ... that the moment Z had met Enver & Co his part of the bargain ended, and he would leave for the US to prepare the road there for Enver & Co.

He further said that Enver had told him last week that he would need some little time to square certain people mentioned in Zed's last letter but that he had fixed the appointment at Lucerne [where Enver's wife had been since the beginning of 1916] for exactly 35 days after the money was placed to his credit at *la Banque Suisse et Française* ... When AK had finished Zed told him, word for word, what his instructions were from his Principals, upon which he calmly said, *'C'est à prendre ou à laisser'*, and notwithstanding all Zed's efforts to re-open the conversation, he remained mute, gave Zed his hat, salaamed him gracefully, and dismissed him.

Z remained on for two days in hopes of running across him, and also to give himself a rest, and as a last resource, before leaving for Paris, Z went to luncheon at his Hotel. AK was in the Dining Room, saluted Z politedly [*sic*], and when he was half way through came and smoked at Zed's table, spoke of commonplace things, and although Zed tried to touch upon the question AK evaded it, wished him *bon voyage*, and started for the door. He stopped short, came back, whispered in Zed's ear *'Tenez l'oeil sur la Mesopotamie'* and walked out.

Note

Before Zed left for Switzerland, I sent him a cutting from *The Times* [reporting a Turkish Cabinet crisis, with Enver's star on the wane] but he did not receive my letter ... until his return. He took an opportunity of showing the cutting to Monsieur Berthelot, Permanent Under-Secretary to the Foreign Office, so as to ascertain his opinion. Monsieur Berthelot told Zed that the French information is quite the contrary of *The Times* report from Athens, and that Enver is after the Kaiser the strongest man in the Central Combine. Much stronger than the Emperor of Austria, and that he is consulted upon everything, and almost always gets his way.

The 'take it or leave it' suggests some cooling on the part of the Turks. In fact, they were anticipating a counter-stroke which would strengthen their hand.

At this stage in the game Lloyd George was still playing a lone hand. He had not raised, at least not as official business, the Turkish peace talks at his newly founded small War Cabinet, nor does Hankey throw any light into this corner. Caillard was unable to arrange his desired meeting; after waiting patiently for over two weeks he returned to the charge in his own hand on 17 August:

I have tried two or three times to see you on Zed's last report, as I am very desirous of discussing that situation with you for a few minutes. There is, too, the question of returning the money if it is definitely decided not to use it – as Zed does not like, in this case, to have it lying at his credit: he points out that he is mortal, and that if he were to disappear, 'difficulties might arise'. On the other hand if, on further consideration, it *is* to be used, there would be no advantage in returning it. I should be extremely grateful if you could manage to see me today, or tomorrow morning, for just a few minutes. I venture to call your special attention to AK's hint to '*tenir l'oeil sur la Mésopotamie*'.

And what was cooking in 'Mespots' that Zaharoff should keep an eye on?

After the capture of Baghdad, the British had consolidated their sway over the outlying green belt and had brought up the railway from Kut, providing themselves with a direct link with the Gulf. But the Turks did not take well to the idea of the City of the Caliphs in alien hands. 'In the late summer,' recorded Sir Charles Callwell, then Director of Military Operations at the War Office, 'it appeared that the Turks under German instigation were contemplating an effort to recover Baghdad.' The 'late summer' was precisely this summer of 1917. Abdul Kerim, rubbing his hands a fraction prematurely at the prospect of some reversal of fortune, had been unable to contain himself, and the hint was gratefully taken. 'This', continued Callwell, 'made [General Sir Stanley] Maude the keener to resume the offensive, and on 28 September he struck his first blow by the capture of Ramadi on the Euphrates.'

It is hard not to feel a certain sympathy for Kerim's subsequent deflation.

Another point is now clear from this latest letter. Zaharoff had not only Morgan's telegrams, but substantial sums of money already at his disposal in his own hands. The $2,000,000 retainer had, of course, to be paid up promptly to secure the negotiations; he had more time to find a further $10,000,000 which would 'pay for everything' and which was conditional on the staged withdrawal of Turkish forces.

That there was money in circulation, and in more than sufficient quantity, is proven by another most curious incident – unsatisfactorily incomplete as our knowledge of it is. The scene is the Treasury. The Chancellor of the Exchequer, Bonar Law, is ensconced with his Private Secretary, J.C.C. Davidson. They have a caller, a director of Vickers, who informs them that he has received a message from the Turkish government to the effect that they were willing to engineer an armistice if a sum of money could be made available.

'I actually handed to —— for payment to Enver as the leader', Davidson recorded many years later, 'a sum of money I think about £780,000, in return for which they promised to negotiate or create the situation of asking for an armistice.'

Unfortunately it is impossible to fix the date, even approximately, for this charmingly casual encounter at the Treasury. And there is the odd sum, peculiarly precise, although it is the random recollection of an old man. It would have made at that time something over $3,750,000, almost twice the total of the retainer. Davidson resurfaces later; he was evidently more closely bound up in the business than he was able to remember.

There is no record of further activity until 27 September when Zaharoff sent notice from the Château de Balincourt that an invitation had been received in Paris that morning 'which will take me to Switzerland in the middle of next week. I will *not*', he emphasized, 'telegraph my departure.'

Despite this touching regard for observing security, he had, as later emerged, overlooked the routine censorship of the ordinary mail leaving France.

Silence descends again. It was not a promising season for the Allies.

In October the Italians, only narrowly escaping the final fate of Serbia and Romania in previous autumns, had been shattered at Caporetto. By the first week of November the full extent of the folly of Passchendaele was evident. The offensive, sanctioned with foreboding by the Cabinet and continued in an unequalled spirit of bland optimism, broken assurances and falsified hopes by the British commander Haig, had come to a squelching halt where it had begun months before – in the Flanders' mud – at a cost of 400,000 men. At the same time in Russia an attempted counter-revolution by moderates let in the Bolsheviks and opened the way to an armistice that would release over fifty German divisions for service on the Western Front. On 14 November, Jaffa fell to the British, working their way up the Mediterranean coast – a very meagre ray of sunshine.

Zaharoff, on the evidence of his weekly accounts promptly paid at the Carlton Hotel, was in London from the middle of October until the middle of November, but communication with Lloyd George still passed through Caillard. In November Caillard wrote once more to the Prime Minister:

I received a note yesterday from Zaharoff, now in Paris, in which he says 'Abdul Kerim will arrive next week and I will be there to meet him.' This note is dated November 18th and curiously enough on November 17th I wrote to Zaharoff that, in my opinion, present conditions in Turkey and information I have recently received concerning Turkish feelings towards Germany point to the probability of this being probably an opportune moment to renew negotiations.

I have also heard that the Turks might ask for an Anglo-French guarantee of their Public Debt, which I believe amounts to somewhere about £150,000,000. I haven't of course an idea of how the English and French governments would view such a proposition, but I informed Zaharoff of the rumour which had reached me, in order that he might not be taken by surprise.

By this time Hankey was aware of the Zaharoff approaches. They were the subject of discussion at the first meeting of the Supreme War Council towards the end of November at which, Hankey noted in his diary, Clemenceau, Prime Minister since the middle of the month, informed Lloyd George that he would make peace with Turkey on any terms, and gave the British premier a free hand to negotiate.

Zaharoff, still according to Hankey, reported that Enver was unwilling to treat. This is curious. Zaharoff might well have been exasperated and close to despair, wary of the Turks' good faith, but he must have considered that he still stood a chance. And there is no confirmation that he had yet met Enver himself. If he had paid another unrecorded visit to Switzerland, it would not have suited Kerim's book to pass on this impression as his opinion; his retainer still hung in the balance.

Zaharoff also reported that the Turks were in a state of great depression. They were short of food and called vainly on the Germans to help them. They were also short of coal, their railway communications in consequence utterly disorganized; this had prevented them from making any attempt to recover Baghdad, on which they had set great store.

The War Cabinet seems simultaneously to have been taken into the Prime Minister's confidence. There was, after all, the need to agree a collective government opinion on the terms to be tendered to the Turks; Zaharoff himself was pressing for explicit instructions regarding the Ottoman Debt* and territorial designs in view of the evolving situation in Russia.

Caillard brought Lloyd George up to date in a note on 6 December. Kerim's anticipated arrival in Switzerland had been delayed; Zaharoff, accustomed for some years to winter in the balmier air of Monte Carlo, had been unwell once more, although he hoped to be sufficiently recovered to be able to travel to join Kerim by the end of that week or early the next. Caillard obligingly offered to put off 'an unhappy time with the dentist' the next morning in order to learn the Prime Minister's views. He was instead received by Bonar Law, who was acquainted with his chief's intentions. (It may have been on this occasion that Caillard left with £780,000. The political concessions had been hammered out – the Foreign Secretary, Balfour, had issued his Declaration which settled the future of Palestine five days before; it remained to determine the cost of a possible arrangement with the Turks.) The heads of agreement, which Bonar Law confirmed to the Prime Minister that same day, ran:

To give as his personal opinion that Allies do not desire destruction of independent Ottoman State nor surrender of Constantinople but freedom of Straits to be secured. Arabia to be independent. Mesopotamia and Palestine to be Protectorates on analogy of Egypt before the war.

Autonomy for Armenia & Syria.

Capitulations to remain abolished and generous treatment to Turkey as regards finance.

It must be doubted whether the Turks would have accepted a 'personal

---

* Caillard now put this at 'anything from £150,000,000 to £2,000,000,000'.

149

opinion' as sufficient guarantee on such grave matters. Perhaps Zaharoff tactfully omitted the reservation.

Two days later Jerusalem was occupied by Allenby's forces, and Zaharoff was off to Switzerland on another errand. Lloyd George, however, was preparing a parallel initiative. There seem to have been any number of Turks, more or less discontented, angling in that neutral country for openings. One such was Mouktar Bey, head of a Turkish Red Crescent mission, who, although a friend of Talaat, inclined towards a settlement with the Allies; another was a Dr Parodi, agent of an opposition faction, who made contact perhaps through the British Minister at Berne, Sir Horace Rumbold. Philip Kerr, Lloyd George's Private Secretary, accompanied by General Jan Smuts, met him there on 18 December.

Parodi admitted to Kerr that any movement for peace had to come from within the ruling Committee of Union and Progress in which the Germanophile section, led by Enver optimistic of a German victory and Talaat confident of a negotiated peace on the basis of the status quo, had the upper hand. The balance of opinion might be shifted, Parodi suggested, if the Allies were to set forth their peace terms in a clear and precise fashion. (This Lloyd George did in a speech early in the new year.) The main concern of the opposition was money: Turkey owed Germany £300,000,000 and would require outside aid to remain independent. (There was as yet no precedent for repudiating war debts.) Kerr was left with the impression that any separate peace with Turkey was not attainable, but he repeated to Parodi, to pass on to his friends, the proposals already outlined by Bonar Law.

This would have confirmed Lloyd George's belief that the surest route to success was to treat direct with Enver. Zaharoff was already working his way to this goal. The next evidence is his own memorandum to Caillard, handwritten in pencil, but not dated. He now had authority to pay over the retaining fees, which he did, thereby setting up a meeting with Enver, who was occupied on a month's tour of the Palestinian and Mesopotamian fronts, for the end of January.

Brother mine,

I have just returned and go to Monaco tonight in an ambulance, for a real rest. I'm ill.

I first saw AK[erim] on Wednesday and repeated to him, almost verbatim, the contents of the letters you wrote me after you had seen your Treasurer [Bonar Law].

He asked me to put it in writing, but I suggested he should take notes himself, as I was too ill (true) to do so and he carefully noted all the items. . . .

I did not go one iota from your letter. He took notes ... and only made one remark when I said Constantinople was not to be given up ... 'This will please.'

It was agreed that I should pay the $500,000 and $1,500,000 into the Bank as originally suggested and this I did the day before yesterday 13th inst.

At meals, champagne and much brandy, made him talk more than on previous occasions, and as your Chairman [Lloyd George] told me to make him talk, I did my best.

He said that at the War Council of the Central Powers, held at Head-quarters last week, the Kaiser presiding, the Germans said that the principle [sic] and perhaps the only great effort was to be made on the Western Front, with every man, beast and arm available and this as quickly as possible, in fact immediately, as the troops coming home from the Russian Front were well accustomed to the cold.

The Germans and Austrians were evidently agreed on this, but Talaat insisted strongly and vehemently upon rapid assistance being sent to Mesopo-tamia and Palestine, the loss of which had entirely destroyed Turkish prestige throughout Islam.

Hindenburg replied that this unhappy state was only temporary and that the moment the Allies were badly beaten on the Western Front, as they surely would, they would beg for peace on their knees and they would not only have to abandon Palestine and Mesopotamia but would be made to give to Turkey Aden, part of the Persian Gulf, Egypt and the part of Greece of which Turkey had been robbed.

This did not satisfy Talaat and as E[nver] agreed with Hindenburg, Talaat went for him, in most violent Turkish and as it looked as if the two were coming to blows, Hindenburg promised Talaat every and immediate assist-ance and the necessary Protocol was signed, but AK said knowingly, 'Bakal-lum', adding 'I will myself give Talaat his coffee.'*

At the same War Council Bulgaria insisted upon a swift and crushing attack on the Salonica Allies, before Greece had time to mobilise and this was agreed to subject to a consultation between the Kaiser and King Ferdi-nand [of Bulgaria] on the following Sunday, in the train.

The Bulgarians said that Salonica Forces, as they are now, are not strong enough to put up a serious defence.

AK said there was a deal of mistrust among the Central Powers, most

---

* A Turkish colloquialism, approximately translated: 'Tell that to the Commander of the Faithful's galley guards.'

of them keeping their secrets to themselves, and this is why the Kaiser and King Ferdinand would talk secretly of the projected attack.

[It never materialised; the Bulgarian army was in no shape, either in morale, or armament, to take the offensive.]

The Austrians said that Germany had not given them all the most solemnly promised assistance against Italy, and that this failure had given the French and English ample time to send troops to help the Italians, thus making the knockout blow very doubtful. Hindenburg retorted almost mockingly 'You only needed a little German bucking-up, to restore confidence in yourselves', and at lunchtime later on said, 'The Italians also needed moral Allied bucking-up.'

[Lloyd George had overriden the generals' reluctance to release men and guns from the Western Front to be rushed to the aid of the Italians after Caporetto. They arrived just in time.]

E told AK that Germany was suffering immensely and could not carry on much longer, and was consequently obliged to try and end the war quickly by beating the Allies on the Western Front and before the Americans could enter the field.

[Kerim then exposed at some length the evil conditions in Central Europe – and the ingenious expedients to counter them: 'cotton for explosives had been advantageously replaced by certain Baltic seaweeds'. Many foodstuffs, ores and minerals were entirely lacking in Germany; there was emaciation and immense mortality among even second- and third-line troops. In Austria-Hungary food was more plentiful, but morale was low. Bulgaria was the best off as she had refused to allow the Germans to despoil the country. The Turks were undoubtedly the worst off in every way, and the people were perishing.]

AK says E has to go to Palestine and Mesopotamia and adds that this will help our affair, but when I asked him in which way, he replied, 'Wait and see'. E's Asiatic trip will take a full month but he had already made the appointment for me to meet him at Lucerne from January 25th–31st and I have agreed to keep the dates.

You *must* give me two or three weeks rest car je n'en puis plus, and then you must send me full instructions based on my original letter about the Turks withdrawing to a certain line and our paying a certain amount and then withdrawing to another fixed line and our paying again and finally opening the Straits.

Are these demons to be trusted? Will men who offer to betray their own country be loyal to us? I do not know how to take AK's talk at dinner before I left. He was drunk and said I was to 'get out' quick and he only had to lift a finger and I would be arrested as a spy, conspiring in a neutral country against friendly belligerents* at the instigation of the Allies. I laughed it out and put it down to drink, and although we parted on the best of terms, it makes me think.

I should add that A K never saw my handwriting nor my signature.

Ever thine,

Zedzed

These, and the ensuing disclosures, must be unique in the annals of the Great War at such a level: a voice direct from the heart of the opposition War Council. At this time the German High Command was supremely confident of victory; or at least of a negotiated peace that did not envisage even a partial renunciation of their annexations by conquest. This was not entirely wishful thinking. The war had still a year to run, and to many thoughtful people on the Allied side there was no end in sight. Even Foch, arch-optimist, confided to Clemenceau as late as the summer of 1918 that the next year would be the decisive one.

The ball was now in the Chairman's court, while Zaharoff was able to restore his flagging spirits by the Mediterranean over Christmas. At the Treasury they were doing their sums. On New Year's day Caillard pressed the Chairman for 'instructions without delay please'. That same day Bonar Law saw Clemenceau, who was aware of Zaharoff's role as intermediary; he still had no objections 'but points out the dangers and recommends precautions'.

The services now had their finger properly in the pie; the War Office sent its recommendations to the Prime Minister a few days later.

1. It is agreed that in the event of a free passage through the DARDANELLES being opened to British submarines and of a favourable opportunity being afforded there to torpedo the GOEBEN & BRESLAU and to return through the DARDANELLES the sum of $5,000,000 will be paid.
2. It is agreed that in the event of all Turkish troops in PALESTINE and on the HEJAZ Railway being withdrawn North of the railway line from HAIFA TO DERA'A a sum of $2,000,000 will be paid and the following guarantees will be given.
   i. The Turkish forces will not be molested while carrying out the withdrawal.
   ii. PALESTINE will not be annexed or incorporated in the British Empire.

* In the German-speaking districts of Switzerland, neutrality was less benevolent – understandably – than in the French and Italian.

iii. All Turkish officials who have been displaced in PALESTINE by the advance of the British troops will receive life pensions equivalent to the pay of their official positions.

This last would appear a quite extraordinary proposition; it had not even been proposed by the Turks. It must also have offended the Treasury; it was excised by a firm blue pencil stroke.

Caillard received this on 9 January. It was the signal for Zaharoff to recommence his packing. Before he left he proposed to have Lloyd George's speech, in which he had tempted the Turks with terms, translated into German for Enver as it was sure to have been misinterpreted by the enemy's press. Caillard, in a letter of 16 January to his 'Cher Ami', suggested also that Zaharoff should stress that the Turks would be allowed to retain their flag in those districts placed under *conseils judiciaires* on the Egyptian model, a point which the Chairman had not mentioned but had now been consulted upon. He sent a copy of his letter – 'The best wishes of all go with you' – to Paris in case Zaharoff had already left Monte Carlo.

An amendment, initialled J.T.D.,* was now rushed from Downing Street to Caillard:

$10,000,000 will be given to secure permanent safe passage through the Dardanelles and Sea of Marmora. This would entail the evacuation of the forts and defences in the Dardanelles and on the islands of the Sea of Marmora and their occupation by British forces. When the above is secured we will endeavour to obtain the revictualling of Constantinople from Southern Russia through the Bosphorus, which would have to be opened.

The reason for this change of heart was that the menace of the two German ships had been removed, one disabled, the other sunk. The way to the Turkish capital was open. But Zaharoff was already on his way.

For what followed we have Zaharoff's own account. Life, he was to find, was not all a bed of roses.

In the train   January 29th, 1918.

My dear C

In order to get through quick I will write each time the train stops and post it en route, if finished.

I left with the Doctor [his personal physician] on 23rd in a saloon car which the French gave me, and which the Italians undertook to deliver to the Swiss Frontier, for which I had to pay 24 1st class tickets.

* (Later Sir) John T. Davies, Principal Private Secretary.

Our trouble began the moment we got into Italy, and before we reached Genoa, our car was invaded by Italian troops who forcibly drove us into the corridor and took possession. We asked the officer in command for protection. In vain.

We had a luncheon basket with some special diet food for me; it was all eaten by the soldiers, and then the knives, forks, plates, etc, etc, divided among the bandits, and finally the basket itself was given by a non-com. officer to a friend who came to meet him at the station. Officer said nothing.

We were four days and four nights getting to the Swiss Frontier, hardly any food except some soldiers' rations, no bed, no wash etc, etc, and useless complaining to officers. When we saw trouble ahead, the Doctor and I divided the cash, each keeping half; mine was taken from me by force, right before the officer.

In the middle of the third night we were dragged out of the train, and on our presenting the letter of the Italian Railway Company and our 24 tickets, the Station Master looked at them, put them in his pocket, and told us to go to H. . . .

[Not perhaps the treatment Zaharoff was accustomed to on the Orient Express; but then the station master, even in better days, was unlikely to be used to an elderly joker travelling on 24 tickets.]

The next morning a Military Chief Doctor, seeing me half frozen and almost delirious, began talking to my doctor, and when he was told our plight, took compassion on us, and actually changed his itinerary to see us safely to the Frontier. Bless that man! I will never forget him and will keep in contact with him.

[It would be nice to know the sequel to this. Zaharoff was never a man to forget a good turn.]

All the above made me very ill, and my Doctor as well, but the idea of being in Switzerland, at last, gave us courage. Alas, my real troubles, my martyrdom, began at its very door.

The Authorities evidently suspected me of something, they searched all my things (I had not a single paper with me, and had learnt my instructions from your Chairman by heart), they stripped us naked and took our clothes into a room to examine them. Cold is my skin's enemy.

It was 7.00 a.m., minus 12 degrees below zero. At about 10.00 o'clock they brought my clothes, the stitches of which were so ripped open that I did not recognise mine. While my Doctor was dressing me, some of these brutes began looking at my bleeding skin; one went away and returned with a quarantine doctor, who declared me to be suffering from a dangerous contagious disease, and consequently not allowed to enter Switzerland, and when I was finally dressed, I was taken by two soldiers to the hospital where I was put to bed. God, what a bed, what a place!

155

In the afternoon two doctors, accompanied by my own, examined me and said I was free to go.

My Doctor discovered that the conduct of the Swiss authorities was dictated by their desire to gain time, pending their communication with Berne and getting a reply about me.

The continuation of this letter in the train was interrupted by Drowsiness and it seems that the doctor had some trouble with me but here I am, and when I finish and post it I'll go to bed.

I continue. We travelled comfortably to Geneva, where I had to meet AK[erim] as arranged and go on to Lucerne with him.

[Zaharoff broke off here.]

As your Chairman is too busy to read all the above, he need only read the following:

We got to Geneva on the evening of 27th, two days later than I expected, but AK said no time had been lost and that instead of going to Lucerne to meet E[nver] he was coming to Geneva next day, and we would all lunch together.

E arrived in the morning, but strongly objected to meeting me, claiming that all his movements were being always watched by the inquisitive Swiss; that AK was badly suspected of intriguing with me, that the Swiss were more Niemtze [Hunnish] than the Germans and in the same breath he strongly advised me not to show my nose outside, because the King of Greece told him only on the previous day that his Staff were boiling to get at me and drink my blood.

I did not see E, but AK kept going backwards and forwards as a sort of telephone, and the following is the pith of these singular conversations.

E said he had not given AK full authority regarding the money, consequently all the money would be returned to me, including AK's share. AK being afraid of E, told him he would return his share to me, but to me he said he would not part with one piastre; he had honestly done his share, and if E was now backing out, through fear, it was not *his* fault.

Many discussions took place about the money. At one time E said he might keep $500,000 for a certain eventuality, but not for himself, as if he came to grief, all that he would need would be a pistol. He afterwards said that he would return all the $1,500,000 and it looks as if he were in earnest because Frs.5,000,000 [just under $1,000,000] have already been placed at my disposal in Paris....

Although the *Breslau* was sunk and the *Goeben* disabled before I left Monaco, I thought it wise to refer to my instructions about them, and I am glad I did so. E said that had these ships still been safe, he could not do what we wanted, because when he, E, found that some of the Turks in the Dardanelles were not up to the mark, he gave over the Straits entirely

156

to the Germans. E says that without making a formal promise, he can arrange for the Turkish armies in Palestine and on the Hejaz Railway to be withdrawn North of the railway line from Haifa to Dera'a, but as he had not a reliable map at hand, he said it would be done 'approximately', but he would not accept payment for this, nor for anything else.

E said twice that he did not know whether the British rule in Mesopotamia and Palestine would not be preferable to German rule, and he emphatically said that if the Germans won this war Turkey would be Germany's vassal. A German victory might seem good to the present generation of Turks, but the inevitable was that they would become German in time. (I have brought back the impression that E is sick of it, and that he is preparing the way to talk to us some day.) He repeated that notwithstanding solemn promises, the Germans had done nothing to relieve Mesopotamia and Palestine, and that Talaat was furious at having been deceived, and had just gone to Headquarters to persuade them to act.

E said that the Kaiser had told him that 'le sort de Palestine et de la Mésopotamie serait décidé sur le front français'.

E's personal opinion was, that so much time had been lost, during which the British had made their Fronts in Turkey so secure, that the Turks and Germans would have a very hard nut to crack.

E said that six months ago he had made every preparation for a separate Peace, and that Talaat was in accord with him, but that when Russia and Rumania began crumbling Talaat told him – 'mais de cela je fais mon affaire'. He regretted that I had not shown confidence in him last summer.

E said he had confirmed his opinion of the sufferings of the Germans and Austrians, of the differences between the two States and Hungary; he actually used the term 'bluff allemand' pretending to be able to hold out for years, and expressed it as his own opinion that the war would be decided by the Americans putting or not their whole heart in it, and quickly.

E certainly means to do away with Talaat in some way or other, and in any case seems to be more friendly towards us than the Germans, and if possible would like to do us a good turn, whether for money or not I cannot tell.

AK said that at times E dreamt of a Turkey from the Adriatic to India, and at others seemed willing to throw up the sponge.

AK repeatedly told me he would not return me the money.

I enclose cheque for the Frs.5,000,000 which E returns, and when the balance comes, I will remit it to you, and although it may not be necessary, I think your Chairman would do well to leave the money in your hands, as we may still need it for the same object.

Next morning I found that E and AK had taken French leave and I immediately took train for France.

I have given my heart and my soul to this scheme and its failure has quite broken me up.

    Toujours à toi,
    Zedzed

AK said of E; 'Il est traître, ne le croyez pas, ne vous y fiez pas, il vous vendra. Dans ce grand monde, pour lui, il n'y a que lui.'

Caillard passed this touching document on to Lloyd George on 4 February. The result, he considered, 'is certainly a great disappointment . . . but he cannot have given up all hope'.

It is difficult to gain an impression from all this of where precisely Enver stood, if indeed he was sure himself. Originally and staunchly pro-German – he even affected the same full moustache as the Kaiser with the ends turned smartly up – he had now become pessimistic about Germany's chances, and sceptical about any further material aid for Turkey in her distress; he was seriously concerned for Turkey's future status, win or lose, yet he still had no sense of urgency to reach an accommodation. This was not the talk of a strong man. His role is passive, docile even.

Talaat on the contrary, although described by General Henry Wilson as 'an oily schemer without principles', emerges as the energetically forceful figure, urging action and assistance, reproaching his allies. There must have been leadership and personality problems within the Committee. If Enver had accepted the British terms at this juncture, could he have carried the majority of the Committee with him? And the pro-German faction, even in a minority, still had the support of sufficient loyal troops led by German officers who could have dealt firmly with any dissidents at the top table.

Enver recognized that Turkey was now on her own and would have to look for support in the not so long term – without our hindsight the time scale would not have appeared so urgent – wherever she could find it. And there was only one alternative source. Resigned and despondent, he does not seem to have had the courage to follow his convictions; perhaps he was just hoping to play for time, to keep the door open. Unlike the outraged Kerim, he was apparently not looking for reward for himself.

Disappointed though he might have been, Zaharoff did not expect an immediate decision. He too was content to leave the door at least unbarred.

15

A Last Throw

When Zaharoff returned from Switzerland 'quite broken up' by the failure of his mission, there was a tonic awaiting him in the post.

His old company had always been an aggressively forward-looking organization, quick to react and adapt. It was already considering its future role in the post-war world. Over coffee and croissants Zaharoff opened a letter which must have offered some small recompense for the discomfort and the affront of which he had been the object on his journey. It was from the chairman, Albert Vickers, imploring him to reconsider the termination of his agreement with them. It was a bracer. Although he had tendered his resignation, it had never been accepted or refused; he was in limbo. (Not, however, a needy limbo; he had continued to draw the same expenses 'if it was necessary to incur' them; he received a round £30,000 in 1917.)

At a recent fully attended board meeting, Vickers wrote,

there was a unanimous wish that I should express to you the Directors' high appreciation of your services, and the great pleasure with which they all look back on the intimate and friendly relations ... between you and the individual members of the Board as well as the Board collectively for the many years ... your connection with the Company lasted; they all hope that these relations may continue for many years to come.

He suggested leaving the discussion of the definite financial arrangements till 'we next have the pleasure of seeing you'.

Although his own answer can never have been in doubt, Zaharoff tarried for over a month before acknowledging the 'very flattering and encouraging' tone of the request. Perhaps he thought that pride required that he should not respond with too much show of haste, but that he was genuinely moved emerged from a charmingly disarming telegram he sent to Sir Trevor Dawson just two days later: 'I sincerely thank you for the sweet letter signed by Chairman which gives me full satisfaction for many years of unhappiness . . . I am grateful to all of you. *Amitiés*.'

Zaharoff was back in the family after two years' exile. And as evidence that he lost little time in recovering his old form, the same John Coffin through whom he had channelled his resignation reported in July to Caillard that 'Sir BZ tells me that he has arranged with you for the sum of £30,000 or £35,000 to be paid on account of his 1% commission.'

For by this time he was 'Sir' – of a sort. On 14 March 1918, he had been created a Knight Grand Cross of the Most Excellent Order of the British Empire – an honorary award in his case as he was a French citizen, although no one, with just one eminent exception, seriously questioned, let alone begrudged, his use of the title; press and public accorded him the right to it without dissent. And he can be said to have earned it; few gentlemen of his age can have acquired it so disagreeably through hours of exposure in his drawers on a hostile platform in mid-winter.

In the meantime Zaharoff's *cape et épée* days were not yet done. At the time that he was picking up the threads with Vickers, he received a mysterious visitor direct from Kerim or Enver – 'a real lady from Switzerland' – who read him a letter in French, allowed him to take it down in dictation, and then burned it. The letter ended on a practical note: 'Give 2,000 francs to the Lady for travel expenses.' The contents of this communication, with a second received from the same source the next day, apart from the intelligence that the Germans had completed five small submarines for despatch in sections by rail to Vladivostock with Russian consent, are not known, but they were deemed of sufficient importance for Caillard to request a meeting with Lloyd George. Two days later Lord Murray of Elibank insisted that Zaharoff himself was very anxious to see the Prime Minister, and would he join them for lunch in a private room at the Bachelors' Club? This stikes an unwontedly urgent note. Hitherto all matters, even those of a delicately confidential nature, had passed by post through a third person. Had Zaharoff received any hot intelligence which justified a visit to London and a meeting with the Prime Minister at short notice?

The German High Command, having resisted the British attempt to clear the Belgian coast, embarked on a decisive bid for victory.

Ludendorff's aim was to strike where the enemy was weak whereas the Allies usually chose to batter their heads against the enemy's strongest points. The preparation for the offensive was accordingly made with great stealth in order to maintain surprise. Aided by fog, Ludendorff launched his attack on 21 March, overwhelmed the British in the Cambrai–St Quentin sector and within a week had penetrated to a depth of forty miles before the impetus slackened. Whether there was any link between Zaharoff's Turkish leak and the German offensive must remain pure conjecture; British GHQ were certainly not prepared for it, but then they habitually ignored even their own intelligence and aerial reconnaissance reports.

Zaharoff was back in London for two months from early June. In the middle of July Lord Murray set up another meeting between Lloyd George and Zaharoff over dinner in a private room at Claridge's. Zaharoff was advocating the resumption of his offensive against the Turks for which he needed to renew his instructions personally from the Chairman. Zaharoff was off again to Switzerland by mid-August.

As he re-embarked, his services were coming to be more highly regarded. He was in line for the Order of the Bath. The timing was exceptional. He had already been honoured five months before, and in the interval there had been, as far as is known, just the one abortive trip to Switzerland, unless he had also purveyed something else of importance. He was thus still wet behind the ears from one knighthood; and he was now being proposed for promotion to one of the more ancient orders of chivalry – and moreover to its highest rank. That there were fears that this sudden elevation might cause comment is evident from a letter from the Foreign Secretary, Arthur Balfour, to Lord Derby, who had been translated to the Paris Embassy in April. 'My dear Arthur,' Derby replied:

Thank you for your letter about Zaharoff. I do not quite know how a GCB for him would be taken. It seems to me a little soon to give him something after having just given him an honour. Would it not be possible to all at events wait until the New Year's list? I think if he was included with other names it would attract less attention than if he was given one special by himself. There is no doubt he is an extremely useful man who evidently wants to play the game by us and has great influence in French Political circles. With regard to calling himself Sir Basil, I presume you will write to him and tell him that he must not do that though of course if you wished it I would see him on the subject when he comes back to Paris. I suppose the reason he is not allowed to call himself Sir Basil is that he has not received the 'Accolade' which I think is the right word for being knighted, by being slapped on the shoulder with a sword!

Leaving aside the somewhat condescending tone from his eminence as the 17th Earl, Derby is incorrect about the use of the title. It was, as we have seen, honorary. It is not, unfortunately, recorded if either the Foreign Secretary or the Ambassador did approach Zaharoff on the impropriety of dubbing himself 'Sir'; in any event it had no effect. No doubt he regarded the subtlety as an irrelevant abstraction. He was duly appointed an honorary Knight Grand Cross of the Order of the Bath on 1 January 1919.

While his rewards were being weighed, Zaharoff was in Switzerland again. As usual he reported on his visit to Caillard, who passed it on to the Chairman on 24 August. Caillard wished, at Zaharoff's request, to discuss with Lloyd George personally 'the presence in Switzerland of another "envoy", and Abdul Kerim's views about money, and Zaharoff's reluctance'.

August 21st 1918

My dear Caillard,

I write this with your gold pen in the train on my returning to France.

I had to wait in Geneva five days for Abdul Kerim, who had gone to Berlin to see E . . . who was just returning from a War Council at the German front.

Abdul Kerim told me E was on top again and that Talaat and the others were nowhere and that E's ascendancy was due to the Turks believing he would very shortly sign peace and give them bread.

[This confirms that Enver had had problems, which might account for the six months' silence since Zaharoff's last mission, but that he had now recovered his position and prestige within the Committee of Union and Progress. The new Sultan, who had succeeded his brother in July, was under his control.]

E had left for Vienna, Sofia and Constantinople and would then come to a general Conseil de Guerre in Berlin at which, for the first time since the war began, the foreign ministers and finance ministers of the Central Powers would be present. . . . E told [AK] he particularly and urgently wants to see me, as the time to deal had arrived, and he preferred dealing with me, as he had not full confidence in the Envoy the Allies had sent to him to open pourparlers.

[Zaharoff had obviously not been informed of any parallel initiative.]

AK either did not know or did not want to tell me who the Envoy is . . . and I must here tell you, Caillard, that it would be a mistake for the Envoy and myself to clash, and please tell your Chairman that as my intervention might interfere with the official Envoy's action, I hope he will agree with me that I should quietly retire, especially as I dislike spending large sums of other people's money. You know I have spent and continue spending my own millions freely for the Allies, but I do not relish handling big amounts, for which I cannot obtain receipts nor render accounts, besides which the official Envoy is in a better position to negotiate than I would be. Kindly assure your Chairman that I will, with much pleasure and with all my energy, assist his Official Envoy and will be most loyal to him.

He [Kerim] said that at the next Plenary Conseil de Guerre to be held in Berlin, the Central Powers would, in all probability, decide to go entirely on the defensive, and withdraw their forces to lines now being prepared, very far back from the present ones in certain sections and that parts of Belgium would be given up. E had told AK that the Kaiser's influence and personality were on the decline and that at the last Counseil de Guerre, Austrian, Turkish and Bulgarian delegates had, for the first time, asserted themselves and had criticized the Germans.

[On 8 August, the British had struck an offensive blow, the first decisive action with tanks, which had a severe psychological effect. Ludendorff later described it as 'the black day of the German Army'. The Kaiser, when informed, remarked: 'The war must be ended.' Ludendorff was pressing for an armistice which he ingenuously hoped might allow him to withdraw the German army intact from the occupied territories.]

Hindenburg and Ludendorff threw the blame on one another, and the Kaiser did not dare to intervene.

The Director General of Artillery, General von Gruger, said they had used, destroyed, and abandoned so much ammunition on the Marne and Montdidier fronts that they were actually short even for urgent needs and that it would take six to seven months to get to normal again.

The Germans told the Austrians, Turks and Bulgars that, for the moment, they could not supply them with guns, ammunition, clothing, boots, saddlery, harness, Maxims, tools, explosives, instruments, aeroplanes, railway material, nor in fact with anything but money, as they had not enough for themselves at present, but impressed upon them repeatedly that they could have any amount of money by simply explaining their needs.

At least half a dozen times AK attacked me for my want of courage and activity and for my folly in not accepting E's conditions, right on the spot, there and then, when he first proposed them to me, as he felt sure that had I grasped E's terms the war would have ended ere this.

[For him to have reported this exchange, Zaharoff was clearly convinced that he had been correct not to accept. The negotiations, anyway, never seem from the evidence to have reached such a positive stage.]

At the last Conseil de Guerre, the Kaiser asked if nothing could be done to separate the Allies or to create trouble between them, when E replied,

'It is the Allies who will separate us,' and this was well received by all but the Huns.

The Emperor of Austria said it was a pity that the only reliable news about the fighting on the French Front came from Allied communiqués, upon which the Kaiser got furious and abused his Austrian Ally with strong language, finishing by telling him that *he* personally was the first cause of so much of their misfortunes, because by his criminal intrigue he had let the Allies know that the Central Powers were not united.

[Peace talks between Austria and the Allies had begun over eighteen months before, first through Prince Sixte of Bourbon-Parma, then through Spanish mediation. Under provocation Clemenceau had publicly revealed the overtures which had effectively ended the exchange.]

Very hard things were said about the German Government and Admiralty having over and over again, and by statistics scientific yet false, assured their own Allies most positively and beyond any doubt that the submarine was doing havoc and was fast bringing England to her knees and that under the very best conditions 100,000 Americans would never reach Europe.

They recalled the fact that the Kaiser, previous to the Americans declaring war, was somewhat disposed to abandon submarine warfare, rather than invite, so to say, the Americans to enter the War, but as the Kaiser was weak on this subject, submarine warfare was voted by 26 votes to 5.

During a hot discussion at the last Conseil de Guerre the Turkish General Izzet Pasha Schishman,* had spat at King Ferdinand, and if anything, the Pasha was applauded.

Austrian, Bulgarian and Turkish Generals and their staff fought so much among themselves at the Hotel Adlon in Berlin that the Police and even the Military had to interfere and now each country's delegates go to separate Hotels when passing through Berlin. AK said E had instructed him to pump me as to the way the Allies intended treating Turkey if things went badly for the Central Powers and to this I replied by writing out for him and E my definite and precise instructions from your Chairman ... and AK said that when I first gave them my instructions E had said that they were fair and not heartless and that in any case they were preferable to the present German heel on Turkey.

I forgot to tell you that just as I was leaving London Monsieur Trochain [Zaharoff's accountant] wrote me that Morgans's New York had credited my account with interest on the sums deposited by your Treasurer. Will you kindly inform your Chairman and your Treasurer and add that I will hold this Interest at your Treasurer's disposal.

AK said quite seriously, 'When you meet E you should have $25,000,000 at your immediate disposal for the big coup, you remember how he could

* Newly appointed Adjutant-General, opponent of Enver, proponent of Turkish neutrality.

not resist the cash temptation last time.' [The evidence does not support this.] To this I replied that I would do nothing of the sort, but that if a proposal were made I would see what it was worth to me in dollars, and I should here tell you, Caillard, that the last time I saw your Chairman he told me he was now prepared to pay. I am not. AK as usual said I was a fool and never ready to grasp gigantic opportunities.

AK asked me what I was prepared to pay for a verbatim report of all the Conseils de Guerre at which the Turkish delegates were present, and on my replying that such reports might be interesting, he said, 'Man, they are worth millions, very many millions.'

AK says it may be two or three weeks before I can meet E and by that time your Chairman may have decided if he will give me any further instructions.

Although we should take cautiously much of what AK has told me, we have to frankly admit that up to now every one of his statements to us have been verified in time, in fact we cannot yet put our finger on a single untruth.

I regret that this report shows that I have not attained anything definite, as I remain, Mon Ami chéri

    Toujours bien à toi

    ZedZed

PS Since my arrival in Paris this morning I have remembered the following:
100,000 marks would be paid for the best method of coping with tanks, but only if the idea is adopted.

[The German military were slow to take up the tank. Only when it had been used against them to such effect in early August did they put it on the 'urgent' list.]

AK said he had been with E to see the trials of immense bombing aeroplanes which were supposed to lift 10,000 kilos tout inclu.

[The Germans were far ahead in bomber development; their heavy bombers could carry loads of 500 kilos for several hundred miles.]

AK asked me about the effect of the Big Bertha guns on Paris and the Parisians, and after we had discussed this subject he said that the Erhart gun works had made guns which carried over 160 kilometres and that two each of these were being built into unarmoured Monitors which were simply fast floating batteries, of which the Germans expected big results against the English.

[Nicknamed after the redoubtable head of the Krupp family, the Paris gun weighed over 140 tons, the barrel being half as long again as a cricket pitch. Its range was 120 kilometres. Bombardment had begun in March 1918 and continued for almost five months, firing approximately every third day. It had some effect on civilian morale. Total casualties were 256 killed.]

Caillard almost certainly did get his desired interview with Lloyd George, in which they agreed on a course of future action. This was doubtless summed up in a letter which Downing Street arranged for Lord Reading, recently returned from the Washington Embassy, to take over to Paris. It was to be delivered to avenue Hoche at once.

For the moment the matter rested. Enver himself had other calls on his time, which was running out for him. In pursuit of short-term gains, he had diverted all troops destined to reinforce the Syrian front to consolidate the territorial advantages won from Russia in the Caucasus by the treaty of Brest-Litovsk. In Palestine the battered wreckage of the Turkish forces, their rail links cut, had been rounded up. On 1 October Allenby entered Damascus and raced on to Aleppo.

There was also less pressure to seek separate agreements with the enemy. The soldiers, the bit between their teeth, would not have welcomed any short cut which might rob them of their hard-earned laurels; peace through victory rather than negotiation had now become a practical proposition.

By the third week in September Caillard informed Lloyd George that Zaharoff had received another invitation to go to Switzerland and would start as soon as his papers were in order. A few days later this was called off by Kerim: they were still of the same mind, but Enver having departed for Vienna, a new appointment would be made. Zaharoff returned to the Château de Balincourt for a breather.

This extended invitation arrived but the French censor delayed Zaharoff's advice to Caillard. (Zaharoff still put his faith in mailbags although Caillard had already warned him that one of his letters had been opened. One wonders what the censor made of all this. If Enver had suspected how casually his confidences were being treated he would have suffered a qualm.) Caillard had in the meantime received a message from the Prime Minister. As a result he wired Zaharoff not to move even if invited by the Turks. This missed him. He had already taken off again; indeed he was on his way home.

In the train going to Paris   October 3rd, 1918

Here I am again, on my return to France, not feeling well, as I caught Spanish fever, which is bad all over the Central Continent.

I reached Geneva early in the morning and two hours later E and AK arrived in an automobile which they had hired at the Frontier, and they immediately sent for me.

E looks very ill indeed with the eyes of a consumptive maniac, besides which he has a bad attack of Spanish influenza. He has aged very considerably and said that he was coming straight from Constantinople and Budapest and felt quite exhausted.

[Both Zaharoff and Enver were fortunate. The 'Spanish' 'flu epidemic of 1918 was estimated to have caused 20,000,000 deaths. The French press made a brave attempt to label it the 'German' 'flu.]

After some preliminary talk E said he presumed he was right in supposing that I represented the French, to which I replied that I represented nobody, but was cooperating with some Allied friends towards a speedy and victorious peace. He said, 'but you are a very prominent French citizen, supposed to be the richest man in Europe, and you live in Paris' – to which I made no reply, thinking it to our advantage to let him continue under that impression.

[Enver enquired about the Allied reaction to the 'Peace Move' concocted at Vienna by the Austrians, Hungarians, Talaat and Enver himself. On Zaharoff informing him that it had been little more than a one-day wonder in the press, Enver added scornfully: 'I told them all along that they were boring a hole in water.']

He said that it was lucky that he had taken a dislike to the soi-disant Allied Delegate – who turned out to be an Austrian Emissary, a 'vile pese-vent'* said he, with an oath, 'but he got nothing out of me'.

[This was presumably Count von Mensdorff, pre-war Austrian Ambassador in London, who opened negotiations with General Smuts in December 1917.]

E twice said sternly, 'Mind, I don't know you and you don't know me.'

At the proper moment I repeated word for word your Chairman's terms about *delivering the goods*, ending up by saying that I was prepared to show my good faith by there and then placing $1,000,000 at his disposal on account.

[The original terms might have been modified. British forces were by then well entrenched along a line far in advance of the Haifa–Dera'a rail-link.]

To my surprise this proposal visibly annoyed him and he said there was a mistake somewhere, for he did not care for money, and wanted none, and that AK had misunderstood him and it was for this reason that he, E, had returned me the money I had placed at his disposal, to which I replied that part only of that money had been returned to me. He became violent and cried out aloud, 'Every piastre has been returned to you', and at this AK, intervening, said that a certain formality at the Bank had delayed

---

* Caillard interpreted this in his own hand in the margin for the benefit of the Chairman: 'Turkish for a pimp.'

the remittance upon which E jumped up and, pushing AK before him, said they would go to the bank, put the matter right, and return in ten minutes.

They shortly returned and E said I would find the money in Paris on my return there, adding, 'I am no Talaat'.

[At this stage, relieved of the monetary burden, Enver became obviously overwrought, even incoherent. He blamed Germany for having driven her own allies 'like swine' and for having 'cruelly abandoned' Turkey. Feeling increasingly sorry for himself, he overlooked his own direct responsibility for withholding reinforcements from the threatened southern fronts. He did not, he said, want Turkey to act alone in making a separate peace; he was on the point of persuading Hungary, 'from time immemorial the closest of friends' with Turkey – an original historical perception – 'to come arm in arm, towing Austria inevitably behind them and automatically breaking the Kaiser's neck'.]

He was very enthusiastic ... and asked me what I thought of it and I naturally expressed great approval, especially as I was really very favourably struck with the idea. He then said, 'This is why you French should help with money; I repeat that we are all exhausted and sooner or later must succumb, and the sooner the better for all concerned. There are chauvinists in Turkey and in Hungary and if we can buy them, we will save blood, money and timing ... and the whole war will end before winter.'

I asked him how much exactly his idea would cost, and he said that although he did not know much about money, he thought that 10 million francs for his Turks and 15 million francs for Hungarians would suffice, in all Frs. 25,000,000.

[That is $5,000,000 – slightly over £1,000,000 – only, including the Hungarians.]

I jumped at his suggestion, and told him that I would, within an hour, place 5 million francs at his disposal, which with the money he intended sending me to Paris, would be sufficient for his Turks. He accepted and the finances were arranged before luncheon.

As to the 15,000,000 francs I promised to arrange that they be at his disposal on my return to Paris. He said he would go at once to Constantinople via Vienna, Buda Pest, Bucharest, Costanza and that if he could dispose of the 15,000,000 francs (through a channel he indicated) by the 20th–25th instant, he would settle with the Hungarians.

I told him I was willing to pay AK handsomely for full reports of the War Council, but he laughed and said, 'I do not suppose *we* will attend many more ...', and talking of War Councils he said the Kaiser was the greatest scoundrel he ever met, untruthful, unscrupulous, false and capable of any crime; he even made the Turks blush by saying, at the last Council, 'that during Peace negotiations, or even after Peace had been signed, my

U-boats would find an opportunity to destroy the English fleet'.

[This remark was underscored in red by Caillard who commented in the margin that it showed the Kaiser in a 'most characteristic Hun frame of mind'. Some such similar scenario was in fact followed – but it torpedoed German hopes The new Chancellor, Prince Max of Baden, appointed by the High Command as liberal window dressing, announced direct to President Wilson that the government accepted his famous Fourteen Points, rather cutting the ground from under the other Allies. Then a week later a German submarine sank the *Leinster* in the Irish Channel. Wilson was offended – some Americans had also been drowned – and insisted instead that an armistice rather than peace negotiations should be settled between the more hawkish military commanders.]

E took the enclosed cutting out of his pocket and complained of it as a mean dirty lie.

[*The Times* reported maltreatment of British prisoners in Turkey by Enver.]

We agreed to take luncheon together, but when I returned from settling finances AK told me E had departed in the same automobile for the frontier and had wished me bon voyage.

I trust you will approve as I have caught the Spanish fever. I will rest and finish this tomorrow if I think of anything else.

Puffing his way contentedly back to Paris, Zaharoff might have been excused for feeling a glow of self-satisfaction. After two years and more of tricky talks with the Turks, he had pulled it off.

In fact, he was in a fix. In Paris, he found Caillard's telegram awaiting him, and he had just paid over to Enver 5,000,000 francs – not quite £200,000 – and cancelled repayment of a similar sum previously outstanding from Enver and Kerim. Still, he might have argued that the subsequent successful completion of his mission was sufficient justification. Caillard certainly thought so. Forwarding this report to Lloyd George on 10 October, he expressed his hope that, in view of its 'great interest and importance', the Prime Minister would agree with him that it was lucky his restraining wire to Zaharoff had arrived too late, thanks to the French censor.

But events were overtaking them. In the middle of September the Allied forces at Salonika, after years of stagnation and wastage, had finally taken the offensive, and by the end of the month the Bulgarians, hungry, worn out and ill equipped, sued for an armistice, thus endangering Austria. It was partly this collapse that spurred the German High Command to parley.

Meanwhile the Turks themselves, their capital now threatened by the forces liberated from Salonika, decided to call it a day and on

30 October signed an armistice on board HMS *Agamemnon*. (General Townshend, a respected prisoner of the Turks since the fall of Kut, was one of their intermediaries with the Royal Navy.)

And that was the end, some loose threads of a financial nature apart, of Zaharoff's Turkish marathon. Unfortunately, there is no indication at any time of Lloyd George's views on the affair, or of his instructions, except that from the middle of 1918 he was prepared to pay up. There is not one mention of the mission in all his voluminous *War Memoirs*, a curious omission. The only reason can be that these were written some years after his fall, which resulted from the disastrous end to the Graeco-Turkish War, leaving him with bitter memories of the Turks, the Greeks and, as he might have seen it, those who had pushed him into the rash adventure. Zaharoff was one of these. In addition, Zaharoff in the meantime had become notorious, quite enough for any prudent Liberal politician to wish to mark his distance. The Prime Minister sought to blame the generals for the breakdown of the negotiations, claiming that the Turks had been dissuaded at the last minute by the publication of a leak by Colonel Charles à Repington, military correspondent of *The Times*, on the pessimistic Manpower Report. There is no evidence for this.

As for Enver, in spite of his loss of hope for the present and his pessimism for the future, he never seemed to be ready for a settlement until the whole edifice was visibly cracking. He had lost all power for action; he drifted. If he had been more resolute, he would have found support for his action close at hand; there was Izzet Pasha, a long-time opponent of the war who was in a commanding position with the army since the summer, and Mustapha Kemal – later to be known as Atatürk – the most successful military leader and friend of Kerim. But personal animosities and jealousies precluded such an alliance.

Unfortunately we know nothing of Zaharoff's reasons for refusing the earlier offer from Enver to which Kerim refers in passing. Perhaps Zaharoff was too timorous in venturing other people's money, about which he showed signs of a fixation, in an engagement which carried too little assurance of success, but as soon as Enver made a firm proposition at their last meeting, he immediately complied without any apparent firm guarantees.

Within weeks of Zaharoff's return to Paris, the Committee of Union and Progress dissolved itself. Izzet Pasha took over the remaining reins of government in order to treat with the British. Kerim joined the Sultan's entourage, and sank with him. Enver, Talaat and Jemal fled on a German warship to Russia. All three met violent deaths, although the latter survived long enough to publish his memoirs. Enver collaborated first with the White Russians, then switched to support the Bolsheviks in the Caucasus. Despatched by them to Turkestan where his dream of an oriental Islamic empire revived, he joined the local rebels and was killed leading a force against the Red Army near Bukhara in August 1922, a year after Talaat had been assassinated in Germany by vengeful Armenians.

Before the Turkish armistice was signed, Zaharoff awoke to his troubles. He had not exceeded his instructions – indeed he evidently enjoyed fairly wide discretionary powers – but affairs had outdistanced him. He was having an uncomfortable time. We are afforded a maddeningly brief insight into this owing to the kindly intervention of his friend Walter Long, Secretary of State for the Colonies. 'My Dear Prime Minister,' he wrote on 22 October,

It is no part of my business but I venture to suggest that Zaharoff should in no circumstances be called upon to pay the £600,000 himself. He has telegraphed instructions to stop payment, but telegrams to Switzerland take a long time & it is possible the money may have been paid. I therefore venture to suggest that if you decide that he is not to find the money himself it would greatly please and relieve him if you were to tell him that the money will be found by the Government.

On the envelope Lloyd George added a petulant: '*Chancellor of X.* I thought you had arranged this.'

And then an old friend, J.C.C.Davidson, Bonar Law's Private Secretary, resurfaces briefly. The next day he wrote to Miss Stevenson, the future Lady Lloyd George:

I have shown Long's letter to the Chancellor. He tells me that Z told him that he could & would stop payment of the £600,000.

I wonder how Long knew about it – I thought only the PM and the Chancellor were aware of Z's Turkish activities.

How was this alarming sum arrived at? Enver was already holding £200,000, to which Zaharoff added a further £200,000 before leaving Switzerland. The further 15,000,000 francs – or £600,000 – for the Hungarians was to be paid on Zaharoff's return to Paris. He must have put this transfer in hand, as he promised, out of his own pocket – an eight-figure sum in present-day values – before clearing it first with London.

The most reasonable explanation is that the Treasury had now written off the initial £400,000 to bad debts – painful as it must have been – and Zaharoff was urgently trying to stop the payment of the second and final instalment. Lloyd George could not have seen Zaharoff's report till late on 10 October at the earliest, that is almost a week after his return to Paris. Zaharoff must then have been summoned to London – he was there by 15 October – to be put in the picture, by which time the £600,000 was on its way to Switzerland. In spite of Long's concern, Zaharoff had already seen the Chancellor and declared himself confident that he would manage to arrest it in time. But he must have experienced a few tense days. The ensuing silence on the matter argues that he succeeded.

What might Zaharoff's reward have been if these negotiations had been concluded earlier? Right up to the late summer of 1918, the results would have brought great material relief to the Allies, and proportionate discomfort to the Central Powers: the loss of the first prop of the Quadruple Alliance, the cleavage of the Dual Monarchy. How many lives might thus have been saved that were otherwise wasted? Haig for his efforts was rewarded with an earldom and a grant of £100,000 from a country which, grateful for the end, was prepared to overlook the means. (Zaharoff had certainly spent as much as that of his own money on bullying the Greeks into belligerency.)

In the same vein it might be added that not one of the Vickers, who had produced the guns, the ships, the planes and the tanks that had made Allied victory possible, received any recognition for their services. (The sole armaments peer, Lord Armstrong, had purchased his title extravagantly many years before.) True, it might be argued, for they had received their own reward, that their companies had prospered – within the limits imposed by the government – though equally the strains and burdens of wartime production created problems which were to dog them in the difficult aftermath of the war.

A not unnegligible interest in this whole history is just how much it reveals of the somewhat perverse character of the leading actor. It is the only adventure of his long life which he never wantonly advertised, even to his intimates; if he had done so, there must have been a passing reference in at least a letter or diary. There was nothing. And it is the only one which can be said with absolute certainty to be literal and truthful.

News of it within their lifetimes was restricted to a cosy circle: Zaharoff himself and Sir Vincent Caillard; the 'Chairman' and the 'Treasurer'; Clemenceau was in on the coup, and the War Office for the nuts and bolts of the terms. Davidson's surprise that another minister – and not the least; the Colonial Office in those days handled all Near Eastern affairs – was in the know is an indication of the extreme discretion with which the matter was treated. Hankey was aware earlier that something was afoot, but was not apparently in the full confidence of the plotters; and his diaries were anyway not published until almost fifty years after the event.

Not one of Zaharoff's obituarists as much as hinted at the drama although they lent uncritical credence to many far-fetched tales. The only contemporary reference that can be traced appeared in the 'Peterborough' column of the *Daily Telegraph* in the week following Zaharoff's death. The writer was shown some papers and letters, presumably in Lloyd George's possession, relating to these 'highly delicate negotiations'. The reason attributed by 'Peterborough' for the breakdown was that Enver 'revealed a distinctly exaggerated estimate of his own importance and the price he asked for his personal goodwill was too high. It was in the neighbourhood of £1 million.' If those were the same papers, the columnist cannot have read them too carefully. The £1,000,000 is near enough the equivalent of the 25,000,000 francs for the Turks and Hungarians; some of this, of course, could have stuck to Enver's fingers, although there is no support for this view in the surviving evidence. As a result of this alleged greed, 'Sir Basil broke off the negotiations and returned empty-handed.' Sir Basil had not broken off the negotiations. He had instead returned with the deal sealed, if not signed. It was just too late.

Oddly, this brief single revelation never seems to have excited any press or biographical interest, then or since. Its next appearance, in which it rated a footnote, was with the publication in 1956 of *Men and Power* by Lord Beaverbrook, who had by then acquired the Lloyd George papers.

In later years when Zaharoff had become the object of obloquy, he never deigned to defend himself by pleading good deeds. With impressive unconcern for present reputation – and posterity – he kept silent.

16

Benefaction

A last wartime adventure, by Biggles out of Buchan, is attributed to Zaharoff. The tale unfolds in a straightforward enough fashion; the plot, like any good sauce, thickens.

'During the war,' Sir Basil related simply,

I went into Germany to discover certain things that Lloyd George and Clemenceau wanted to know, in the uniform of a Bulgarian doctor.

I paid heavily for that uniform, and the man who sold it died. Well, I got the information and I was in the train making for the frontier when to my horror I noticed that a German officer, sitting opposite, hardly ever took his eyes off me.

For three solid hours I was obliged to remain there, with his eyes boring into me. Whenever I looked up I found him staring at me, and certain papers in the lining of my coat began to burn a hole in my chest. [He must have regretted that he had not trusted to his good memory as he had already done in neutral Switzerland.]

At last, when the frontier was at hand, I could bear it no longer. I asked him why he was so interested in my appearance.

'Herr Doktor,' he said, twisting his moustache, 'You must pardon me if I annoy you, but you are exactly like my sister's husband, who has been reported missing.'

God in heaven! I could have kissed the man on both cheeks, I was so relieved.

I wired to the Quai d'Orsay, of course, as soon as I was over the frontier, and when I reached Paris all I thought of was driving straight home to a bath – I hadn't had one for a fortnight – but the stationmaster was on the lookout for me.

'There is someone who wants to see you,' he said with much mystery, and led me to the official waiting-room, where Clemenceau threw himself into my arms and kissed me as I had wished to kiss that fantastic German.

When we had talked he said: 'Now you must go over at once and tell Lloyd George. He is waiting for you.'

'But my friend,' I protested, 'I must have a bath first.'

'You can have your bath in London,' he said, and I was hurried into the first train with a new order in my buttonhole, to be greeted in London by Mr. Lloyd George with the GCB in his pocket.

They say that the information I brought ended the war.

So much for that. This information is said to have triggered the final assault on the Hindenburg Line.

Foch's great offensive got under way on 26 September 1918. Zaharoff had returned to Paris from Switzerland at the end of August. There he waited for urgent clarification from London and instructions for future action before another meeting was set up with Enver within the next two or three weeks. He would have been most unlikely to risk losing contact for a fortnight with the Turks, whose summonses gave him only short notice. His next invitation, which arrived no later than 20 September, found him in Paris. Prior to September his time can now be accounted for as far back as the first week in June when there was no consideration being given to bracing thoughts of an offensive; the Allies rather were fighting desperately to hold off successive German offensives.

The recipient of this recital, recorded fifteen years after the event, was the traveller and author, Rosita Forbes. The shower of orders that awaited his return may be accepted as embellishment, or excused, as it has been by those who have sought to justify the tale, as the fading memory of an old man on the grounds that the GCB was not conferred on him 'until 1921'. On the contrary, this is the one part of the whole adventure which is plausible; the myth-makers managed only to confuse themselves. Lloyd George would have known perfectly well since the summer of 1918 that the Bath was in the pipeline – though hardly in his pocket – but was not to be formally announced until the following January.

As for the other, he was created a Grand Officer of the Legion of Honour on 30 June 1918, on the recommendation of the Minister of Foreign Affairs for extraordinary services to the Allies, but he had been in London for the three preceding weeks and would not leave until the middle of August.

Other doubts resurface. 'You're not to write a single word about me until after I'm dead,' Basil Zaharoff admonished Forbes. 'Promise or I won't talk.'

It is barely credible that a man who had carefully destroyed all his personal papers three years before would break the habit of a lifetime to indulge in just such autobiographical prattle to which he so objected. Why did he not instead regale Rosita Forbes with an account of his Swiss trips? It is this that suggests that, cornered by a personable but pertinacious woman, he satisfied his whimsical humour, and her thirst for original revelation.

There is another more practical objection. Through his Turks he was familiar with the most confidential deliberations of the enemy Supreme War Council, supplemented with the frankest information on the morale and condition of Germany. What more can he have hoped to garner by risking his neck?

It was long known that Zaharoff had supplied information of great value to the Allies – Clemenceau himself was witness to this – and some means had to be established by which he obtained it. A specious case was made out of this to explain the escapade of the pseudo-Bulgar medico. Lloyd George is said to have come into possession of two pieces of related information from The Hague. Ludendorff, the German commander, glooming over his prospects, took 'encouragement from the fact that Basil Zaharoff, who is in a position to know, has counselled the Allies against expecting to defeat us this year [1918]. If Zaharoff really thinks this, it gives us time to recover, but everything depends on the Russians.' The Swedish Ambassador on the other hand reported that 'Basil Zaharoff has changed his mind on the subject of a further campaign in 1919 before victory can be achieved. He is very much concerned at the possibility of Socialist revolts in sympathy with the Bolsheviks, and now believes that Germany cannot resist both the Allies and a revolution inside her own territory.'

Zaharoff was accordingly quizzed in Paris by Lloyd George in front of Clemenceau: 'Which of these versions is correct? What do you really believe?'

Zaharoff replied:

It is true that I don't think Germany could possibly be completely and militarily beaten until next year. It is also true that if we have to wait as long as that the Bolsheviks may take advantage of us. Remember Berlin is in some ways an easier prize for the Communists than it is for us. *We* could not reach Berlin by defeating the German armies before next spring, but the Bolsheviks might capture power there long before that. But the only accurate answer to these surmises can be got from Germany itself.

So far, so good. This is doubtless a reasonable representation of his views.

Lloyd George swooped on this. 'Then,' he said, 'you must go there and find out.' Clemenceau thought this sally a huge joke, but Zaharoff gravely replied that if the two Allied leaders wished him to go to Germany, it could be arranged. Lloyd George took him at his word.

This conversation is alleged to have been passed to one of the editors of the elusive *Documents Politiques de la Guerre*, on which so much of the legend hangs, by Clemenceau's son, Michel, 'who was acting as an adviser to the French Premier'. Michel, later at least employed by Zaharoff, never enjoyed such confidence. Before the war he had been involved in a scandal over government contracts, his father refusing even to speak to him until Michel joined up in 1914. The *Documents* nevertheless proceed to elaborate the plot.

Zaharoff insisted on laying a false trail. It was to be put out that he was off to Athens. A chance Bulgarian military doctor was kidnapped in Switzerland and brought back to France by the agent Nadel, where he was grilled on his habits, family and career, his friends and his foes, and his past. The two men were of course the same height and build so as to spare Zaharoff's tailor fussy fiddling with alterations; and both men wore beards, although Zaharoff had to restyle his – which it must be supposed he had regrown. Facially, however, there was no similarity so Zaharoff was obliged to avoid all contact with anyone the Bulgar knew, or might have known – a tricky conjecture. In return for his co-operation the doctor was promised his freedom and a golden handshake; instead, he was poisoned.

What happened in Germany is not clear but we are told that it is certain he went to Berlin and Potsdam where he 'seems to have remained strictly incognito' – the whole point of the disguise. He also sent a secret message to Herr Krupp through an emissary to warn him that unless an armistice could be arranged, he might find his factories confiscated by the Bolsheviks. (He might more safely have done this from Switzerland.)

There is not one whit of evidence in support of any of this. But even without it his record of service to the Allies is impressive enough. T.P. O'Connor, in the course of an obituary notice on Zaharoff's old friend, Albert Vickers, who died in July 1919, described Sir Basil, in perhaps an excess of loyalty, as 'the man who contributed more money, more brains and more ardour to the defeat of the Germans than any individual man in Europe'.

And it was to O'Connor that he confided: 'Whenever I spend money I think how best I can spend it to the advantage of my fellow men.' This has an odiously smug ring to it but there is no doubt that he was addressing himself to the common weal. *Le Temps* claimed that he contributed 50,000,000 francs to the Allied cause, roughly equivalent to Alfred Nobel's £2,000,000 legacy. It is impossible to account for most of this.

In May 1919, Zaharoff was in London to be invested by King George V at Buckingham Palace with the insignia of a Knight Grand Cross of the Bath. (Did he this time request gracious permission to style himself 'Sir Basil'? Information of such a sensitive nature is strictly confidential but fifteen years later Sir Harry Stonor, Groom-in-Waiting and friend of Zaharoff, related to Sir Robert Bruce Lockhart that the King 'hates latter [Zaharoff] and objects to him using his title of 'Sir' as his GCB, given for bringing back very valuable information from Berlin during the war, is only honorary'. There is, however, a teasing indication in the Foreign Office archives that Zaharoff's use of the title was questioned in 1928 and that authority to do so was confirmed four years later, that is, two years before Stonor's intimation of the monarch's distaste. Sir Basil was the possessor of a signed photograph of Queen Mary and it is unlikely that that tartar in a toque would have made such a gesture if the recipient had been guilty of the least impropriety.)

While in London he took the opportunity to telephone the Rector of the Imperial College of Science for the latest news of a benefaction which had been simmering for three years. Following his bent, Zaharoff had presented Asquith in the summer of 1916 with a cheque for £25,000 for research into flight. The Prime Minister passed this on to the Air Board, which in turn approached the Vice-Chancellor of London University. Insensible to the priorities of war, a year elapsed before Imperial College was sounded out. There was still little sense of urgency. The first candidate the College had in mind was ironically killed in an air crash and the matter lapsed. No expression of gratitude or even acknowledgement had been passed to the donor. So it may be imagined that Sir Basil's inopportune call to intimate that he would like to visit his 'chair' caused consternation in the cloisters in South Kensington. Fobbed off, Sir Basil brooded over the ingratitude as much as the inaction.

Then in November he wrote to the College suggesting that they return his money as it was clearly not being put to any use. The next day he had a change of heart: he suggested the money should instead be distributed to the London hospitals – with accrued interest.

By now thoroughly alarmed, the College approached Winston Churchill, Secretary of State for Air, for assistance. There followed ten days of suspense which the College, stung to action, confidently filled with hatching plans to spend the money they looked like losing. Then came reprieve. Zaharoff informed Churchill that, as he had personally taken the matter in hand, he was reassured that the funds would 'no doubt' be usefully applied. After this wobbly take-off, the Zaharoff Chair of Aviation, the first in the United Kingdom, taking precedence over Cambridge by two years, has been filled by a succession of distinguished scientists and academics. But it was a close-run thing.

Before even this matter was happily resolved, Zaharoff took a side-step into fields somewhat removed from his trade. In a gesture of pure philanthropy, just one week after the armistice was signed, he founded the Marshal Foch Chair of French Literature at Oxford. For Oxford this was as revolutionary as the Maxim; modern languages were a recent innovation. The senior chair in a (comparatively) modern language was the Jesus Professorship – of Celtic; after the turn of the century the Romance and German languages and literature were deemed worthy of attention; French, unusually, went unhonoured. As the correspondent of *The Times*, rhapsodizing across the road in the bar of the Randolph, put it, French was 'for the first time enthroned in Oxford while the benefactor modestly veils his name'. But this endowment too, again worth £25,000, almost foundered on the insistence of the donor that the professor must be approved by the University of Paris.

In October 1920, this munificence was rewarded with an Honorary Doctorate in Civil Law in a solo ceremony, a year after the Allied leaders Joffre, Pershing, Haig, Beatty and others, and a year before his friend Clemenceau, achieved similar distinction.

There is an ironic twist to this foray into the campus: for just once the legend was over-generous to his memory. Biographies and the *Encyclopaedia Britannica* ascribe to him a twin Field Marshal Haig Chair of English Literature at the University of Paris. It would have constituted a happy conjunction if it had existed. He did, however, in December 1926, after he had heard that the Rector of the University had twice called cap in hand at avenue Hoche, send him 50,000 francs from Monte Carlo once the 'precarious position' of the University had been conveyed to him.

Two years after his Oxford début, his liberality was again imposed on. The petitioner was an enterprising Parisian publisher, Bernard Grasset, the 'Napoléon de la librairie'. Although he already had under his banner such stars as François Mauriac, André Maurois and Jean Giraudoux, he foresaw that future success could only be assured by offering the largest sums to young hopefuls to tie them down at the least cost to his house. He determined to establish his own literary prize to rival, and if possible to eclipse, the Goncourt and Femina awards. Confidently predicting that the nouveaux riches were anxious to be forgiven for their wealth by their generosity, he approached Sir Basil in May 1921, intimating that 'the great interest of the Zaharoff creation is that it will suddenly bring to light a talent quite unknown'. For such a revelation he proposed a sum of 150,000 francs to assure a suitable prize for three years. Sir Basil countered with an offer of 100,000, of which Grasset would offer 15,000 francs to the author (three times the value of the Prix Goncourt) and earmark the balance for publicity. Zaharoff considerately only insisted that the jury members should be paid for their drudgery.

Paul Bourget of the Académie Française agreed to preside over the Grand Prix Balzac which was announced by Zaharoff's Agence-Radio. The publication of the successful work would, it was promised, be undertaken by Bernard Grasset. Proust was the first to see through this: it smacks more of a Prix Grasset, he wrote to a friend, than a Prix Bourget. The Syndicate of Publishers was similarly aroused by the danger to its other members whose authors were withdrawing their manuscripts to submit them for the Balzac. The ensuing polemic created all the publicity for which the promoters can have wished.

In October 1922, the jury announced that the prize was to be shared between Émile Baumann and Jean Girardoux. There was some deception. The authors were accepted as deserving of the highest recognition – all except for the one that had fallen to them, founded to aid an unknown and unpublished writer. It was remarked that the two laureates were published by Grasset. The jury fell out. The innocent benefactor, 'a questionable European politician', was himself reviled for annexing the great name Balzac for a pittance and for 'not daring to give his own name to his prize'. In March 1924, the reconstituted jury spoke out again. The second award was to be divided among three authors. Critics pointed out that all three were again from Grasset's stable, one even having been seduced from a rival house after he had submitted his offering. Grasset threw in his hand; fiction was anyway flourishing. It is not known whether Sir

Basil managed, or even tried, to retrieve the unspent portion of his prize. On unfamiliar ground, perhaps he never realized he had been taken for a cruise through the cultural jungle.

Another act of sounder sense is documented. Finding himself in Toulon in 1912, he was distressed to see the streets swarming with sailors at an evident loose end. There were, he was informed, few leisure facilities (of the type he had in mind) for sailors or soldiers and those that existed, run by rival Catholic and Protestant missions, were of a forbidding confessional character; for the entire Toulon naval base there was just a two-room complex supported by charity drives and lotteries. He therefore offered 300,000 *francs-or* to build a clubhouse with accommodation for the navy. The ground was reserved, the (Greek) architect chosen, when war broke out. Four years later 300,000 paper francs in a deposit account had depreciated; the plans had to be modified, new land chosen. The President of the Republic laid the first stone in 1923, and work was only finished three years later.

He was also credited by the reference books with providing similar comforts, *foyers du soldat*, to complement the *cercles du marin*, for the land army. There is no record of this, yet another case of the legend overleaping itself. One reason for such confusion was that he preserved the same discretion in his public munificence as in his private life. When word of his generosity leaked out, it provided at least the raw material for good stories. Wandering one day in the summer of 1919 in the Zoological Gardens in Paris, where Escoffier had made a name for himself during the Prussian siege, he noticed that the buildings were in a state of decay after years of wartime neglect. Worse, in the cat compound the famous lion Whiskey, mascot of the Esquadrille Lafayette, was palpably rheumatic. Sir Basil complained to a keeper, who summoned the director, Professor Mangin. Zaharoff expostulated, Mangin explained. Profoundly touched, Sir Basil drew out his *portefeuille* and wrote out a cheque on the spot for 250,000 francs. Thinking he had to deal with a crank, the unworldly professor put it away in a drawer until months later an assistant found it and hopefully sent it off to the Ministry of Public Works. The real Professor Mangin existed at the Museum of Natural History to which Sir Basil, prompted by one of the brothers Barthou, gave 500,000 francs for the immediate embellishment of the Jardin des Plantes. In spite of the name, these gardens also harboured a menagerie, including big cats, although their names are not recorded. It is to be hoped that all the inmates were suitably rehoused.

Sir Ronald Storrs recorded how he was the recipient of another of these cases of instant impetuous giving. In September 1919 he was picked up in Paris for the eighty-five-minute bumpy drive to Balincourt. Lunch was *en famille*. 'Zaharoff, the millionaire of my dreams, was lying out with one foot swathed for classic gout, and with an electric bell-push in the cedar tree communicating with the secretary. He pushed it when I had shown him my Jerusalem plans [for an ecumenical heritage fund] and at once wrote me off a cheque for £500.'

A whole miscellany of other donations and favours is attributred to him. Across the Channel he presented 100,000 francs to the Ministry of Public Instruction to facilitate the publication of learned works hard hit by the rise in the cost of printing, and acquired some Mozart manuscripts for his adopted country; he contributed generously to a war hospital in Biarritz and probably to clinics in Greece, financed the Interparliamentary Union in Paris and gave 200,000 francs to the National Committee on Sports towards the cost of French participation in the Antwerp Olympics (1920) or, according to another source, the Amsterdam Olympics (1928). He is generally believed to have contributed 1,000,000 francs to the 'Save the Franc' fund in 1926 (the franc was only finally stabilized two years later at less than one-fifth of its pre-war value) and a similar sum to the 'Paris poor'. He is also supposed to have offered a palatial building for the Greek Legation in Paris but retracted his offer when informed that the gift would be subject to tax. In London his liberality seems to have been restricted to a gift of £5,000 to the Westminster Abbey Fund.

This was not all a one-way trade. In 1919 he had joined the elite ranks of the Grand Cross of the Legion of Honour, the highest award in the gift of the President of the Republic, limited to eighty holders. Louis Renault, by contrast, one of France's greatest wartime arms manufacturers, was made only a humble officer of the order in 1918.

He had another agreeable surprise. At the beginning of the war he had sent his gold plate to the Bank of France to be melted down as a gesture to the war effort, and then thought nothing more of it. One morning he opened a letter from the Bank to advise him that they had not taken advantage of his offer. The plate was returned to him intact. (He nearly lost it again. A few years later, when Rosita Forbes was lunching with him in the avenue Hoche, the tête-à-tête was interrupted by an emissary from the Bank of England. He had come to request Sir Basil to deposit a million in bullion in the London vaults to prop up the gold standard. Rosita Forbes was dismissed by her host: 'My dear, would you not like to use the motor this afternoon?' The man from the Bank, however, went away without the plate.)

When Sir Basil came over to London for his investiture, in May 1919, he brought the Duchess and her two daughters with him to share his triumph. They crossed the path of Colonel Repington, military correspondent of *The Times*, who had heard his name 'often abroad, and with some awe'. 'Lady Cunard's box at the Opera,' he noted in his diary, 'where I found Lord and Lady Carisbrooke, Lady Worthington, the Spanish Duchesse Marchena, Lady Acheson, Lady Hamilton, and some men, including Sir Basil Zaharoff whom I was glad to meet. He is the mystery man of the war to most people, but not to our Ministers, with whom he is in close touch.' Sir Basil invited Repington to lunch in a private room at the Carlton Hotel:

A large party. Lord and Lady Farquhar, Sir George Younger, the Duchesse Marchena and her two daughters – of whom I found the unmarried one, Mlle. de Bourbon,* very clever and outspoken – Lady Cunard, Mrs. Walter Long, the Max-Mullers and Sir Vincent Caillard who has almost broken down from overwork but is mending I am glad to hope. A bouquet of wonderful malmaison carnations for every lady. Found the Duchess very quick-witted, well-informed and agreeable. Sir Basil Zaharoff told us many interesting tales.

Repington's circle of acquaintance included Lady Diana Manners, a beauty famous for her rendering of a mute Madonna in Max Reinhardt's *The Miracle*. When Lady Diana married the diplomat Duff Cooper that year, Sir Basil blessed them with a cheque for £250, thus topping the Aga Khan's contribution to the kitty – a welcome gesture, it represented some five months' salary at the Foreign Office. He was more generous to Elizabeth Asquith when she became engaged to Prince Antoine Bibesco; she received, it is said, a box of white lilies accompanied by a cheque for £1,000. (Zaharoff remained on close enough terms with the former Prime Minister to receive a printed copy of a Romanes lecture Asquith had delivered, which Sir Basil read 'with avidity and am now rereading *con gusto*'.)

He was a guest of Lloyd George at Chequers. On this occasion his friend Nellie Melba auctioned an album of autographed photographs of celebrities for charity. The bidding stopped at £250. Dame

---

* Angèle de Bourbon married Jean, son of Count Léon Ostrorog, at Balincourt in 1920. During the war Sir Basil had offered her hand to Commander Sir Dennistoun Burney, the inventor of the paravane, with a retainer of £100,000 a year as an inducement. Burney always later regretted not having accepted; he consoled himself with the design and construction of the airship R 100 in partnership with Vickers.

Nellie, determined to reach a round thousand, offered to sing songs at £50 a time. After just a pair of airs even this attraction failed to work on the pockets. Sir Basil stepped into the awkward silence, so it is said, and made up the difference. (He was not quite so generous; his bank ledger reveals that he came up with just £100 for Melba in August 1919.)

All this rash giving gave rise to the wildest rumours about his reputed wealth. He suffered the hazards of such a reputation, being regularly touched for charities by duchesses downwards in amounts from £500 to twenty guineas.

Although Sir Basil was not a sociable man, he was a member of the Prince of Wales' creation, the Marlborough Club, from at least 1926. His friends and fellow members, Vincent Caillard and Lord Murray, must have prevailed on him (or the committee) that he was clubbable material.

While he was still in a generous mood, one of his more endearing propensities was to offer empty thrones to his acquaintances. As a sales technique it was original; it would have offered many advantages to have one's own man in such a place. His motive was certainly not that of any romantic royalism. 'Kings are out of date,' he once remarked. 'I believe in the dictatorship of brains and ability, not of chance.' All his considerable powers of persuasion, however, did not suffice to fill any vacancy.

He was first tempted into this novel field before the war. In 1912 he put up Prince Christopher of Greece for the Portuguese throne. He was 'very anxious for me to accept it', wrote the candidate, 'and promised unlimited financial support. I answered that the proposition did not tempt me. In the first place, the deposed King Manuel was one of my closest friends, and I wondered what part Mr. Zaharoff had played in the events preceding his abdication; it was rumoured to be an active one . . .' The Prince had a more compelling reason: he was so bald, he regretted, that a crown would be sure to slip.

(Zaharoff was not called on to play any part in Manuel's departure. The King owed his unpopularity to his suspected infatuation with the little French dancer, Gaby Deslys, who just managed to escape from the country by train one step ahead of the vengeful mob.)

Two other thrones were later offered to Prince Christopher, Lithuania and Albania. His wife's fortune – she was the American tinplate heiress Nancy Leeds – made him a desirable catch for such impoverished places.

In Albania, indeed, there was something of a scramble, a gold rush in reverse. A sovereign was seen as the token of true independence for a fledgling state in much the same way as a national airline in a later age. The Albanians' own preference ran to an English office-holder as that country had less of an axe to grind than most in the area. The first informal offer was made to Aubrey Herbert, who had been largely responsible for Albania's establishment in 1913. Money was the stumbling block. 'If I had fifty thousand a year,' he mused, 'I think I should take Albania.' The successful entrant was Prince William of Wied, a friend of Herbert's family, the Carnarvons, who lasted six months.

There followed an interregnum during the European hostilities until in 1920, having cleared their territory of Italians, the Albanians became once more absorbed in the matter. They turned to Herbert who discussed their problem with Maurice Hankey and Philip Kerr, Lloyd George's Private Secretary. It was proposed to shift the case on to the young shoulders of the League of Nations but this was ruled out lest they should have an American foisted on them who might have difficulty in finding the place on the map. For a brief moment there was a profusion of pretenders, one clique favouring an Egyptian aspirant, one the Duc de Montpensier, another the Duke of Abruzzi. Lord Howard de Walden received an offer; but he was too comfortably off at home to be lured away. An English adventurer who happened on the scene tendered the crown, which was not in his gift, to the Duke of Atholl on the grounds that his personal pipers would be popular.

Zaharoff is alleged to have favoured any candidate approved by the British government, which meticulously refrained from bestowing any endorsement, as a method of checking the pretensions of a wealthy American oil magnate, Harry F. Sinclair. Sir Basil's object was to block an extension of American interests in the Balkans, and in Albania in particular, where his stake coincided with British interests, the Anglo-Persian Oil Company. (In the following year Anglo-Persian did acquire a provisional concession in the area.) The matter was discussed between Lloyd George, Venizelos and Zaharoff. The latter suggested that the affair should be placed in the hands of Maundy Gregory, the notorious broker in honours. Unfortunately one stipulation was that any candidate should dispose of an income of £10,000 a year, and none of them had such means, let alone the little extra to pay Gregory a commission.

In the end the wily Zog, Minister of the Interior and real power under the throne, profited by this confusion and slipped into the vacant seat himself.

Zaharoff is also said to have financed the attempt of the Emperor

Karl to make a come-back in the autumn of 1921, though this was categorically denied by the Emperor's secretary, Baron von Werkmann, on the practical grounds that 'If he had really financed the Habsburg movement, it might have got on better.'

17
Slump

From the first days of the war the primary preoccupation of the British government was production of arms and munitions, but even as this problem was in the course of being ironed out, it faced the practical matter of profits. The pre-war concept of 'fair market value' for goods was scrapped in favour of consideration of the cost of production, subject to the rigorous examination of the new Ministry of Munitions. Once the control of prices was enforced, the control of profit was tackled. A formula was agreed which limited the net profit of the arms manufacturers to no more than 20 per cent above the profits for the last two years of peace. (The Board of Trade had wanted to reduce this to 15 per cent, the companies successfully held out for the higher figure.) A subsequent Finance Act then taxed the excess of wartime over peace-time profits.

In 1913 the profits of Vickers had been just over £900,000; in the first year of war they barely passed the one million mark and in 1915 were only slightly higher. After that, partly through overwork but also through inadequate control, the accounts department cracked – the Royal Ordnance factories similarly suffered – and the profits for the four years 1916–19 were lumped together at a figure of just under £4,500,000. The company thus never reached the limit of the 20 per cent increase; it did not even quite reach the lesser limit proposed by the Board of Trade.

The central powers were less constrained. Krupp, basking in the admiration of the general public as much as the military, earned double its peacetime profits in the first year of war; a tax on war profits

187

was only introduced in 1916. Profits in France were more modest – with one exception, the plant established by the American inventor Benjamin Berkely Hotchkiss which reaped rewards greater than any other European company. United States armaments firms showed themselves more sensitive to this issue. They disguised their profits by deft book-keeping; the real figures, which turned out to be almost double those published, were only revealed at a Senate enquiry fifteen years later.

Almost a year before the armistice Vickers turned its attention to the challenge posed by the conditions of the post-war world. A Peace Products Committee, with 'no false dignity, no illusions', even came to consider, in an example of flagrant sexual discrimination, the relative selling merits of 'boy rabbits (squeaking)' and 'girl rabbits (non-squeaking)'. They thus faced the future in a buoyant and expansive mood. Great hopes were pinned on locomotives and merchant ship-building for Barrow; Crayford, the home of the Maxim, turned to sporting guns – and sewing machines; Dartford to furniture, wooden toys and washing machines; the Wolseley works planned a luxury mass-produced car at £800 such that 'no American car could compete with'.

The euphoria of peace was short-lived; it was followed one year later by the slump. A further problem, shared by the other traditional arms manufacturers, was that their peacetime products were too highly priced; ironically, they found it difficult to reduce the exceptional standards required to manufacture weapons down to the lower, and less costly, standards acceptable in the civilian sector. As shipping freights fell, orders for new vessels were suspended or cancelled, and although a modest start was made to refurbish the fleet, these orders too were halted by the government as a concession to the Washington Naval Conference. These natural calamities were compounded by Vickers' acquisition of the Metropolitan Company, which had itself absorbed British Westinghouse. The aim was to create an enterprise to match the electrical empires of AEG and Siemens in Germany and General Electric in the United States, the same field Maxim had deserted thirty years before for armaments. The price paid – £13,000,000, the largest transaction ever in the United Kingdom – was too high. To aggravate these misfortunes the direction of the company too was ailing; Tom Vickers had died in 1915 and Albert had followed four years later; Vincent Caillard was tiring. Under these conditions profits slumped to half their wartime high; in 1920 the momentous decision was taken to pass the dividend.

Abroad there were loose ends to tie up, claims resulting from the slightly incestuous pre-war relationship between the largest arms companies. Vickers lodged two small claims against Deutsche Waffen, the Loewe family firm, in respect of machine-guns and parts sold up to the war which the Germans countered with a claim for £75,000 representing a share in the profits of guns sold by the British company in the territories covered by their marketing agreement. This led to acrimonious negotiations through the Enemy Debt Clearing House which resulted in Deutsche Waffen withdrawing its claim in return for a payment of £6,000 in full settlement of all accounts. The case of the patent agreement with Krupp for shell fuses was more bizarre. The Board of Trade in 1916 had suggested that Vickers should apply to the Board for suspension in its favour of any Krupp patents, and in January 1919 had further requested that Vickers pay to them all sums which would otherwise have been payable to Krupp, in exchange for an indemnity against any claims from Essen. In July 1921 Vickers received a formal claim from Germany for royalties at one shilling a fuse, a total of £260,000, for the period 1914–17. The defence was taken over by the government law officers and dragged on for some years until a compromise was reached whereby Vickers paid Krupp £40,000 in royalties for the Krupp fuses incorporated in British shells returned in earnest to the Germans and their allies.

In Paris Sir Basil must have been watching this transformation of his old company with gloom and foreboding, as much the new and unfamiliar lines as the dipping profits. (Although Zaharoff, the all-rounder, is made to say on stage that it was 'Chance, which forty years ago happened to set me down in a munition firm instead of in a chocolate factory', it is difficult to imagine him achieving the same success with bunnies as with bombs.) In June 1919 he had come to a new agreement with Vickers. He was reappointed foreign adviser on £5,000 a year – increased to £6,500 the following September – and three-quarters of 1 per cent of the profits.

His overseas empire, however, was crumbling. His Russian preserve had been cut off in 1917. Japan remained as ever outside his orbit; Italy for the moment maintained its prosperity although it faced losses in the future. Spain remained the one gem in his crown. By 1917 the first stage of the reconstruction of the Spanish navy had been completed with the building of three first-class battleships and other smaller units, and the Spanish government was then prepared to undertake the final phase with the construction of further warships, including submarines, and their armament. SECN (La Naval) was awarded the contract for this second naval programme in which Placencia shared as a subcontractor, the sole foreign ventures to continue to pay dividends throughout the first decade of peace.

In Turkey Vickers and Armstrong regained possession of the Ottoman Dock Company and took over the operation with the help of an overdraft from the National Bank of Turkey, but after the end of 1921 the company lost money and the British pulled out two years later, not before clearing the overdraft of some £30,000.

While the doors to some markets were closing, new prospects were (at first sight) opening. Despite the uncertainties of the post-war world, the outlook of the triumvirate at Vickers – Douglas Vickers, who had taken over the chair in 1919, Vincent Caillard and Basil Zaharoff – remained staunchly cosmopolitan; they saw no reason why the formula which had served them so well in the years before the war should not be repeated, and with the continuing decline in the home market it anyway offered a chance at a straw. New frontiers were being drawn but the professed priority of their inmates to achieve self-proficiency in arms production fuelled false hopes; their ambitions overran their budgets.

Schneider was also pursuing a policy of expansion. Indeed, alone of all the large arms firms, it was able to maintain its wartime prosperity and now, after the dismantlement of Krupp, it found itself in the privileged position of being the largest armaments works on the Continent. It was under French protection, with all the trading benefits that this umbrella conferred, that the new-found states of Central Europe began to organize themselves. Schneider acquired the majority holding in Skoda, which had been disposed of by the new Czech government, and it established a strong presence in Poland; Vickers, accommodating itself to this situation, teamed up with Schneider for the construction of munitions factories in that country and took the plunge on its own in Romania and Yugoslavia at the request of their governments. But the total profits and fees were trivial. Conditions were not propitious; when the arms firms proudly showed off their latest weapons at the British Empire Exhibition at Wembley in 1924–5 they attracted only the attention of their critics.

Romania was the only one of these fresh fields in which Zaharoff interested himself. At arm's length, he set about carving the company a niche in much the way he had in pre-revolution Russia. The key to his operation was Prince Stirbey, the long-reigning favourite of Queen Marie and Grand Master of Ceremonies at the court. The Vickers agent, Dr E.Madge, had acquired as assistant Georges Bonesco, a former commercial attaché at the Romanian Legations in London and Washington; from 1920 he also acted as *The Times* correspondent in Bucharest, although not a conspicuously successful one ('Bonesco sends the official declarations of Romanian politicians,' a senior member of the staff complained, 'which, you will admit, are far from being the proper contribution for *The Times*'). On the intervention of Prince Stirbey, who enjoyed a commercial as well as a ceremonial monopoly, Bonesco lost his post with Vickers and was replaced by Captain E.G.Boxshall, Stirbey's son-in-law. Boxshall went on to become Stirbey's nominee for chairman of Resita, the sole steel company in the country with interests in civil and military programmes, in which Vickers bought an interest for £45,500. Zaharoff kept in touch from his sanctuary in Monte Carlo where he entertained Prince Stirbey in style. He did not, however, build up any false illusions about the prospects. The idea of the Romanian government, he wrote to Douglas Vickers, 'is to utilize Resita to a certain extent, but not to a great extent ...'. Despite this note of caution, Vickers built up its investment to £107,000 and set up new works at Copsa Mica and Cugir. The business, however, was, in the words of J.D.Scott, the Vickers historian, 'mainly negative'. Payments for government contracts fell behind, the railways, dependent on Resita for material, assuming the interest charges. The British company extricated itself in 1934.

Another example of a *Times* correspondent doubling as an arms agent surfaced in old Serbia. Roland Bryce, nephew of Lord Bryce, a pre-war ambassador in Washington who had himself served in 1921 in the British Legation in Belgrade, was appointed *Times* man and Vickers agent with an assignment to sell submarines. As he did not speak Serbian, his journalistic duties were performed for him by the daughter of a White Russian general, the woman being at the same time an employee of the official Yugoslav Press Bureau, which effectively ensured that none of his despatches contained anything that might upset the reactionary Pashich regime. However, there being no market for submarines, first Vickers and then *The Times* dispensed with his services.

Zaharoff himself felt less of an urge to travel to such far-flung outposts unless the occasion and an exceptional commission (and even that was a secondary consideration now he had acquired a taste for political power) might warrant the effort. He was after all in his seventies, an elder statesman in the company hierarchy. The map of Europe had changed, the familiar dynasties were disappearing, the old politicians dropping out. Not that he considered retirement. He was diversifying. He was also indulging in dreams of empire. This was to be paid for with 100,000 lives.

18

Eastern Reproaches

While Zaharoff was weaving his grand design for the post-war world, his spirit hovered over the table of the Versailles Peace Conference – and prevented the principals spilling each other's blood.

His scheme was conceived on an immodest scale. Anticipating the shape of the new world, he sought to fashion an alliance of greater and lesser powers to contain Bolshevism; British firms were destined to be the main force for moulding and controlling the Middle and Far East, while Schneider was to be the linchpin of a grand alliance of francophile nations ringing Germany, although he privately insisted that Europe could not prosper until Germany once again became a thriving state.

His interests in the Middle East coincided perfectly with Lloyd George's ambitions, and came increasingly into conflict with French objectives. It was on this issue that the most violent clashes between the British and French leaders took place. These had erupted even before the war's end; perhaps, indeed, the two statesmen felt less constrained about indulging their mutual antipathy over an issue which for Clemenceau at least was secondary.

The core of the trouble was the Sykes–Picot agreement of May 1916 which had portioned out the territories of belligerent Turkey. Lloyd George was convinced that Picot had got the better of Sykes, 'a worried, anxious man', who had signed away Syria and Mosul. The prize was oil. This was succinctly settled in December 1918 when Clemenceau and Lloyd George met at the French Embassy in London.

'Well, what are we to discuss?' asked Clemenceau.

'Mesopotamia and Palestine,' replied Lloyd George.

'Tell me what you want.'

'I want Mosul,' replied the Prime Minister.

'You shall have it,' said Clemenceau. 'Anything else?'

'Yes, I want Jerusalem too,' continued Lloyd George.

'You shall have it,' replied his accommodating host, 'but Pichon [Foreign Minister and loyal friend] will make difficulties about Mosul.'

Still, this entente gave rise to continuing friction. Clemenceau, after one such incident, described 'old George [the Frenchman was himself seventy-eight] doubling up his fists and squaring off. If Wilson had not intervened, I would have given him a clip on the chin with a *savate* stroke.' After another altercation Lloyd George rose and seized Clemenceau by the collar. After Wilson had separated them, Clemenceau offered Lloyd George reparation with pistols or swords – 'as soon as he should have acquired a domicile in Paris'.

The French premier was a noted handyman with both weapons but this threat was as imminent as a Greek Kalend (his apartment in the Rue Nitot was provided by courtesy of the French government). It has, however, been interpreted as a firm challenge, after which Lloyd George was said to have begged Zaharoff to go to Clemenceau and offer his apologies, thus averting 'an almost total breakdown between the French and British viewpoints', let alone damage to the ageing principals.

Zaharoff had his eye on the Thracian road to the east which led to the oil-wells. He fervently desired to see Greece a great power. With the collapse of the Young Turks, the empire was headless and fit for plucking; Zaharoff for his share coveted the Ottoman possessions in Europe as well as ancient Byzantium. This, however, had been promised to tsarist Russia by the Sykes–Picot team and that claim now had somehow to be blocked. Although the Bolsheviks had withdrawn from the war and thus weakened their claim to the Turkish capital, it had still to be formally renounced. Zaharoff, through the mediocre militarist Wolfgang Kapp, commanding a band of freebooters on the disputed eastern front of Germany, indicated to the Bolsheviks where this secret document might be found in their archives. It was duly discovered and published, to the consternation of the signatories. In return for an assurance that the Bolsheviks would make no claim on the city, Sir Basil had 'by devious means' ensured that the campaign in support of the White Russians was called off. Further, he even contrived to divert the munition supplies destined for the Whites to be delivered instead to Greece for use against the Turks.

This surreptitious dealing with the Soviets was incautiously un-covered by Sir Basil Thomson, head of the Special Branch. Having fallen foul of the old Greek, Thomson was pressured by the Home Secretary, Edward Shortt, to retire voluntarily under threat of other-wise summary dismissal. *The Times* printed Thomson's own protest over this treatment for which no reason was offered by the government to an indignant House of Commons. Thomson's departure was not a result of any persecution but a straightforward matter of prestige and procedure. He would not accept the findings of a Cabinet com-mittee report on the secret service that he should subordinate himself to the Chief Commissioner of Police. The only mystery is why the government did not quite openly explain itself. It seems that the decision to force Thomson out produced a sharp division in the Cabi-net with Shortt, who backed the committee's report, opposed by the Conservatives Walter Long and Bonar Law; it may be that an assur-ance was given to all parties to withhold any explanation in order to avoid spotlighting this disagreement within the Coalition.

Another intelligence chief, the energetic Admiral Hall, is also said to have fallen victim to Zaharoff's backstairs influence, although no clear motive is advanced except that he was referred to inexplicably as 'one of Zaharoff's biggest enemies'. His fate was not to be invited to attend the Peace Conference which he had expected to do as head of the intelligence bureau in the suite of Admiral Sir Rosslyn Wemyss. Zaharoff, it is alleged, had written to Clemenceau: 'You must convince Lloyd George that it would be wholly undesirable for Admiral Hall to go to Versailles.' In fact 'Blinker' owed his absence to no one but himself. He had made enemies in Fleet Street and among the civilian staff of the Admiralty and there was still rancour in high places for his circulation of the Casement diaries; he had compounded this by canvassing too freely his opinion that Lord Beatty should replace Wemyss as First Sea Lord, which would hardly have recom-mended him as a loyal aide.

Once having used Kapp to sow discord and push his own plans, Zaharoff then betrayed his *putsch* to German intelligence through his friend Canaris, then ADC to Defence Minister Gustav Noske, whom he promptly deserted in the crisis. This was obliging of him, but quite unnecessary. The German General Staff was not only already aware of Kapp's plot but viewed it with a benevolent eye. The farce, which ran for one week, was finally starved into submission by a general strike after the government had fled the capital in disarray.

Zaharoff next proceeded to reinforce Lloyd George's existing ambitions in the Middle East with promises of valuable concessions for British interests in Romania and Macedonia, where Anglo-Persian did indeed come to have concessionary interests, and in Asia Minor once it had been cleared by his Greeks. (He is also said to have reinforced this appeal with a contribution to Lloyd George's Party Fund.) Lloyd George was delighted with this prospect. Zaharoff was determined that the favour should be returned.

'I want a free hand', he informed the Prime Minister, 'to direct matters in the Middle East. The crisis is near. And I want you to support every Greek move against the Turks.'

And for good measure he requested an assurance that Cyprus, annexed to the British Crown in 1914, would be duly ceded to Greece. On this count the Welshman was more canny, promising merely that the wishes of the inhabitants would be taken into 'most sympathetic and careful consideration'.

However, Lloyd George responded more positively to the other demands. Sir Basil remembered this as the happiest day of his life. 'Lloyd George had come to see me,' he recounted to Rosita Forbes. 'He was leaning against that table in the hall, waiting for his hat, when he said to me, as if it were nothing: "So it's your birthday today, is it? Well, go along and tell your friend, Venizelos, that I make you a present of Asia Minor."'

Sir Basil could not have chosen a more willing partner for his adventure, but he still required a slight push along the path to empire and the east. Zaharoff provided it in May 1919 by producing with a flourish a Turkish proclamation summoning the faithful to a massacre of the Christian population of Asia Minor. This revived old fears. Next month a Greek army, 20,000 strong, landed at Smyrna in what was intended by the powers as a preventive, and provisional, occupation. Taking their cue from the supposed Turkish intent, the Christians reversed roles and merrily set about massacring the Moslems.

The pill had been made still more unpalatable to the Turks by the Treaty of Sèvres of August 1920, imposed upon the Sultan and soon repudiated by the emergent Nationalists, which assigned to Greece not only the whole of Thrace, that is, Turkey in Europe, but Smyrna and its hinterland, and internationalized Constantinople and the Straits. While the Turks might have resigned themselves to their defeat at the hands of the British in war, that 'Greeks should conquer Turks', wrote Winston Churchill, 'was not a decree which any Turk would recognize'. Now, with the Greeks swarming on to their soil, they prepared to resist.

The green light to the Greeks was to cause a falling out among the former Allies; it was disputed within the Cabinet itself and was opposed by the military advisers. Field Marshal Sir Henry Wilson charged that Lloyd George had become 'so enmeshed with Zaharoff and the Jews' that he had been 'forced to back the Greeks against the Turks which will result in the loss of India and Egypt', and also, he considered, 'the total ruin of the Greeks . . . Who', he asked, 'is paying for Greek mobilization?'

Others were beginning to put the same question. Although the mass of the House of Commons was apathetic, a lone voice of protest was heard, that of Aubrey Herbert, a Turcophile who retained an admiration for Venizelos.

In June 1920, he quizzed the Prime Minister whether Sir Basil Zakharoff [sic], KCB [sic], was consulted with regard to the Turkish Treaty. The reply was a frosty negative. Waiting a week, he ventured to ask why Sir Basil Saharoff [sic], GCB, GCMG [sic], was not consulted. Bonar Law, leader of the House, regretted that he did not understand the object of the question.

'Is it not a fact', pursued Herbert, 'that this distinguished Greek gentleman paid for the Smyrna expedition out of his own pocket and controls the greater amount of the shares of Vickers Maxim?' (The Hon. Member was also some ten years behind with news of industry.)

'I was not aware of these facts,' replied Bonar Law in unusually jocular vein, 'but I wish he would defray the expenses of our troops garrisoning Constantinople.'

The Fates now took a hand. Venizelos, his conviction of full British support confirmed by Lloyd George, returned to Greece in triumph after the signing of the Treaty of Sèvres; his escape from an assassination attempt at a Paris station only added a sparkle to his saviour's halo. His complacency was short-lived. Alexander, who had taken the place of his father Constantine on the throne, was unexpectedly bitten by a malicious monkey in his palace grounds and died from blood poisoning. The sympathy aroused by this unusual end resulted in a rise in the popularity of the monarchist party. Venizelos, wily as he was, had lost touch with the people owing to his repeated absences abroad about their business. Over-confident and careless, he was badly beaten at the polls. Lloyd George peevishly remarked that the result made him despair of democracy.

Paul, Alexander's younger brother, refused the vacant throne. Legend relates that it was then offered to Prince Sixte of Bourbon-Parma. The Prince, naturally wishing to sound out the acknowledged king-maker, sought an introduction to Sir Basil through Edmund

Blanc, who declined on the ground that he had less influence over the Greek than his brother Camille, a partner of Zaharoff in the Monte Carlo Casino. Camille consented on condition that the postulant would grant him the franchise for a casino in the shadow of the Acropolis. This the Prince graciously accorded. Sir Basil's advice to Camille Blanc was, however, less encouraging. 'One Monte Carlo is enough for this world. And as for Prince Sixte, he is better off where he is – the Faubourg St Germain.'

This jockeying was anyway irrelevant. King Constantine was recalled to the throne by plebiscite. This gave all the parties concerned a chance to reconsider their hands.

The French were prompt to profit. Clemenceau* had resigned in January 1920 and had been succeeded by a previous and periodic premier, Briand.

The steady growth of the British presence in the Middle East and the loss of the Mosul oil-fields, although they had been assured a share of the product, rankled with the French. More rationally they showed a greater appreciation of the strength of the Nationalist revival, quite apart from the political wisdom of refraining from exacerbating relations with Islam, a view shared alike by Winston Churchill, the War and Foreign Offices, and not least the India Office. Without a word to their ally, the nationalist Radical, Franklin-Bouillon, was despatched with a consignment of cognac to come to a separate arrangement with the Turks. This combination succeeded; the Nationalists achieved recognition and arms, supplied by France and paid for by the Soviets who had already made their own peace.

British policy was less positive. The government prepared to abandon Greece without a thought of appeasing Turkey. In November 1920 Lloyd George was insisting that there was little difference between his own and French policies regarding the Greek King's return, that both recognized that the Greeks were entitled to select their own rulers; in the next breath he was proposing to inform the Greeks that the Allies did not approve of the appointment of Constantine and 'that if he is appointed they will not regard Greece in the same friendly spirit as they otherwise would'. Churchill approved this sentiment, considering that the ousting of Venizelos had wiped the slate. 'It is not every day that moral creditors are so accommodating,' he crowed, '... and if Constantine returned to the

* When Clemenceau lost office, he also lost the use of the official Rolls-Royce which the British government had considerately put at the disposal of the Président du Conseil. On the first morning of his retirement, a radiant Rolls was waiting in the road outside his home in the rue Franklin, a parting present from Sir Basil.

throne, Greece would receive no further financial assistance of any kind from the Allies.' Sir Basil, looking for the silver lining, took a more resigned view. 'Let them have Constantine, if they want him,' he is said to have declared. 'He'll rake our chestnuts from the fire and when he is finished, we'll dethrone him. We did it once and we can do it again.'

This coolness did not deter the Greeks. The newly restored King shared all Venizelos' annexationist ambitions and was, moreover, now freed from all Allied restraint. He dusted off his spurs and set out for the front. His army in Asia Minor now numbered over a quarter of a million men, constituting the largest Hellenic expeditionary force since classical times. Although they enjoyed only a slight superiority in numbers, they held an overwhelming advantage in field and machine-guns, tanks and planes, in spite of French efforts to rearm the Turks. In July 1921 this force took the offensive. Within ten days they had reached and taken Eskishehr, just fifty miles from Angora (later Ankara), and thrown the Turks back across the River Sakkaria. On 5 August, Mustafa Kemal assumed supreme command. The bitter battle that then ensued lasted for twenty-two days and nights and ended in a Greek withdrawal to Eskishehr, where both sides, exhausted, dug themselves in. Having lost their chance of outright victory, the Greeks hung on for a year.

As the situation in the Middle East soured, critics on both sides of the Channel sought a scapegoat. Sir Basil fitted the role. The constant sniping flushed him out. He came forward with a public statement for the first and last time in his life, that he had not seen Lloyd George since the spring of 1919 (he had been in London in May) 'nor has any communication, verbal or otherwise, passed between us since then'. The Foreign Office confirmed this. Its statement did nothing to stem the scepticism.

Zaharoff's *Times* obituary stated that 'at one period he was said to be bearing the cost of the Greek Army from his own pocket'. More precisely, Aubrey Herbert declared in the House of Commons that Sir Basil had contributed £4,000,000 out of the same pocket to maintain the Greek armies. Excessive as this might seem, it was still a drop in the Aegean, however welcome, against the occupation costs which were running at £250,000 a week. His old friend Skouloudis confirmed that he did finance the Greek cause out of sheer love of country; a fellow politician, Gounaris, on the other hand, complained that Zaharoff 'didn't give a drachma'. Gounaris, by then Prime Minister, was in London from October 1921 until the next February desperately trying to secure a war loan for his country. His plea was ignored. If Sir Basil had been anxious to help, his assistance in the market would have been far more beneficial than any personal financial contribution he could afford, but there is no evidence that he lifted so much as a finger. He was in London himself for the last ten days of October and may well have seen Gounaris to discuss the prospect; evidently he declined his aid, either from lack of confidence in the new regime or from pique at the ingratitude shown to Venizelos. And he may have had an additional reason for dragging his feet – doubts about Lloyd George's own future. Early in 1922 T.P. O'Connor had written to him: 'My own impression is that the Coalition is breaking up, that an election within a few months is almost certain, that the results are very uncertain – probably Conservatives at the top with a small majority, Labour next, Liberals at bottom.' That thought must have sobered Sir Basil.

Gounaris must have wondered where he stood. While Curzon was urging the Greeks to rely on the good offices of the Allies to extricate them from their impasse in Asia Minor, Lloyd George, who had staked his reputation on this adventure, misleading the Cabinet and the country, was privately urging them through Philip Kerr to stand firm and refuse any settlement. The Prime Minister's 'known and evident partisanship', wrote Churchill, 'created in Greek minds a sense of vague and potent confidence'.

Captain the Hon. Aubrey Herbert resumed his labours in the House. Although he did not want to mention names, he protested, there was one that he would mention, 'one of the strong supporters of our Greek policy. The result of that Greek policy has been that the whole of the East is in chaos, and that Great Britain has made enemies throughout the entire East ... and if the Government at any time decide upon giving a bar to Sir Basil Zaharoff's GCB, I think we ought to be told the reason for it.' (The British Embassy in Constantinople was of the opinion that Herbert was 'not quite sane on the subject of Sir Basil Zaharoff'.)

The pack took up the cry. Lord Rothermere's *Daily Mail* urged that 'this Levantine must be taught that the English nation was determined to be master in its own house', while Lord Beaverbrook demanded that the 'doors of Government offices should be shut to him and his agents'. Simple chauvinism apart, these proprietors, courted and ennobled by Lloyd George, doubtless found such stern stuff a convenient distraction, allowing them to vent their disapproval of the whole adventure without directly criticizing the Prime Minister, from whom Rothermere was still expecting promotion to the peerage and posts for himself and his family as the price of his paper's support.

Sir Basil chose this moment to make an attempted irruption into press proprietorship himself, perhaps prompted by the mangling he was receiving at the hands of the media. The move was otherwise inexplicable; he had just successfully shed his own *Excelsior* – and considered himself well out of it.

His views on the press are quite formal. 'You say you are in the throes of bringing out a new paper,' he wrote to O'Connor who had informed him of his plans to revive *T.P.'s Weekly* at this time, 'and I am really sorry for you, for in my opinion a newspaper is a terrible disease.' Yet here he was making a bid for *The Times*, which was up for sale following the death of Rothermere's brother, Lord Northcliffe, in August 1922. There were rival groups in the hunt, many of which centred round Lloyd George, who is said to have fancied himself as editor. The Prime Minister offered Sir Campbell Stuart, the Canadian managing director and Northcliffe's executor, a peerage if he could arrange it; Zaharoff instead proposed to put 'a large slice of shares' in Stuart's way if he helped him.

'This quite remarkable figure,' Stuart recorded, 'the mystery man of Europe ... did not seem to understand young men who preferred ideals to fortunes, and in me he frankly admitted he had met a type of individual he had never known.' (Sir Basil was more likely to have faltered in the face of such unaccustomed modesty.)

He told me that he did not intend to interfere, if proprietor (I had heard these words before), but [John] Walter and I should be the absolute rulers, and financially I should be very rich. It was not pleasant to have to reply that while I realised the position I occupied could have allowed me to become wealthy I felt that I had a far greater duty to perform which was to see ... that *The Times* should now and forever pass into suitable hands, and that I did not consider that those hands were his. Zaharoff bore no ill-will, and from this strange conversation came a disinterested friendship that lasted until he died.

In view of the late press lord's blatant meddling and megalomania, Sir Basil might have been excused for thinking this a harsh judgement. (Wickham Steed, the paper's editor, once found his boss chewing a cigar and swilling a mixture of champagne and brandy in his bed at the Hotel Plaza-Athenée, raving at *The Times*. 'Sir Basil Zaharoff was the real ruler of England; he was the man behind Lloyd George. He would expose them all.')

Some of this brouhaha predictably filtered across to Paris where the British Prime Minister's predicament was not regarded with great regret; differences were already emerging over the question of German reparations. Zaharoff came to be seen as the Anti-Christ by the Catholic right and the embodiment of the old enemy, *perfide Albion*, by the republican left, and behind him both parties discerned the hand of that 'redoubtable and almost autonomous institution, the [British] Intelligence Service'. Former President Poincaré, who replaced Briand as premier in January 1922, is even alleged to have considered Zaharoff's expulsion from France, but was balked by his naturalization. Caught in the crossfire of party polemics, it is small wonder Sir Basil became disillusioned with the tribe: his 'admiration for politicians waned, and with regretful philosophy he observed that sooner or later they nearly all suffered from an exaggerated idea of their importance'.

The newly elected Senator Henri de Jouvenel, editor-in-chief of *Le Matin*, friend of Briand and foe of Clemenceau, condoled with England in her misfortune. After a ritual insinuation concerning Zaharoff's relationship with the Tiger, he magnanimously conceded that:

we do not reproach the financier, who is at home everywhere, with having exploited the political influence he has acquired, here and elsewhere, to the advantage of his native country. The scandal consists solely in the support which is given to him, for his home is neither France, nor England. The nations are to be pitied which allow themselves to be harnessed to the service of international finance. . . .

When England has calculated what a policy *à la* Zaharoff, from Egypt to India, will cost her, she will also, without a doubt, be ready to make her peace with Islam. She will then be able to count on our good services, should she desire them. . . .

Such sensible advice was not about to extricate the Greeks, who had stubbornly repudiated mediation in favour of a military decision, from their perilous situation in the Anatolian uplands.

Time was running out. The Turks too were newly intransigent in spite of the fact that the former Allies had abandoned the provisions of the Treaty of Sèvres. The Greeks made one last attempt to force the hand of the British. They switched two divisions from Asia Minor to Thrace, demanding permission to enter Constantinople which would have given them strong leverage on the Turks. This was denied them. In spite of this, Lloyd George, playing his lone hand, made a speech in the House of Commons of such blatant encouragement to the Greeks that they were once more persuaded that the British government would rescue or support them in their straits.

On hearing that the Greeks had depleted their forces in Anatolia, Mustafa Kemal, disguising his intentions from the enemy as Allenby had once done against the Turks, attacked on 26 August 1922. He vowed to reach Smyrna within fourteen days to drive the Greeks into the sea. He was one day out. Fast as they advanced, the Turks never caught up with the remnants of the Greek army, who scorched the earth – and not a few Turkish civilians with it – in their path. (Many of the Greek soldiers, recent refugees, were also Turkish subjects and feared the consequence of capture.)

Brilliantly executed as the offensive had been, the Turks owed a measure of their success to failings in the Greek command. The coalition government which had succeeded Gounaris in May had appointed a political general, Hajianestis, to command; an eccentric who suffered from bouts of belief that his body was made of glass and would snap if he stood up, he directed the battle from the safety of a chair on the coast. Although relieved of his command after battle had been joined, the news of his appointment never reached his successor, General Tricoupis, before he was captured with his staff.

Only days before Kemal reached Smyrna, Zaharoff made one last-minute attempt to save his countrymen. He prevailed on T.P. O'Connor to implore Lloyd George to 'do something for the Greeks'. But it was already too late. The Prime Minister deplored the situation, but protested his helplessness. His friends cravenly blamed Venizelos' potent eloquence for their ever having backed the wrong horse.

As Smyrna burned, the work most probably of Armenian arsonists, the Greek government resigned and King Constantine was once more forced to leave the country. Eight of his ministers and advisers were tried by court-martial by the vengeful revolutionary régime which assumed power; six, including the deluded Hajianestis, were shot, the luckless Gounaris being dragged from his sick bed and given a heart stimulant to keep him upright before the firing squad. Great Britain, which had tacitly backed the Greeks while denying them the means, thereupon withdrew her Minister from Athens.

There was now, indeed, a threat of war with Turkey as the victorious Nationalist armies came face to face with British troops at Chanak by the shores of the Dardanelles. This crisis provided the final nail for the coffin of the Coalition, already in trouble at home over Ireland. Lloyd George fell, the Liberals foundered.

An urgent problem facing the new Greek regime was the influx of refugees, approaching a million and a half wretches, driven out of Asia Minor. The government succeeded in raising a loan of £10,000 which was guaranteed and administered by the nascent League of

Nations. Sir Basil for his part in the fiasco is said to have given 'several thousand pounds' to the American Near East Relief Fund and an aide was reported in Paris to have let it drop that he had organized a French syndicate to operate a casino in the Kaiser's former residence on Corfu, the profits of which would be shared with the Refugee Resettlement Commission. If so, nothing came of this amiable idea.

Meanwhile Sir Basil had disappeared, which in itself aroused suspicion. The French and British press, having discovered a likely bugaboo, were not about to let him go. After all, any man who, in the view of the Beaverbrook press, could hardly estimate his own wealth because it so permeated the financial arteries of Europe that every move of the political nervous system rested on his fortunes, must be considered of legitimate interest to any guardian of the public conscience.

There thus began a curious, though one-sided, game of hide-and-seek. Having pinpointed the man most responsible for Britain's predicament, *Le Matin* reported: 'Sir Basil is expected in London this week. England should not believe the danger is over.' The deepest mystery, announced the *Sunday Express*, surrounded Sir Basil Zaharoff's 'comings and goings between London and Paris. No doubt the sinister Greek comes to London on "private business"' – in which case, it was remarked, he had forgotten his golf clubs – '... Nonetheless his private business is the fate of nations, the plans of governments and the marching of armies.' The *Weekly Dispatch*, however, revealed that 'while everybody was searching for Sir Basil, the Greek multimillionaire was staying quietly in London . . . any number of people were passing him by [in Piccadilly] and not one recognized him. That shows the mystery in which he moves. . . .'

The mystery in fact is more simply explained by his absence, sufficient reason why so few were able to recognize him. He was in London staying at the Carlton for two weeks in the beginning of November 1919, and again at the end of October 1921. Such evidence as there is, admittedly of a negative character, indicates that he did not visit the country in either 1922 or the next year; there were no hotel bills and, more conclusive, no cheques cashed by his valet Short or his secretary Macdermott, without whom he never displaced himself. At the time he was reported in London on this occasion, he was on the way to Bucharest.

This animated speculation continued throughout the course of the conference which had opened at Lausanne to resolve all the outstanding grievances between the recent combatants and the Allied powers, at which Venizelos, in the role of roving ambassador, represented his country. Sir Basil had no interest in its proceedings, although he was accused of torpedoing it on one occasion by insisting that the pre-war Vickers' concession for the Bosphorus docks and arsenal should be renewed by the Turkish government. (It had already reverted to Vickers and was by then losing money. Vickers' interests respecting conditions of jurisdiction were overseen at Lausanne by Count Léon Ostrorog, their European legal adviser.)

After the sudden collapse of Greece's imperial fantasies, a small but efficient Greek force had been constituted under General Pangalos* on the Thracian frontier. This had greatly strengthened Venizelos' hand at the conference table; it was here that the spectre of Zaharoff was once more spotted. 'New War Plot' shrieked Beaverbrook. In a roundabout way *Le Matin* reported in January 1923 that the Turkish press had announced that the 'mystery man of Europe' was rearming the Greeks in preparation to retrieve their honour and their homes in Eastern Thrace. The *Tewid Efkiar* was cited as saying that Sir Basil had shipped 150,000 rifles to Salonika; the same source had learned from Athens that Zaharoff had raised money from the Greek colony in Paris and had let Venizelos know that he was ready to support financially a revolutionary government in his country. A Belgrade source divulged that the republican movement, centred on Salonika and headed by Venizelos and General Pangalos, was financed by the Greek bankers, Zaharoff and one Benakis, and that armed clashes were feared between republican regiments and those still loyal to the monarchy.

There was, indeed, some fire behind this smoke. Vickers applied to the Foreign Office in July 1923 for authority to export thirty machine-guns to the Hague. The company did not respond to a request for information on their ultimate destination. They instead re-applied for a permit to export the same quantity of guns to Salonika, which was refused. This transparent operation inclined the Foreign Office to believe that Vickers were deliberately trying to evade the embargo on the export of war materials, to which some hand added the footnote: 'No armament firm has any morality. In this case Vickers are stupid too.' Vickers 'respectfully' pleaded that their inability to supply the order would result in loss of employment and that the guns would anyway be obtained from another European source whose government was less scrupulous. This cut no ice.

In May *Le Matin* again swung the spotlight on to him; for a man of mystery, motive was not necessary to make news. 'Sir Basil Zaharoff

---

* Two years later Pangalos was to become an unusually interventionist dictator, going so far as to issue a solemn decree regulating the length of ladies' skirts.

suddenly returns to Paris. The Greek multi-millionaire, whose presence in London has been so eagerly canvassed this morning suddenly
returned to Paris as mysteriously as he went to London some days
ago.' When the newshounds lost the scent, it was enough to report
that he was ill and, after he had disappeared from sight for days,
the first rumour of his death was circulated. Three days later he was,
unseasonably for him, in Monte Carlo.

For the rest of the summer Sir Basil contrived to elude the vigilance
of the press. This was deemed insupportable. When the Lausanne
Treaty was at last signed in July 1923, it was solemnly recorded that
'the old man's horse passed the post first, but he was not there to
lead it in'.

There was no such animal.

Up till then the Greeks had certainly still harboured hopes for
Eastern Thrace, and it is also true that Salonika was a hotbed of republican fervour, a cause which Zaharoff was about to abandon – if he
had ever embraced it.

The catalyst for this change of sentiment was Queen Marie of
Romania, grand-daughter of Queen Victoria and mother-in-law of
the recently and insecurely enthroned King George of Greece, the
son of Constantine who had died in exile at Palermo. Warm-hearted
and generous, she had a taste for leopard skins, on which many a
good-looking foreign military attaché had slipped, and theatrical cos-
tumes. She now set about wooing the old Greek, a quarter of a century
her senior, with all her energy and talent. Sir Basil played hard to get.

'She came to see me in this house when Romania wanted a loan,'
he told Rosita Forbes. 'She had lovely hands . . . she sat in that
chair where you are sitting, with her veil thrown back looking like
a nun who'd eaten an apple off the tree of knowledge, but I said
only that I would consider the matter.

'I can see her now, sweeping out of the door, so sure of herself
that she said: "We will send a train for you."

"It may be that I shall not come."

"You will," she said.

"And did you go?" asked Rosita Forbes.

"Yes, but I kept the royal train waiting . . . while I made up my
mind."'

Queen Marie's main motive for seducing the Greek – and to keep
her image fresh in his mind she left a large signed photograph behind
her – was to make use of his influence over Venizelos in order to
secure the Greek throne. Sir Basil was in one of his playful moods
when he spun this tale. In Bucharest he let it be known that he was

there at the invitation of the Prime Minister. His personal links with the country went back certainly as far as the war when Captain Willie Walford, brother of the Duchess of Marchena's son-in-law Leopold, had been assistant to the British Military Attaché, Lord Thomson, who had also basked in the royal favour. And he was on close terms with Prince Barbo Stirbey, an even longer-standing royal favourite, and brother-in-law of Ion Bratianu, virtual dictator of Romania from 1922. Apart from Vickers' stake in the Resita steel plant, Sir Basil had developed a personal interest in oil. However, the preoccupation of the Romanian government, of which Ion's brother Ventila was Finance Minister, was the stabilization of the currency, which had fallen to a thirtieth part of its pre-war value, and the consolidation of the external debt. Preceded by his reputation, the brothers Bratianu were looking to Sir Basil to re-dress this state of affairs. He arrived in the Romanian capital in November 1922. His notoriety sparked intense curiosity, not least among the British diplomats. The *Moniteur du Petrole Roumain* speculated that if he could succeed in settling the country's finances, it was 'more than likely that [he] would not remain inactive' in the matter of oil concessions. He was not the first in the field. Walter Long, who had retired as First Lord of the Admiralty with a viscountcy the previous year, headed one rival syndicate; Anglo-Persian and Standard Oil were dangling large loans, to be secured on the government's eventual royalties and share of profits, in exchange for concessions.

As Sir Basil declined to clarify his own intentions to the press, the British Legation put its ear to the ground. The results must have confused it if it was not aware of his penchant for adding a zest of local colour to his curriculum vitae. A 'quite reliable source' reported that Sir Basil claimed to have been born at Jassy of a Romanian mother, Mavrogordato (the name, indeed, of one of his banking partners). A 'sure source' revealed that Sir Basil's sister had been governess to a local girl of good family, Miss Negroponti, after Zaharoff had lost all the family money in unfortunate speculations in his early days. And through the indiscretions of a lady-in-waiting, the Legation heard that Zaharoff had promised the King to use his influence with Venizelos to shore up the Greek throne in return for royal support for Sir Basil's plans, a consolidation loan and a con-cession for state oil lands. On the strength of his word, Zaharoff was rewarded with the Grand Cross of the Star of Romania. The diplomats considered all this unlikely; possibly Zaharoff had been misled by the King's 'trick of bowing and looking agreeable without saying a word'. The consolidation loan – for £2,500,000 – had, in fact, already gone through. Zaharoff's role had been that of a 'mere intermediary' between the Romanians and Helbert Wagg & Co. acting through the British Overseas Bank, for an introductory commission. There were soon charges flying around, levelled by 'a leading intellectual liberal', that this had been improperly excessive, and that the grand total of commissions and expenses had reached £830,000. The Prime Minister defended himself: commission had not exceeded 1.5 per cent and Zaharoff was anyway a friend of the King of England and of Lloyd George, Barthou and other leading statesmen. Sir Basil also succeeded in diverting a further loan of £4,000,000 which was being negotiated with France, in the direction of his principals. But, although the Legation still suspected that he had an eye on oil (he was known to be connected with Anglo-Persian in France), Lloyd George had now fallen and the Romanians estimated that Zaharoff's influence had declined. He had, in an opinion attributed to the Secretary-General of the Ministry of Finance, 'manqué le train'.

Sir Basil was, however, as good as his word with Venizelos. He summoned his friend to Monte Carlo to intercede with him. There is no first-hand account of this meeting, though there is no doubt it ended in tears. Zaharoff pleaded on account of all the aid he had pledged to Greece: Venizelos, taken aback by the sudden volte-face, countered that it had been accepted in the cause of liberty and in the interests of Greece. 'Are you then capable of working *against* the interests of your country?' Zaharoff is said to have asked. This was the signal for an exchange of words. Venizelos swept out of the suite at the Hôtel de Paris and departed the same night for Athens. He left Sir Basil in no conciliatory mood. 'He tried to get the better of me,' he related to Prince Christopher of Greece. 'No man has ever done that yet, though some have tried and regretted it.'

They never met again. A few years later, when informed that Venizelos wished to visit him in Paris, Zaharoff summarily dismissed the idea. 'Let him go, this Cretan, there is nothing in him. If only he would realize it is time he retired.'

It is most probable that this meeting took place in the spring of 1923. Venizelos at that date had no direct influence over Greek domestic affairs, and he could not have foreseen that he would be called back. However, in October 1923 a counter-revolution was nipped in the bud and although there was no evidence of the King's complicity, republican sentiment, and General Pangalos' pressure, was so great that the government invited the King to leave the country until the national assembly should have decided the future of the crown.

207

It is possible that Zaharoff's words had had some effect, for Venizelos, untypically in the light of his past high-handed treatment of the throne's incumbents, on his return to power in January advocated a plebiscite to settle the constitutional state of Greece. Overborne, he resigned. (An eventual plebiscite in March 1924 found in favour of a republic in the ratio of roughly two to one, but King George had his revenge; he was returned by yet another plebiscite within Sir Basil's lifetime in a reaction to a botched military coup to reinstall Venizelos.) Did Venizelos attempt to extort too high a price for his support? Did he also reproach Zaharoff for his own loss of power during the late war with Turkey, and for not having done enough to succour Greece? Or, improbable as it might appear, did he see in Sir Basil a possible rival to his own continuing ambitions? In January 1924 the Paris press picked up a report from Athens of Sir Basil's rumoured intentions. 'Will Sir Basil Zaharoff, the banker, be invited to be President of Greece?' the French papers enquired.

Privately, exasperated finally with their love of faction, he expressed his disenchantment with the country and its inhabitants. Venizelos, he declared to Queen Marie, was 'a broken vessel'.

'And Greece?' enquired the Queen.

'That is almost all over. I have burned my boats on both sides there. I do not wish to hear Greece, or the Greeks, mentioned ever again. I have finished with them for ever. They are out of my system.'

19

Banker, Oilman,
Middleman ...

The Graeco-Turkish war was seen as Zaharoff's most bitter defeat – to his pocket, his influence and his prestige. There were many in Britain, and more in Greece, who blamed him for dragging the two nations into such a humiliating disaster. Most men, it is argued, would have capitulated gracefully at that age – he was past seventy – and retired quietly to an anonymous retreat. But those who thought this episode marked his end were soon to discover that he had remarkable powers of recovery. He was destined to exchange 'the mirage of a Greek empire' for 'the substance of an oil empire'. There were those, not the least clamorous, who discerned his shadow behind each move in the battle between American, British and French interests to secure a share in Middle East oil. The legend runs that, disguised under a French hat, he first tried to lay his hand on France's sources of oil only in order to deny these to her; then to exclude all American trusts, namely Rockefeller's Standard Oil of New Jersey, from the Middle East sources of supply and, having achieved that, to pull off his hat-trick to create a monopoly over the French market in conjunction with the British group, Anglo-Persian. Quite a fistful of ambitions for any septuagenarian.

His real interest was very much more modest. Essentially, except for the foray into Romania, it was confined to France and limited to the promisingly profitable realms of transport and distribution. There is no record anywhere that he exercised any influence on oil policy.

But before embarking on his career as an oilman he mixed in other

209

matters. Both as a launching pad and as an umbrella for his schemes, Zaharoff provided himself with a bank – a stalking horse, as it was seen by his critics, for his political ambitions.

Since 1916 he had figured on the list of the two hundred most important shareholders of the Banque de France. (He retained this listing for just ten years.) His holding must have been substantial as he achieved this rank even before the transfer of £50,000 to the Banque in August 1918. This was itself seen as a trespass and was picked up in the Chamber, presumably inspired by fear that Zaharoff might insinuate himself for election as one of the fifteen Regents of the Banque who were required to be of French nationality. Deputy Jean Bon, on 26 July 1918, had already questioned Finance Minister Louis-Lucien Klotz, friend of both Zaharoff and Clemenceau, on this point.

Bon: 'Take the list of the two hundred chief shareholders who take part in the General Assembly [of the Banque de France]. Will you look at the name that comes last in the list. It is Zaharoff.'

Klotz: 'Monsieur Zaharoff is a Frenchman.'

Bon: 'He is not a Frenchman. On 12 July 1918, on the recommendation of the Ministry of Foreign Affairs, he received a decoration as "member of the Board of Directors of the firm of Vickers-Maxim and a great friend of France". Next day *Le Temps*, too, wrote that Monsieur Zaharoff was certainly a great friend of France, but that he was no Frenchman.'

Klotz: 'Newspapers can make a mistake.'

Bon: 'Can you give me the date when Monsieur Zaharoff was naturalized?'

Klotz: 'I haven't it with me. But the Chamber no doubt will believe me when I assure it that Monsieur Zaharoff is a Frenchman and has performed most important services to France and her Allies.'

The Banque de France, however, was unsuitable for his scheme; he attracted too much of the limelight (apart from the inherent difficulty, it might be thought, of persuading the other 199 major shareholders to follow him along his tricky path).

There was also the Banque de l'Union Parisienne, now one of the two most powerful banks in France, in which Zaharoff and Schneider–Creusot were said to be partners. Some went so far as to claim that this bank was under the influence 'mainly' of Zaharoff, 'who in the gay world of Paris was the representative and incarnation of the British oil and industrial interests . . .'. Something still more discreet was therefore needed.

A modest enough house, Banque Mayer Frères et Cie, was transformed in January 1918 into a joint-stock company and capitalized at 10,000,000 francs under the name of the Banque de la Seine. Among the subscribers were Basil Zaharoff with a mere 200 shares of 500 francs (but paid for in sterling, not by then a negligible attraction), Francis Barker and the Walfords, father and son; also Maurice Carrier, a colleague on Le Nickel, and Ambroise Mavrogordato of a Balkan banking family (a young relation, perhaps his son, succeeded Bonesco as *The Times*' correspondent in Bucharest, his official address in the Romanian Press Bureau being given as the Vickers office). In 1919 the Banque de la Seine was transformed into a limited company and the capital raised to 30,000,000 francs – and doubled the following year – in which Sir Basil now emerged with over 20,000 shares worth almost 10,500,000 francs, a substantial stake. He was joined by the Banque Thalmann, former partners of Vickers in pre-war Turkey, and Nicholas Piétri, a Corsican banker, friend and later executor of Clemenceau. The bank president was Léon Pissard, a Frenchman from Constantinople; Léon Ostrorog also appeared on the board. Such a fraternity would appear to the innocent (or naive) as a natural combination; in the current climate of opinion, they were regarded as Zaharoff's 'men of straw'. (A case could be made out for Carrier in this role. Zaharoff passed him amounts totalling £11,000 in 1918 and 1919 which might have covered the purchase price of Carrier's shareholding in the Zaharoff empire.) The composition of this board, proclaimed the more chauvinist circles, marked their 'vassalage' to the 'Zaharoff–Vickers' group. The Mayer brothers, Pissard and Piétri were indeed also directors of Vickers France, which was incorporated in 1919 but which was never more than a correspondent office.

It was under the shelter of this façade that Zaharoff, it was darkly hinted, was about to launch his initiative to draw the French government by sinister combinations into a policy at home and abroad which, if it had succeeded, would have placed France under the political and economic tutelage of England.

This at least was the grand scenario as seen from Paris.

His first move in this direction was to found the Banque Commerciale de la Méditerranée in March 1920, which duly set up shop in Constantinople, still occupied by the Allies. The principal shareholders in the Banque de la Seine were again in evidence, but Zaharoff's presence alone was enough to convince the morbidly suspicious that the new bank's objects were political. In the course of the year the capital was rather more than doubled to 30,000,000 francs, this time largely subscribed by the Banque de la Seine.

The next step in this progression was the formation of a French company designed to absorb the Vickers naval dockyards in Turkey. Vickers and the Thalmann bank took the largest parts; Ostrorog and Caillard too made their appearance on the board. The capital was to be boosted from a modest one to fifteen million francs. The motive alleged for this manoeuvre was to lay hands on the entire Turkish munitions and naval shipbuilding industry. This was hardly required: the group already enjoyed a monopoly in this field. Instead, such change of domicile would seem to be an unexceptionable precaution in view of the unsettled situation inside Turkey and the political estrangement with Britain brought about by Lloyd George's encouragement of the Greeks. It affected neither the composition nor the activities of the Turkish operation, the pre-war enterprise in which Vickers shared a 40 per cent stake with Armstrong. Ultimately the viability of such a venture depended on guarantees of orders from the host country. In post-war conditions these were not sufficient to keep the company afloat. The British partners withdrew in October 1923, the French company staggered on until it wound itself up three years later. In the interval it had tried to win control, according to alert French sources, of the Anatolian Railways in company with the American General Electric Company and other 'oligarchic' western groups. Zaharoff in the same year was reported by the Foreign Office, at a time when Greece's finances were in disorder and the drachma had lost over 90 per cent of its gold value, to have headed a syndicate to relieve the Greek government of the state railways and to promote a hydroelectric scheme, concessions which were considered to be a condition of a foreign loan 'of a private character'. The offer lapsed as the political situation was only slightly more stable than the currency. He was also believed in Paris to have cornered the eastern tobacco monopoly, Tabac d'Orient et d'Outremer.

All this was venture capital with a vengeance, but before any of it could be put at risk, the entire political landscape had changed dramatically.

Once the flames of Smyrna had died down, Zaharoff was said to have been behind an attempt to recreate a Balkan alliance to present a common front to Turkish nationalist ambitions. This was to be achieved by a consortium of Greek bankers offering a carrot – a sum of £15,000,000 was mentioned – on generous terms to Romania, Bulgaria and Yugoslavia. Aid from such a source encountered 'a measure of distrust' on the part of the Bulgarians in spite of an offer of an outlet to the Aegean through the railroad to Dede Aghach on the borders of Western and Eastern Thrace, the very territory in dispute at the Lausanne conference. Lord Beaverbrook's wide-awake watchdog discerned in this a plot by Venizelos and Zaharoff to pull the Greek chestnuts out of the fire, which would enable them, protected by British troops in the neutral zone of the Straits, to hold on to Eastern Thrace. These good intentions likewise foundered.

It is not easy to perceive exactly how any of this was calculated to lead France by the nose. She had decided where her interest lay and adhered to it. There were those, notably André Tardieu, Clemenceau's disciple, who in his new paper *L'Echo National* deplored any policy which might lead to a clash of interests with Britain, but the same people were not sorry to witness Lloyd George's troubles at home. 'As for France,' remarked Clemenceau when the Prime Minister finally fell, 'it is a real enemy who disappears.' Sir Basil would have had to be more surrealistic than optimistic to have hoped to deflect the entire French military, political and diplomatic establishment. There is no evidence that he was so naive.

With so many balls in the air, it is surprising that he had any time for other matters. But oil was still on his mind.

Sir Basil's early interest in oil might well have been inspired by his friend Walter Long who, from the Colonial Office, established and ran the Petroleum Executive in the later years of the war.

The British had been aware for some time of the possibilities of oil in Algeria and it was in Oran and Algiers that another friend, Lord Murray, the former Master of Elibank, acting for the giant construction group, S. Pearson, and backed by the Admiralty, succeeded in acquiring a concession of just under 300 square miles; an application for a concession for ten times that had been refused after repeated opposition in the French Chamber. A French company was formed to exploit this situation, of which 67 per cent of the capital was to come from French pockets, who would provide at least two-thirds of the direction. These trustees of the national interest turned out to be old friends: Léon Pissard, Maurice Carrier and Nicholas Piétri.

Thus it was interpreted by those so inclined that three of the five French directors were 'inspired by English influences'. These suspicions were voiced by Roger Mennevée in his *Documents Politiques, Diplomatiques et Financiers*:

By 1920 twelve wells were in operation [in Algeria]. Then in an extraordinary way borings were suddenly unsuccessful although they were made in an area which was extremely promising. Later they all had to be abandoned, a circumstance which in interested circles gave rise to some very queer rumours. It was known that it was in the interests of the foreign oil trust that France should not discover any oil wells on her own soil or in any of her colonial territories, for then she would remain permanently under the control of the foreign oil producers.

What is beyond any doubt is that Zaharoff was associated in some capacity with the Pearson group, and that this bore fruit. He received personal payments in unequal amounts suggesting commissions of over £13,500 in 1918 and a lesser sum of over £5,000 the following year. Small beer, perhaps, but the yeast was active.

Zaharoff had therefore plugged the Algerian breach. He next turned his attention to metropolitan France.

The French oil industry, so far as it existed at all, was ripe for reform. Calouste Gulbenkian, Royal Dutch–Shell's adviser in Paris, described it as 'a monopolistic association of grocers'. The country was dependent on her allies, America in the main, for petroleum products and transportation.

Before the end of the war, the major problem was tanker tonnage; within weeks of coming to power Clemenceau supported a vigorous shipbuilding programme. It is even probable that Zaharoff, with his ear to the political foreground, anticipated this. A strange story is told by his old friend, Sir George Owens-Thurston. During the war Zaharoff walked into Thurston's office at Vickers and casually enquired if he could purchase a shipyard in Britain. There happened to be one on the market. He thereupon wrote out a cheque and christened his buy the Forth Shipbuilding Company. This story, with the swift response of the chequebook, has all the familiar hallmarks of the legend. Yet it had some basis in fact. In order to escape heavy duty and excess profits tax, Thurston disloyally revealed, Zaharoff arranged for a French company to be formed to act as an intermediary with Continental buyers. The ships were sold at a profit of £40 per ton, of which the Forth company was allowed to retain only an eighth part. In this way, claimed Thurston enviously – he was himself embarking on bankruptcy – Zaharoff made a million when a million was still a million.

The sums are suspect. It would have been hard to find a buyer at those inflated prices even in a buoyant market. There is, however, strong circumstantial evidence of some similar sly scheme. Just days before Clemenceau had promised action, the Compagnie de Transit de Caen was registered with capital so insignificant as to suggest a shell operating company by Alfred Delpierre, a former *chef de bureau* at the Ministry of Marine. And two commonplace names, Maurice Carrier and Leopold Walford, appeared on the board.

And the Forth company was real – and rewarding. In May 1916, the year of the company's registration, Zaharoff paid £15,000 to Forth; next year he received several small payments in the region of £1,000 and in 1918 he returned similar sums to Forth. His reward came later that same year with a payment to him of £100,000, followed in the next year by a final settlement of £74,589. This was a profitable flutter, even on the profit Forth was permitted to retain, a suspicion shared by others; a writ was issued three years later for the recovery of a share of the departed treasure and which was only served by the Foreign Office after considerable delay and expense. It is likely, however, that he let his friends in on this coup. Otherwise inexplicable payments from Zaharoff to Caillard, Barker, Dawson and Thurston, as well as to Leopold Walford, are recorded, a total of almost £60,000 in 1918 with a further £70,000 shared among them the next year.

Certainly he was interested in the construction to the detriment of the operational side of the business: commission was his *métier*, not management. He was shortly suspected of having practised this preference on another front.

Some time after the founding of the Banque de la Seine, he acquired control of a small shipping company, the Société Navale de l'Ouest, which operated sixteen ships. Under the Zaharoff regime the capital was increased progressively from 3,000,000 to 40,000,000 francs. His own original stake was in the process diluted by this development until, by 1921, he gradually withdrew from the picture, leaving behind him some questions. *La Tribune de Paris*, in the wake of the annual general meeting of 1923, suggested a possible source of the company's problems. The price of construction which Sir Basil had imposed on the company, the paper speculated, resulted in heavy burdens which hindered its operation and led it, more or less rapidly, but surely, to the abyss which swallowed up the millions of the unlucky share and debenture holders. The paper then pointed the finger more precisely. When Zaharoff negotiated with Vickers for the building of a number of ships, he received a commission of £7 per ton. (This is a more reasonable figure, representing very approximately some 5 per cent of the construction cost.) The paper hinted that as much as 200,000 tons was involved ... No such ships were commissioned at Barrow during this period. There remains, however, the mysterious Forth Shipbuilding Company, whose brief period of activity may have coincided with the French company's construction programme. But by December 1921, following the depradations of its old management, the company had been reconstructed, with the naval architect Owens-Thurston as the sole survivor of the old guard. Indeed the only clue to Zaharoff's prior presence was a typical conceit: 'ZED' prefixed to the company's telegraphic address.

And by 1923 his credit was fully stretched and his bank was also in difficulty. Before that unhappy time, he had one more function in mind for the Société Navale. This did at last concern the Anglo-Persian Company, British Petroleum as it became.

Sir Basil had pinned his hopes on the expected boom in tanker traffic and in 1919 had concluded a contract with the Anglo-Mexican Oil Company for the French trade, but in this he was acting in the capacity of a carrier. He now wished to expand into the distribution sector, and for that he needed to go into partnership with a supplier. But this was to be self-defeating. The large combines, once they had gained a foothold in the market place, showed a natural preference to carry their produce in their own fleets – and commission their own ships. There was no room for the middleman. It was this which sapped the trading account of the Société Navale de l'Ouest.

The one source of supply for petrol to which France had a claim in the Middle East had been relinquished by Clemenceau in exchange for a nebulous understanding that she would reap an indeterminate share. One of the principal aims of French diplomacy in the immediate post-war years was to translate this intent into liquid matter.

The concessionary rights to oil in the pre-war Ottoman Empire had been acquired by the Turkish Petroleum Company after negotiations into which the British and German governments had been directly drawn. Anglo-Persian held half the capital in this company with the remaining share held equally by Royal Dutch–Shell and the Deutsche Bank representing German interests. This arrangement went into cold storage for the duration of the war, though not before Churchill had acquired a majority holding in Anglo-Persian for the British government. Gulbenkian worked on French fears that without their own sources of supply they must always be at the mercy of *Les Trusts*; he suggested that they should request the British to transfer to them the former German holding in the Turkish company. This seemingly straightforward proposal suffered from the same obfuscations that afflicted all Anglo-French relations. Pichon, Clemenceau's Foreign Minister, saw this gesture as an example of 'inter-allied collaboration'; the Foreign Office considered such an action 'quite untenable'. In the midst of misunderstanding, the Quai d'Orsay was tempted to regard the Sykes–Picot agreement, assigning France the rights to

Mosul, as still valid. In the end the British interests, apprehensive of American intervention, agreed to the proposal in order 'to get the French on our side and so prevent the oil question coming up before the Peace Conference at all'.

This was formalized by treaty at San Remo in May 1920 at which France won a 25 per cent participation in the Turkish Petroleum Company. It equally provoked immediate hostile reaction from the State Department which demanded an 'open door' policy (so long as they were on the wrong side of it) and 'equal opportunities for all' as spelt out in the mandates of the League of Nations (to which they did not belong). It was Gulbenkian, his Five Per Cent intact, who persuaded the others to make room for their late ally; he picked up a quarter interest for them, surrendered by Anglo-Persian in what became the Iraq Petroleum Company.

The hand of Zaharoff was clearly discerned in this battle for oil. His intrigues antagonized many powerful forces in the United States; the 'mischievous and damaging manner ... in which he tricked' them did 'irreparable harm to the relations of friendly countries'. There is not the least evidence that he had even the tip of his finger in the pie.

There remained the French market to corner. The position in France was that she was still largely dependent on American supplies. Moreover, as the franc depreciated in value against the dollar, her import position became more desperate.

American oil interests had not, naturally, taken this 'rebuff' from the Greek lying down. Standard Oil counter-attacked: their man, Edward Tuck, acquired a minority holding in the Banque de la Seine in 1920, gaining 'a foothold in the enemy's camp'. (He must have regretted this but, although the investment turned sour, his friendship with Zaharoff survived.)

In August of the same year a sanguine Zaharoff assured Philippe Berthelot, Secretary-General at the Quai d'Orsay, of his intention to supply all the oil for France's needs. He had yet to find the means. Then, in his first active intervention in the industry, he promoted in October the association of Anglo-Persian, which had not yet any stake in France, and two small native refining and marketing companies to form the Société Générale des Huiles de Pétroles. In his wake he brought his bank and the Société Navale de l'Ouest. Of the 100,000,000 franc capital, French sources provided 55 per cent, and of these the Société Navale was the largest shareholder, followed by some half-dozen banks of which the Banque de la Seine was the leader and the Banque Commerciale de la Méditerranée the least. Zaharoff's own holding was worth 3,000,000 francs; handfuls of shares were also held by his omnipresent 'men of straw', Maurice Carrier and Nicholas Piétri. These three, together with Paul Mayer of his bank, sat on the board. Standard Oil and Royal Dutch–Shell made similar matches with French oil interests.

This was acclaimed in London. 'Wizard Greek's Oil Coup', heralded *The Star*. 'Fights Americans: Ensuring French Supply'. The French media were not so grateful.

Despite this flourish the results of this French company for its first decade were discouraging. By the end of the next year, when it was decided to double the capital, the French partners were unable to find the money and Anglo-Persian's holding was increased to a three-quarter interest.

Sir Basil was also reported to be forming other companies to work a fleet of tankers under the French flag; a number of tankers, it was claimed, were under construction in British yards, 'an enterprise which Sir Basil's connections with Vickers should make profitable'. This was the Association Pétrolière, created in July 1921, in which Anglo-Persian, the Société Générale des Huiles and the Société Navale took roughly equal parts, Piétri again appearing on the board with the minimum qualification – one share. There is still no evidence, however, that any tankers were ordered from Vickers. These would have brought relief to Barrow, where 'the birds were nesting in the cranes'.

Sir Basil's personal fortunes, tied to those of the Banque de la Seine, went through a severe crisis after the Greek defeat in the east. 'The collapse of Greece seems to have shattered Zaharoff's power,' *Action Française et Etrangère* gleefully reported. 'Will he at last pack up and go? Things are going badly for the Banque de la Seine. Its shares have fallen from 500 to 225. Why doesn't Monsieur Zaharoff stop the rot? He was able to pay 400,000,000 francs for the Greek army and he hasn't 10,000,000 for his bank?'

The bank was poorly. Sir Basil first tried to introduce bureaucracy and blue blood, a former *Prefet* of the Seine and the Vicomte de Breteuil, whose *Informations Politiques et Financières* hoped would reform the bank's bad habits, stem imprudent investments as well as eliminate 'foreign political influences'. This public relations exercise was inadequate and in 1925, the establishment facing a further crisis, its remaining assets were put into a new Société Parisienne de Banque, founded in association with the Banque Robert Schumann. Sir Basil took a small stake worth 2,000,000 francs (perhaps all that was left of his 10,000,000 franc holding in the Banque de la Seine); Sir Trevor Dawson of Vickers was even more chary. Léon Pissard, Maurice

Carrier and Nicholas Piétri retained their seats on the new board but when, to the relief of the financial community, the latter retired for 'exclusively personal reasons' a year later, this act was taken to mark 'the definitive retreat of the Zaharoff–Vickers group' from French soil.

20

Monte Carlo and Marriage

'Why I bought Monte Carlo, no one knows.' Quite one of the best throw-away party lines, and most certainly, however regrettably, apocryphal.

Legend accretes to Monte Carlo like burdock to a St Bernard. Monte Carlo was the Casino; in the absence of other taxation, it carried the administration and the judiciary, education and the small police force – and the reigning family of Grimaldis. Add to this a zest of Zaharoff, then the task of unravelling his role in this muddle is an ungrateful one.

Sir Basil had been quietly enjoying the winter delights of these sunny acres since well before the turn of the century, comfortably conserved in the Hôtel de Paris which, in the view of no less a gourmet than Nubar Gulbenkian, offered the best cuisine and the best cellar in Western Europe. Neither little wars nor the Great War disturbed this custom – until Zaharoff died there at the onset of one winter.

This predilection for the Principality gave rise to the most persistent of all legends surrounding his life: that he was the owner of Monte Carlo and drew vast revenues from its gaming tables. He was for just once quite formal about this alleged relationship, and forthright in his views on gambling. On one of the very rare occasions when he received a newspaperman, he explained:

You will probably be greatly surprised to learn that I have not, and never have had, anything to do with gambling at Monte Carlo. My only interest in Monte Carlo is in its sunshine. That is the only reason that I often go there. As a matter of fact, I have never been inside the Casino.... I have

220

higher interests in life than to take people's money from them through gambling.

There can be no doubt that that statement represented his views on gambling; it is 'a fool's substitute for life', he said on another occasion. And it was clearly understood that his secretaries, Macpherson ('The Scots are the most dependable race on earth') and the Yorkshireman Theo Macdermott, faced instant dismissal if they were found at the tables. It is also probable that he never set foot in the Casino; he disliked noise and crowds. However . . . the legend is too persistent.

Zaharoff induced his friend Clemenceau in July 1918 to confect a 'secret' treaty which effectively detached Monaco from French sovereignty and, worse, deprived the 'national finances of important and legitimate receipts' and further pledged France to give financial help in the event, remote as it must have seemed, of a failure of the Casino. The guilty couple tried to slip this through, suitably clouded in the language of conveyance, by incorporating it into the small print of the Versailles Treaty. It was first published in Monaco next August but did not reach the ears of the French Chamber until the following summer. That impulsive politician, Senator Gaudin de Villaine, who had exposed the illicit wartime trade in nickel, denounced it, if he had indeed correctly interpreted its terms, as an 'act of treason'. The explanation by Poincaré, in his reincarnation as premier, that the treaty had not been submitted to the Assembly for approval until the other signatories of the Peace Treaty had been informed and consulted was considered unacceptable.

It is not clear at what stage the suspicion stirred that Zaharoff was behind this but, once suspected, his presence was inevitably seen as a typically brazen example of encroachment by British imperialism on France's glamorous backdoor-step.

It appears that French policy behind the revision of the treaty was based on quite other grounds. Prince Albert's son, Louis, was middle-aged and unmarried – and there was no bride in prospect. The next in line was Prince William of Württemberg, Duke of Urach. Although he was a Monegasque by birth, the French government refused to consider his candidacy. The alternative was annexation, but that raised a vexing problem: under existing French law, it would have entailed the closure of the Casino, and the ruin of the locality. (There is no record that any consideration was given at that stage to changing French law.)

In the golden age of the Casino, the days of Russian Grand Dukes (and corrupt war ministers) and American railroad barons, the Casino had registered a net profit in the last years of peace of some three-quarters of a million pounds in spite of additional onerous burdens, including the building of the opera house, imposed by the terms of the renewal of the concession in 1912. War clouds cast more than a slight shadow over the tables so, although Monaco maintained strict neutrality, the Casino closed its doors. Before the last shot was fired it was business as usual, but with the post-war boom in chips, expenses accelerated to a dangerous level. The reigning family too had expensive tastes and when the Prince demanded two million francs over and above his regular stipend, the company declared itself unable to pay. The indignant ruler insisted on an audit. This revealed mismanagement and extravagance. It was considered, however, essential to proceed discreetly with the reorganization in order to avoid damaging talk of retrenchment and economy.

In such a delicate situation Sir Basil would have been the obvious candidate for axeman. One of the first measures of control credited to him was the insistence on two signatures on all cheques signed by the management. In the face of this humiliating restraint, Camille Blanc, whose father, a waiter at the Bad Homburg casino, had been first granted the concession, made a dignified exit early in 1923. Two days later a cheque for £1,000,000, bearing the famous signature of Basil Zaharoff, was presented at a London bank. (The name of the payee was left teasingly blank by the author of this tale, but there was disappointment in store; the transaction would have left Sir Basil, give or take the odd pound, £999,500 in the red at the Bank of England, or a mere half million if incautiously drawn on Barclays.)

This manoeuvring, however it was accomplished, let in Zaharoff's 'confidential agents', Alfred Delpierre, his accomplice from the Compagnie de Transit de Caen, as president of the Société des Bains de Mer, the company operating the concession, and René Léon as the new manager. (Léon, after an Oxford education, had moved to a Wall Street banking business where he gained useful experience floating loans to South American states.) In addition Zaharoff brought in Léon Barthou, brother of the former Prime Minister and future Foreign Minister, Louis, both of whom were close friends.

It has been suggested that the shares to which Delpierre owed his position were assigned to him by Sir Basil on the condition that he surrender them if and when he abandoned his functions. This is a reasonable supposition. It is not improbable that Zaharoff also held shares in his own right, if not in his own name.

The new regime overturned the old paternal provident system under which those who had lost their all were awarded a pension of ten to fifteen francs a day, not from philanthropic concern but to eliminate the discouraging spectacle of the less fortunate punters haunting the pavement outside the gambling rooms. Henceforth losers were paid two months' severance pay on the spot, and a single ticket to Paris. Free entry was abolished, the lowest stakes were doubled and the staff was trimmed.

In spite of this he remained a most disinterested promoter of the tables. There is an old story of a bright young thing accosting him on the terrace.

'Sir Basil, the Casino does belong to you, doesn't it? Can't you tell me how to make some money?'

'In the first place, madame, the Casino does not belong to me alone and, in the second place, I am unable to tell you how to make money. But I can tell you how to save it.'

'Tell me, how?'

'By staying away from the gaming rooms.'

The originality of this advice does not seem to have affected the Casino's fortunes. Revenues rose until in the spring of 1925 the company was able to distribute a dividend of more than 100 per cent, the equivalent of some 43,500,000 francs. That year represented the high-water mark in the prosperity of the Casino, which was now suffering from the competition of rival establishments at Cannes, San Remo and the new casino built at Nice by Frank Jay Gould. A price war predictably erupted. Profits and share prices slumped.

The less imaginative estimates credit Zaharoff with a shareholding of just over 500,000 francs in the Société des Bains de Mer. This would appear a more realistic figure than some of the wilder stories suggested. One precise claim was made that he sold his holding in April 1926 for £3,400,000, most of this being taken up by Daniel Dreyfus et Cie. If there was any foundation for this, the only charitable explanation is that French francs were confused with pounds sterling.

Yet another source explained his interest on the grounds that he advanced a loan to the Casino during the lean years of the war – a round figure of £1,000,000 is floated – against a mortgage which was later converted into debentures, the last batch being surrendered in 1926. There may, indeed, have been some basis of truth in this. Another story is that when he disposed of his holding, he 'kept' only the Hôtel de Paris. Zaharoff's stake in the Casino must remain a matter of surmise and supposition. Despite his protestations, it is most probable he was a shareholder, albeit in a minority. He acquired his stake when the share price was relatively low and sold it at its peak round about 1926. At that date, and even long after, the press repeatedly reported consternation among directors, officials and shareholders on rumours that he had withdrawn his interest. These owed much to the legend. The legend himself sat back, tight-lipped as a Swiss bank, refusing enlightenment, alternately irritated and amused by the speculation.

Arcane motives were imputed to him to account for his ever setting up his fief in Monte Carlo. It was said that what attracted him was not the lure of dividends from the Casino but the fantasy of controlling a tiny kingdom, a substitute for Greece; that all his life had been spent in quest of a country to call his own. Great powers fascinated him, he is alleged to have claimed, but ultimately bored him; it was more fun to play with small states. Greece was too cosmopolitan for this purpose. 'But Monaco, now there is a territory one can control easily; one could transform it overnight and make it into a veritable fairyland.' Notwithstanding this ambition he managed to maintain close and friendly relations with Prince Albert, who clearly saw no serious threat to his throne from that quarter.

A final romantic theory was evolved that Sir Basil acquired the Principality in order to lay it at the feet of his bride as a wedding present.

In the autumn of 1923 Sir Basil received news that the ever-frail Duke of Marchena had entered into a decline. The state of his health was another mystery. The belief that the Duchess was bound inescapably to a mad duke added poignancy to the legend of faithful but frustrated love. Ten years later the foreign editor of the *Evening Standard* issued an internal memorandum relating to a report that the Duke had died after spending some years in an asylum: 'This information is incorrect and should not be repeated.'

The Duke had already collected the attributes of an ogre; a dispassionate correspondent of the *Sunday Express* admitted that it would be 'wrong to say he was "hideously ugly"'. Whatever he was, an ill-favoured invalid or a doited Adonis, the Duke died at Neuilly-sur-Seine in a clinic on 17 November 1923. He was buried in the small chapel at the Château de Balincourt.

Now, after some thirty-five years of loyalty on the one hand, of patience on the other, the couple, the Duchess now fifty-five and Sir Basil rising seventy-five with the aid of a stick, were at last free to become man and wife.

After a decent interval of mourning the ceremony was performed in 'extraordinary secrecy', which may be interpreted as a quiet family affair, in the tiny *mairie* of Arronville, near Pontoise, on 22 September

224

1924. So as not to suffer the loss of the prerogatives and precedent of 'Madame la duchesse', the Duchess had persuaded her brother-in-law to put her plight to Alfonso XIII. In June she had been awarded the life title of Duchess of Villafranca de los Caballeros. Sir Basil chose not to assume, as he might have done, his wife's rank.

Sir Basil was at once seen by the legend as a possessive and reclusive husband, installing a 'personal bodyguard of some dozen servants in charge of his mansion', and making them 'keep a twenty-four-hour watch on the grounds'. There was certainly such activity each summer as to arouse curiosity: unusual shipments, cased and handled with great care, passed through the gates; gangs of men, many of them speaking foreign tongues, moved around in purposeful activity.

The Château de Balincourt, largely rebuilt on an old site in the seventeenth century, had passed into various hands, and out again, usually through enforced sale for debt. At the end of the last century King Leopold of the Belgians acquired it for his mistress, and later morganatic wife, Blanche Delacroix, who presented him with two sons and received in exchange the title of Baroness Vaughan. When the King died in 1909, La Vaughan switched her devotion to the gambling table. The uncertainties of this trade persuaded her to consider letting her home to the Duchess of Marchena in 1915, who had been without a country retreat since Sir Basil had abandoned the Château de l'Échelle to the Germans. She bought it in January the following year.

The Duchess, a keen gardener, took the landscape in hand. She engaged a Venetian designer, Rafaeli Mainella, who, working under the close eye of his patron, laid out a great parterre in an intricate design of clipped box, highlighted each year by 40,000 bedding begonias, overlooked by colonnades and a bronze equestrian statue of Velasquez. He cleared vistas leading to romantic follies and introduced a profusion of gazebos and false-fronted belvederes; he installed pavilions set amidst water gardens, and topped the lot off with tons of imported statuary, balusters and urns from the south. For ten summers two, and sometimes three, teams of workmen laboured for four months to establish order in nature. Eleven gardeners reigned over this *urbs in rure* – and also tended to Sir Basil's table; ten acres of orchards, kitchen gardens and glass provided melons and other favoured fruit for the house in and out of season.

That summer, as usual, the newly weds were surrounded by their family; Angèle and Jean Ostrorog shared their roof, Cristina and Leopold Walford a neighbouring property. Old friends paid them visits: Sir Basil's colleagues, the Dawsons and Caillards; the red-bearded H.E.D.Blakiston, long-time Master of Trinity College, Oxford, who had been Vice-Chancellor at the time Sir Basil had founded the Foch Chair; Reginald McKenna, now chairman of the Midland Bank, would call when his affairs took him to Paris, as would Saemy Japhet, the banker. Edward Tuck of Standard Oil was a regular visitor from his house at Malmaison.

French leaders came and went in their fashion, Louis and Léo; Barthou, former Finance Minister Klotz and Georges Clemenceau himself, forever gloved because of eczema of the hands. Marshal Pétain made one descent. 'Quelle beauté!' he exclaimed, regarding the pleasing prospect. 'It is so charming I would like to be buried here' – a pretension which caused the disrespectful younger ladies to giggle.

Haughty as he might appear, Sir Basil, known as Bim by those on familiar terms, still had his mischievous side. As the days shortened at Balincourt, he affected not to notice the gloom that encroached over the dinner table, or, despite the complaints of fellow diners, to understand the sudden need for artificial light. This foible was too much for the octogenarian George Paget Walford, Cristina's father-in-law, who one day left the table in mid-meal and near darkness. He was discovered later at his home in nearby La Chapelle, munching biscuits. 'I hope I don't get these fads', he grumbled, 'When I get old.'

As winter approached it was time to make the move to Monte Carlo. Bim, with his grandchildren and their keeper, would take the crack Train Bleu from Paris. The Duchess would follow in her car. They were joined by Short, Sir Basil's valet, Theo Macdermott, who brought his own piano down for the long winter, and Jean Dumenc,* his personal chef (who treated the hotel guests to his art after ministering to his master), with his wife, who helped out in the cloakroom. (The history of the Hôtel de Paris relates that Zaharoff was excessively fond of eggs, which he consumed in impressive quantities. If so, he managed to conceal this little weakness from his family, although he did favour a fresh almond omelette, a pleasantly *croustillant* contrast.) The party occupied top-floor suites Nos 111–15, Sir Basil's being well sound-proofed in advance of each visit even though his secretary had mastered his scales. He was not permitted to overindulge his penchant for reclusion. That perennial courtier, Sir Harry Stonor, often took neighbouring rooms at the hotel; old Nellie Melba was attracted to lunch; and from further afield there were occasional calls

---

* A former pupil of Escoffier, he founded L'Écu de France in London after Zaharoff's death.

from Lloyd George, Lord Inchcape and the now venerable and venerated T.P.O'Connor. The only ripple of ill-humour to disturb this easy rhythm came when Sir Basil would be pursued by the persistently obtrusive press; on one occasion the old duellist smashed the camera of an incautiously close photographer with his stick.

This idyll was cut tragically short. The Duchess's health began to fail. T.P.O'Connor, who had been to stay in January 1926, said on his return to London: 'She is obviously dying, but she doesn't realize it. Basil manages to keep the bad news from her.' One month later she was dead.

Even in his personal grief his legend pursued him. 'Forty years' patience,' he is cited as saying, 'and then to be rewarded with a year and half of marriage. It is a meagre dividend for a man who has invested so much in one passion.' Even in love, concluded the legend, Zaharoff could not resist thinking in terms of dividends.

A mawkish adventure is attributed to his mourning. Two days after the funeral Sir Basil undertook a last sentimental journey. From Monte Carlo he caught a train to connect with the Simplon Orient Express on its eastward-bound run to Athens. Once aboard at Milan he locked himself in his usual compartment No. 7 and drew the blinds. He ordered a frugal meal – salad, yoghurt and a bottle of champagne – to be sent along to him, but declined to have his bed made up and dismissed his secretary with orders that he was not to be disturbed till morning.

He showed an odd concern for the hour. When the train had passed Salzburg he rang again for the attendant.

'The time,' he enquired, sitting erect and staring ahead of him, 'the exact time.'

'By the empire's time,' replied the irreconcilable veteran, 'it is now exactly half-past two, your Excellency.'

'Switch off the lights – all of them – and leave me instantly.'

It had been at 2.32 on the same line just thirty-nine years earlier that there had come that frantic scream and call for help in the night from a distraught young bride.

There was no reply at dawn to the secretary's usual triple knock. Braving the danger, he entered and found his employer still sitting erect, eyes half closed, the involuntary tremor of his thin yellow hands betraying the only signs of life. To cap it he was sitting in the cold; he had turned off the heating to sharpen his reveries.

There was no such theatrical affectation about his true feelings. With simple dignity and tenderness he wrote a short note in French from Monte Carlo to Mainella to thank him for his letter of condolence on the death of his wife. 'The mortal remains of the Duchess will remain here at the Church Saint-Charles until the beginning of May, because as she felt the cold, I do not want to conduct her to Balincourt in such weather, and I would like there to be leaves on the trees and flowers on the ground.'

21

Run-Down

A shadow from his past fleetingly brushed Sir Basil a few months after his seventy-fifth birthday. He reported matter-of-factly to Vincent Caillard that he had visited Petrograd – 'Retrograd' he concluded sadly – where he had found that officials and banks close to the Soviet leadership were anxious for Vickers to return and take over the Tsaritsyn arsenals.

This much is probable. The company's management and design expertise would have been welcome.

The current status of the works was rather obscured than clarified by two memoranda presented to Zaharoff. They were 'drawn up in English by somebody who does not know the language very well'. (One wonders why he did not insist on a sight of the Russian originals.)

Successive governments, from the tsarist through to the Soviet, had considered plans to acquire the works for the state. In 1917 the 'control packet of shares' had been sold through the International Bank of St Petersburg, one of the original investors, to the Sormovo-Kolomna steel works, another of Vickers' partners in Tsaritsyn. Vickers, along with the other shareholders, was said to have been compensated with Sormovo-Kolomna shares and 'a small sum of money'. In March 1918, 'the change of regime notwithstanding', it was decided to purchase the works for the state at a cost of 63,000,000 roubles, worth some £1,600,000 at the then rate of exchange. This sale was a formality, if not a fiction, banks and industrial undertakings having already been expropriated. This 'payment' was nonetheless seen to constitute recognition of Vickers' claims.

Vickers was now to be offered the chance to obtain repossession of the Tsaritsyn arsenals, or their value in cash. This prospect had been dangled before Sir Basil, he informed Caillard from Monte Carlo in February 1924, by a Comrade Shaikevich, principal director of the International Bank of Petrograd, which 'having friends among the Bolsheviks ... can obtain advantages'. Zaharoff summed up the proposal: 'It really comes to this: The Banque International and the Sormovo-Kolomna Company would put their shares at the disposal of Vickers, and would indicate to Vickers how to make their claim, and would prepare their Soviet friends as to how they should handle Vickers' claim. . . .' He pronounced himself 'very favourably inclined' in view of recent international recognition of the Soviets, and his hope that 'Russia will begin to open up again'. He might more seriously have envisaged the recovery of other substantial debts, notably Vickers' 10 per cent holding in the Nicolaieff shipyards, design fees and royalties as well as £170,000 still outstanding on the battle-cruiser *Rurik*.

Zaharoff was perhaps lulled into this fantasy by Lenin's new economic policy. Forced to acknowledge a severe defeat on the economic front owing to the hostility of the peasants and the failure of world revolution, Lenin had introduced laws legalizing private trading and inviting the return of foreign investors and concessionaires. Lenin had been able to impose this on a reluctant party, but Lenin had died the month before Sir Basil passed this proposition to Vickers. And even under this more benevolent regime, the Soviets had still refused to consider the restoration of property to foreign interests, or to pay compensation for the seizures, still less to recognize the debts of the tsarist government.

A more sceptical Caillard wrote back within the week to caution him, raising the spectre of 'special considerations', and, not wishing to commit himself to paper, sent out a man from Vickers to confer with Sir Basil in Monaco. Shaikevich had evidently hinted that a draft contract already existed between the Soviet government and Vickers for the resale. The couple now asked for a sight of this document. The last laconic record of this business simply stated that 'an endeavour was made to buy and obtain a copy of the alleged contract without success'.

Unable thus to provide any evidence of his good faith, Comrade Shaikevich, emulating the Boojum, softly and silently vanished away.

Many, many years and one hot and cold war later, an incoming chairman of Vickers, familiarizing himself with the company's affairs, was informed that 'Zaharoff reported that the Russians were now proposing to pay Vickers 63 million gold roubles for their confiscated interests, but nothing came of this, and one can hardly imagine it would be any good trying again!' (In 1987, following an Anglo-Russian accord, Vickers lodged a claim on the former Imperial Russian assets for £783,167.4s.2d.)

What might have taken him back to his old haunts? Was he hoping to collect royalties in the more relaxed economic climate, or was there a personal motive? He must have left for Russia shortly after the death of the Duke of Marchena in November 1923; he was back in Monte Carlo by the following February. Only urgent business would have persuaded him to exchange the Mediterranean sun for the rigours of the Russian winter. He was married again in September. There is an unexpected, and inexplicable, sequel to his visit. In the following year, a lady and her daughter presented themselves before the British Consul in Moscow requesting repatriation. Satisfied with their bona fides, the Consul complied (the loan was later written off by the Foreign Office). Her name was Mrs Z. Z. Zaharoff, a style reminiscent of his old Cypriot pseudonym, which might have been retained by the first Mrs Zaharoff, the former Emily Ann Burrows, who had dropped out of his life forty years before in somewhat embarrassing circumstances. She would now have been rising eighty. English (and destitute) she must have been to qualify for aid, yet she made no public claim on Sir Basil. The matter remains another mystery.

If there had been a serious chance of it at the time, Vickers would have been happy to recover even part of their debt. The view from the boardroom was bleak. The depression was most severe nationwide in steel and shipbuilding. The Washington Naval Treaty of 1922 did nothing to help: the politicians proposed a limitation in tonnage and a naval holiday for the construction of capital ships for a period of not less than ten years. If the British did not wholeheartedly concur, neither did they vehemently demur, and as a gesture they suspended work in hand on four battle-cruisers. The Americans extraordinarily had even demanded that no more warships should be built in private yards; the Admiralty mildly protested that they considered the armaments and shipbuilding capacity of the private sector 'necessary and desirable' – and, their Lordships might have added, less costly.

Sir Basil is supposed to have prompted this reluctant confession by suggesting that Vickers should request an annual subsidy to maintain its naval works: he expected that this would be refused but in exchange would wring from the government a recognition of the right to build privately. If this was so, the record is no longer available. It is true that towards the end of the year the Admiralty placed orders for two battleships, the *Nelson* and *Rodney*, of which Vickers received its due share.

The Vickers board, the prospect of better times ever remote, even receding, began to shape a controlled retreat from their over-exposed position. In the two years 1923 and 1924, £2,750,000 was written off against reserves. This was recognized as penny pinching. The next year Reginald McKenna, a former Chancellor, was invited to head an enquiry to examine the position of the company and to submit recommendations. The result was a massive reduction in capital by almost £12,500,000; the shares were written down from £1 to 6s 8d, close to their actual market value. (Sir Basil, of course, was reported to have lost another fortune by the way.) The Beardmore shipyards, which had faced even harder times, were disposed of in 1926; the Whitehead torpedo works at St Tropez had already been shuffled off on to the French steel company Firminy; Vickers France was wound up; and the Wolseley car company, which had piled up successive losses, was sold to Mr Morris for almost three-quarters of a million pounds. Douglas Vickers, the last of the family in the firm, now aged sixty-five and chairman of eight years' standing, stepped down and was replaced by General Sir Herbert Lawrence, a banker by marriage and former Chief of Staff to Haig.

But Armstrong Whitworth was in a worse way. With £6,500,000 in debts to the Bank of England, the company declared a moratorium of five years on debentures. Its shares, worth as much as £3 before the war, dropped to as low as 2s 6d at the news. The Admiralty, however, were alarmed at losing their armament capacity. A merger was inevitable, Vickers the obvious partner.* The agreement was signed on the last day of October 1927, with Vickers playing the lead role. 'It would be hard', *The Times* commented, 'to name an amalgamation in industry of equal importance.'

Just two weeks before this marriage, the new chairman of Vickers had presented to Sir Basil an ornately chased gold cup inscribed 'as a mark of great appreciation of the valuable work which he has done for them and of their sincere gratitude and high esteem'. Dated 12 October 1927, it was to celebrate the completion of fifty years' connection with the company from those first modest origins at £5 a week with Nordenfelt in Athens.

---

* Montagu Norman, the Governor of the Bank of England, faced with the bleak proposals from the Vickers team, would have preferred the conversations, in the words of J.D. Scott, Vickers' historian, to have been more 'personal, elusive, and discreet to the point of mystification'. There is no record of any direct dealings between Norman and Zaharoff which, Scott concludes, 'must always be a matter of regret to students of negotiations considered as one of the fine arts'.

In the same summer, too, Sir Basil had been called upon to perform one unusual and unpleasant duty, a singular illustration of the unique position he occupied in the company of which he had never been a director. His old friend, Sir Vincent Caillard, now aged seventy, was not considered the man for the new times envisaged by the company reorganization put in hand by Sir Mark Jenkinson, one of the new breed, an accountant with wartime experience in the Ministry of Munitions. Sir Basil was delegated by the board to intimate as much to Caillard. The operation was executed with merciful despatch.

Sir Basil saw Caillard in Paris in the middle of August 1927 and put the board's proposal to him that if he 'will give me his resignation ... he will receive from the Company £20,000 in cash and £4,000 per annum for life, which', added the prudent Greek, 'I have assumed is free from income tax.' As he pointed out to Jenkinson, 'the meeting between two such old friends was, as you can imagine, very painful, and in the course of the conversation I told Sir Vincent of your very friendly feeling towards him and your desire to do the right thing ...'. Two days later Jenkinson informed his envoy that the chairman had agreed these terms. 'Needless to say, I am very grateful to you for your kind help in this matter for there is no one able to handle such a delicate matter, without hurting, as yourself.' In another two days Sir Basil had told Jenkinson that Caillard had accepted the proposal and was tendering his resignation that same day.

Sir Vincent died three years later. Frank Barker was already dead. Trevor Dawson, the last link with the company's heyday, followed his colleague Caillard quite suddenly the following year. The one survivor from the golden years showed no sign of letting up.

At the same time that Jenkinson was enlisting Zaharoff as his executioner, he prepared a draft letter which he intended to send to Sir Basil after General Lawrence had approved it. He had had drawn up a statement showing the amount of commission at 5 per cent on all outstanding orders. 'The profit on these orders', he hoped to say, 'will not allow payment of this commission and also cover Head Office charges but on the other hand we cannot let you personally be out of pocket.' The future was grim: 'Prices are so "cut" that it is difficult to secure an adequate return on the capital of the company' and that for the future they could not afford such commissions unless the ratio of profit could be increased, 'but as regards the past, we are entirely in your hands, and whatever "lump sum" you suggest will be accepted by us'.

There was little activity in his account at the Bank of England after 1922; that year may have marked the occasion of his last visit of any length to those shores. Occasional glimpses of his affairs surface, revealing an obsessive preoccupation with his accounts and commissions. An offer was made by Vickers to Sir Basil, and promptly accepted, of a contribution of £10,000 per annum towards office and other expenses to commence from 1 January 1927; this did not include his commission or the 'usual half yearly accounts for expenses'. It would appear to have been a most generous provision, perhaps intended in place of a pension, in view of the depressed state of the country and the company, not to speak of his diminishing mobility. He was not yet reduced to living off candle-ends.

Spain was still by far the healthiest of the surviving overseas operations, the one with most bustle and commensurate benefit: there were the Sociedad Español de la Construcción Naval, which for twenty years had been engaged on building the armada; and Placencia, the old Maxim–Nordenfelt subsidiary of which Sir Basil was a director. These companies, heavily dependent on the Spanish government, also fed largely off each other. La Naval was the smaller company's main customer, while Vickers in turn received orders from La Naval worth some £1,000,000 in the first decade of peace, mostly for heavy-gun mountings.*

This cross-fertilization provided a very profitable field for commissions, and Sir Basil profited. He received a cut on all orders placed with La Naval by the Spanish government and the Electric Boat Company; and on all orders placed by La Naval with Vickers and other outside contractors such as the Whitehead Torpedo works; and on all orders received by Placencia, mostly but not exclusively from La Naval. On top of this there were 'our Spanish friends' to look after: these local commissions ranged from $6\frac{1}{8}$ per cent – $5\frac{1}{8}$ per cent for orders placed with Placencia by La Naval – down to $2\frac{1}{2}$ per cent for such etceteras as dual sights (perhaps a necessary aid for the accounts department, threatened with double vision). The same Dons could be accommodating, by default. 'I should say', Zaharoff advised his company, 'that, after all these years, as my Spanish friends have not claimed commission, we need not give the matter any further consideration.'

From these sources alone Sir Basil received in the fifteen years

---

* These were the most costly and meticulously engineered items of essential equipment for a capital ship of which armament represented roughly one-third of the construction cost. A 14-inch gun quadruple-armoured mounting, taking two years in the making, compared in bulk to a four-storey house complete with lifts; it weighed some 1,550 tons, was 60 feet deep and had to manage guns with 54-foot barrels, each weighing 80 tons and firing a shell of three-quarters of a ton.

following the war approximately £125,000 as commission paid without deduction for either British or Spanish taxes.*

He may also have been part-paymaster for some of the local Spanish commissions and sub-commissions – or less straightforward favours. In November 1925 he acknowledged a statement of the Spanish account from Vickers with 'a cheque for four hundred thousand pesetas [about £10,000], with which I am doing the needful'. Old habits – or lifelong clichés? – die hard, and this one was to land him in trouble again.

While Placencia's business flourished and considerable payments were made out of profits to Vickers in 1928 and 1929, La Naval's debt to Vickers, aggravated by the fall in the value of the peseta, mounted. Vickers agreed to suspend payment for the sake of old ties but the increasing sickness of the currency raised the debt to more than £500,000 by 1931. In answer to the alarmed calls from the creditor, discussions were started for some scheme of reconstruction but settlement, the civil war intervening, was not reached until almost ten years later.

Spain was also seen as a potential market for other Vickers hardware: tanks and planes (the company had acquired the Supermarine works of Schneider Trophy fame in 1928). The company continued to turn to Sir Basil for advice in his eighties. 'The Spaniards are difficult people to deal with,' he advised the chief of the aviation division, 'and if we press them, they immediately shut up like oysters, and think that we are endeavouring to force them, and my policy has always been to induce them to believe that they are having it entirely their own way, and this line of conduct has hitherto been most successful and satisfactory. ...' He urged the same caution on Sir Noel Birch, a former Master-General of Ordnance, who had reinforced the board. 'Above all they are shy of new faces.'

But he began soon to despair of even this privileged preserve. 'Remember that at present the only matters concerning the Spanish Government are politics.' The country had already embarked on the path that was to lead to the popular front and civil war.

---

* There is a record of just one payment ever made by Zaharoff to the Inland Revenue – £439 10s in 1924. This is not, of course, evidence that he never paid any tax.

22

Senate Committee, Royal Commission

The health, the continued existence even, of Vickers rested on a contradiction. 'Our interests', General Lawrence pointed out at the first general meeting under the new regime, 'are mainly in connection with armaments ...' and yet the Committee of Imperial Defence had simultaneously laid down a policy based on the assumption that there would be 'no major war for ten years'. That the company was able to maintain a dividend at all was due to the fact that the combination of Vickers and Armstrong had produced the 'only ... fully fledged armament firm' left in the country, and it therefore received a high proportion of whatever orders were forthcoming. The Barrow yard was kept going on a reduced diet of cruisers, destroyers and its speciality, submarines – and parts thereof.

A further blow to the order book was the Treaty of London of 1930 which refroze many of the restrictions of the Washington Treaty. Admiralty expenditure at once fell by almost a third and, although replacement of the fleet already tending towards obsolescence was allowed, the rate was limited; under the Treaty this would not have been achieved for fifteen years, that is by VE Day. A handful of orders from overseas, principally from Chile and Brazil, helped to keep the yards open. Merchant shipbuilding, facing keen international competition, was an even more painful subject.

Sir Basil had done his best. In December 1929 at Monte Carlo he had managed to secure orders for two 27,000 ton liners for P & O, the *Strathaird* and *Strathnaver*, for Barrow. This had been a stroke of chance in the most literal sense. 'Had it not been that I

236

was in a generous frame of mind owing to my having won 100 francs in the casino,' claimed Lord Inchcape, P & O's Scottish chairman, 'I might have squeezed a little more out of Sir Basil than I succeeded in doing.' Sir Basil's sense of timing had not deserted him.

By the mid-1930s a distant gleam of light, the signal for the end of disarmament, was discernible. It coincided exactly, and not accidentally, with an orchestrated crescendo of opposition to the private manufacture of arms.

There were several strands to this – the moral, the political and the supposedly practical. One considered that the manufacture of all and any arms was immoral; another that the profit motive in the manufacture of arms was immoral – the so-called 'vested interest in war' – and the other that the private sector was less competent than the public sector. (And this at a time when costs of naval shipbuilding in private yards were 10 per cent cheaper than in the Royal Dockyards, which did not even have the capability to build modern battleships.)

The ammunition for this offensive had been obligingly provided by the League of Nations, whose Covenant stated categorically that the members 'agree that the manufacture by private enterprise of munitions and implements of war is open to grave objections'. The British government had never agreed to any such thing but, surprisingly, they had accepted the formula, which was quite contrary to their own oft-repeated policy; perhaps they thought it wiser, or easier, to acquiesce and ignore it than to argue endlessly and aimlessly over it.

This controversial clause led straight to the setting up by the League of a Temporary Mixed Commission on Armements which spawned a First Sub-Committee to consider private manufacture. This body in turn gave birth to the famous six points of objection: that armaments firms fomented war scares; attempted to bribe government officials; disseminated false reports; controlled newspapers to influence public opinion; organized international rings to accelerate the arms race by playing one country off against another and to increase the price of arms to governments. These allegations did not represent any findings of the Sub-Committee, but by repetition they acquired an absolute authority. They resurfaced at the Disarmament Conference at Geneva in 1932 and were repeated in the House of Commons.

The first barrage, however, came from across the Atlantic, and for quite different motives. This was the age of the isolationist.

But before the embers of this national introversion flared up, the octogenarian Sir Basil, increasingly frail, was reportedly chosen by the European arms-makers to represent their point of view in Washington on the eve of the Disarmament Conference. In view of his controversial character, every effort was made to keep his mission secret. Nonetheless it was rumoured in February 1932 that he had arrived in the Potomac on board J.P.Morgan's yacht *Corsair* to call upon President Hoover. This part of the story was easily disproved; the *Corsair* had never left New York. The American press corps in Europe was immediately alerted; one report established that he had all along been at his usual winter haunt in Monte Carlo, another that he had been spotted in London. There was no denial from the White House but an intimate of the President, asked for his private opinion on the mysterious visit before indiscretions were institutionalized, is said to have obliged: 'President Hoover meant nothing but good for the American people by inviting Zaharoff to call upon him. What was more natural, with the World Disarmament Conference impending, than that the President should want the advice of the world's leading munitions agent?'

This disappearing trick was seen as typical of Zaharoff's tactics. What better method, it was asked, to ensure a secret than to leak a false story and then leave it to the world's press to confound the rumour?

As the international situation darkened with Germany's withdrawal from the League of Nations and the collapse of the Disarmament Conference, American fears of embroilment deepened. In this atmosphere a Senate Committee set itself up to investigate the munitions industry under the chairmanship of an outspoken isolationist, Gerald P.Nye of North Dakota. (His degree of isolation might be gauged from one of his first questions: 'Who is Zaharoff?') The Committee's assistant legal adviser was later to make more of a name for himself: Alger Hiss.

The declared objective was to hunt for proof of a conspiracy that the armaments makers, in league with Wall Street and British propagandists, had deliberately instigated the late war for the sake of the profits. The undeclared objective was a determination to steer America clear of entangling alliances which might involve her in the quarrels of the Old World. The Committee, armed with powers to impound documents, burrowed for two years. One of the first targets to emerge was an American armaments company which was known to have close links with an overseas company. This was the Electric Boat Company, the other was Vickers. There was talk of patent monopoly, of formenting an arms race between Chile and Peru, of irresponsible business practices and, of course, of Basil Zaharoff.

The Electric Boat Company owed its pre-eminence in the submarine market to the original basic Holland patent. From its founding it had had a licensing agreement with the British company. Owing to their higher building costs, royalties on foreign orders were the company's lifeblood. In 1927 alone twenty-four 'submarine boats' were under construction in European yards – six of them in Zaharoff's Spanish yards – while the only submarines built in the United States between the completion of war contracts and 1934 were four boats for Peru. In practice this meant that Electric Boat received 40 per cent of the profit on submarines built in the Vickers yards in Britain, and 50 per cent on those built by Vickers in yards elsewhere. Between 1902 and 1934 this arrangement had brought in just under £1,500,000 to the American company on 170 boats completed during this period. Without these, as Henry Carse, Electric Boat's chairman, testified, there would have been no Electric Boat Company, 'because that is the only thing that kept us alive'.

It transpired that Zaharoff had acted as Electric Boat's European agent from at least 1912 and moreover had his own royalty agreement with the founder, Isaac Rice, and Albert Vickers by which he received 5 per cent of the selling price of submarines put together by his 'pet baby', La Sociedad Español de la Construcción Naval; even when Electric Boat and Vickers reduced their royalties to 3½ per cent each in the depression, Sir Basil's remained at the original figure. The total commission paid to Sir Basil from 1919 up to 1930 came to just over three-quarters of a million dollars – a 'very onerous burden' in the eyes of Electric Boat, a very fitting one in the eyes of the recipient.

Twice the American company attempted to remonstrate with the indomitable Greek on the size of his fee. 'I don't believe either fundamentally or originally', Carse told the Senators, 'there is any reason for such an allowance. My predecessor granted it when he was giving away everything.' Carse admitted, though, that he had talked to Sir Basil, whom three days earlier he had described as the 'greatest man living', in Paris in 1923, and had settled the dispute. 'Sir Basil convinced me of the justice of the commission.' Not so thoroughly, however, that he did not have another try the next year. Sir Basil's short response that it was the proper allowance to make brooked no mere quibble.

'Did he convince you?' asked Senator Bennett Champ Clark, who had previously shown interest in whether George V was a shareholder in Vickers.

'Yes, sir,' replied Carse.

'Mr Z' continued to steal the scene.

'I am astonished', remarked Senator Homer T.Bone at one point, 'the United States did not give him some honour.' (He had just confused the Bath with the Garter.)

'We had testimony,' replied Senator Nye, 'that in 1919 the President accorded some honour to him.'

This good impression was soon spoilt for the Senators. Another of Sir Basil's fateful jaunty letters was read before the Committee.

Gentlemen,

I beg to acknowledge receipt of your letter of 3rd inst., bringing my cheque for Frcs 391,497.68 on Madrid, with which I am doing the needful.

I now avail myself of this opportunity to say good morning to your President, in the hope that Mrs Carse and Master Carse are in excellent health.

The Senators jumped on this.

Sen. Nye: 'What is the meaning of that language "with which I am doing the needful"?'

Carse: 'I do not know.'

Sen. Clark: '. . . What did you understand that this remittance was for?'

Carse: 'I did not understand anything about it. I do not ask people what they are doing. It is none of my business.'

Sen. Clark: 'That phrase was just a meaningless phrase to you. . . .'

Carse: 'Yes, it did not mean anything. He never told me what his expenditures were.'

Sen. Bone: '. . . does the language "doing the needful" have any particular significance in a country like Spain?'

Carse: 'I do not know. I do not know what he did with it . . . One can make all sorts of guesses and have all sorts of dreams, and so on . . . . You are asking me for facts. I do not know anything about what he did with the money. From what I know of Sir Basil, I would rather think that he kept it for himself.'

(It should be added that Zaharoff, fond as he was of the phrase 'doing the needful', used it in a variety of senses, sometimes to indicate that he would return some benign service or favour, or even in those far-off days as a storekeeper in Cyprus to boast of clearing his shelves of some slow-moving article.)

Through ignorance and lack of preparation, Carse was made to appear devious and evasive. He professed to be unaware that the original patent-pooling agreement for submarines between Vickers and his company had been not only approved, but actively encouraged by the Admiralty. No witnesses were called from Vickers in clarification. The impression left by the proceedings was that of two powerful arms companies conspiring to deceive the government of one of them. In the absence of such explanations, compounded by Carse's dismal showing, many other questions went unanswered. Little wonder that the worst interpretation should have been put on them. They received an immense amount of airing on both sides of the Atlantic and, although Electric Boat was exonerated ('You have been mighty decent with us ... mighty clean in the way you have dealt with the Committee,' acknowledged the Dakotan), their effect on public opinion in the United States was dramatic.

The Nye Committee recommended by a majority of one that certain arms firms in the United States should be nationalized. This proposal fell on stony ground. But the consequences were more serious. Anti-war Bills proliferated, others proposed to enforce neutrality on the country. The President was obliged to bow to this pressure and accept an Act imposing an embargo on the export of arms in the event of war. Roosevelt wanted to discriminate between an aggressor and his victim but the isolationists would have none of it. He was forced to accept a compromise: the embargo would be discretionary, but once imposed it would apply to all belligerents. This act was to prove a constant source of embarrassment to the administration, and a more damaging inconvenience to Britain in her time of greatest need.

Much of this sound and fury awoke a responsive chord in certain British breasts, where a considerable industry of propaganda against private manufacture of arms had been cultivated, notably by the League of Nations' Union and the Union of Democratic Control. In this charged atmosphere the revelations of the Nye Committee, as interpreted by the headlines, acted like a gas poker on a Catherine-wheel. The sparks began to whizz.

Part of this reaction was founded on political prejudice just a short step from acute schizophrenia, but it was also echoed by a sympathetic strand in popular feeling which somehow saw the issue as a natural extension of the wish formally to interdict war. This opposition, if emotional, was earnest, and eventually effective.

Questions were asked in Parliament, most of them drawing on the correspondence thrown up by the Nye Committee, most of them aimed at Vickers, which had not yet had an opportunity to put its case. Major Attlee, Leader of the Opposition, proposed that Britain should set an example by prohibiting forthwith the private manufacture of arms, a practice he compared with prostitution, the moral equivalent of the slave trade. The Liberals more coolly put in a plea for an enquiry. It is difficult to understand the national government's motives for refusing this, but refused it was in a glittering speech by Sir John Simon, the Foreign Secretary.

He dealt severely with the 'grossest misrepresentations' of the abolitionist propaganda, he ran concentric rings around the plodding Leader of the Opposition. Did Mr Attlee, then, approve of state brothels? Should not the slave trade have been nationalized? It was a brilliant display – and he entirely misjudged the temper of the House; *The Times* even labelled his performance 'unfortunate'. A fortnight later he retracted it. He apologized to the House for having given the wrong impression and come to the wrong conclusion; he apologized so profusely, indeed, that he was in some danger of becoming for once almost a popular figure. He promised that after all there would be an enquiry in the shape of a Royal Commission.

It was to be neither a white-washing operation nor 'a fishing expedition in dirty waters'. The chairman was a slightly deaf eighty-year-old retired appeal judge, Sir John Eldon Bankes. The members included Dame Rachel Crowdy, wartime commandant of the VADs (Voluntary Aid Detachment) in France and an official of the League of Nations; an authority on international law; two businessmen, one a prominent figure in the Co-op movement; the former war correspondent, Sir Philip Gibbs, and the Liberal journalist, J.A.Spender, who twenty years before, as editor of the *Westminster Gazette*, had defended the conduct of Liberal ministers in the Marconi scandal and the sale of honours.

As the Commission opened, Vickers' image could not have been worse. The chairman General Sir Herbert Lawrence, a stern unbending character, did nothing to improve it. The prejudice against the private manufacture of arms, he declared in the company's General Statement, was 'the expression of an honourable, but perhaps mistaken, ideal respecting the sanctity of life and the iniquity of war'. This caused a sensation of shocked indignation. As a result Vickers soon found itself in the dock.

It was Gibbs who, with professional curiosity, probed the most persistently into the Zaharoff legend, whose owner was fifteen years short of his century.

This interest had been anticipated by members of the Vickers board, who considered Sir Basil something of a political liability in the prevailing climate of opinion. Their latest recruit, Colonel A.T.Maxwell, a young banker and barrister, put their case to the chairman. General Lawrence at once reacted very firmly. 'The day I leave the chair they can do what they like. Until then we will keep the arrangements that we have made.' Colonel Maxwell's impression from this was that

General Lawrence, although personally he disliked very much the publicity and the mystery-man side of Zaharoff, had a high sense of what the company owed to his abilities.

General Lawrence soon found himself at a loss to describe Sir Basil's exact relationship with the firm: he had become by dint of long service an institution.

'Would he have been officially recognized as one of your agents?' asked Sir Philip Gibbs. 'I mean, would he have signed an agreement with your firm? He must have done, of course.'

'I do not think so,' replied Lawrence. 'I should certainly say not. I do not think he was ever accredited in any sense by a signature of the firm.'

'But in order to draw his commission,' Gibbs persisted, 'you would have had to have a formal agreement with him?'

'I think he would have, probably. I have no knowledge of it.'

The effect of this uncharacteristic bumbling was to give an impression of evasiveness. Indeed his company seemed to have very little idea itself of where all the parties stood. The Commission had been told that Sir Basil had ceased to have any connection with Vickers in 1924, yet a letter dated the following year had been produced at the Senate enquiry in which Sir Basil specifically referred to 'the interests of my firm of Vickers'.

Sir Philip Gibbs was as much concerned with Zaharoff's image as his activities. He was, he claimed, 'regarded as a very sinister figure stalking through the Courts of Europe'.

'He is rather an expansive person,' replied Lawrence, doing his best to put him into perspective, 'and talks rather at large.'

Gibbs worried away at commissions like a bull-terrier with a recalcitrant bone. What method of payment had been arranged? Was he paid by commission on orders received by Vickers?

'So far as we are able to trace,' replied Frederick Yapp, a recent director whose father had served as company secretary to the old Maxim–Nordenfelt firm, 'Sir Basil Zaharoff did originally receive a commission on orders which he obtained from us.'

'And he is still one of your agents?' asked Gibbs.

'In Spain only.'

'With regard to Sir Basil Zaharoff,' continued Sir Philip, 'who is rather an important figure in the world, and will go down in history, there is no doubt, I imagine you will agree, that his value to you was very largely his influence in political circles of Europe and the world. Do you agree with that?'

'I do not think we have anybody like that today,' replied Yapp.

'You have nobody to succeed Sir Basil Zaharoff?'

'Nobody.'

'Do you mean from the social point of view?' interposed Sir Charles Craven, Vickers' caustic managing director.

'I mean,' said Gibbs, 'from the political-interest point of view, friends of prime ministers, friends of politicians, and of those who rule the destinies of mankind. . . .'

It was left to Sir Maurice Hankey to put the positive case for the private manufacture of arms. He was in a peculiar position. He was a senior civil servant; he was careful to explain that he did not commit the Prime Minister, and yet he clearly spoke for the government and represented the views of the defence ministries and other concerned departments. He took a strong line from the outset, condemning the 'lack of balance and perspective' and the 'vagueness and exaggeration, inaccuracy and insinuation' which characterized the case against private manufacture.

Hankey's evidence largely influenced the Royal Commission's report issued in October 1936, arguing that the reasons for maintaining private manufacture outweighed those for its abolition. The Report advocated more rigid control by the government over the export of arms and, in time of war, conscription of labour.

The demon king was not invited to take the stage himself, but if his French citizenship, age and frailty precluded this, neither was he invited to submit his testimony. The legend of the 'merchant of death' had been the subject of wide speculation and investigation for well over a decade, time enough for the prosecution to prepare its case. Yet among the many witnesses and multitude of written submissions by a wealth of national and international alliances and leagues, federations and associations, councils and conferences, spokesmen for political factions, religious organizations, trade unions, promoters of women's rights and even, oddly, upholders of temperance, not one was able to point to any impropriety on Sir Basil's part.

And the political climate, too, had changed. It was no longer possible wilfully to ignore the war clouds surging up again over Europe which no amount of wishful thinking and well-meaning intentions would blow away. Just one month after the Report appeared, the Berlin–Tokyo–Rome axis had been cemented, the Anschluss was only a year away.

Sir Basil himself survived publication by only a matter of weeks.

23

Last Lust

A fter the Duchess's death the bereaved husband retired
once more into his shell. Three months after his loss he
formally adopted his two stepdaughters; in the same year
they were divorced, the younger reverting to her maiden
name, Angèle de Bourbon. She cut a dashing figure, a brilliant horse-
woman and keen shot (Sir Basil bought her a pair of Purdeys, though
she found them too heavy). She was also a confirmed rallyist; three
times competing in the Monte Carlo in the *époque héroïque*. Cristina
Walford's divorce was one of convenience to safeguard her heritage.
Judging from the repeated handouts in larger and lesser amounts
Sir Basil heaped on him through the years, money clearly ran too
fluently through Leopold's fingers. Even after the formal break, they
remained a devoted couple – and Sir Basil continued to allow himself
to be touched regularly and in moderation.

Although he rarely ventured out himself, and never to dine, Sir
Basil still entertained on a modest scale in Paris. The occasional English
visitor remarked disapprovingly that the rooms were kept at a tropical
temperature with all the windows shut. Old Clemenceau came round;
President Doumergue dismissed England at one lunch because of
the 'ludicrous and economic experiments of the Labour government
which will surely ruin her'. His host took leave to disagree. Turks
still visited, ill at ease and uncomfortable in their new bowler hats
(the wearing of the fez had been made a criminal offence under Atatürk's reformist zeal).

The gold service was de rigueur. Its owner was at one time, we
are told, held in high esteem by the gourmets of Europe. He himself

invented a dish called *Bananes Zaharoff* which some French christened *Bananes à la Mystère*, an ancestor of the *Bombe Surprise*. Stories were told of his sending out emissaries all over the world in search of choice and rare recipes; of aeroplanes bringing strange sea-food from distant quarters of the earth ... (The same source, possibly having fed too well on strange sea-food, also noted, amid the magnificent French furniture, 'Bayeux tapestries' – a pleasant surprise.)

All that distinguished the house from its neighbours was the profusion of flowers in glass-covered window boxes; gloxinias were a favourite. Although he now spent little time in Paris, they gave pleasure to the people who passed. During the threatened May Day demonstrations of 1930 he was said to have returned home to find his servants removing the display of blooms for fear the glass might be smashed. 'Leave the flowers,' he instructed them. 'They are the pride of the *quartier*. They shall not be deprived of them.' The appreciative horde cheered as it filed past the house.

Flowers filled the house. His table was often decorated with an arrangement of petals. 'But they won't last,' someone objected. 'Nothing does,' he pointed out.

A traditionalist to the core, his motorcars were the one visible note of nonconformism. The make was modest. As a friend of the family he loyally stuck to Renaults all his life with just one exception: his very last car was a Packard (the French agent, brother-in-law of René Léon of the Monte Carlo Casino, was another friend). His motors were always painted in the same livery of Oxford blue picked out in yellow. But what was most noticeable was that by the late 1920s he still favoured an old pre-war box-like model. This was not for reasons of economy, rather for ease of entry; Sir Basil was not obliged to stoop unnecessarily. However, their exceptional endurance was not owed entirely to the good offices of Baker, the chauffeur, but to the simpler expedient of replacing them regularly. The production line was interrupted to turn out an antique model made to measure.

Although he led a quiet life from choice, Sir Basil nonetheless managed to enjoy the odd amatory adventure – the 'brief Indian Summer of his last romance', though it more closely resembled a lusty winter.

It is clear that he had a reputation for gallantry even at a ripe age. The most unlikely evidence of this is offered by the systematically selfish and petulant Violet Trefusis. In 1920, months after her unusual elopement with Vita Sackville-West, she taunted her lover that she was about to become the mistress of Basil Zaharoff. There was little enough danger of that but the threat was calculated to cast the wretched Mrs Nicolson into a decline. It is not less strange that the old man and the minx were incontestably acquainted. In the previous year or two, Zaharoff had paid two amounts – £250 and twenty guineas, suggesting donations to charity for which he was an accustomed target – to Violet's mother, Mrs Keppel. In early December 1919 he paid one hundred guineas to 'Trefusis'. This might have been an overdue cheque for a wedding present (Violet had married the unfortunate Denys Trefusis that June). But at this time Vita and Violet were together in Monte Carlo, gambling recklessly at the Casino while waiting to be offered a cruise on Venizelos' yacht. Certainly the two girls were too obsessed with each other's charms to spare much of a thought for an old Greek. His gift, doubtless accompanied by a homily on fickle chance, was more probably the indulgent gesture of a family friend.

The object of his final infatuation, born Edmée Dormeuil at Le Havre, had married in 1914 at the age of eighteen a rich tea planter from Ceylon, Sir Theodore Owen, her senior by some forty years. She subsequently led the old gentleman a song and dance, achieving in the process some ephemeral fame on the London and Paris stage under her maiden name until she was ineluctably widowed. She was in many respects a very lucky young lady; on one occasion she discovered a diamond ring worth £6,000 in an omelette. Unfortunately this chance was counter-balanced by an uncontrollable streak of extravagance. (Her luck would not last for ever and 'when fortune deserts me', she recalled having told Sir Basil at her appearance for a hearing in bankruptcy in November 1936, 'you will die'. She was right.)

The young bride had first marked Zaharoff down when he was lunching alone at his table at the Carlton Hotel. The waxen clearness of his complexion and his steely gaze made the deepest impression and from the curious, rather old-fashioned severity of his dress, she knew him to be a man of consequence.

It was only in the year after she lost her husband in 1926 that she was reminded of him again and, a slave to impulse, wrote him a note recalling their first encounter. She was fortunate once more. Sir Basil's secretary was ill so that the great man himself happened to glance through his immense mail. Yes, he replied, he vividly remembered 'the little girl in pink with the golden curls' whom he had seen at the Carlton twelve years before who had stared at him with such big round eyes until the colour rose in her cheeks.

A strange courtship by correspondence proceeded, on his side usually dictated from the Hôtel de Paris. (When he did use his own hand, he had a care for the medium; he was too easily overcome.

'I shall write in pencil now because the ink has given me black ideas, for which I ask your pardon.') She followed up with flowers while he reciprocated with rose trees and out-of-season asparagus from the south. She was not backward in offering a series of fetching photographs, begging in return with unkind emphasis for a recent likeness. He complied, but his heart had mounted to his mouth. He quickly regretted this impetuosity. 'Sweetie Mine,' he implored, 'I am trembling with anguish at what you will think of me when you have seen what is left of me. Be merciful. ...'

The cumulative effect of this long-range relationship began to take a hold on him. 'I am quite mad about you and can think of nothing else.' He planned to meet her halfway in Paris – 'This is an adventure. I throw caution to the winds ...' – in spite of the inconvenience due to the need to change his habits and leave Monte Carlo at least a month earlier than was his wont. But he still had his doubts. 'I begin to think of your disappointment when first you meet me, a middle-aged gentleman' – he had clearly not been quite frank about his age – 'bald, with white hair. You will say to yourself that this is May and November!'

He had now been poring over the trio of photographs once again. 'Beautiful Lady!' he gushed. 'I do love the little feet in the whole-length photo, and after seeing them I will take off your shoes and then your stockings and kiss the tiny little darling feet and feel their soft delicate skin.'

Despite this effusion, she reproached him for being too cautious and reserved in his letters. 'Cherika,' he protested in reply, 'Don't bé cruel!' She also prudently asked him whether he wanted his letters back. 'I cannot forget the great insult in your last letter,' he replied in an unnaturally incautious moment. 'Fancy asking me if I want my letters returned to me! You don't, I imagine, want me to send back your letters, do you? Never! They are far too precious to me. ... I really do not deserve such a suggestion from you.' (They were quite as precious to Lady Owen.)

Their first face-to-face was finally fixed for the end of March 1928. Although she can have had few illusions about the fate which awaited her, she was naturally curious about where she would be received. '*Tout sera naturel,*' he promised her. 'I will not receive you in a drawing room, *visite d'étiquette.* You will come to my library *(intime) ou je suis toujours dans ma solitude. Le dîner sera simple, comme si j'étais seul, les vins aussi. Il n'y aura aucun changement dans ma vie habituelle.* You would not love me if I gave myself airs. *Le "célèbre" service d'or massif est sur la table depuis un demi siècle et il y sera pour toi,*' he reassured her. He likewise commanded her to wear a simple pink dress with no jewels. (She never accepted jewels on principle – unless they turned up in an omelette.)

He promised to pick her up for dinner in the 'little coupé' at 7.25, but at the last moment his courage failed him. The car was empty. On the seat which he would have occupied was a bunch of red carnations to welcome her in his stead.

She was not disappointed. Sitting in almost deathly immobility at the far end of the room, his eyes glowed at his young guest from a face the colour of old wax. He rose slowly and bowed. She smiled and then, in his thin, rather high-pitched voice, he said: 'You are lovelier than I thought you would be. It is good of you to come.'

She at once started off on the wrong foot after the formalities, casting her chinchilla coat, which had cost another £6,000, carelessly over the back of a chair near the fire. 'My dear little lady!' he reproached her. It took a time to break the ice; the footmen interfered with the intimacy. Her host was, however, so she judged, the more nervous of the two and she tried to put him at his ease by wheedling out of him the secrets of his life. She had only moderate success.

After coffee they repaired to his private study once more where very soon whatever constraint that remained between them disappeared. The time came when their casual talk slurred into easy silences, and suddenly the strangest lover she had ever known took Lady Owen into his arms.

That, she assured the readers of the *People*, was the first of many meetings but even at that distance of time – one week after his demise – she did not feel justified in describing 'the intimacies of a friendship that was very dear to me', particularly as she was, after all, 'scarcely more than a girl' – or anyway in her thirties – 'at the time'. However she kept something up her sleeve for other audiences. 'His ardour as a lover was that of a young man ... He was a great lover, yet he was not of the wild and indiscriminate type. Deep down in his heart there was abundant virtue. ...'

However, all good things have an end. Sir Basil had, she supposed, set her on a pedestal too high for a girl of her wayward impulse and emotion. The day accordingly came when, in all loyalty, she felt bound to tell Sir Basil that she had found another lover, young and strong and, it may well be believed, altogether different. He took the news with quiet and tragic dignity. His St Martin's summer had ended. (It might be noted that the saint's symbol is a goose.) There were no reproaches, but the breach was final.

The same wayward impulses got her into deeper trouble. She was shortly sentenced to five years for a *crime passionel*, the attempted murder by shooting of the wife of her lover, an Alsatian doctor. It was reported in the press that Sir Basil had never ceased his attempts to interest successive ministers of justice in her case; she was pardoned after two and a half years by the incoming President Lebrun. She later encapsulated her experiences in print – *Flaming Sex: A Book with a Moral*.

After Edmée Owen had passed on to fresh pastures, Sir Basil settled down once again to a routine more befitting his age.

It was about this time that talk got about that he was committing his own memoirs to paper. That gave rise to emotions ranging from indignation to panic. And then a mysterious fire broke out at the avenue Hoche. The Paris papers reported that the fire brigade had everything under control within half an hour, although the valuable furniture was seriously damaged. The cause of the fire was ascertained; the owner of the house, without due precaution, had been burning a great mass of papers in the grate.

Two days later the press had more information. The cinders were all that remained of Sir Basil Zaharoff's memoirs. On the morning of the outbreak a servant, who had been in the house for years, had absconded with them. The fugitive was apprehended the same evening in the Bois de Boulogne in the act of negotiating with an unknown man who made good his getaway. The compromising packet was returned to the owner and Sir Basil that night decided to disembarrass himself of the inflammable matter. One Paris newspaper offered £1,000 for any page of the manuscript which might have survived. There was no response. It was also reported elsewhere that the faithful Macpherson had been offered £2,000 to purloin any diaries, an offer which he reported to his master. This may well have decided him.

In fact, the destruction of his papers and the fire were two quite distinct incidents separated by some years.

He explained his motives to Lady Owen. 'You are right in saying that burning my memoirs was like parting with old friends, but of late I have read several memoirs of people who have passed on to the other world.

'They all seem to have left behind them disagreeable sayings about other people. But my memoirs were written for my own pleasure. . . . I think that they belonged to me and that I had the right to destroy them.

'I did so because I did not want to leave anything unpleasant behind me. It was a struggle and needed much determination and courage, but I felt that it had to be done. . . .'

250

It was also a matter of the deepest regret to posterity, although their survival would have strangled a small industry at birth.

He related to Rosita Forbes how he had executed the deed as there was 'too much trouble in them. I put them into the kitchen stove and I ruined my best umbrella ramming them down. It took all day to burn them, and my daughter came in just as it was finished and was furious with me. She tried to pull out the last pages and they fell on the floor charred . . . So now I have no life records but my memories – of the adventures that were the dreams of my life.'

The fire in his home, a more serious conflagration, took place in 1930. If he had been in his bedroom instead of his study, he might well have gone the way of his late memoirs. As it was, much damage was done. It may well have been in this blaze that the silver model of a cannon – not gold as legend records – of which image-makers made such a symbolic ado, was melted down. The firemen threw many portable possessions through the windows into the courtyard where the next morning his daughter rescued a heavy metal desk lamp, not solely for its sentimental value: it was in *or massif*.

The surprise is that anything at all was saved. A Glaswegian eyewitness recorded that two firemen first arrived on bicycles and immediately set to work – to take notes. It was ten minutes even after the complete brigade arrived before hoses were playing around. The crew, evidently unsteady at the late hour, were falling over the hose, which one of them managed to coil around his neck.

Having rid himself of his own work, he was in no mood to welcome the speculations of other considerate (and hopeful) biographers. Whenever he received offers of manuscript biographies for sale, he would return a printed card: 'M. Zaharoff n'ayant plus de voix, ne peut pas chanter.'* Still, the gradual appearance of such unauthorized volumes caused him exceeding annoyance, though he never made any attempt to correct the legend. If he had wanted panegyrics, as one biographer suggested, he knew the price.

Sir Basil had not sunk into torpor. Well past his eightieth birthday he continued to concern himself with the wider affairs of the world, and in particular the rise of Nazism. He can only have viewed the mouthings of the pacifists and isolationists as pitiable and, more important, passé, the proceedings of the enquiries into the structure of the armaments industry as largely irrelevant to the changing order.

He is reported to have seen Georges Mandel, the former head of Clemenceau's private cabinet who had inherited some of his old chief's

* Wordplay on 'sing' and 'blackmail'.

spirit,* to urge him to forge closer ties with Spain to forestall German intrusion. He told Mandel to:

pay less attention to *les jeux des mots* of Fascism and Nazism, but to concentrate on where France's real friends were. You won't find them simply divided into opposite camps, but in some very strange places. Germany will dominate Europe again if France, Britain, Italy and Spain do not seek alliance with the right forces in Germany. Those forces, those real friends, are not in the so-called underground democratic camp – that doesn't exist, as no German is a genuine democrat – nor are they to be found among those of Hitler's entourage who pretend to be friends of Britain but enemies of France (they only seek to divide). You keep dossiers, M.Mandel, and I tell you that you should add into the list of possible friends in time of need: Admiral Canaris, of the Abwehr; General von Kleist, of the German High Command; Baron von Thyssen, the industrialist, Juan March, of Majorca, on the Spanish side, and the Spanish officer, Beigbeder. If Britain and France were wise, they would immediately try to bring all these people on to their side: it could be done. But for this purpose the Italians must be kept in the dark; you cannot trust them, for they pass everything on directly to the Nazis now. Only when they see that there are other and better forces in Germany working with Britain, France and Spain, as ought now to be the case, will they take notice and swing over.

This conversation cannot be confirmed from any evidence, but it is plausible; the banker and industrialist Juan March was certainly a friend of the Zaharoff family. But Sir Basil was out of step with prevailing sentiment. Several more years were to pass before Fritz Thyssen and Ewald von Kleist became alive to the danger. The General, a confidant of Colonel Oster, Canaris' aide, then visited London to interest a receptive Churchill, an initiative which was thwarted by the placatory Nevile Henderson in Berlin, and after a distinguished military career, paid for his indiscretion with his life; Thyssen, one of the Nazis' earliest paymasters, was luckier, fleeing before the outbreak of war with the lament, 'What a *Dummkopf* I was.' But Sir Basil would seem to have been mistaken over Colonel Juan Beigbeder's sympathies; as Spanish Foreign Minister in 1940, he mixed himself in the plot to kidnap the Duke of Windsor.

The role of Canaris is more obscure. There is no clear evidence that the Greek and the German knew each other, but it is probable

* Briefly Minister of the Interior in 1940, he fled with Daladier to North Africa to continue the struggle from there but was ignominiously returned as a deserter. One of the leaders of the Jewish community in Paris under the Occupation, he refused to leave for his own safety, was handed over to the Germans and perished in a concentration camp.

that their paths had crossed in Spain during the war, and they would have had one bond in common: Canaris was proud of his descent from the Greek admiral and hero of the struggle for independence. There is no doubt either that he shared Sir Basil's misgivings about the Nazis.

There is another letter attributed to Juan March, to a friend in Madrid.

There is now no question that Spain must be rescued from the Republican mob as swiftly as possible. Doubtless the Germans and Italians will support us, but it is not in Spain's long-term interest, nor in that of France, or Britain, or even Italy, to allow Germany to call the tune. And she will want to call the tune, to be the master of Europe – that is the price she demands for rescuing us from Bolshevism. This is a job we must do for ourselves. Hitler is the enemy of the survival of any real independence among European nations. He wants not merely a living space and colonies, but the power to dictate to all. His is an unhealthy regime and bodes ill for the future. Basil Zaharoff, who knows his Germany and who has tried to get along with the National Socialist riffraff agrees with me. More important, Canaris thinks the same, and does not love, nor trust his new masters. He is our best ally in Europe at the moment. Zaharoff is too old to have much influence now, but he is wise and could save us all from putting too much faith in the Germans. For once Zaharoff is not questing for commissions; he is horrified at the idea that Germany may once again perpetrate another world war.

Canaris* is not what he seems. He has learned a lesson and will now merely hold on to his powers in the intelligence world to find out Hitler's plans and to thwart him until some new rulers can be brought to power. Spain needs Britain as an ally, perhaps more than France, because Britain is stable, but no one will now listen to Zaharoff, whom they mistrust, and no one will listen to Canaris because he is head of intelligence. That is the tragedy of it all.

If this is a close representation of his thinking, Sir Basil can only have quietly despaired. There was no role left for him. He was a lonely old man with a past and a reputation. The thought must have embittered his last years.

And his time was running out.

---

* Admiral Wilhelm Canaris took his secrets to the scaffold with him on 9 April 1945, weeks before the next war ended.

24

Exit

His own family was shrinking. His sister Charikleia had died in 1928, followed by Zoë; Sevasty, who had served as a nurse through the war, 'my third and last one, and life companion here', died at the end of 1932. None had married.

The press had already begun to kill off their brother. Sir Mark Jenkinson would kindly send him newspaper cuttings speculating on his precarious health. 'It is evident I have amused the public,' Sir Basil replied. 'Now that the newspapers find that I no longer interest the readers, they either make out that I am retiring, or am dying, and I should tell you that as far as Vickers – my Alma Mater – is concerned, I hope to die in harness.'

The European press kept this up for a full ten years. On each prediction of his death from different capitals, Sir Mark would send him a sympathetic telegram, only to receive a cheerful reply. In January 1932 he was rumoured to be seriously ill with 'flu. 'I have just received your telegram,' wrote Sir Basil. 'The Press endeavour to kill me half a dozen times a year. I think I once told you not to believe these reports until I myself informed you of my death, for which I am in no hurry.' Next March he was again reported seriously ill in Monte Carlo; that summer a Bucharest sheet gave out that he was 'dangerously ill and was on his death bed', followed by a report from London that he had died. Next morning this was contradicted from Paris: 'Today Sir Basil felt as well as ever and went for a ride in his electric bathchair in the park of his beautiful country seat, Château Balincourt.'

'It was not the death rattle they heard,' he is said to have remarked

254

to friends. 'It was the rattle of the Remingtons* firing off my obituary.'

The natural hazards of old age and the unsatisfied curiosity of the newspapers were not deemed adequate as an explanation for this speculation. Some suitable motive had to be uncovered. It was made out that the old man took a macabre delight in inventing and encouraging these reports in the hope of provoking some enemy into an embarrassing indiscretion.

Life at his beautiful country seat, surrounded by his adopted daughters and their families, was well ordered and punctual, the daily routine invariable: breakfast in bed at nine o'clock in company with Pater, Fragonard and Boucher, when his mail and the newspapers would be read to him by Macdermott (he did not tolerate the wireless); a ride in his motor, from which he rarely descended, around the local markets, the Grand Cross of the Legion of Honour in his lapel, a white piqué stock around his neck. At 12.30 the bell would ring to give a half-hour warning of lunch. Meals were not easy: 'On m'appelle le taciturne,' he used to say. The children, overawed, would sit in silence. 'Don't all talk at once,' he would tell them. Uncertainly, the chatter would start up, then gather way. 'Don't all talk at once,' he would next admonish them. A subdued silence would fall again. High standards at the table were maintained *en famille*. Melon from the garden was always on the menu, with a fish or egg dish followed by the main course, dessert before the cheese in the English fashion, with fruit, coffee and Chartreuse, a rare cigar, the band boldly embossed 'ZZ', and, a final treat, a stuffed *pruneau d'Agen* from Fortnum's. The meal was most likely accompanied by a Latour 1919.

Sir Basil would then take his siesta and at four o'clock would ride round the gardens in his electric carriage with his valet Short, or take a row on the lake with Macdermott, sweets for children of the estate in one hand, bread for the swans in the other. After this exercise Short would read to him, mostly history. At 7.30 the bell would go again to warn of supper. And so to bed.

Even in this quiet haven, his legend did not leave him alone. In October 1935 the Italian press revived the shade of the arms king. British sources were accused of supplying arms to Abyssinia on the curious grounds that Stanley Baldwin, Sir John Simon, Ramsay MacDonald and the Archbishop of Canterbury were all shareholders in Vickers, and that this motley gang was 'guided' by Sir Basil Zaharoff.

In October, in 'excellent health for his age and remarkably alert', he celebrated his eighty-seventh birthday quietly in Paris. He left

* E. Remington & Sons, gunmakers, pioneered the first efficient typewriter model.

almost immediately for the winter sun. He was spotted in Monte Carlo wrapped up in his rugs in his bathchair being wheeled along the Promenade des Anglais. (It is to be hoped the chair fitted in the car for the ten-mile trip to Nice.)

On 26 November 1936, he went for his usual drive and dined with his daughter Angèle in his rooms at the Hôtel de Paris. It was his custom to have a hot bath drawn for him each evening and leave it overnight so that by the morning it had reached exact room temperature. On the next morning, Friday, he was found dead in the bath by Short.

The ultimate irony of his life was that following so many years of speculation on his origins, his date and place of birth on his death certificate were confidently given as 20 October 1850 in Phanar, that quarter of Constantinople where the rich Greek merchants and bankers had led their sheltered lives. (This was shortly corrected by affidavit, witnessed by Léon Barthou, which established the 'perfect identity of person between Monsieur Zakarie (Zacharie), son of Basil or Basile Zaharoff, and the person called ZAHAROFF Basil' born at Mughla on 6 October 1849.)

It might have been said that he had finally settled his accounts – except for one conventional detail. At the time of his death, he was owed £17,500 in outstanding commission on his Spanish business.

At 3.00 a.m. the next day a motor-hearse left Monaco. His last voyage, with two drivers alternating, ended at Balincourt at midnight. At a small family service – the family embracing also the household and outdoor staff and the estate workers – conducted by a Greek Orthodox priest imported from Paris, Sir Basil Zaharoff was laid to rest beside his Duchess in the private chapel in the grounds.

The Mayor of Arronville provided the only recorded burial-day tribute. 'He was generous and unfailingly polite ... when he first came here my predecessor told him there were no poor in the district. When Sir Basil found out that the Mayor was wrong he was always ready to put his hand in his pocket.'

This was not mere graveside cant. A sequel to *The Times* obituary from 'J.G.K.' stressed the same compassion. 'The side of Basil Zaharoff's character which made a strong appeal to me and to the few whom he honoured with the title of "Friend" was his intense sympathy for the poor, the sick and the sad. ...' Describing himself as the 'beggarman' for the Great Ormond Street Hospital for many years, on five occasions Sir Basil had sent him cheques of £1,000 each to endow cots, a benefaction that escaped all the usual publicity.

As the obituaries rolled off the presses, the legend flowered and flourished, fed by flights of fantasy and garbled facts. And it enjoyed a long season.

He was barely in the ground before the headlines crowed 'Ghost of Zaharoff Keeps Shares Down.' Vickers shares were lagging behind in the general rise of steel and engineering; the reported reason was selling from Sir Basil's estate. Three hundred directorates were ascribed to him at the height of his power; he was credited with a precise 298 decorations from thirty-one nations.

The vultures also gathered, attracted by the prospect of pickings.

The first on the scene from London was Hyman Barnett Zaharoff, alias Haim Manelowitsch Sahar, claiming to be the lawful son of the house. He was robbed of his proof; the body was already buried. It was suggested that he might have been deliberately balked as there was no evidence that Sir Basil had not died two days earlier than the world had been told. 'I am not satisfied with my present legal arrangements ...' he told the press. 'By the time the French courts have reopened ... I expect to have made new arrangements and also to have secured the financial assistance of a group of people in London who are interested in seeing my claim established.' No more was heard of that.

In Romania, a Pascu B. Zaharoff, a rival claimant as a son, by Georgita Marinescu, sought the assistance of the British Legation to establish his right to the inheritance. A nineteen-year-old Olga, one of the Boston Zaharoffs, an expectant grand-niece, asserted that she and her sister had been left the fortune under a will which had vanished. Frank Miller, a seventy-five-year-old Detroit grocer, claimed to be Sir Basil's brother; he recognized him by a little piece of bone in his ear. An even less convincing claimant was an Armenian tobacco blender, Saddick Chachaty, whose father had been another of Sir Basil's brothers. Two 'sisters' surfaced, Iphigenia Zaharya, eighty, and Melpomeni, some years younger, inhabiting a wooden house on the Sea of Marmora; the elder offered to share her portion with the Greek government, the younger with Atatürk, if their plan should succeed. This play for sponsorship also fell down. All these hopefuls had left it rather late to establish their kinship only after the passing of the patriarch.

Sir George Owens-Thurston, appearing four months later at the London Bankruptcy Court, believed he was a legatee under a missing will. (He had not done badly without it. Between 1917 and 1919 he received almost £30,000 from Sir Basil, whether in director's fees, split commissions or partly for old times' sake is not known.)

And what did the will that was not missing hold? Speculation on the extent of his wealth was an understandably popular pastime with the press. Sir Basil was not one to disabuse them. The most conservative estimate put it at no less than a round £30,000,000. Without being so precise himself, Sir Basil nonetheless is reported to have told a friend at Balincourt: 'I am the seventh richest man in the world.'

This figure seems to have been born out of a statement attributed to a certain J. Ridgely Carter of Morgan Harjes & Company in 1931. 'Zaharoff is a client of ours and is worth perhaps £30 million.' This was a most unusually forthcoming statement for a banker (and diplomat; he had served many years in the American Embassy in London) to utter within earshot of a third party. Morgan Harjes was the Paris house of J. P. Morgan, of which Carter was a partner, although the name of the company had been changed well before 1931, on the death of the other partner Henry H. Harjes, to Morgan et Cie. It is not apparent that Carter issued a disclaimer – or an apology for his indiscretion – and certainly Zaharoff had been a client. Considerable sums were transferred to and from Morgan Harjes through his accounts: £102,000 was placed at the Bank of England through Morgan Grenfell under the instruction of Morgan Harjes as early as 1917, and in 1921 and 1922 transfers of just under £40,000 went the other way. One legend maintained that Japhets in London, Rothschilds in Paris and the Imperial Ottoman Bank 'housed enough gold to enable him to match his fortunes with Ford and Rockefeller'. Little of it was his metal, although Japhet was warm. He was welcomed as 'the most prominent of our shareholders' at a house-warming in their new City premises in October 1924.

Certainly by the standards of the day he had a fortune, but it is more difficult to tell where it came from and where it went. There is an indication only of his cash flow in his ledger at the Bank of England. The most active years were 1917, 1918 and 1919. In that period over £950,000 entered his account by one door and left by another. Of this £115,000 only came from Vickers with further similar amounts from Forth Shipbuilding and Morgan Harjes, but the bulk, in excess of half a million pounds, arrived more discreetly, entered as 'Paris', 'Cash' (more than a quarter of a million in one payment) and 'Post'. It did not lodge there long. In the same years over half a million dribbled out again in some ten various payments to Barclays Bank, and there the trail ends. The records have not survived.

From the early 1920s the transactions dwindled to more imaginable amounts, mostly tokens to assorted charities. By the time of his death his credit balance stood at just £745 8s.

He was saddled by hearsay with losses of between £3,000,000 and £4,000,000 in his declining years; this may or may not have included the milk that was spilt with the Greek adventure in Asia Minor. As if that were not enough, he informed his little friend, Lady Owen, that during the war he had given two-thirds of his entire fortune to France – and, what is more, 'never regretted it'.

His investments were not always happily chosen. The Banque de la Seine had turned sour; he lost more money in west Canadian lumber. Klotz, Clemenceau's Finance Minister, was commonly supposed to have acted as his financial adviser. This would explain his ill-fortune. It was Klotz who presided over the rapid decline of the franc by allowing the French unfunded debt to snowball in 1919 in the unrealistic expectation that it would be recovered through German reparations. Clemenceau, who had no time or inclination for economic considerations, lamented: 'Just my luck to get hold of the only Jew who can't count.'

Making every allowance for all these losses, it is still not reasonable that his wealth at its apogee ever reached anything like the reputed fortune.

A possible explanation that at least satisfies the legend was given in the months following his death. 'One who had been on intimate terms with Sir Basil and his family for several years' allegedly claimed that he had 'disposed of the great part of his fortune about eight or ten years ago. The money has since been tied up in a trust in Luxembourg. What is now left in his will is only what he needed to keep up his mode of living, which for years past, though lavish, was never spectacular.'

His estate in Britain was valued for probate at £193,103, his French estate was worth perhaps three to four times as much. Still, in pre-war terms, that was more than a competence. He bequeathed all his worldly goods to his legally adopted daughters, three-fifths to Cristina Walford of 22 Kensington Palace Gardens, two-fifths to Angèle de Bourbon of 120 rue de Longchamps. To the younger sister he also left Balincourt and the house in avenue Hoche. Balincourt, overclouded with memories of a martinet mother, stood empty for thirty years.

His entire staff inherited the equivalent of half of all they had earned in their years of service with him. The joy with which this news was received was moderated by the notary announcing that such gifts were subject to death duties; then, with a theatrical sense of timing, he put them out of their distress with the news that these would be paid by Sir Basil's daughters.

His resting place was disturbed just once. On 22 January 1937, thieves broke into the family vault. Sir Basil was undisturbed but the grave robbers smashed their way into the Duchess's coffin. A fortune in jewels, including a diamond and emerald necklace of inestimable value, was believed to be buried with her. The rumour of this treasure no doubt arose from his habit of stopping by the vault each day to pay his respects with a silent prayer over the Duchess's remains. No one was prepared to swallow such a story; what was more natural than that he should be keeping an eye on the cache? The intruders were deceived.

25

Epilogue

If Basil Zaharoff remains a figure of chiaroscuro, it is as he intended. Indeed, had he not exceeded his allotted span, there would have been no sulphurous legend on which to throw light. (The tag, 'the Mystery Man of our day', was first coined in the right-wing *National Review* only in 1921.) He was doubtless surprised, certainly displeased, by the intensity of this sudden interest in him. Despising convention, caring not a fig for present reputation or posterity, he compounded the fascination through his stubborn regard for strict privacy which, combined with a strong streak of Baron Münchhausen in his character, served to confound and confuse the curious. Neither, heaped with calumny, did he once stoop to justification. In this manner he fostered a legend, and if this is picaresque, his life was barely less so, although even now it may be doubted whether what is known of him represents more than the tip of the iceberg; there must be many secrets still lurking in the woodwork of war ministries and admiralties around the globe – potential fodder for a crop of PhDs.

He would not be especially remarked in the ranks of other late-Victorian and Edwardian plutocrats, self-made and often alien implants, for the most part an acquisitive and ruthless breed of new men with new mores, in his case offset by more amiable qualities. His two most evident traits, once he had settled down and scattered his wild oats – he was not more unscrupulously opportunistic than the young Disraeli – were loyalty and generosity to those in his intimate circle, difficult ones for the legend to acknowledge. There were two enduring threads in his life: Vickers, his 'alma mater', and a greater Greece. Outside these passions his coterie was limited but, excepting Venizelos, survived the wear of time and the fluctuations of fortune. A pronounced philanderer, he was refreshingly free from Victorian hypocrisy, and yet remained faithful to his Duchess for forty years.

If a man may be judged by his friends, the most revealing relationship was that with Walter Long. A Tory Member of Parliament, he was the last of Macaulay's 'fox-hunting squires'; seventy-three Longs had sat in the House in over 550 years. Forced by ill-health to resign the First Lordship of the Admiralty in 1921, he died three years later. *The Times* obituarist held him up as 'a remarkable example of the influence which sterling honesty and straight-forwardness of character can command in public life . . . incapable of a single mean or unworthy action'. The Liberal *Manchester Guardian* on his retirement paid tribute to him as 'loyal, honest, shrewd . . . all those things we sum up in the word "gentleman" . . . liked and trusted even by his opponents'. It is inconceivable that such a 24-carat character would have tolerated the intimacy of a man who fell much below this exacting standard.

Blessed with unlikely tact and consideration, Basil Zaharoff had his own standards of sensibility. He clung to his friends even in adversity. Unforgiving of slights, real or imaginary, he never forgot or failed to return a kindness. To Lord Bertie, British wartime Ambassador in Paris, he confided his admiration for Lloyd George, but did not admire 'his behaviour to Asquith,* for whom he expressed great friendship as a straight and just gentleman'. This was not a fawning posture: Lloyd George was already Prime Minister, Asquith in the political wilderness.

His long life spanned a period of the greatest advance in weapons technology prior to the nuclear age. When he was still a boy, armies fought their wars with muzzle-loading muskets – the percussion cap had barely superseded the flintlock – and bronze cannon with a slow rate of fire and limited range and accuracy; the fleets, fully rigged, still sheltered behind wooden walls. In the last year of his life the Spitfire flew; the first King George V class battleship of 35,000 tons was laid down within months of his death. Basil Zaharoff played his not inconsiderable role in the development of this lethal revolution at the same time that he contributed to the creation of a company which grew into the greatest and most innovative armaments manufac-

* After the family had left Downing Street, some of Margot Asquith's letters continued to be sent to No. 10. They were returned by Lloyd George's secretaries with 'Not Known' written across them.

turer in the British Empire, the mainstay of that arsenal which sustained the Allied war effort through the most murderous conflict in history.

Such a *métier* attracted no opprobrium until well after the dust had settled in Europe. The export of arms, quite apart from the commercial benefits to the country at a period of progressive decline in trade, was regarded by each government as essential in maintaining that additional capacity for the hour of need which home demand alone could never sustain. Despite this, the British arms makers were left to fend for themselves in the resulting struggle for markets, while their French and German competitors were actively championed by their governments in the wider national interest.

The ethics which commonly prevailed in most overseas markets were not those traditionally associated with Whitehall (Westminster had less inflexible mores). Competition was intense, commissions abusive, corruption endemic − conditions which were not confined to the trade in arms. While such were resented as irrelevant or inflationary, they could not be ignored; the alternative was to abandon the market altogether. And neither was indulgence in such practices a certain recipe for success; it was no more than an entrance fee for the arms race. Performance and price were determinant factors. Basil Zaharoff best succeeded in those countries, notably Russia and Spain, where he exchanged his role of agent for that of entrepreneur and importer of technology and expertise with investment in indigenous enterprises, accelerating the industrial development and independence of the host state.

Much has been made of the parallel between Basil Zaharoff and Andrew Undershaft. The comparison is otiose. It must be doubtful if Shaw had even heard of the Greek when he wrote *Major Barbara* in 1905. Later critics of the 'arms traffic' fastened on to the 'true faith of the Armourer' propounded by Undershaft: 'To give arms to all men who offer an honest price for them, without respect of persons or principals ...', which his one-time wife, Lady Britomart, countered with her own counsel to restrict them 'to people whose cause is right and just, and refuse them to foreigners and criminals'. Such a simplistic and selective policy would have precluded the export of all arms whatsoever outside the Dominions. In the case of Vickers alone, although it might have denied the Maxim gun to potential foes (and future allies), if the foreigners had been as disobliging as to follow suit then the British would have been denied in turn access to patents for armour plate, aeroplanes and time and percussion fuses for shells.

263

Less often quoted was Undershaft's recipe for happiness, that 'you must first acquire money enough for a decent life, and power enough to be your own master'.

Certainly his advice was unexceptionable, but it was Zaharoff's misfortune that chance decreed he should achieve that desirable state through the sale of arms rather than humbugs or hot-water bottles. If Sir Basil had developed any sense of public relations he might, anticipating a future US Secretary of Defense, have retitled himself an 'international logistics procurement executive'. (The one compliment he escaped was to have an incandescent cocktail named after him in the manner of another reserved but altogether less sympathetic figure.)

He well understood the politician's trade, and viewed the tribe with scant esteem. 'Begin on the Left ...', he advised the young Robert Boothby, 'and then, if necessary, work over to the Right. Remember it is sometimes necessary to kick off the ladder those who have helped you to climb it.' Politics played no part in his programme. His friendships ranged through the party spectrum from High Tory to Irish nationalist. In the unique case of Greece, where his emotions enlisted him in the cause of politicians pursuing a nationalist policy of expansion through conflict, he contributed to the greatest misfortune of his compatriots.

As for his fabled political acumen and prescience, the evidence is mixed. The majority of the views attributed to him are of doubtful authenticity, and undated. He manifested a shrewed understanding of the nature of the First World War and of the combinations and susceptibilities of the French Third Republic; and he showed a timely, and far from widely shared, awareness of the menaces of Bolshevism and Nazism.

His role as an *éminence grise* is harder still to gauge. 'I admire power that is secret and doesn't advertise itself', he had admitted to Rosita Forbes. Such traffic is too often intangible and rarely acknowledged. In small matters, his playful boasting struck even his friends as implausible; in great matters he was the soul of discretion. He avoided any breath of suspicion in the recurrent political scandals of the Edwardian age on both sides of the Channel. In the pre-war decades, at the zenith of his career, there is no evidence that he had access to the ears of statesmen in London or Paris. Such influence as he may have exercised at the courts of Spain and Russia was legitimate and mercenary, directed at winning orders in competition with the diplomatic pressures of rival companies working through their embassies. His wartime services had been honoured in discharge of any further obligations; and those who were even aware of these services had left the driving seats of power in the aftermath of the war. He was himself a survivor from an older vanished world, on the way to becoming a legend in his lifetime. Old friendships lingered on, the great still flocked to his table to gawp at the gold plate,* attracted by the aura of power, or simple curiosity. He did little to dispel the impression. He proceeded, noted Sir Campbell Stuart, managing director of *The Times*, 'always with an air of mystery, always with an air of secrecy'. He later had cause to rue this contrivance when he began to attract the unwelcome attention of press and parliaments. In September 1918, *The Times* military correspondent, Colonel Repington, dined with the earthy and eccentric French Rothschild, Maurice, with whom he discussed the alleged 'Jew influence' around Clemenceau, in which he included Basil Zaharoff. Rothschild dismissed the others – Georges Mandel, the bankers Stern, Perreire, even Rothschilds themselves – as small fry. 'Zaharoff of Vickers', he added, 'was another matter. He had vast influence and great wealth.' Whatever the substance of this charge, such a reputation was alone sufficient to ensure a respectful audience, and the survival of the legend.

If he appears a paradox, it is that he presented his mask to the world, revealing his face only to rare intimates. His kindly disposed secretary considered him forbidding but lovable; approachable yet inaccessible. 'He never mellowed', a mere acquaintance recorded, 'as so many men will do under the spell of wine and conversation,' and that acquaintance 'never succeeded in penetrating that enigmatic personality'. And yet a close banking associate found that 'his friendship and his hospitality towards those who are congenial to him is simply unequalled' and his charm unforgettable. Despite an outlandish flamboyance and a schoolboy's relish for subterfuge, he earned and retained the trust and respect of his employers, stern steel masters, for an unparalleled half-century.

Sir Basil offered his own explanation of the origin of the legend. 'If I put down one, thus,' he said one day, sitting at his desk with a notepad, 'it means one. If I put down another one and then again I put down one, it makes a hundred and eleven. Yet I have simply put down three ones. That is the way rumour grows.' He suffered a further misfortune to become the target of the partisan passions of the Third Republic which identified him as the right arm of cross-Channel 'imperialism'. And the legend grew long legs. Even before he was discovered by the US Senate committee, he was seriously

---

* This was acquired, after Zaharoff's death, by King Farouk of Egypt.

seen across the Atlantic as a 'combination of Haroun-al-Raschid, Genghis Khan and Napoleon', which did little to detract from his fascination.

A more serious rationale for his reputation was advanced by the *Manchester Guardian* in his obituary. 'Although there is no good reason to suppose that his business methods were either more or less moral than those of other men, it was widely thought that because he was the personification of a bad system' – a view, however, rejected by the Royal Commission – 'he must also have been a bad man.' Any moral judgement is superfluous. It is indisputable that, in the words of a friend and colleague of thirty years' standing, he 'really was an extraordinary man'.

Chronology

1890   Constantinople, Spandau, Cadiz, Lisbon; Chile, Peru, Brazil, Argentine.
Appointed foreign adviser by Maxim–Nordenfelt for two-year term. Nordenfelt, bankrupt, emigrates to Paris.

1891   May, minimum fee, excluding commission, £1,000 p.a.
Founds Express Bank, Paris; agent for American Bank Note Co.

1892   September, contract renewed indefinitely; minimum guaranteed commission of £1,000 p.a. December: Athens, Constantinople.

1893   1 per cent commission on orders from French government. South America.

1894   Guarantee of commission withdrawn.
Acquires Château de l'Échelle, near Roye.

1895   June, given six months' notice.
October. Sigmund Loewe appointed managing director of Maxim–Nordenfelt to stem losses.
New contract: 1 per cent commission on all orders from Europe.
Winters in Monte Carlo each year.

1896   Confirmed as director of Placencia de las Armas. Krupp acquire Germania naval dockyard, Kiel.

1897   Rewarded for services in Russia and Spain.
Vickers & Sons acquires Barrow Naval Construction & Armaments Co. Ltd and Maxim–Nordenfelt Guns & Ammunition Co. Ltd to form Vickers Sons & Maxim Ltd.
Awarded half of 1 per cent commission on whole of company's business.
Armstrong Whitworth merger.
Graeco-Turkish War.

1898   Awarded nine-tenths of 1 per cent of profits, plus expense allowance of £1,000 p.a. Avenue Hoche, Paris, acquired.
Spanish–American War.
Loss of Spanish fleets.

1901   Deutsche Waffen: exclusive rights to manufacture and sell Maxim guns outside British Empire, France and US.

1902   Payment of £34,000 received from Vickers. £25,000 holding in bankers S. Japhet & Co.
Vickers acquires half share in naval shipyards, Wm Beardmore, Glasgow.
Vickers licensed to manufacture Krupp time and percussion fuses.
Chile orders *Libertad.*

1903   Payment of £35,000 received from Vickers.

1904   Payment of £40,000 received from Vickers.
Russo-Japanese War.

1905   Payment of £86,000 received from Vickers.
Remuneration fixed as equal that of junior managing director.
Director of Vickers–Terni, Italy.
Russia orders *Rurik.*

1906   Lends £100,000 to Vickers. Russian Tula arsenal

acquires licence to
manufacture Maxims.
Vickers, with Armstrong,
purchases controlling share
in Whitehead Torpedo Co.
Vickers–Terni constructs
arsenal, La Spezia.

1907 Brazil orders *São Paulo*.

1908 French citizen. November:
Chevalier, Legion of
Honour.
Vickers, Armstrong and
John Brown found
Sociedad Español de
Construcción Naval, Spain.
Young Turks revolution.

1909 Founds Chair of Aviation,
University of Paris.
Loans S. Japhet & Co.
£100,000.

1910 Founds *Excelsior*, Paris.
November: acquires licence
to manufacture French
R.E.P. monoplane for
Vickers.

1911 Russia: Vickers win
contract for Nicolaieff naval
shipyards on Black Sea.
Maxim retires.
Appearance of reputed son,
Haim Manelovich Sahar.
Marriage of Duchess of
Marchena's daughter,
Cristina, to Leopold
Walford.

1912 European agent for US
Electric Boat Co.
Vickers and Armstrong win
contract for Turkish arsenal
and naval shipyard. Turkey
orders *Reshadieh*.
October–December. *First
Balkan War. Young Turk
coup d'état*.

1913 Forms French Whitehead
Torpedo Company;
director, Le Nickel.
Vickers constructs Tsaritsyn

arsenals on Volga.
June–July. *Second Balkan
War. Enver Pasha, Turkish
War Minister*.

1914 January. Russian arms
company Putiloff affair.
Officer, Legion of Honour.
August. *Secret alliance
between Turkey and
Germany*. Göben *and*
Breslau *enter Dardanelles*.
November. *Allies declare
war on Turkey*.

1915 December. Asquith accepts
offer to buy neutral Greek
government for £1.4
million. Founds Agence-
Radio, Athens.

1916 January. Offers resignation
to Vickers.
June. Proposes to HMG to
buy up Turkey for £4
million.
Acquires Forth
Shipbuilding Company;
shareholder, Banque de
France
Duchess of Marchena buys
Château de Balincourt.

1917 May. Meeting in
Switzerland with Enver
Pasha's envoy, receives
Turkey's conditions for
armistice.
June. *Greece declares war on
central powers*.
July and December.
Meetings with Turkish
envoy, Switzerland.

1918 January. Requested by
Vickers to reconsider
resignation.
Founds Banque de la Seine,
Compagnie de Transit de
Caen.
Meets Enver Pasha, Geneva,
with British peace terms.
March. GBE.

Treaty of Brest-Litovsk: Turkey recovers all territory lost to Russia.

June. Grand Cross, Legion of Honour.

August. Meeting with Turkish envoy, Switzerland.

3 October. Return from Switzerland with Enver's acceptance of terms and money.

15 October. London to report success.

30 October. *Turks sign armistice.*

1919 January. GCB. Grand Cross, Legion of Honour.

May. *Greeks land at Smyrna.*

June. Reappointed foreign adviser to Vickers at £5,000 p.a. plus three-quarters of 1 per cent of profits.

November. Chair of Aviation, Imperial College of Science; Marshal Foch Chair of French Literature, Oxford.

Acquires Société Navale de l'Ouest.

1920 Founds Banque Commerciale de la Mediterranée, Société Générale des Huiles de Pétrole.

September. Salary increased to £6,500 p.a.

October. DCL, Oxford University.

Angèle de Bourbon, daughter of Duchess of Marchena, marries Jean, son

1921 of Count Léon Ostrorog. Founds Association Pétrolière.

August. *Greek advance on Ankara checked.*

1922 August–September. *Turks retake Smyrna, Greeks driven out of Asia Minor.*

November. Bucharest; Romanian loan.

1923 *Treaty of Lausanne.*

17 November. Death of Duke of Marchena.

1924 February. Bolshevik approach to Vickers.

22 September. Marriage to Duchess of Marchena, newly created Duchess of Villafranca de los Caballeros.

1925 Banque de la Seine merged into Société Parisienne de Banque.

1926 25 February. Death of Duchess of Villafranca. Adopts stepdaughters, Angèle and Cristina.

1927 1 January. Salary increase to £10,000 p.a. plus expenses.

November. Vickers–Armstrong Whitworth merger.

1934–5 US Senate Special Committee Investigating the Munitions Industry.

1935–6 Royal Commission on the Manufacture of and Trading in Arms.

1936 27 November. Death at Monte Carlo, burial at Balincourt.

Select Bibliography

BALFOUR, J.P.D. (Lord Kinross), *Ataturk: The Rebirth of a Nation* (1964)
BEAVERBROOK, Lord, *The Decline and Fall of Lloyd George* (1963)
BERTIE, Viscount, *The Diary of Lord Bertie of Thame 1914–18* (1924)
BONSAL, Stephen, *Unfinished Business* (1944)
BROCKWAY, Fenner, *The Bloody Traffic* (1933)
BRUUN, Geoffrey, *Clemenceau* (Harvard, 1943)
BURNS, Emile, *Karl Liebknecht* (1934)
CALLWELL, Major General Sir Charles, *F.M. Sir Henry Wilson: His Life and Diaries* (1927)
CHRISTOPHER of Greece, Prince, *Memoirs of H.R.H. Prince Christopher of Greece* (1938)
CHURCHILL, W.S., *The World Crisis: The Aftermath* (1929)
COMPTON-HALL, Richard, *Submarine Boats* (1983)
CONSTANT, Stephen, *Foxy Ferdinand, Tsar of Bulgaria* (1979)
COOKRIDGE, E.H., *Orient Express* (New York, 1978)
DAVENPORT, Guiles, *Zaharoff: High Priest of War* (Boston, 1934)
DJEMAL, Pasha, *Memoirs of a Turkish Statesman* (1922)
FERRIER, Ronald W., 'French Oil Policy, 1917–30', *Enterprise and History*. Edited by D.C.Coleman and Peter Mathias
FORBES, Rosita, *These Men I Knew* (1940)
FYFE, Hamilton, *T.P. O'Connor* (1934)
HOLT, Edgar, *The Tiger* (1976)
JAMES, Admiral Sir William, *The Eyes of the Navy: A Biographical Study of Admiral Sir Reginald Hall* (1955)
JAPHET, S., *Recollections From My Business Life* (privately printed, 1931)
LEE, Arthur Gould, *Helen: Queen Mother of Rumania* (1956)
LEWINSOHN, Dr Richard, *The Man Behind the Scenes: The Career of Sir Basil Zaharoff* (1929)
LLOYD GEORGE, David, *War Memoirs* (1936)
LOCKHART, Bruce, *The Diaries of Sir Robert Bruce Lockhart 1915–38*, ed. Kenneth Young (1973)
MACKENZIE, Compton, *First Athenian Memories* (1931)
MANCHESTER, William, *The Arms of Krupp* (1969)

271

MAXIM, Hiram, *My Life* (1915)

McCORMICK, Donald, *Pedlar of Death* (1965)

MENNE, Bernard, *Krupp Deutschlands Kanonkönige* (Zurich, 1937)

MENNEVEE, Roger, *L'Homme Mystérieux de l'Europe* (Paris, 1928)

MOTTELAY, P.Fleury, *Life and Work of Sir Hiram Maxim* (1920)

MURPHY, William Scanlan, *Father of the Submarine* (1987)

NEUMANN, Robert, *Zaharoff: The Armaments King* (1938)

NOEL-BAKER, Philip, *The Private Manufacture of Armaments* (1936)

PALEOLOGUE, Maurice, *Journal 1913–14* (Paris, 1947)

PHOKAS-KOSMETATOS, C.P., *The Tragedy of Greece* (1928)

RIDDELL, Lord, *Intimate Diary of the Peace Conference and After* (1933)

RIDDELL, Lord, *Lord Riddell's War Diary 1914–1918* (1933)

ROSKILL, Stephen, *Hankey: Man of Secrets 1877–1918* (1970)

SCOTT, J.D., *Vickers: A History* (1962)

STORRS, Sir Ronald, *Orientations* (1937)

THOMSON, Sir Basil, *The Allied Secret Service in Greece* (1931)

TREBILCOCK, Clive, *The Industrialization of the Continental Powers* (1981)

TREBILCOCK, Clive, *The Vickers Brothers: Armaments and Enterprise 1854–1914* (1977)

WATSON, D.R., *Georges Clemenceau* (1974)

YOUNG, Gordon, *The Rise of Alfred Krupp* (1960)

Miscellaneous Publications

Royal Commission on the Private Manufacture of and Trading in Armaments, 1935–36. Minutes of Evidence and Report.

Special Committee Investigating the Munitions Industry, United States 73rd Congress, 1934–35.

Documents Politiques, Diplomatiques et Financiers (Paris).

Source References

I have adopted the now standard usage to avoid the distraction of footnotes or numbered references in the text. Source references are prefaced by the number of the page on which the source is quoted, followed by the catch phrase with which to identify the passage. Where the sources are books listed in the Select Bibliography, they are referred to simply by the surname of the authors, followed by the Volume numbers in Roman numerals (where appropriate) and the page numbers; where more than one book by the same author is given in the Bibliography, a brief indication of the title is added, i.e. Lord Riddell's *Intimate Diary of the Peace Conference and After* is referred to as Riddell, *Intimate Diary*. Where the references are from books not listed in the Bibliography, the author's name and full title of the work is given.

I have, where I have thought it useful, noted the primary source for the reference cited in the published work from which I have quoted; similarly, I have indicated where no primary source is recorded.

The following abbreviations have been used to refer to other sources:

BE. Bank of England Ledgers. Statements of Sir Basil Zaharoff's personal account are complete from 1916 to 1936.
CUL. William Shaw Papers, Rare Book and Manuscript Library, Columbia University.
DPDF. *Documents Politiques, Diplomatiques et Financiers*, Paris.
LG. Lloyd George Papers, held for the Beaverbrook Foundation at the House of Lords Record Office.
PRO. General correspondence of the Foreign Office, Public Record Office, Kew. While the Index offers teasing glimpses of Sir Basil Zaharoff, the relevant documents themselves are too often missing, their absence marked 'File not selected for preservation'.
VA. Vickers Archives, now at the Cambridge University Library.

Prologue

p. xvii   Störmer. McCormick, 169. No source indicated.
p. xvii   'sinister influence'. McCormick.
p. xvii   Senator Gerald P. Ward Nye. Special Committee Investigating the Munitions Industry, 1934–5.

p. xvii 'Millions died.' *Daily Herald*, 28 November 1936.
p. xvii 'recruiting agent.' *Reynolds*, 29 November 1936.
p. xvii American author. Davenport, 3.
p. xvii *High Priest of War*. Davenport.
p. xvii *Pedlar of Death*. McCormick.
p. xvii propagandists. J.T.Walton Newbold, *The War Trust Exposed* (1913). George Herbert Perris, *The War Traders: An Exposure* (1913).
p. xviii H.G.Wells. *The Work, Wealth and Happiness of Mankind* (1932), 618.
p. xviii 'an enigma.' McCormick, 14.
p. xix 'admire power'. Interview with traveller and author, Rosita Forbes. *Sunday Chronicle*, 29 November 1936.
p. xix 'natural dignity.' Japhet, 131.
p. xix Clemenceau. Quoted by Ferdinand Tuohy, *Daily Mail*, 28 November 1936.
p. xix passed into fiction. Basil Zaharoff appeared by name in the play *Versailles* (1932) by Emile Ludwig, and it has been made out that he served as the model for Andrew Undershaft in Shaw's *Major Barbara* (performed 1905, published 1907). He figured largely in Upton Sinclair's sociological series *World's End* and, within the last five years, in Morris West's *The World is Made of Glass*, Duncan Kyle's *The King's Commissar*, Jonathan Black's *The Plunderers* and Sidney Sheldon's *If Tomorrow Comes*.

Chapter 1: Origins and Youth

p. 2 'My father.' Lady (Edmée) Owen. *The People*, 29 November 1936.
p. 2 'almost forgotten.' Rosita Forbes. *Sunday Chronicle*, 29 November 1936.
p. 3 'We were poor.' Rosita Forbes. Ibid.
p. 3 Recollections of Zaharoff's parents. Private source.
p. 3 Bertie, II, 141.
p. 4 'plenty of English.' CUL. London, 9 January 1880.
p. 4 'difficult to believe.' Christopher, 112.
p. 4 French obituarist. *Larousse Mensuel*, no. 365, July 1937, 753.
p. 5 'lucky all my life.' Christopher, 115.
p. 5 'I began.' Lady (Edmée) Owen. *The People*, 6 December 1936.

Chapter 2: Nuptials and Newgate

p. 6 'cornflower blue.' Christopher, 114.
p. 6 Henrietta Greenslade. *Sunday Dispatch*, 13 December 1936, 11 December 1938.
p. 8 London trial. Much mystery, with dark hints of missing papers, has been wilfully attached to this case. It was fully reported in *The Times* of 16 December 1872, and subsequent issues of 21 and 28 December 1872; 4 January and 4 February 1873. The confusion originated with Neumann (*Zaharoff the Armaments King*, first published in Germany in 1935) who mistakenly attributed a report of the trial to *The Times* of 17 January 1873.

Subsequent biographers repeated this error, thus creating all the elements of the mystery.

p. 10 'reconstituted from memory.' Lewinsohn, 31–6.

p. 11 'bizarre theory.' Neumann, 58. McCormick, letter from Basilius Demitrios, 31.

Chapter 3: Island Interlude

p. 13 Merz. McCormick, 33. *Documents Politiques de la Guerre*.

p. 13 sporting guns. McCormick, 35.

p. 14 Sir George Owens-Thurston, chief naval architect to Vickers for twenty years. *Daily Express*, 28 November 1936.

p. 14 Sir Harry Luke. *Cyprus* (1957), 83.

p. 14 Storrs, 534.

p. 14 John W. Williamson. Letter from his daughter, Mrs Adrian de Lavison, 31 July 1936. Quoted by McCormick, 37.

p. 14 'great credit.' CUL. 29 August 1879.

p. 14 'ignorant idiot.' CUL. 22 October 1879.

p. 15 'humble apology.' CUL. 13 April 1880.

p. 15 'irresistible longing.' Mackenzie, 313.

p. 15 'my dear Monsieur.' Lewinsohn, 47.

p. 17 'appoint Zaharoff.' Ibid., 58.

p. 17 contested this. VA. Microfilm 19a. Folder 553.

p. 18 'very grateful.' CUL. Athens, 21 April 1881.

p. 18 father died. There is a tomb at the Monastery of Christ on Prinkipos in the Sea of Marmora, in the name of Basil Zaharoff, died 1878, and his wife Helena, died 1879. Alexandre Sgourdeios to author.

p. 18 'My affair.' CUL. Alexandra Hotel, Hyde Park Lane, London, 15 August 1879.

p. 19 'hide and seek.' Ibid.

p. 19 'zig-zag.' CUL. 92 Piccadilly, 19 December 1879.

p. 19 'lose all scent.' CUL. 29 August 1879.

p. 19 Footnote. *Evening Standard*, 14 August 1879.

p. 19 'humbugged.' CUL. Grand Hôtel, Paris, 4 February 1880.

p. 19 'badly managed.' CUL. Alexandra Hotel, London, 15 August 1879.

p. 19 'have the bugger.' CUL. 92 Piccadilly, 2 January 1880.

p. 19 'taken to the place.' CUL. Constantinople, 29 July 1879.

p. 19 'most profitable.' CUL. 92 Piccadilly, 25 December 1879.

p. 20 'Roi de Prusse.' CUL. Ibid.

p. 20 'making a God.' CUL. Limassol, 9 November 1879.

p. 20 'what a lark.' CUL. 92 Piccadilly, 30 January 1880.

p. 20 'treated me.' CUL. London, 29 August 1879.

p. 21 'very good thing.' CUL. Limassol, 9 November 1879.

p. 21 'utter a word.' CUL. 92 Piccadilly, 25 December 1879.

p. 21 'excused myself.' CUL. 92 Piccadilly, 9 January 1880.

p. 21 'regular service.' CUL. Alexandra Hotel, London, 15 August 1879.

p. 21 'buy a boat.' CUL. 29 August 1879.

p. 22 'go to h.ll.' CUL. Limassol, 28 October 1879.

p. 22   'damned first.' CUL. Ibid.
p. 22   'better than expected.' CUL. Limassol, 20 November 1879.
p. 22   'boxed and fixed.' CUL. 92 Piccadilly, 16 January 1880.
p. 22   'most economical.' CUL. 92 Piccadilly, 23 January 1880.
p. 22   'said repeatedly.' CUL. 92 Piccadilly, 2 January 1880.
p. 22   'Greek clique.' CUL. Alexandra Hotel, London, 15 August 1879.
p. 23   'Rothschild received.' CUL. 92 Piccadilly, 19 December 1879.
p. 23   'another form.' CUL. 92 Piccadilly, 9 January 1880.
p. 24   'lend assistance.' CUL. 92 Piccadilly, 16 January 1880.
p. 24   'The Liberals.' CUL. 92 Piccadilly, 30 January 1880.
p. 24   'word of honour.' CUL. Alexandria, 17 March 1880.
p. 25   'God bless.' CUL. Limassol, 31 March 1880.
p. 25   'pushing and cheek.' CUL. Larnaca, 13 April 1880.
p. 25   'poor Cypriotes.' CUL. 92 Piccadilly, 30 January 1880.
p. 25   'd—d place.' CUL. Larnaca, 13 April 1880.
p. 25   'My dear old.' CUL. Larnaca, 19 May 1880.
p. 25   'till the matter'. CUL. Beirut, 14 June 1880.
p. 25   'Venus herself.' CUL. Beirut, 21 June 1880.
p. 26   'passed bankruptcy.' CUL. Larnaca, 17 August 1880.
p. 26   'that old dog.' CUL. Larnaca, 30 October 1879.
p. 26   'I'll lick those.' CUL. Larnaca, 28 October 1879.
p. 26   'little breezy.' CUL. 92 Piccadilly, 9 January 1880.
p. 26   Maltass. CUL. Beirut, 21 June 1880.
p. 27   'very great confidence.' CUL. London, 29 August 1879.
p. 27   'far as Smyrna.' CUL. Limassol, 5 November 1879.
p. 27   Dear Paolo. CUL. Zaharoff to Paul Samuel. Limassol, 9 November 1879.
p. 27   'no use putting.' CUL. Limassol, 9 November 1879.
p. 27   George Rossides. CUL. 92 Piccadilly, 23 January 1880.
p. 27   'doing people.' CUL. Limassol, 5 November 1879.
p. 27   'very shocked.' CUL. Château de l'Échelle, Roye, Somme, 29 August 1897.
p. 28   'disagreeable affairs.' CUL. 92 Piccadilly, 2 January 1880.
p. 28   'moment I leave.' CUL. Paris, 4 June 1881.
p. 29   Anaemia. CUL. Hôtel Castiglione, Paris, 16 June 1881.
p. 29   'have Tassilaki.' CUL. Alexandria, 17 September 1881.
p. 29   French Rothschilds. CUL. Paris, 22 July 1881.
p. 29   'nearly decided.' CUL. Paris, 7 July 1881.
p. 30   Panama Canal. CUL. Paris, 24 July 1881.
p. 30   'Search for ZZ.' CUL. Ibid.
p. 30   'dear old Gibbs.' CUL. Alexandria, 13 August 1881.
p. 31   'always well.' CUL. Alexandria, 19 August 1881.
p. 31   'have nothing to do.' CUL. Alexandria, 1 October 1881.
p. 31   'Want to get.' CUL. Alexandria, 17 September 1881.
p. 31   'A fellow like.' CUL. Rossmore Hotel, Broadway, New York, 13 December 1884.
p. 31   'reached $20,500.' CUL. Grand Hotel de Roma, Madrid, 29 October 1887.
p. 32   'find out quietly.' CUL. Paris, 7 July 1881.
p. 32   'fail to understand.' CUL. New York, 13 December 1884.

p. 35   *New York Times*, Sunday, 4 October 1885. 'Zacharoff's Two Wives, A Bigamist Exposed and Deprived of his Bride'.

p. 35   'female fiend.' CUL. New York, 31 December 1884.

Chapter 4: Submergence

p. 36   'plainly anti-social.' Noel-Baker, 347–8.

p. 36   'sold a submarine.' Rosita Forbes. *Sunday Chronicle*. Op. cit.

p. 36   'less reliable source.' *Documents Politiques de la Guerre*. These were supposedly compiled by a trio: MM. Roger Mennevée, René Tarpin and Barthe. The latter was a *député* for a time in 1919; the first was editor of the strident *Documents Politiques, Diplomatiques et Financiers*. The privately printed *Documents Politiques de la Guerre* consist of correspondence and reconstituted verbatim conversations of leading statesmen – and Basil Zaharoff. Their authority is questionable.

p. 37   'If only someone.' Quoted by McCormick, 48–9.

p. 37   Tom Vickers. The meeting was recorded by Mrs Orbach, daughter of Sigmund Loewe. Scott, 39.

p. 38   'fashion of making war.' Georges Blond. *La Grande Armée* (1979), 34.

p. 38   Patent No. 693 of 1881 for Submarine or Subaqueous Boats. *Brassey's Annual* (1887), 158.

p. 39   'deck to strut.' John P. Holland. Quoted by Richard K. Morris. *John P. Holland* (USNI Annapolis 1966).

p. 39   paid £9,000. Captain G. Togas, HN, to author.

p. 39   persuaded Hassan. Murphy, 118. William Scanlan Murphy's *Father of the Submarine* (1987) gives the first complete account of the trials and tribulations of these early submarines.

p. 40   'no naval use.' Murphy, 144.

p. 40   *The Times*, 24 September 1888. Murphy, 177.

p. 41   'low-class.' Rear-Admiral Sir Reginald Bacon. *From 1900 Onward* (1940), 50. First flotilla commander of submarines.

p. 42   six boats. Trebilcock. *Vickers Brothers*, 106.

p. 42   Albert Vickers. VA. Electric Boat Co. Letter Book, 19 May 1901.

p. 42   'guided absolutely.' VA. Ibid., 6 February 1903.

Chapter 5: Arms and the Men

p. 43   Footnote. Duke of Cambridge. Quoted by Scott, 28.

p. 44   Patent No. 1739 of 1873. Nordenfelt Patent No. 1488 of 1881.

p. 44   arms contracts. VA. 687–93.

p. 45   'worship God.' Maxim, 1.

p. 45   Footnote. MSS 'Maxim Nordenfelt Days and Ways. Memories of 1892–97'. Recalled by a Septuagenarian, G. R. Field. VA. Historical Document 52–H–1.

p. 46   gun trials, Spezia, Vienna. Maxim, 198–205. Neumann, 87–9; Lewinsohn, 68, 71–3; McCormick, 55.

p. 49   Maxim 'furious'. Rosita Forbes. *Sunday Chronicle*. Op. cit.

p. 49   'S. America.' CUL. Buckingham Palace Hotel, no date (?23 August 1886).

p. 49   justifiable grumble. CUL. Ibid.

p. 50 'getting on famously.' CUL. 53 Parliament Street, 8 December 1886.
p. 50 Sir William Pearce. CUL. 53 Parliament Street, 13 July 1887.
p. 50 'persuade the Greeks.' CUL. 3 rue Treilhard, Paris, 1 August 1887.
p. 50 'very nice one.' CUL. Ibid.
p. 50 'an annuity.' CUL. Grand Hotel de Roma, Madrid, 12 December 1889.
p. 50 'notable events.' CUL. Grand Hotel de Roma, Madrid, 9 June 1888.
p. 50 bought Barrow. Ibid.
p. 51 Nordenfelt shareholders. Murphy, 176.

Chapter 6: First Love

p. 52 'sickly scion.' Neumann, 267.
p. 52 'saddest face.' Rosita Forbes. *Sunday Chronicle*. Op. cit.
p. 53 temptress. Lady (Edmée) Owen. *The People*, 6 December 1936.
p. 53 'an extraordinary man.' Sir George Owens-Thurston. *Daily Express*, 28 November 1936.
p. 53 'Socorro.' Cookridge, 113.
p. 53 'Monsieur, please.' McCormick, 63. Paul Brancafort, *L'Intransigent*, 2 April 1957.
p. 54 Albert's nephew. VA. Colonel J. Leslie to Viscount Knollys, 1 January 1958.

Chapter 7: Bagman

p. 57 Spandau trial. Mottelay, 21.
p. 57 Friedrich Krupp. Maxim, 268.
p. 57 'flattering the wife.' Rosita Forbes. *Sunday Chronicle*. Op. cit.
p. 57 Grand Duke S. Neumann, 95.
p. 58 Protestant. Maxim, 213.
p. 58 'purity and fluency.' Sergei Sazonov. *La Russe Libre*, Paris, 1924.
p. 58 T.P.O'Connor. *Sunday Dispatch*, 8 October 1922.
p. 58 Another friend. Owens-Thurston. *Daily Express*. Op. cit.
p. 58 'the mysticism.' Christopher, 112.
p. 59 'real English.' Maxim, 222.
p. 59 September 1888. VA. Maxim–Nordenfelt Minute Book.
p. 60 present of £500. CUL. Grand Hotel de Roma, Madrid, 12 December 1889.
p. 60 'stronger man.' Rosita Forbes. *Sunday Chronicle*. Op. cit.
p. 60 into liquidation. Murphy, 182.
p. 61 September 1892. VA. Maxim–Nordenfelt Minute Book.
p. 61 Henry Poole & Co. Ref. UZ6, p. 477.
p. 61 'handsome man.' Christopher, 113.
p. 61 Krupp's star salesman. Manchester, 425.
p. 62 slack periods. VA. 'Maxim–Nordenfelt Days and Ways'. Op. cit.
p. 63 Sigmund Loewe. Scott, 45.
p. 63 axe fell. VA. 'Maxim–Nordenfelt Days and Ways'. Op. cit.
p. 64 'want cheap work.' CUL. Château de l'Échelle, 23 August 1894.
p. 64 'what frankly.' CUL. 54 rue de la Bienfaisance, 2 January 1895.
p. 64 'too idiotic.' CUL. Château de l'Échelle, 23 August 1894.
p. 64 'Royal Commissioner.' Avenue Hoche, 14 March 1898.

p. 65 first man. VA. Microfilm 19a, 553.
p. 65 boasted to colleague. VA. 570. Zaharoff to Sir Robert McLean, 15 April 1929.
p. 65 solo spin. Mottelay, 178.
p. 66 'I would like.' *Li Hung-Chang's Scrapbook*, compiled and edited by Hiram Maxim (1913), ix.
p. 66 King of Denmark. Maxim, 220.
p. 67 Nasr-ed-Din. Kenneth Rose. *Superior Person* (1969), 224.
p. 67 obsolescent stock. VA. 'Maxim–Nordenfelt Days and Ways'. Op. cit.
p. 67 'no waste'. *Westminster Budget*, 17 November 1893. 'Mr Cecil Rhodes's Despatch'.
p. 67 'invaluable for.' A. Bott. *Our Father* (1931), 122, 212.

Chapter 8: Arms Amalgamated

p. 69 'optimistic, daring.' T. P. O'Connor. *Daily Telegraph*, 16 July 1919.
p. 69 honourable burial. Neumann, 114.
p. 69 'supply ships.' Scott, 44.
p. 70 over 63 per cent. Trebilcock. *Vickers Brothers*, 123.
p. 71 well rewarded. VA. Vickers Sons & Maxim Minute Book.
p. 71 Purdeys. VA. Colonel J. Leslie to Viscount Knollys, 1 January 1958.
p. 71 Grace, Lady Napier & Ettrick. *Daily Sketch*, 31 August 1921.
p. 71 Japhet, 80. Laurie Dennett. *The Charterhouse Group*, 76.
p. 71 figure which fluctuated. Roy Jenkins. *Asquith* (1964), 92.
p. 72 the Maxim division. Trebilcock. *Vickers Brothers*, appendix B, table 3, 158.
p. 72 *'principal actionnaire.'* DPDF. February 1928, 38.
p. 72 Vickers family holdings. Trebilcock. *Vickers Brothers*, appendix B, table 11, 163.
p. 73 Deutsche Waffen. Japhet, 91.
p. 73 Senatorial enquiry. *Hearings before the Special Committee Investigating the Munitions Industry*, US Senate, 73rd Congress.
p. 73 bribe officials. *Report of the Temporary Mixed Commission on Armaments*, League of Nations Document No. A.81, 1921.
p. 73 *Royal Commission on the Private Manufacture of and Trading in Arms*, 1935–6.
p. 73 Vickers' historian. Scott, 81.
p. 74 China and Japan. *See* Clive Trebilcock, 'Legends of the British Armament Industry: A Revision', *Journal of Contemporary History*, 1970, no. 5, 17.
p. 74 'greasing wheels.' VA. Zaharoff telegrams.
p. 74 Trebilcock. *Journal of Contemporary History*. Op. cit., 18.
p. 74 'terrible odds.' VA. Microfilm 307. Zaharoff to Albert Vickers, 28 July 1910.
p. 75 Göltz. Manchester, 187.
p. 75 'too disgusting.' VA. Microfilm 214. Sir George Buchanan, 20 May 1913.
p. 75 'loans.' Noel-Baker, 144.
p. 75 Zaharoff to Dawson. VA. no. 786.
p. 75 Zaharoff to Thaine. Ibid. 23 March 1907.
p. 76 Zaharoff to Thaine. Ibid. 13 August 1909.
p. 76 Zaharoff to Dawson. Ibid. 3 May 1908.

p. 76 Douglas Vickers. VA. Commissions to Zaharoff, 23 May 1901.

p. 77 July 1905. VA. Vickers Sons & Maxim Minute Book.

p. 77 Owens-Thurston bankruptcy, March 1938. *Daily Express.*

p. 77 offer in 1913. VA. Caillard to Zaharoff, 10 March 1913.

p. 78 'very platonic.' Arthur Raffalovich. *L'Humanité*, 30 December 1923.

p. 78 *Evening Standard.* Pollock, Paris correspondent, *c.*1933. British Library, Colindale. Zaharoff box.

p. 78 'terrible winter.' VA. Letter Book 33. Albert Vickers to Zaharoff, 13 January 1911, 6 March 1911.

p. 78 A. de Bear. *Sunday Express*, 6 December 1936.

Chapter 9: Eastern Empires

p. 80 'is peculiar.' CUL. 54 rue de la Bienfaisance, 13 March 1897.

p. 80 'worth the candle.' CUL. Avenue Hoche, 14 March 1898.

p. 81 Legend pretends. McCormick, 47.

p. 81 25,000 guns. Richard Lewinsohn. *The Profits of War through the Ages* (1936), 146.

p. 81 £45,596. Trebilcock. *Vickers Brothers*, appendix B, table 8, 162.

p. 81 Senator Thurston. Hudson Strode. *The Pageant of Cuba* (1935), 140.

p. 81 Roosevelt. Hugh Thomas. *Cuba* (1971), 364.

p. 83 'lazy, hypocritical.' Paléologue, 6.

p. 84 arms firms manipulated. *Report of the Temporary Mixed Commission on Armaments*, League of Nations. Op. cit.

p. 84 sober biography. Bruun, 114.

p. 85 'jeune fille.' *The Times*, 28 November 1936.

p. 85 Senator Dupuy. *Financial Times*, 28 November 1936.

p. 85 Zaharoff's secretary. A. de Bear. *Sunday Express*, 29 November 1936.

p. 85 Albert Vickers. VA. Letter Book 33. 11 November 1910.

p. 86 destroyers in parts. Owens-Thurston. *Daily Express*. Op. cit.

p. 86 Tula arsenal. VA. Document 735.

p. 87 defence programme. *Trebilcock. Industrialization*, 281–3.

p. 87 private factory. VA. Microfilm 215.

p. 87 Nicolaieff agreement. VA. Document 735.

p. 88 Raffalovich. *L'Humanité*, 30 December 1923. For another sidelight on Zaharoff in Russia see Robin Bruce Lockhart. *Reilly: Ace of Spies* (1967), 64.

p. 89 Albert Thomas. *Journal Officiel*, 19 March 1914.

p. 89 Putiloff. Neumann, 135; McCormick, 89–90; Noel-Baker, 367.

p. 89 *L'Echo de Paris*, 27 January 1914.

p. 89 *The Times*, 28 January 1914. St Petersburg: 'We are able to state from information received from official sources that this report has not a word of truth in it.'

p. 90 Deputy Thomas. Cited by Paul Faure. *Si Tu Veux Paix*, ch. VIII.

p. 90 Union of Democratic Control. *The Secret International* (1932).

p. 90 'allusions correct.' VA. Zaharoff to Jenkinson, 28 July 1932. Microfilm 19a, 553.

p. 91 Liebknecht. Reichstag, 18 April 1913. Cited by Jean Huteau. *Les Cahiers des Droits de l'Homme* (1932).

p. 91 'great French newspapers.' Louis Launay. *Bourse et République* (1922).
p. 91 'great effect.' Noel-Baker, 247.
p. 91 Krupp newspapers. Liebknecht. Reichstag, 18 April 1913, 11 May 1914.
p. 91 Schneider newspapers. *Vlaanderen*, Ghent. 14 January 1933.
p. 92 'stroke of luck.' Constant, 233.
p. 92 Albert Vickers to Dawson. VA. Letter Book 31. 19 January 1910.
p. 92 impossible price. Owens-Thurston. *Daily Express*. Op. cit.
p. 93 his own pocket. *The Times*, 28 November 1936.
p. 93 $2,500,000. *Encyclopaedia Britannica*, 1955. Zaharoff, Sir Basil.
p. 93 'never posed.' Christopher, 115.
p. 93 secretary. A. de Bear. *Sunday Express*, 6 December 1936.
p. 93 'foreign Greek.' CUL. Château de l'Échelle, 29 August 1897.
p. 94 'restless, subversive.' Phokas-Kosmetatos, 318.
p. 94 'persuasive, plausible.' Roskill, II, 143.
p. 94 swallowed in part. Djemal, 72–4.
p. 94 *Meisterstreich*. Bernard Menne. *Kruppe Deutschlands Kanonkönige* (Zurich, 1937), 300.
p. 95 Zaharoff to Albert Vickers. VA. Microfilm 307. 28 July 1910.
p. 95 Vickers' bonds. Scott, 85.
p. 95 *Kölnische Zeitung*. Neumann, 143.
p. 96 500 million francs. Bernard Menne. Op. cit., 301.
p. 96 Léon Rénier. Theodore Zeldin. *France 1845–1945: Taste and Corruption* (1980), 173.
p. 96 paid for in francs. This accusation was made by Paul Faure in 1932 (*Journal Officiel*, 11 February). Secretary of the French Socialist Party and Deputy for Le Creusot, the home of Schneider, he lost his seat in the same year.

Chapter 10: Friendly Relations

p. 98 archives of the Yard. Davenport, 52–3.
p. 98 Secret Service. *Financial Times*, 28 November 1936.
p. 98 Nadel. McCormick, 103.
p. 98 'Basilius Zacharias.' Ibid., 70.
p. 98 Haim Sahar. Neumann, 32–7.
p. 100 add to his fortune. *Financial Times*. Op. cit.
p. 100 de Bear. *Sunday Express*, 6 December 1936.
p. 100 James Dunn. VA. Letter Book 33. Albert Vickers to Zaharoff, 14 January 1911.
p. 101 Thyssen. Noel-Baker, 143.
p. 101 PM was asked. (later Sir) Herbert Williams MP. *The Times*, 3 December 1936.
p. 102 Jellyfish. VA. Letter Book 33. 28 November 1910.
p. 103 record time. Compton-Hall, 170.
p. 103 Owens-Thurston. *Daily Express*. Op. cit.
p. 104 University of Paris. Louis Liard. *Les Bienfaiteurs de l'Université de Paris* (Paris, 1913), 21.
p. 104 Darmstädter Bank. Japhet, 102–3.
p. 105 'elegant aircraft.' Scott, 74.

p. 105 'very desirous.' VA. Aviation file. Zaharoff to Barker, 16 November 1910.
p. 105 'want to treat.' Ibid. Barker to Zaharoff, 17 November 1910.
p. 106 'avoid handling.' Ibid. 7 December 1910.
p. 106 'huskies.' Trebilcock. *Vickers Brothers*, 114.
p. 106 Chevalier, 15 November 1908; Officier, 12 January 1914.
p. 107 Tom Vickers. Scott, 83.
p. 107 Whitehead. Scott, 84.
p. 108 Senator Gaudin de Villaine. Neumann, 165–6.
p. 108 Zaharoff in Brest. McCormick, 131.
p. 109 Possehl. Neumann, 166–7.

Chapter 11: Private Lives

p. 111 Lloyd George, I, 124.
p. 111 Zaharoff to Sazonov. *Documents Politiques de la Guerre. see* Note, Chapter 4, page 36.
p. 112 'wild uncertainty.' Scott, 100.
p. 112 'thousand young men.' *The Times*, 5 June 1916.
p. 112 'machinery was winning.' Karl Friedrich Nowak. *The Collapse of Central Europe* (1924), 101.
p. 113 'convince McKenna.' McCormick, 98. Letter from T.P.O'Connor to H.McGuire, 29 November 1909.
p. 113 'if at all.' Report of the Royal Commission on the Private Manufacture of and Trading in Armaments, 1935–6 (HMSO Cmd. 5292), appendix V.
p. 114 (missing) French. *Documents Politiques de la Guerre*. Op. cit.
p. 114 hold over Lloyd George. McCormick, 112.
p. 115 'old, stooped.' Fyfe, 236.
p. 115 'thought coldly.' Janet Flanner. *Paris was Yesterday* (1973), 60.
p. 115 'considerable speculation.' Bruun, 113.
p. 115 'sometimes sinister.' Holt, 149.
p. 115 Georges Wormser. Professor J.-B. Duroselle to author, 26 September 1985.
p. 116 'formidable enemy.' McCormick, 112. *Documents Politiques de la Guerre*. Op. cit. Correspondence of Michel Clemenceau. M.Marcel Wormser, curator of the Musée Clemenceau, whose family has a long tradition of service to Clemenceau, and Professor Duroselle, the statesman's biographer, have no knowledge of these documents.
p. 116 'far greater.' McCormick, 121. Letter from T.P.O'Connor to H.McGuire.
p. 116 Paris police files. Watson, 246.
p. 116 *L'Echo National*. DPDF. No. 3, March 1928.
p. 116 Foreign Office. PRO P 2254/2/117.
p. 116 *T.P.'s Journal*. Fyfe, 237.
p. 117 valet Albert. Bonsal, 74.
p. 118 'probably finest.' Lockhart, I, 305.
p. 118 'strong spoke.' VA. Zaharoff to Caillard, 30 March 1915.

Chapter 12: War Service

p. 119 Briey. *Assemblée Nationale. Chambre des Députés, Session de 1919. Procès-verbaux de la Commission sur le rôle et la situation de la métallurgie en France:*

défense du Bassin de Briey. Also *Rapport de la Commission d'Enquête* (Fernand Engerand).

p. 119   fought six months. 'If, in the first days of the war, the French had penetrated to the depth of a dozen kilometres in Lorraine, the war would have been ended in six months by the defeat of Germany.' *Leipzige Neueste Nachrichten*, 10 October 1917.

p. 120   Albert Thomas evidence. Noel-Baker, 44.

p. 120   'extremely agitated.' McCormick, 124. *Documents Politiques de la Guerre.* Op. cit.

p. 120   General Malleterre. Noel-Baker, 43.

p. 121   'same French source.' McCormick, 144. M.Barthe, joint editor of *Documents Politiques de la Guerre.* Op. cit.

p. 121   'surreptitious trade.' Brockway, 65.

p. 122   'known my value.' Rosita Forbes. *Sunday Chronicle.* Op. cit.

p. 122   Colt Patent Firearms. VA. 786. Vickers to Union Development Co., New York, 31 December 1919.

p. 123   well-meaning admirer. *Sunday Dispatch*, 8 October 1922.

p. 123   Riddell. Friend of Lloyd George, chairman of the *News of the World*, founder of George Newnes. Riddell. *Intimate Diary*, 175.

p. 123   'jusqu'au bout.' Bertie, II, 141.

p. 124   'half-peace.' Clemenceau. Archives of the Senate, *Commissions des Affaires Etrangères*, 19 April 1918.

p. 124   Zaharoff to Venizelos. McCormick, 126. No sources indicated.

p. 124   military attaché. Compton Mackenzie. *My Life and Times: Octave 5* (1966), 41.

p. 124   Submarine. This adventure first surfaced in the *Daily Telegraph* obituary (28 November 1936). It was later 'confirmed' to McCormick by Sir Guy Gaunt, British Naval Attaché in Washington during the First World War. Although Gaunt raises the danger of being stopped at sea by U-boats in his memoirs (*The Yield of the Years*, 1940), he does not cite this very good story as an example.

p. 124   Lyautey. McCormick, 128.

Chapter 13: Aegean Stables

p. 127   'neither pro-German.' Lee, 41.

p. 127   Constantine's warnings. *Le Temps*, 5 October 1915; *Sunday Times*, 22 February 1922. The Allies considered these a German manoeuvre to bluff the Entente.

p. 128   'internment camp.' Liddell Hart. *A History of the World War 1914–1918* (1930), 207.

p. 128   Asquith. The Bodleian. Asquith Papers, vol. 29, folio 206. January 1916.

p. 129   'wildly imaginative.' Phokas-Kosmetatos, 41.

p. 129   *Embros.* Lewinsohn, 126.

p. 129   'enterprises of extortion.' Phokas-Kosmetatos, 43.

p. 129   'devilishly cunning.' Neumann, 172.

p. 129   'mental aberration.' Phokas-Kosmetatos, 42.

p. 130   'Thanks to.' Lee, 55.

p. 130   'secret known.' Roskill, I, 239.

p. 131   dud missions. Storrs, 314–15.

p. 131   'republican views.' Sarrail. *Revue de Paris*, 15 December 1919.

p. 131   'take Tino.' Callwell, I, 259.

p. 131   Footnote. Bertie, II, 22, 29.

p. 131   'France's action.' Phokas-Kosmetatos, 278.

p. 132   'not the intention.' Lee, 49.

p. 132   'guns and riff-raff.' Bertie, II, 72.

p. 132   'Greeks are ready.' Lee, 55.

p. 132   'seen Arras.' Lee, 56.

p. 132   Greek politician. Lewinsohn, 129.

p. 132   'known in Britain.' Lee, 64.

Chapter 14 : Talking Turkey

p. 135   'under no circumstances.' Barbara Tuchman. *The Guns of August – August 1914* (1962), 163.

p. 136   'force the Turks.' (Admiral Wilhelm Souchon.) 'La Percée de SMS Goeben et Breslau', *Les Marins Allemands au Combat* (Paris, 1930), 47.

p. 137   'even victorious.' Maurice Paléologue. *Un Grand Tournant de la Politique Mondiale 1904–06*, 84.

p. 137   'pretty sure.' Roskill, I, 239.

p. 138   Hall's biographer. James, 62.

p. 140   'Zaharoff's services.' VA. Submission in evidence to the Royal Commission.

p. 140   'man of secrets.' Roskill, I, 239.

p. 142   'much excited.' Fitzherbert, 192. William Ormsby Gore to Lord Robert Cecil.

p. 142   Herbert presented. Ibid. Foreign Office 371/3057, no. 148986.

p. 142   These records. LG. Box F/6/1–3. Caillard to Lloyd George, memorandum, 27 June 1917.

p. 144   '$xxx'. Ibid.

p. 145   'If the money had.' Ibid. Caillard to Lloyd George, 17 August 1917.

p. 146   *The Times*, 17 July 1917.

p. 147   'actually handed.' Robert Rhodes James (ed.). *Memoirs of a Conservative: J.C.C. Davidson's Memoirs and Papers 1910–37* (1969), 90.

p. 147   'will *not*.' LG. Box F/6/1–3. Zaharoff to Caillard, 27 September 1917.

p. 148   Ottoman debt. LG. Box F/6/1–3. Caillard to Lloyd George, 6 December 1917.

p. 148   Hankey noted. Roskill, I, 466.

p. 149   Bonar Law. LG. Box F/30/2/27. Summary of Chairman's Personal Views, 6 December 1917.

p. 150   Parodi admitted. Lloyd George, V, 2482 and appendix, 2505.

p. 150   'Brother mine.' LG. Box F/6/1–3. Zaharoff to Caillard, undated.

p. 153   'instructions without delay.' Ibid. Caillard to Lloyd George, 1 January 1918.

p. 153   Bonar Law saw. LG. Box F/30/2/28. Law to Lloyd George, 1 January 1918.

p. 153   War Office Memo. LG. Box F/44/345. Copy to Caillard, 9 January 1918.

p. 154   '*Cher Ami*.' LG. Box F/6/1–3. Caillard to Zaharoff, 16 January 1918.

p. 154   J.T.D. amendment. LG. Box F/44/3/47. Memorandum from 10 Downing Street, undated.

p. 154   'IN THE TRAIN.' LG. Box F/6/1–3. Zaharoff to Caillard, 29 January 1918.

p. 156   'Niemtze.' A variation – *niemec*, *nyemetz* – of a Slav language expression in the pejorative sense 'Hun'. Dr Dorothy McEwan.

p. 158   'great disappointment.' Ibid. Caillard to Lloyd George, 4 February 1918.

p. 158   'oily schemer.' Callwell, I, 128.

Chapter 15: A Last Throw

p. 159   'unanimous wish.' VA. Albert Vickers to Zaharoff, 20 January 1918.

p. 159   'very flattering.' VA. Zaharoff to Albert Vickers, 25 February 1918.

p. 160   '*Amitiés*.' VA. Zaharoff to Dawson, 27 February 1918.

p. 160   'BZ tells.' VA. Memo, Coffin to Caillard, 28 July 1918.

p. 160   'lady from Switzerland.' LG. Box F/6/1–3. Zaharoff to Caillard, 21 September 1918.

p. 160   Murray. LG. Box F/41/5/19. Murray to Lloyd George, 23 February 1918.

p. 161   Murray. LG. Box 41/5/25. Murray to Lloyd George, 14 July 1918.

p. 161   Derby. LG. Box 52/2/27. Derby to Balfour, 17 August 1918.

p. 162   'another envoy.' LG. Box F/6/1–3. Caillard to Davis, 30 August 1918.

p. 166   'papers in order.' Ibid. Caillard to Lloyd George, 21 September 1918.

p. 166   wired Zaharoff. Ibid. Caillard to Lloyd George, 10 October 1918.

p. 169   *The Times*, 23 September 1918.

p. 171   'no part of my business.' LG. Box F/30/2/52. Long to Lloyd George, 22 October 1918.

p. 171   'shown Long's letter.' Ibid. Davidson to Stevenson, 23 October 1918.

p. 173   *Daily Telegraph*, 30 November 1918.

Chapter 16: Benefaction

p. 174   'went into Germany.' Rosita Forbes. *Sunday Chronicle*. Op. cit.

p. 175   Rosita Forbes (Mrs A.T.McGrath). The envelope containing these revelations was sealed, marked 'Not to be opened until the death of Sir Basil Zaharoff has been confirmed beyond all possibility of doubt' and confided to the care of the National Provincial Bank, South Audley Street in October 1933.

p. 175   GCB not conferred. Appointed Honorary Knight Grand Cross of the Order of the Bath (Civil Division) on 1 January 1919. As an honorary appointment, however, it would not have been included in the New Year's Honours List.

p. 176   Ludendorff, Swedish Ambassador, McCormick, 156. Michel Clemenceau to René Tarpin, one of the editors of the *Documents Politiques de la Guerre*. Op. cit.

p. 177   O'Connor. *Daily Telegraph*, 16 July 1919.

p. 178   'Whenever I spend.' Neumann, 265.

p. 178   gracious permission. 'I am afraid that I am not permitted to release any information concerning the honours received by Basil Zaharoff. This would include anything concerning whether he had petitioned the King.' Oliver Everett, Librarian, Royal Archives, Windsor Castle, to author.

p. 178 Lockhart, I, 305. Entry for 11 September 1934.

p. 178 Zaharoff's use. PRO. Use of title by, T13122/13122/372. File not selected for preservation.

p. 178 was confirmed. PRO. Authority to use title Sir, T14499/14499/372. File not selected for preservation.

p. 178 Imperial College. Adrian Whitworth, Librarian, to author.

p. 179 *The Times*, 21 November 1918.

p. 179 'insistence of donor.' Hebdomadal Council Papers. Nos. 111, 11 October–13 December 1918, p. xxvi. Oxford University Archives HC/M/3/52.

p. 179 FM Haig Chair. Laurent Morelle, *conservateur* des Archives Nationales, Rectorat de l'Académie de Paris, to author, 16 September and 22 October 1985. 'J'ai fait de nouvelles recherches au sujet de l'énigmatique Chaire Field Marshal HAIG de l'Université de Paris. Le résultat s'est avéré aussi négatif que lors des premières investigations.'

p. 179 50,000 francs. Ibid. Zaharoff to Rector, 16 December 1926.

p. 180 Prix Balzac. Gabriel Boillat. *Revue d'Histoire Littéraire de la France, Notes et Documents*, 880–908, 576–85.

p. 181 Cercle du Marin. Private source.

p. 181 Foyers du Soldat. '... il n'a été trouvé aucun renseignement sur les dons'. General Delmas, chef du Service Historique de l'Armée de Terre, to author.

p. 181 Zoological Gardens. Davenport, 212–13.

p. 181 Jardin des Plantes. Catherina Hurtache, *conservateur*, Bibliothèque Centrale, Musée National d'Histoire Naturelle, to author.

p. 181 Storrs, 381.

p. 182 Ministry of Public Instruction. *Morning Post*, 18 February 1921.

p. 182 Mozart MS. *Daily Express*, 14 January 1921.

p. 182 Biarritz, Interparliamentary Union, Olympics. Neumann, 266.

p. 182 'Save the Franc.' *Petit Bleu*, 16 November 1927.

p. 182 Westminster Abbey. *Daily News*, 3 October 1922.

p. 182 Hoche tête-à-tête. Forbes, 148. 'The story is a good one ... but, you will not be surprised to learn, it is thought here to be a bit far-fetched.' Henry Gillett, Archivist, Bank of England, to author.

p. 183 'Cunard's box.' Charles à Court Repington. *The First World War 1914–18* (1920), 521.

p. 183 Footnote. Dennistoun Burney. Michael Behrens to author.

p. 183 £250. Philip Ziegler. *Diana Cooper* (1980), 107. BE.

p. 183 Elizabeth Asquith. Davenport, 212.

p. 183 *con gusto*. Bodleian. Asquith Papers, vol. 32, folio 251. Zaharoff to Asquith, 29 June 1918.

p. 184 Melba. Davenport, 212; Neumann, 266. BE.

p. 184 'out of date.' Rosita Forbes. *Sunday Chronicle*. Op. cit.

p. 184 'very anxious.' Christopher, 116.

p. 185 'had fifty thousand.' Fitzherbert, 122.

p. 185 English adventurer. J.S.Barnes. *Half a Life Left* (1937), 104.

p. 185 Zaharoff's object. McCormick, 187.

p. 185 Emperor Karl. Neumann, 289.

Chapter 17: Slump

p. 188 Peace Products. Scott, 137.
p. 188 loose ends. Ibid., 147 ff.
p. 189 'chocolate factory.' Emil Ludwig. *Versailles* (1932), 89.
p. 190 Romania. Scott, 148.
p. 190 Bonesco. VA. Evidence to Royal Commission.
p. 191 Bryce. Ibid.

Chapter 18: Eastern Reproaches

p. 192 'anxious man.' Riddell. *Peace Conference*, 25.
p. 193 'I want Mosul.' Roskill, II, 28.
p. 193 firm challenge. McCormick, 167.
p. 194 Thomson pressured. Ibid., 173.
p. 194 Cabinet committee report. Roskill, II, 235.
p. 194 'biggest enemies.' McCormick, 161.
p. 194 'convince Lloyd George.' Ibid. No source indicated.
p. 194 replace Wemyss. James, 176.
p. 194 betrayed Kapp. McCormick, 169.
p. 195 Party Fund. Ibid., 212. Barthe, *Documents Politiques de la Guerre*. Op. cit.
p. 195 'free hand.' Ibid., 177. No source indicated.
p. 195 'come to see me.' Rosita Forbes. *Sunday Chronicle*. Op. cit.
p. 195 'conquer Turks.' Churchill, 354.
p. 196 'enmeshed with Zaharoff.' G.R.Searle. *Corruption in British Politics 1895–1930* (1987), 286.
p. 196 'total ruin.' Callwell, II, 282.
p. 196 quizzed the PM. Herbert. House of Commons, 14 June 1920.
p. 196 waited a week. Ibid., 23 June 1920.
p. 196 Prince Sixte. Davenport, 233–4.
p. 197 Footnote. radiant Rolls. Private source.
p. 197 Lloyd George insisting. Riddell. *Intimate Diary*, 251. Entry for 27 November 1920.
p. 197 'moral creditors.' Churchill, 388–9.
p. 198 resigned view. Davenport, 236. No source indicated.
p. 198 'any communication.' *Sunday Express*, 21 August 1921.
p. 198 Skouloudis. Lewinsohn, 137–9, 152.
p. 198 'give a drachma.' McCormick, 181.
p. 199 'My own impression.' Fyfe, 305.
p. 199 'strong supporters.' Herbert, House of Commons, 17 July 1922.
p. 199 'not quite sane.' PRO. E7150/3181/44.
p. 200 'terrible disease.' Fyfe, 284.
p. 200 'slice of shares.' Paul Ferris. *The House of Northcliffe* (New York, 1972), 279.
p. 200 'quite remarkable figure.' Sir Campbell Stuart. *Opportunity Knocks Once* (1952), 99–100.
p. 200 'expose them all.' Ferris. *Northcliffe*, 263. Op. cit.
p. 201 'admiration waned.' *The Times*, 28 November 1936.

p. 201   Senator Jouvenel. Neumann, 233–4.
p. 202   Hajianestis. Balfour, 314.
p. 202   'do something.' Riddell, *Intimate Diary*, 385. Entry for 3 September 1922.
p. 202   luckless Gounaris. Leonard Mosley. *Curzon* (1960), 248.
p. 203   French syndicate. Davenport, 234.
p. 204   'War Plot.' *Daily Express*, 22 October 1922.
p. 204   'stupid too.' PRO. E4655/15/44.
p. 205   *Le Matin*, 15 May 1923.
p. 205   old man's horse. Neumann, 258.
p. 205   'came to see me.' Rosita Forbes. *Sunday Chronicle*. Op. cit.
p. 206   *Moniteur de Pétrole*. Cited by *Morning Post*, 8 November 1922.
p. 206   'quite reliable.' PRO. C4040/4040/37.
p. 206   lady-in-waiting. PRO. C16588/13/19; C16638/405/37.
p. 207   'intellectual liberal.' PRO. C21283/42/37.
p. 207   'better of me.' Christopher, 115.
p. 208   Paris press. *Daily Mail*, 2 January 1924.
p. 208   'broken vessel.' McCormick.

Chapter 19: Banker, Oilman, Middleman

p. 210   Since 1916. Secrétaire du Conseil Général, Banque de France, to author.
p. 210   £50,000. BE 1918.
p. 210   'gay world.' Neumann, 204. Karl Hoffmann. *Oelpolitik und Angelsachsischer Imperialismus.*
p. 211   Banque de la Seine. DPDF. March 1928, 88.
p. 211   'vassalage.' Ibid.
p. 212   General Electric. Ibid., 92.
p. 212   'private character.' PRO. C6021/2264/19.
p. 212   Balkan alliance. *Western Gazette*, 4 January 1923.
p. 213   wide-awake watchdogs. *Daily Express*, 22 October 1922.
p. 213   'As for France.' Watson, 279.
p. 213   Algeria. DPDF. March 1928, 95.
p. 214   Gulbenkian. Ferrier, 243.
p. 214   Owens-Thurston. *Daily Express*. Op. cit.
p. 214   Forth Shipbuilding. BE 1916–19.
p. 215   issued writ. PRO. T13657/13657/317. Not selected for preservation.
p. 215   *Tribune de Paris*, 1 September 1923.
p. 216   'interallied collaboration.' Ferrier, 244. Pichon to Paul Cambon, French Ambassador in London, 17 December 1918.
p. 216   'quite untenable.' Ibid. Memo, 6 January 1919.
p. 217   'get the French.' Ferrier, 245.
p. 217   'mischievous manner.' McCormick, 185. Zaharoff's 'occult role' in oil is also elaborated in *The Secret War* (1935) by Franck C. Hanighen (co-author of *Merchants of Death*) and Anton Zischka, 56–61.
p. 217   'foothold.' Neumann, 225; McCormick, 187.
p. 217   France's needs. Ferrier, 252. Zaharoff to Berthelot, 5 August 1920.
p. 218   *The Star*, 28 October 1920.

p. 218 'Basil's connections.' *The Times*, 28 October 1920.
p. 218 birds nesting. Scott, 144.
p. 218 *Action Française*. Neumann, 236.
p. 218 *Informations Politiques*, 11 June 1923.
p. 219 'exclusively personal.' DPDF. March 1928, 94.

Chapter 20: Monte Carlo and Marriage

p. 220 'bought Monte Carlo.' Davenport, 286.
p. 220 a newspaperman. *Daily Telegraph*, 26 October 1926.
p. 221 'fool's substitute.' *Sunday Dispatch*, 29 November 1936.
p. 221 instant dismissal. Private source.
p. 221 'secret' treaty. DPDF. June 1923, February 1928.
p. 221 Senator Gaudin de Villaine. 'What is the exact nationality of this Grand Cross of the Legion of Honour?' Written question 17 October 1922, supposedly unanswered. DPDF. February 1928.
p. 223 old story. Neumann, 279.
p. 223 Hôtel de Paris. Acquired by the Société des Bains de Mer in 1929.
p. 224 'but Monaco.' McCormick, 201. Zaharoff to Sir Charles Mendl, former Press Attaché, British Embassy, Paris.
p. 224 *Evening Standard*. Memo to Newsroom and sub-editors, signed C. W. Sutton, 25 September 1933. BL Colindale, Zaharoff box.
p. 224 *Sunday Express*, 28 February 1926.
p. 224 'extraordinary secrecy.' Neumann, 276.
p. 225 'personal bodyguard.' McCormick, 197.
p. 226 'Quelle beauté.' Private source.
p. 227 'obviously dying.' McCormick, 198.
p. 227 'years' patience.' Ibid. Zaharoff to Mendl.
p. 227 mawkish adventure. Cookridge, 120 ff.
p. 228 Zaharoff to Rafaeli Mainella, 18 March 1926. Private source.

Chapter 21: Run-Down

p. 229 'not know language.' VA 1219. Zaharoff to Caillard, 10 February 1924.
p. 230 'special considerations.' Ibid. Caillard to Zaharoff, 16 February 1924.
p. 230 'Zaharoff reported.' VA. F. Scott to Sir Charles Dunphie, 23 May 1961.
p. 231 Mrs Z. Z. Zaharoff. PRO. K8230/8230/238. File not selected for preservation.
p. 231 Sir Basil prompted. Lewinsohn, 180.
p. 232 controlled retreat. Scott, 143 ff.
p. 232 *The Times*, 4 November 1927.
p. 233 '£20,000 in cash.' VA. Zaharoff to Jenkinson, 16 August 1927.
p. 233 'delicate matter.' VA. Jenkinson to Zaharoff, 18 August 1927.
p. 233 'prices "cut".' VA. Reorganization of Vickers. Draft letter, Jenkinson to Zaharoff, 17 August 1927. There is no indication, such as an acknowledgement, that this was sent.
p. 234 'usual half yearly.' VA. Royal Commission. Board Minute, 28 February 1927.
p. 234 'our Spanish friends.' VA. 787. Zaharoff to Dawson, 1 July 1929.

p. 235 approximately £125,000. Ibid. Jenkinson to Zaharoff, 30 May 1932.
p. 235 'doing the needful.' Ibid. Zaharoff to Cartwright, 30 November 1925.
p. 235 Placencia to Vickers. Paid £40,000 in 1928, £20,000 in 1929.
p. 235 'difficult people.' VA. 786. Zaharoff to McLean, 15 April 1929.
p. 235 'Above all.' Ibid. Zaharoff to Birch, August 1929.
p. 235 'Remember that.' Ibid. 7 September 1931.

Chapter 22: Senate Commission, Royal Committee

p. 236 'fully fledged.' Scott, 183. M.M.Postan. *British War Production* (HMSO, 1952).
p. 237 'generous frame.' *Daily Express*, 19 July 1931.
p. 237 *Report of the Temporary Mixed Commission on Armaments*, League of Nations, doc. A.81, 1921.
p. 238 'Hoover meant nothing.' Davenport, 298–9; McCormick, 213.
p. 238 *Hearings before the Special Committee Investigating the Munitions Industry*. United States 73rd Congress, US Government Printing Office, Washington, 1934–5.
p. 242 'fishing expedition.' Philip Gibbs. *The Pageant of the Years* (1946), 410, 425–9.
p. 242 John Simon. House of Commons, 8 November 1934.
p. 242 *Royal Commission on the Private Manufacture of and Trading in Arms, 1935–6.* Minutes of Evidence and Report (HMSO, Cmd. 5292). Scott, 245 ff.
p. 242 Colonel Maxwell. VA. Royal Commission.

Chapter 23: Last Lust

p. 245 'ludicrous economic.' Forbes, 147–8.
p. 245 'high esteem.' J. Emrys Jones. *Sunday Dispatch*, 9 September 1934.
p. 246 'leave the flowers.' Ibid.
p. 246 most unlikely evidence. James Lees-Milne. *Harold Nicolson* (1980), I, 153.
p. 247 'fortune deserts.' Lady (Edmée) Owen. *Empire News*, 29 November 1936.
p. 248 '*tout sera.*' Edmée Owen. *Flaming Sex* (1934), 133.
p. 249 Zaharoff and Lady Owen. *The People*, 29 November, 6 December 1936.
p. 249 'ardour as lover.' Owen. *Empire News*. Op. cit.
p. 250 Paris papers. Neumann, 283.
p. 251 'too much trouble.' Rosita Forbes. *Sunday Chronicle*. Op. cit.
p. 251 Glaswegian eyewitness. *Daily Express* (Glasgow), 21 April 1930.
p. 252 'pay less attention.' McCormick, 230. Report of conversation given by Mandel to René Tarpin, compiler of *Documents Politiques de la Guerre*. Op. cit.
p. 252 '*Dummkopf.*' Fritz Thyssen. *I Paid Hitler* (1941), 157.
p. 253 'now no question.' McCormick, 229. No source indicated.

Chapter 24: Exit

p. 254 'my third.' VA. Microfilm 19a, 553. 3 November 1932.
p. 254 'amused public.' Ibid. Zaharoff to Jenkinson, 2 November 1927.
p. 254 'Press endeavour.' Ibid. 5 January 1932.

p. 255 suitable motive. McCormick, 227.
p. 255 '*Le taciturne.*' Private source.
p. 255 87th birthday. *Daily Telegraph*, 21 October 1936.
p. 256 death certificate, No. 311. In author's possession.
p. 256 owed £17,500. VA. Spanish Commissions.
p. 256 Mayor of Arronville. *Sunday Dispatch*, 29 November 1936.
p. 256 *The Times*, 4 December 1936.
p. 257 'Ghost of Zaharoff.' *Star*, 28 November 1936.
p. 257 'am not satisfied.' *Reynold's*, 1 August 1937.
p. 257 Olga Zaharoff. *Manchester Daily Express*, 3 March 1938.
p. 257 Miller, Chachaty, two sisters. *Daily Express*, 2 December 1936.
p. 258 'seventh richest.' *Daily Mail*, 30 November 1936.
p. 258 Ridgely Carter. *Sunday Express*, 1 February 1931.
p. 258 'Japhet's in London.' Davenport, 292.
p. 258 'most prominent.' Japhet, 122.
p. 259 'just my luck.' Watson, 354.
p. 259 'intimate terms.' *Daily Telegraph*, 18 February 1937.
p. 259 entire staff. Private source.

Epilogue

p. 262 'remarkable example.' *The Times*, 27 September 1924.
p. 262 'loyal, honest.' *Manchester Guardian*, 27 September 1924.
p. 262 Footnote. Lees-Milne. *Nicolson*, I, 180. Op. cit. Margot Asquith to Harold Nicolson, 29 October 1922.
p. 264 'Begin on the Left.' Lord Boothby. *I Fight to Live* (1947), 21.
p. 265 'never mellowed.' Christopher, 114.
p. 265 'simply unequalled.' Japhet, 131.
p. 265 'way rumour grows.' *Financial Times*, 28 November 1936.
p. 266 'and Napoleon.' Davenport, 25.
p. 266 *Manchester Guardian*, 28 November 1936.
p. 266 friend and colleague. Sir George Owens-Thurston. *Daily Express*, 28 November 1936.

Index

Birch, Sir Noel, 235
Blakiston, H. E. D., 226
Blanc, Camille, 197, 222
Blanc, Edmund, 196–7
Blühm, Heinrich, 9
Bon, Jean, 210
Bone, Senator Homer T., 239
Bonesco, Georges, 190, 211
Bonsal, Stephen, 117
Boothby, (Sir) Robert, (later 1st Baron), 265
Borbon, Angèle de, 78, 95, 99, 183, 225, 245, 259
Borbon, Cristina de, 78, 99, 118, 183, 225, 245, 259
Bosshardt Bros, 109
Bourget, Paul, 180
Boxshall, Captain E. G., 191
Brassey, 2nd Baron, 50
Bratianu, Ion, 206
Bratianu, Ventila, 206
Breteuil, Vicomte de, 218
Briand, Aristide, 128–9, 130, 197, 201
Brown, John, & Company, 82, 87
Bryce, Roland, 191
Bülow, Friedrich von, 61
Burney, Commander Sir Dennistoun, 183n
Burrows, Emily Ann, 6, 7, 9, 10, 12, 13, 19, 34, 35, 114, 231
Burrows, John, 7

Caillard, Sir Vincent, 77, 87, 95, 114, 140, 160, 183, 184, 188, 190, 212, 215, 225, 229–30; Turkish peace talks, 144–5, 146, 148, 149, 153–4, 158, 162, 166, 169, 172; retirement, 233
Callwell, General Sir Charles, 146–7
Cambridge, Duke of, 43n, 46
Canaris, Admiral Wilhelm, xvi–xvii, 194, 252–3
Carrier, Maurice, 211, 213, 215, 218
Carse, Henry, 73, 239–41
Carter, J. Ridgely, 258
Cassel, Sir Ernest, 46, 51, 69, 88, 104, 134
Chambers, Sir Thomas, 10
Christopher of Greece, Prince, 4, 58, 93, 184, 207, 265
Churchill, (Sir) Winston, 127, 135, 179, 195, 197, 216, 252
Clark, Senator Bennett Champ, 239, 240
Clemenceau, Georges, 120, 124, 148, 153, 164, 172, 179, 192–3, 197, 213, 264
on Zaharoff, xix, 117
Zaharoff's relations with, 115–16, 175–7, 194, 197n, 221, 226, 245
Clemenceau, Michel, 115, 177
Clemenceau, Paul, 115
Coffin, John, 140, 160
Colt Patent Firearms Company, 122

Comité des Forges, 119, 121
Commerell, Admiral Sir John, 59, 65
Compagnie de Transit de Caen, 214
Constantine I, King of the Hellenes, 93, 126, 127, 131, 132, 156, 197–8, 202, 205
Cooper, Lady Diana, see Manners, Lady Diana
Coventry Ordnance Works Ltd., 113
Craven, Sir Charles, 244
Crowdy, Dame Rachel, 242
Curzon of Kedelston, 1st Marquess, 199

Darmstädter Bank, 104
Davidson, (Sir) J. C. C. (later 1st Viscount), 147, 171, 172
Davies, (Sir) John T., 154
Dawson, Sir Trevor, 75, 76, 107, 112, 160, 215, 218, 225, 233
Delacroix, Blanche, see Vaughan, Baroness
Delpierre, Alfred, 214, 222
Demidoff, Prince, 129, 131, 132
Derby, 17th Earl of, 161
Deutsche Bank, 90, 216
Deutsch Waffen und Munitionsfabriken, 63, 81, 91, 109, 189
Disraeli, Benjamin (later 1st Earl of Beaconsfield), 18, 24
Djemal Pasha, see Jemal Pasha
Dormeuil, Edmée, see Owen, Lady
Doumer, Paul, 87
Doumergue, President Gaston, 245
Drake, Oliver P., 48
Drebel, Cornelius van, 37n
Dreyfus, Daniel, et Cie., 223
Dumenc, Jean, 226
Dunn, James, 100
Dupuy, Senator, 85

Eady, Griffin, 138
Ebert, Friedrich, xvi
Edward, Prince of Wales (Edward VII), 39, 46, 57, 65, 67
Electric Boat Co., Holland submarine, 41, 86, 239; agreement with Vickers, 41, 240; Zaharoff's relations with, 42, 239; Sociedad Español de Construcción Naval, 82, 234, 239; US Senate Special Committee, 73, 238–41
Elibank, Alexander Murray, Master of (1st Viscount Murray), 101, 114, 160, 161, 184, 213
Elliot, Sir Francis, 15
Enver Pasha, 135, 136–7, 142–6, 147, 148, 150, 151, 156–8, 160, 162–5, 166–9, 170–1, 173
Escoffier, 181
Esnault-Pelterie, Robert, 105–6

Lampsas, 37
Lansdowne, 5th Marquess of, 123
Laurier, Sir Wilfrid, 102
Law, Andrew Bonar, 147, 149, 150, 153, 194, 196
Lawrence, General Sir Herbert, 232, 233, 236, 242, 243
Lawrence, Colonel T. E., 139, 141
League of Nations, Temporary Mixed Commission, 73, 237; Union, 241
Lenin, V. I., 230
Léon, René, 22, 246
Leopold II, King of the Belgians, 118, 225
Li Hung-Chang, 66
Liebknecht, Karl, xv–xvii, 91
Libertad, 82
Limpus, Admiral A. H., 136
Lincoln, Ignatius Timothy Trebitsch, 114
Lloyd George, David (*later* 1st Earl), 56, 111, 112, 113, 123, 127, 176, 185, 196, 200, 213, 262
  Zaharoff's relations with, 113–14, 160–1, 175, 176–7, 183, 195–6, 198, 227
  Turkey, peace proposals, 142, 144–5, 146, 148, 149, 150, 151, 154, 158, 162, 166, 169–70, 171, 173
  Versailles Peace Treaty, 192–3; Graeco-Turkish war, 195, 196, 197, 198, 199, 201, 202
Lockhart, Sir Robert Bruce, 118, 178
Loewe, Ludwig, 63
Loewe, Sigmund, 63, 108
Long, Walter, 1st Viscount, 171, 194, 206, 213, 262
Ludendorff, General Erich von, 161, 163, 176
Luke, Sir Harry, 14
Luxemburg, Rosa, xv–xvi
Lyautey, Marshal L. H. G., 120, 124

MacDermott, Theo (secretary), 203, 221, 226, 255
Mackenzie, Compton, 130
McKenna, Reginald, 113, 130, 140, 226, 232
Macpherson (secretary), 221, 250
Madge, Dr E., 190
Mainella, Rafaeli, 225, 227
Malleterre, General, 120
Mandel, Georges, 251–2, 264
Mangin, Professor, 181
Manners, Lady Diana, 183
Manuel II, King of Portugal, 184
March, Juan, 252, 253
Marchena, Francisco de Borbon y Borbon, Duke of, 52–4, 78, 224
Marchena, Duchess of, *see* Muguiro y Beruete, Maria del Pilar

Marie, Queen of Romania, 205, 208
Maude, General Sir Stanley, 147
Mavrogordato, Ambroise, 211
Max of Baden, Prince, 169
Maxim Gun Co. Ltd., 46, 51
Maxim, Sir Hiram, 43, 45, 62, 65, 66, 69; character, 45, 49; gun trials, La Spezia, 46–7; Steinfeld, 47–9; Spandau, 57; sales missions, Russia, 57–8, Turkey, 58–9; flight, 65–6
Maxim-Nordenfelt Guns & Ammunition Co. Ltd., 51, 57, 60, 64, 66–7, 72; acquired by Vickers, 69
Maxwell, Colonel A. T., 242
Mayer, Paul, 218
Melba, Dame Nellie, 183–4, 226
Mennevée, Roger, 213
Mensdorff, Count von, 167
Merry del Val, 60
Merz, Charles, 13
Metropolitan Company, 188
Michael Nicolayevich, Grand Duke, 83, 86, 103
Mills, Algernon, 63
Morgan, J. S., & Company, 143, 164
Mouktar Bey, 150
Muguiro y Beruete, Maria del Pilar, Duchess of Marchena, 52–4, 78, 183; Zaharoff's meeting with, 52–4; marriage to, 224–5; death, 227
Mulliner, H. H., 113

Nadel, 98, 177
Napier and Ettrick, Lady, 71
Nasr-ed-Din, Shah of Persia, 67
Naval Construction & Araments Co. Ltd., Barrow, Nordenfelt submarines, 39; Holland submarines, 239; acquired by Nordenfelt, 50; acquired by Vickers, 69; profits, 72; *Libertad, São Paulo*, 82; *Reshadieh*, 136; *Rurik*, 76n, 86; First World War, overseas orders, 139; post-war, 236–7
Nickel, Le, 107–8, 211
Nicolaieff, Société des Ateliers et Chantiers, 87, 90, 230
Noel-Baker, Philip, 36, 75
Nordenfelt Guns & Ammunition Co. Ltd., 44–5; Maxim merger, 51
Nordenfelt, Thorsten Vilhelm, engages Zaharoff, 17, 35; submarines, 38–41; gun, 44; company registered, 44; Barrow Shipyard, 50; retirement, 60; Paris lawsuit, 60, 63
Nordwell, Baron de, 83
Norman, Montagu, 232n
Northcliffe, 1st Viscount, 200

Submarines, Canada, 103; George Garrett,
38, 40; Germany, First World War, 164,
Kaiser on, 169; Greece, 39; 'Holland',
41, 82, 86, 239; 'Nordenfelt', 38–41;
Russia, 36, 40–1, 86; Turkey, 39–40;
Vickers, delivery and profit, 42;
agreement with Electric Boat Co., 41,
239, 240
Sykes, (Sir) Mark, 192, 193
Symon, Randolph R., 46

Tabac d'Orient et d'Outremer, 212
Talaat Bey, 135, 136, 142, 143n, 150, 151,
157, 158, 162, 167, 170–1
Tardieu, André, 85, 116, 213
Thaine, Philip, 75, 76
Thomas, Albert, 89–90, 120
Thompson, Robert Lawrie, 62
Thomson, Sir Basil, 137, 194
Thomson, Lord, 206
Thurston, Senator, 81
Thyssen, Baron, 101, 252
Townsend, General Sir Charles, 170
Trefusis, Violet, 246–7
Tricoupis, Charilaos, 18
Tricoupis, General, 202
Trochain, M., 164
Tsaritsyn, Russian Artillery Works Company,
88
Tuck, Edward, 217, 226
Turkish Petroleum Company, 216, 217
Turot, Henri, 129

Union of Democratic Control, 90, 241
US Senate Special Committee Investigating
the Munitions Industry, 73, 238–41

Vaughan, Baroness, 225
Venizelos, Eleutherios, 93, 94, 124, 126,
127, 128, 131, 133, 185, 195, 196, 197,
204; quarrel with Zaharoff, 207–8
Vickers, Albert, and Zaharoff, 42, 55, 78, 85,
92, 94, 100, 102, 159, 239; Maxim Gun
Co., 46; Maxim-Nordenfelt Guns &
Ammunition Co., 63; character, 54, 69;
Vickers Terni, 83; Le Nickel, 108; death,
178, 188
Vickers-Armstrong Ltd., formation 1927,
232
Vickers, Douglas, 76, 190, 191, 232
Vickers [Sons & Maxim, 1897–1911] Ltd,
formation, 69; company results, 71, 77,
139; shareholdings in, 72; licensing
arrangements with, Deutsche Waffen,
81; Electric Boat Co., 41, 240; Krupp,
57, 68; royalties, 81, 86; aviation,
105–6, 235; subsidiaries, 107
in Canada, 103; in Greece, 92; in Italy, 83;

post-war, 189; in Japan, 83, 86; in
Romania, post-war, 190–1; in Russia,
86–8; post-war, 229–31; in Spain see
Sociedad Español de Construcción
Naval, Placencia de las Armas; in Turkey,
92, 94, 135; pos-twar, 190, 212
First World War, warns Admiralty of
Krupp purchases of nickel, 109;
production, 111–12, 122; profits, 187
Post-war, royalty claims, 189; and
Metropolitan Co., 188; post-war
conditions, 188, 190, 236; attempt to
export arms to Greece, 204; naval
shipbuilding, 231–2; reorganization,
232; merger with Armstrong
Whitworth, 232; and US Senate Special
Committee, 238–9, 240; and Royal
Commission, 242–4
Vickers Sons & Co. Ltd., 64, 68–9
Vickers Terni, Societa Italiana d'Artiglieria ed
Aramente, 83, 189
Vickers, Colonel T. E., 37, 54, 107, 188
Villafranca de los Caballeros, Duchess of, see
Muguiro y Beruete, Maria del Pilar
Vogel, Lieutenant, xvi

Wagg, Helbert, & Co., 207
Walford, George Paget, 118, 211, 226
Walford, Leopold, 118, 211, 215, 225, 245
Walford, William, 206
Walter, John, 200
Waterlow, Sir Sydney, 8
Weizmann, Dr Chaim, 141–2
Wells, H. G., xviii
Wemyss, Admiral Sir Rosslyn, Baron Wester
Wemys, 194
Wendel, Françoise de, 119
Werkmann, Baron von, 186
Whitehead, Robert, 38, 107
Whitehead Torpedo Co., 69, 107, 232, 234
Wied, Prince William of, 185
Wilhelm of Austria, Archduke, 47
Wilhelm I, German Emperor, 57
Wilhelm II, German Emperor, 92, 109, 127,
135, 151, 157, 163–4, 169
Williamson, John W., 14–15
Wilson, Field Marshal Sir Henry, 131, 158,
196
Wilson, President Woodrow, 141, 169, 193
Witt & Co., 32
Wolseley, Field Marshal Sir Garnet (1st
Viscount), 13, 46
Wolseley Tool & Motor Car Co., 69, 188,
232
Wormser, Georges, 115, 116
Württemberg, Prince William of, 221

Xenos, Stefanos, 32–3